James P. Cot

The Rose of Camelot

Book One
of The Rose of Camelot series

by

James Philip Cox

authorHOUSE™

1663 LIBERTY DRIVE, SUITE 200
BLOOMINGTON, INDIANA 47403
(800) 839-8640
WWW.AUTHORHOUSE.COM

First published by AuthorHouse 09/22/05

ISBN: 1-4208-6610-9 (sc)
ISBN: 1-4208-6611-7 (dj)

Library of Congress Control Number: 2005905447

Printed in the United States of America
Bloomington, Indiana

This book is printed on acid-free paper.

For Lynne.
You always knew I could. You are, in many ways, the inspiration for Rose.

The Rose of Camelot:

being the Adventures of a young Girl
who dreamed of becoming a Knight
in King Arthur's Court

Chapter 1

"Rose! Michael! Time to come to supper!" Poppa called as he made his way from the fields to the cottage. He checked inside the barn and saw an incredible sight. It appeared that a small pile of hay had come to life as it rumbled and tossed, and small grunts came from within.

"God preserve us, not again," he prayed as he moved to the jumbling mass.

"Rose! Michael! Come out from there, and be quick about it!" he yelled.

Presently, a small towheaded lad about eight years old with blood running from his nose crept out, followed by a slightly taller, gangly girl with bright red hair two years his elder.

"Michael! Rose! Have you two been fighting again?" he asked, already sure of the answer.

"She started it," said Michael ruefully.

Their father sighed and stared down at his red-haired daughter. "Rose, Rose, Rose ..." he said shaking his head sadly. "How many times have I told you, 'tis not seemly for a girl to fight."

Rose puffed herself up indignantly and met her father's eyes. "He told me I was left by fairies, and that I wasn't really his sister!" she said with choked emotion.

How like her mother, the man thought to himself. When given a choice in how to express her feelings, most often it would be

1

anger that came foremost. Oh, tears she could cry, and had when occasion called for it – a skinned knee or a bee sting or some such physical trauma. But, when it came to *feelings*, now that was a different story.

"Michael, you know that isn't truth. Tell your sister you're sorry."

"But it *is* true," Michael insisted as he wiped the bloody snot from his face. "I've got light hair, and you've got light hair, and momma ..."

"You were too young to remember, but your mother's hair was red, too, but lightened over the years before her passing." He felt a small sting at that last part, after all these years. Been gone most of their lives, and yet Michael still seemed to remember her, though it was the fanciful memory of a child who'd never really known his mother and not the real woman indeed.

The look in Rose's eyes lightened, and her face relaxed ever so slightly at that.

"Did she really, Poppa?" Rose asked.

"Well, 'twasn't the bright fiery red you possess, my stripling, but yes, she had red hair, too."

"I ... I don't remember ... very well," Rose said quietly, and he could hear guilt behind it as she said it.

"'Tis all right, stripling. 'Tis fine." Her father comforted her, taking her around the shoulders in a hug. He put a hand on Michael's head and tussled his hair. "This bright young lad remembers well enough for us both."

Michael made a wry face and shook himself away. "I still say she's a changeling," he shouted and ran to the cottage.

Poppa sighed again and took his Rose by the hand as they made their way across the yard.

Ah, Mary, how I wish you could see how your children have grown! he thought to himself as memories wrenched at his heart. *Sure but that you'd be proud of 'em both.*

2

Poppa set to ladling out the evening stew as Rose put out the cups and knives, and Michael tore off chunks of bread for each of them.

"As fine a feast as any in the kingdoms!" he'd say, as he always had no matter how meager the meal.

Once the three were finished eating, Poppa sat by the hearth, lit his long clay pipe, and had himself a smoke as he stared into the fire. Michael and Rose cleared away the dishes, washed and dried the plates, and put them back in the cupboard. Then, as was their wont to do, they sat by their pa and asked him for a tale before they went to bed.

"Tell us a story, Poppa!" Michael cried and climbed onto Poppa's lap. Rose curled up at his feet, legs drawn up and arms wrapped around them as she gazed into the fire and let her mind escape into the images her father's stories would conjure up.

"And what tale would you hear of me tonight, my weeds?" he asked. This was part of the tradition. They all knew a story was coming, and that Poppa would tell them whatever it was they asked for. In this, at least, he could be generous. Words soothed, calmed, and pleased, and they were free.

"Tell us again of how the High King came to his throne!" Rose asked.

"Yes!" piped Michael. "And how you were there to see him draw the sword from the stone, and how Merlin was there, and how all the kings and knights and ladies had to pay him his respects, and ..."

"Peace!" Poppa cried. "Mayhap I should let you tell the tale, for you're already halfway through 'fore I've even begun!" He laughed.

"Yes, whist, Michael!" Rose said.

Poppa drew a long draw from his pipe and waited for dramatic effect before beginning.

"Well, as I'm sure you recall from hearing this tale so many times," he said, "the old High King had passed away and named no heir, and all the land was in turmoil."

"Because of all the greedy, evil kings!" Michael chimed in. Rose made a face and stuck her tongue out at her brother before turning back to the fire.

"That's right, my fine lad," Poppa continued. "Because of the greed and ambition of all the evil lords and petty kings who desired land and riches for themselves.

"All the land was in turmoil, and many a person began to curse the foolishness of the old king for not having named an heir afore he up and died." He paused to take another drag from his pipe before going on.

"Now, in the midst of winter, before Christmas tide, in the great old church in London there appeared a large stone with letters in gold set upon it. And upon the stone sat an anvil. And thrust through both stone and anvil was the fairest sword any man had ever seen. And the words set in the stone read ..."

" 'Whosoever draweth forth this sword from this anvil and stone is right wise King of all England by right and birth,' " said Rose half to herself.

"Shall I let you two tell this tale?" Poppa asked good-humouredly.

"No, Poppa. Go on. I'm sorry," urged Rose. This time it was Michael's turn to thumb his nose at her, but she simply ignored it.

"Well, as your sister said, quite rightly, the writing on the stone said that whoever could draw it forth was the rightwise king, and so all the lords and knights and lesser kings held a great tournament to see who would have the privilege of trying to draw the sword. And they held the contests for many days, and every knight who won the tournament would be given his chance to pull the sword free and claim the kingdom as his own. But every knight and lord who tried failed.

"Then, on New Year's Eve, a certain knight and his two sons, who had come from the northern parts of the kingdom – not very far from here – one Sir Ector, and his son Kay and, so far as everyone believed, Kay's younger brother, Arthur, as

4

his squire – attended the tournament that day. But Arthur, in all the excitement and glory of that place, forgot his brother's sword for the tournament! Such a thing could not be! And so he ran back to the hostel, but it was closed up fast for everyone was at the fair. So he ran through the streets of London until he came upon the sword sitting in the churchyard, and he thought to himself 'Well, here is the fairest sword I have ever seen! And my brother deserves no less from me, and he shall have it for the contest!' And, without a thought, Arthur ran up and pulled the sword out of the anvil and stone as easy as you might draw breath and ran back to the tournament.

"When he got there, he gave the magnificent sword to his brother, Kay, who knew it for what it was. But Kay feared they may come to trouble, and he hurried with it under his cloak to his father to ask, as all wise children should." He paused while Michael rolled his eyes, but Rose sat entranced, and then he went on. "And wise old Sir Ector asked Kay how he came by the sword. And Kay answered him that he knew not how, but that his younger brother, Arthur, had given it to him. And Sir Ector asked Arthur 'Is this true? Did ye draw the sword from the stone?' And Arthur, being a loving and dutiful son, answered him 'Yes, Father.'

"Sir Ector was stunned and, like Saint Thomas, had to see for himself before he would let himself believe such a thing, and so he told Kay and Arthur to go with him back to the church and see if Arthur could put the sword back in the stone. And, of course, Arthur did. He slid the sword as easily into the anvil and the stone as if they were made of water. Then Sir Ector asked Kay to try to draw the sword from the anvil and stone, and of course Kay could not. Then he asked Arthur to try again, and Arthur pulled the sword free as if it were air!

"Now, Sir Ector was a very kind and loving man, and he knew the truth of Arthur's parentage, and knelt down before him, and motioned for Kay to do likewise. And Arthur was amazed and asked 'Father? Brother? Why do ye kneel down before me? How can this be?'

"And Sir Ector said 'This can be because ye are truly not my son.' Then Sir Ector told both Kay and Arthur how Merlin had come to him one night with a babe swaddled against the cold, and asked him to safeguard Arthur until such time as Uther, the High King, might rightfully send for him and make Arthur known as his son and heir. But the old High King died before he could make his wishes known, and so Sir Ector had raised and loved Arthur as if he were his very own.

" 'And this self-same Merlin, I am sure,' said Sir Ector, 'is the one who made this sword and anvil and stone, and declared the truth in letters of gold, knowing that one day, you, Arthur, would come and pull it free.'

"And Arthur wept, and Kay wept, both for joy and for loss, for Kay felt as if he had lost a brother while he had gained a king, and Sir Ector wept for the loss of a son likewise. And Arthur said, 'Father – for so you shall always be to me, and Kay my brother – what can I do for you? How can I ever repay all you have ever given me?'

"Then Sir Ector said ..."

"I know, I know!" exclaimed Michael. " 'If it please you, my lord and king, for the love and kindness we have given you, that you might grant that Kay shall be made knight and serve you as your satchel!' "

"That's 'seneschal', you dolt!" Rose replied with a roll of her eyes and a sigh. Michael always seemed to enjoy breaking the magic of their father's stories. Couldn't he just see the knights in their shiny armor, and the wonder of the magical world in which they lived?

"That's correct," their father went on. "So, Arthur declared that Kay shall be his first knight and have the place of seneschal within his household, and that Sir Ector and his wife would be welcome to move into the palace and reside there with him all of their days."

"But what about the other knights and lords," Michael asked impatiently. "What about how mad they all got, and they all went to war and refused to accept Arthur as their king ..."

"Whist! Enough, now," said Poppa. "I think that's enough for one night," he said as he lifted Michael from his lap and patted him on the bottom to scoot him off towards the loft to bed. "I can see 'tis no night for storytelling as I keep getting interrupted by boggins who can't sit still."

"Aw, Poppa," whined Michael.

"Yes, Poppa, please don't stop now," implored Rose. She knew the story so well, but there was something special in hearing her father tell it that made it somehow seem more vivid, more real.

Poppa stopped and looked at his two children: Michael who stood shifting from foot to foot restlessly while putting a pout on his face; and Rose who had that faraway glint in her eyes, and almost a sadness, a yearning, that reminded him again of her mother and brought a dull pang to his chest. How could he say no?

"No more chiming in?"

"No, Poppa," Michael promised. Rose's eyes lit up.

"Well, I guess a little more would be all right, then," he said with a grin and put aside his pipe. Michael climbed back up onto his lap, and he resumed. "Now, as you know, when it was revealed to the attending lords and knights that a mere boy had drawn the sword, there was a great deal of consternation over it. 'How can a boy be king?' some asked. Others said, 'What right does this boy claim to draw the sword? He's not even a knight!' There was a great deal of unhappiness and dissension."

"Weren't you there, Poppa?" Michael asked. Rose shook her head angrily.

Poppa smiled and gave his boy a playful poke. "Yes, I was there, and I saw as Arthur drew the sword before all the assembled onlookers. Time and again, he would slide the sword into the anvil and stone like any other knight would sheath his weapon in a scabbard. Then lord after lord, and knight after knight, would push their way forward and seize the sword and pull with all their might – to no avail. Every one of them failed. Then Arthur would draw the sword and cheers would go up from the crowds.

"But, some men are as stubborn of will as an ox, and refused to accept the evidence before their eyes.

" 'This is some trick of Merlin's!' they claimed. 'For who but Merlin could have placed this stone here with a sword sticking out of it?' And believe me when I tell you, there were more than a few there who were inclined to believe this, for who trusts wizards and their strange ways? For many of those who protested, however, it had more to do with their own plans and ambitions than it did with the legitimacy of Arthur's claim, however presented."

"And then Merlin came ..." Michael broke in. Rose scowled, but Poppa simply clamped a hand over the boy's mouth and went on.

"Then Merlin came, and he told how such a thing had come to pass. He told the lords and knights how he had helped Uther gain access to the Duke of Cornwall's wife, the beautiful Ygraine, the very night her husband, Duke Gorlois, was killed in a raid on Uther's camp. And how the Lady Ygraine believed Uther to be her husband, that no shame might fall upon her, for she was a good and faithful lady. Merlin told how, when the babe was born, he brought the suckling to Sir Ector to be raised with Ector's own child, the noble Sir Kay – God bless him and keep him! And there, upon a Holy Bible, Sir Ector swore that this was all fair and true. And Merlin asked the Archbishop of Canterbury to hold a coronation for Arthur right then and there. But many of the knights assembled demanded that Arthur be knighted before he was crowned, and so it was decided that Arthur's coronation would be postponed until Candlemas. This seemed to appease the more ambitious lords who still hoped to claim the High Kingship themselves, and so it was delayed. And then delayed again when no consensus could be formed until the holy time of Easter. And Easter came, and the lords pressed for yet a further delay, and it was not until Pentecost that Arthur's crowning took place."

"Did you see that, Poppa?" Rose asked with shining, eager eyes.

"No, sweetling. But I have heard the tales, grown in the telling I am sure, as have you." With that he reached down and while cradling her brother with one arm he tweaked her nose. "It was a magical experience, with cloth of gold and white samite everywhere. And all the kings and knights in their polished best armor. And the ladies dressed in long flowing gowns, with wimples flying. So much rich materials one could have sailed a fleet unlike any the world has ever seen with all the cloth I hear tell of!" Poppa smiled wryly.

"But," Poppa took on a serious tone suddenly, for effect, "the magic of that day wouldn't last. It wasn't many weeks before the ambitious lords broke with Arthur, and the land slipped once again into war. One by one, Arthur went forth and conquered each kingdom, until, now, at last, we have a little peace. It took him two years before he had conquered, killed, or converted enough lords to his cause that Arthur felt secure in his throne and could settle down to begin his reign."

"And the lords who broke from him were: King Lot of Orkney, and the King of Scotland, and King Mark of Cornwall, and the one known only as the King of a Hundred Knights," Michael went on sleepily. It was a tale he'd heard many times before, and he seemed to have a knack for remembering such things.

Poppa stood slowly. He lifted the young boy gently and carried him to the loft to put him to bed.

"That's right," he said quietly. "As well as the Duke of Cambenet, and King Uryens of Gore, and the King of Ireland ..." he continued.

"And King Nentres, and the King of Northumberland..." Michael kept listing dreamily as he slipped into slumber.

Poppa came back to Rose as she sat gazing into the fire, her eyes far away. He shook her shoulder gently to rouse her, and lifted her into his arms. Rose nuzzled her face into his chest as she was carried, like her brother, up to the loft they shared to sleep in.

"And what do you see when you look into the fire, my stripling?" Poppa asked.

9

Rose yawned and gave her Poppa a kiss on the cheek while she slipped under the wool blankets and smiled. "Oh, Poppa! I see everything as you talk about it. And it's the most beautiful thing in the world!"

"And I suppose you want to be one of those fine ladies, wearing a long gown and a silly cone with the wimple?" Poppa said as he brushed some of the straw matting away from her head.

"Oh, no, Poppa!" Rose replied. "I want to be a knight and help good King Arthur keep peace in his kingdom!"

Poppa smiled at that. It was a silly wish, of course, for who had ever heard of a girl becoming a knight? *But,* he thought to himself, *if anyone could do it, it would be you, my wild Rose.* He kissed her on the forehead one last time, and climbed downstairs to make up his own bed.

The memory of Rose's mother was quite fresh that night, and so Poppa as he got himself ready for bed, knelt down at the foot of their four-poster bed – one of the only such in the entire county so far as he knew – and felt around for the latch that opened a small space under the floorboards. He reached down and took out a small, wooden box, finely crafted, and opened it. Inside was a slender silver pendant on a fine silver chain. It had belonged to Rose and Michael's mother, and he recalled how on her death bed she had told him it should pass to Rose when she was of age. Rose had been seven then, and was with him as she passed. Michael was in the other room, being watched by the neighbor women who had come to sit with the family until Mary's passing.

Ah, how I miss you! Poppa thought to himself. He recalled how they met, and the sacrifices both had made. *You even gave up your name to be with me. "Branwen." After all this time, I have always been aware of how half of me seems missing. Still.*

He reached under the floor space and drew out another object – a bundle wrapped in old leather, and tightly tied with a length of leather cord. Poppa ran his hands over it, remembering, then shook his head and replaced both the bundle and the pendant. He closed the covering and blew out the candle as he climbed into bed.

Wherever you are, Mary, I love you still! And we have fine, strong children!

Chapter 2

Summers came and went, and life on the farm went on peacefully as it should. Poppa took Michael with him to market, though he sometimes let Rose come along as well. He wanted Michael to learn how to barter with the merchants who sold their produce, for he wanted the boy to be able to take over one day.

Rose grew strong and lean doing her share of chores about the farm milking cows, churning butter, cooking and cleaning. Poppa taught her and Michael how to fish, and they spent many a lazy afternoon down by the pond. Poppa would sit under the great oak that grew out over the pond and smoke his pipe, more often than not falling asleep, while the two children splashed about the shoreline. They probably frightened away more fish than they ever caught, but they did catch fish often enough, and would have a wonderful meal that evening when they got home.

Poppa taught them a lot of other things as well to help eke out their living during the leaner months. How to lay snares for rabbit and other small game. How to hunt for eggs, and how to catch birds, and how to light a fire with flint and steel. Michael never really caught on very well, though he could recite back Poppa's instructions word-for-word after only one hearing. Rose, on the other hand, learned everything very quickly. She could lay snares better than Poppa, and had a quick wrist and deadly aim with small stones to bring down birds.

"You think with your body, Rose," Poppa told her one day. She had been feeling discouraged because of Michael's uncanny memory, while she herself had to struggle to pay attention. She felt as if her body kept wanting to run out and *do* something, that it wanted to just start doing whatever it was Poppa was trying to explain. And, to be honest, she was also frustrated with how slow Michael seemed at actually doing anything. Poppa seemed to pay more attention to her brother because he was slower, and it hurt a little that Michael got more attention.

Rose looked up at her Poppa and shaded her eyes with her hand because the sun was behind him. Poppa stepped forward a bit so that his body would block the sunlight, making it easier for her.

"It's just that ..." Rose started. "It's just that, I wish ... I wish I could remember everything like Michael does. You never have to tell him anything twice, and I seem to need to be told over and over again. I feel so stupid around him!"

Poppa stroked her hair, and said, "I hardly need to tell you something 'over and over again.' Why, once you've actually done it once or twice, you take off like a bolt of lightning! Poor Michael and I have to run just to keep up with you! I must confess you often leave *me* feeling like an idiot."

Rose smiled. "Oh, Poppa," she said. "I don't either."

Poppa paused to check and see how Michael was doing. The boy was trying to set out a snare to catch rabbit or squirrels and sat talking to himself, going over things step-by-step. He usually wound up needing Poppa or Rose to show him how to tie the knots, though, or else he'd wind up getting himself tangled up with the line, or trip the snare as soon as he released it.

"I'm serious, my stripling!" Poppa smiled. "You ... it's an amazing thing to watch the way you do things. You take to your chores like running water – that's the only way I can describe it. You just seem to *flow* through your chores. You hardly ever stop to think *how* you should be doing something, you just *do* it. Once you've seen me do something and then you sit down and copy my what I've done, you master it just like that!" Poppa snapped his fingers.

Rose felt warm from her Poppa's praise and hugged him tightly.

"I love you, Poppa!" she said as she squeezed him.

"I love you, too, my wild Rose," Poppa answered. "Now go and help your brother. If I'm very much not mistaken, I think he's managed to get his fingers stuck in his own trap!"

Rose shook her head and raced off to help extricate her brother. "Oh, Michael!"

Michael only smiled at them both and giggled. Poppa sometimes wondered if the boy did such things deliberately, knowing that either Rose or he would be there to rescue him.

Nothing ever seems to get the boy's spirits down, Poppa thought. *I wonder where he gets that from?*

Now Rose, she took after her mother, in more ways than one. And Michael, well, he had his mother's knack for mental things. A trait or a skill, Poppa was never sure which really, but one that was renowned amongst the initiates of Avalon such as Mary was.

As for himself? Well, he had his own knack more along the lines of Rose's for physical things – using tools, hunting, fighting.

Fighting? God, but it's been a long time since I've thought about that! Poppa ran his hand along his ribs, remembering an old scar that ran along his left side. *Is that something I should teach the boy, too? No. Not Michael. Poor lad, he'd probably get himself hurt on his own sword or spear if he handled weapons the way he handles farm implements!* Poppa chuckled. *Dangerous enough letting him handle a small knife to cut vegetables or to skin a squirrel!*

Rose had helped Michael out of his own snare, and was sitting re-laying his snare for him. Michael waved at Poppa and smiled. He pointed at Rose as she finished his job for him.

"Next time I'll leave you out here with no food until you catch something on your own!" Poppa shouted to him good-naturedly. He picked up the brace of rabbits Rose had captured earlier and signaled for the children to follow him home. "We'll come back tomorrow and see if your sister has left anything to catch!"

On Michael's eleventh birthday, Poppa had a special surprise in store for the boy. Over the past year, the boy had begun to lose some of his clumsiness, though he was still no match for Rose when it came to physical skills. But Poppa felt secure enough in taking Michael out on a more serious hunt for larger game. So, for Michael's birthday, Poppa came out of the barn carrying a large boar spear, hefting it lightly.

Michaels' eyes grew wide as he saw what Poppa carried, and he said to him, "Is that …? Am I …? Do you really think …?"

Poppa laughed at the boy's sudden inarticulateness. "Now, we're not going after any boar, mind you," he told Michael. "But, for larger game, or a wild sow perhaps – yes, I think you're ready to learn."

Michael let out a whoop of delight. Rose came out onto the porch to watch as Poppa took Michael out into the middle of the yard and began to show him how to hold the weapon. Michael was awkward, and Poppa kept showing him over and over again how to carry the spear, how to set it, and how to brace it properly. Rose felt jealous of Michael's instruction. She sat and watched as she churned butter, longing to have a try at wielding the great weapon herself. But Poppa would never allow it, she felt, as he deemed it "too dangerous" for a girl. The smaller things, the snares and birds and such, he didn't mind showing Rose, and even delighted in her skill and success. But not in this.

"Brace it like this," Poppa showed Michael again how to plant the butt of the spear, holding it in a manner that allowed it to be moved and directed easily, yet still maintain its stability.

Michael took the heavy spear and nearly toppled over as he made a clumsy attempt at imitating Poppa's maneuver. Poppa stepped aside and watched, shaking his head. Rose wondered where he found the patience.

"What's that?" Michael said and pointed toward the horizon where sunlight glinted and shimmered.

Poppa squinted, and Rose stepped out into the yard and shaded her eyes trying to see what it was Michael had spotted.

Poppa took the spear from Michael. "What do you see?" he asked the boy. "Your eyes are sharper than mine."

Michael squinted as well. "It looks like sunlight on metal," he told Poppa. "Lots of little specks."

"What is it, Poppa?" Rose asked. Poppa seemed suddenly tense, his usual playfulness forgotten.

Poppa waved her to be quiet and crouched down putting his ear to the ground.

"What do you hear?" she asked him.

"Footsteps – lots of them. Thousands," he paused. "An army." Poppa sat up, his face clouded with a frown.

"Really, Poppa?" Michael asked excitedly. "Soldiers? A real army? Let's go see!" He turned to race away, but Poppa stopped him.

"No!" he said sharply. Michael turned back confused. Poppa stood and realized that both children were looking at him with concern. He put a weak smile back on his face and said, "All right. We'll go take a look. You've never seen a real army before. It'll be like a parade."

"Yes!" Michael was overjoyed, and Rose felt her heart leap with excitement.

"Me, too?" Rose asked.

Poppa looked at her, and Rose could see his eyes seemed sad even though Poppa was acting like it was okay. "Yes, of course. You, too."

"Rose, hurry up!" Michael shouted as he raced off toward the main road. Rose ran after him, and Poppa followed more slowly. He kept the spear in his hand and walked with it like a walking staff, feeling suddenly very old.

The line of men stretched quite a ways in both directions by the time they had reached the road. Rose was thrilled at the sight of the men wearing their suits of armor, the footmen in their quilted suits of heavy cloth, and the sergeants in suits of studded leather. She saw dozens of swordsmen in coats of heavy chain mail, and the knights!

How grand they look! Rose was enchanted by the men on horseback in suits of heavy plate armor, their lances carried high with pennons snapping in the breeze. They wore surcoats of varied colors, bearing the insignia of the houses to which they belonged.

"Isn't it wonderful, Rose?" Michael asked in wide-eyed astonishment.

Rose merely nodded, trying to take it all in, to capture the sight so that she might keep it forever.

Most of the village had turned out to watch the army as it marched south – merchants and farmers, housewives and children. Poppa frowned as he watched, not sharing in the children's excitement.

"Where away?" he shouted to a line of footmen bearing pikes as they passed.

"We go to give our regards to the King," came a reply. A captain on horseback rode past, scowling at the sight of Poppa with his spear, demanding to know who in his command had answered, and then beating the man with his riding crop when the guilty party was made known.

"Let that be a lesson to you all!" he shouted as he returned to his place. "Any man who speaks without permission will be given ten lashes and serve on latrine duty for a fortnight from here on out. Understood?"

Rose and Michael were shocked at the sudden violence of the captain, the magic of the moment broken.

"Ready to go home, now?" Poppa asked.

"Oh, not yet, Poppa, please! It's my birthday!" Michael pleaded.

Poppa looked down at Rose. "And what about you, my Rose? Have you seen enough?"

Rose looked up at her Poppa, disturbed by his sudden sadness, and felt torn. Part of her wanted to stay and watch until the very last man had passed over the horizon, emblazing the memory on her mind. But part of her was terribly upset by the manner in which the soldier had been beaten merely for having spoken without permission. It spoiled what was an otherwise wonderful experience.

"Well ..." Rose replied. "It is Michael's birthday, after all, Poppa. For his sake, is it okay?"

Poppa saw how she pleaded with him with her eyes. And he saw how Michael waited eagerly for him to say, "Yes."

"All right," Poppa said. "We'll stay. For your brother's sake." He smiled at Rose, and she felt relieved because whatever had been bothering Poppa seemed to leave him then.

Rose took her Poppa's hand, and together the three of them watched as the army continued past them on its way south. They stayed until the last horse had gone by, and the sun was setting as they turned to make their way back home.

Michael practically danced on the way home. He recited the list of names of houses Poppa pointed out to him from the insignia the men wore on their surcoats.

"The rebel kings!" he said as he scampered along. "Wasn't it wonderful, Rose, to see them in all their glory?"

Rose walked in a dream, the vision of the men and their armor, the horses and brightly colored banners, playing over in her mind. But the one incident kept intruding and cast a shadow over the brightness of the day.

"Hm? Yes. Oh, yes ... it was, of course!" she said to him.

"Thank you, Poppa!" Michael exclaimed as he ran and gave his pa a big hug before running ahead again.

Poppa brooded as they walked home, but broke out of it momentarily to acknowledge the boy's affection.

When they reached the cottage, Poppa went inside, put on his hunting cloak, and threw together a few things into a knapsack, which he then slung over his shoulder. He paused, considering taking out the bundle of leather, and of what it held, debating with himself for a moment before shaking his head and hurrying into the common room where Rose was setting out supper.

"Going somewhere, Poppa?" she asked, surprised.

Michael saw, too, and looked disappointed. "Where are you going, Poppa?" he asked. "Aren't we having a special supper?"

Poppa's heart wrenched, but he felt a pressing need to be away and couldn't explain it to them. He wasn't sure why he was doing what he was about to do, but he couldn't deny he felt it to be important enough to leave them alone for a few days.

He touched the boy's head and kissed him on top. "Yes, we made your favorite supper for your special day, Michael. Of course we did! But ..." Poppa paused, torn. "But Poppa has urgent business and must be away for just a few days. I'll hurry and be right back, and then I will take you hunting. All right?"

Michael pouted but said, "Sure, Poppa. All right."

"Rose?" Poppa said to her. "You know what to do should there be an emergency? The neighbors ..."

"Of course, Poppa," Rose replied. After all, they had been left on their own before.

Poppa gave her a quick hug and took one last look at his children, putting aside the emotions that came up, and strode quickly out of the house. Rose and Michael stood on the porch watching him go.

"What do you think that was all about?" Michael asked Rose.

Rose shrugged and put her arm around her brother leading him back inside to eat. "Come on, now – before your supper gets cold. Poppa will be back soon," she said to him.

Poppa moved with great speed through the fields and woodlands, heading south and a little east. He traveled with urgency, following little known paths and animal trails. Speed was of the essence, he knew, and the rebel army would not travel any faster than its supply train, so he had a slight advantage. Still, on foot, it would be a couple of days to reach his destination

– an old Roman outpost, barely manned any longer, as the Empire withdrew its forces from the isle of Britain to help fight the barbarian hordes which had threatened or sacked the great city before. From there, he hoped to send word by courier further south, alerting Arthur to the massive army heading his way. If, that is, the Roman auxiliaries were willing to help him – *and that was a big "if."*

He camped overnight, lighting a small fire just long enough to cook a squirrel he brought down and skinned, and then slept sitting up, his back against the bole of a tree and the boar spear in his hand. His rest was undisturbed, however, and he began at daybreak, practically running through the forest.

Finally, after another uneventful night, the forest began to thin out as he neared the outpost. It was a simple wooden palisade, a temporary fortress that had been used and maintained far longer than originally intended, but not deemed important enough to make more permanent and rebuild in stone. Poppa saw few sentries and took a deep breath before walking out into the clearing and making his way to the main gate.

The guards at the gate stopped him, their heavy pilums barring his way. Poppa was relieved when he saw that the men posted here were relatively young. It meant it was less likely he would be recognized, and might have a better chance at conducting his business and getting home without much difficulty.

"Right," said one guard. "What business have you here?" He eyed Poppa suspiciously. The man was clearly no merchant, and visitors to the fort were extremely rare.

"I have need to speak with your commanding officer," Poppa answered. It was best to be direct and as honest as possible. "I have news that must be relayed to the King immediately."

The guard raised an eyebrow. "The King's business, eh? And what might that be, if you don't mind my asking?"

Poppa felt angry at being questioned, but knew the man was only doing his job. *I would have done the same in my day*, he thought. The man stood to be disciplined if he disturbed the captain without good reason. It was expected that the lower-downs could handle most things on their own and trust their judgment if something seemed beyond their prerogative. *Best to be as forthcoming as possible. It really doesn't matter who takes word to Arthur, so long as somebody does.*

"The rebel lords are marching south," he said simply. Now it was a matter of loyalty – whom did Rome back now?

The two guards exchanged glances. The senior officer furrowed his brows, but said with a heavy sigh, "Better follow me."

Poppa was both glad and worried by the admittance. The longer he remained, the greater the chances he would be recognized by some of the older auxiliaries. But he also knew that only he could convince the soldiers here of the need to send a messenger. It would be so much easier to just leave and hope they would check out his story on their own. If, that is, they supported Arthur's claim to the throne. But, no, he would have to take his chances and hope for the best.

The guard escorted Poppa into the camp and took him to a low, small wood building set into the wall. This would be the commander's office. Poppa swallowed and said a quick, silent prayer before he ducked through the low doorway and entered the dimly lit office.

Behind the table sat a man with short-cropped hair, dressed in the red-dyed, gold embroidered tunic of a Legionary commander. His face was slightly grizzled, covered with stubble, and he had dark hair slightly greyed at the temples. He looked up in surprise at the visitor and squinted in the shadowy light that crept in to the office from narrow, shuttered windows.

"By the gods!" he exclaimed as his face registered recognition of who his visitor was. "*Lucius?*"

Poppa's heart hammered in his chest, and he wished he still had a weapon, but had been forced to leave his spear with the other guards at the gate. He braced himself, ready for anything.

"Lucius, it is you, isn't it?" the commander stood and came around the table to get a better look. Suddenly, Poppa found himself in a tight bear hug, the commander slapping him on the back. "By the gods!" he said, and shook his head in disbelief. "We thought you dead by now!"

Poppa relaxed and was relieved. *Thank you, Jesus!*

"Good to see you, too, Claudius," he said to the other man. "And, to be honest, I thought I'd be dead before this, too."

The commander laughed and waved away the younger soldier. "Away, away! I know this man, and I will deal with him myself. Back to your post!"

The soldier saluted, and the relief was plain in his face as he headed back to the main gates.

The older man sat down again in his chair, laughing at the joke. "Or, I suppose, you were pretty sure you'd wind up dead if anyone recognized you, eh?" Claudius ran his hand over his hair.

Poppa leaned against the doorway. "I must confess, I am a little surprised by your reaction," he told Claudius. "Desertion is a capital offense, or have the rules changed since I was in command?"

Claudius got up quickly, and waved for Poppa to be quiet. He ducked his head outside and looked both ways hurriedly before taking Poppa by the arm and offering him his chair. Claudius sat on the edge of the table and offered Poppa a cup, then poured him some wine.

"I'd join you, but I have only the one cup," he said. "Oh well ..." and he proceeded to take a swig from the bottle.

Poppa sipped the cup. The wine was bitter, poor stock, imported from Tuscany though, and it brought back memories.

"They're not taking care of you as well as they used to," he said to the other man.

Claudius shook his head in agreement. "Not like in the old days," he replied. "Gods! 'The old days?' Have I gotten so old?" He looked at Poppa. "Lucius! I still can't believe my eyes."

"Lucas, now, if you recall," Poppa corrected him.

"Oh, that's right – after your baptism, and all that, right?" Claudius remembered. "Can't say that I admire your choice of faiths, but then – who's to say? Maybe all gods are one god, I don't know."

Poppa took another sip of the bitter wine. "It's not for my faith that I risked coming here," he informed the older man. "I have news, urgent news that must get to Arthur, the High King."

Claudius looked at Poppa as he considered. "The High King, eh? I'm not sure that's any of our affair, Luciu – *Lucas*. Rome hasn't meddled in the affairs of Britain for some time, now, as you well know."

"I know," Poppa replied. "But this king is different. That's all I can tell you. The hope of the future lies with him – whether it be a bright one or a dark one depends on much. Not the least of which is whether or not you will send word to him that the rebel lords are marching." Poppa looked at Claudius intently, and tried to impress upon the older man the import of what he was saying. "Were I still Lucius, I could order you to send word – and believe me, my old friend, I would do it. This is that important."

Claudius frowned at being reminded of their old relationship, the difference in position they once held.

"As you haven't called for the guards to come and drag me away, or ordered my execution, I assume you recall that I once held your respect and loyalty?"

"That was when you still owed your allegiance to Rome," Claudius answered. "And when I still owed my allegiance to you as my centurion."

Claudius got up and took another swig from the bottle as he paced the small office thinking. "Oh, who am I kidding?" he said. "I still respect you, Lucius – for the man you were. I don't know why you deserted – only that being the kind of man you are, it surely wasn't done lightly. And I trust you. Gods help me, but I do! This will probably get me in a lot of hot water with the emissaries of Rome, but I'll do it."

Poppa felt greatly relieved. So much was at stake here, and at least he had done what he could. The rest was up to God.

"Hail, Caesar!" he said as he downed the last of his wine.

"To Caesar!" Claudius toasted and drank a deep drought as well.

Poppa stood and embraced the older man. "Thank you, old friend. For the love you once bore me."

Claudius held Poppa by the forearms. "You're welcome, Lucius. May your god watch over you! And he'll need to if you ever show your face around my door again!" He looked Poppa in the eye. "You know the others who are still around probably wouldn't be as understanding as I, right?"

Poppa understood.

"Then farewell, Lucius who is now Lucas!" Claudius saluted Poppa in the old Roman manner, and Poppa returned the salute.

"Farewell, my friend. And may God keep you as well! May you know peace and find a happy retirement, for the days of Rome are fading, my friend. Sadly."

Claudius nodded. "Aye, that they are. But what times they were, eh? Quickly, now, before anyone else recognizes you!"

Poppa ducked under the doorway, and Claudius escorted him to the gate where he recovered his spear. With a final salute, he departed, and headed back home as swiftly as he could. With satisfaction he heard Claudius give the order for a messenger to mount up and carry word south "as though the hounds of hell were at his heels!"

Chapter 3

Carados roared in frustration as he spurred his horse and his men onward. His great battle axe dripped blood and gore as he shouted orders at the army in retreat. He didn't know who had betrayed them, but Arthur and his force of twenty thousand had ambushed him and his fellow rebel lords and their army of fifty thousand men near the Forest of Bedgrayn. The rebel army had laid siege to a castle near the forest, and left a small force to occupy it while they went on toward where they believed Arthur was encamped. Arthur had attacked at night while Carados and his men camped, resting before the next day's march and anticipated battle. Two of Arthur's knights, Ulfius and Brastias, brave men he conceded, had struck quickly and deeply with a mere three thousand men, but killed more than twice that number in the confusion and darkness. The rebel lords, once the light began to arise and they could see each other, mounted a fierce counter attack. They carried the battle to Arthur's camp, causing heavy casualties on both sides. However, Sir Kay succeeded in wounding King Lot, a grievous wound to his head leaving the man half-blinded from the blood dripping into his eye. And Arthur struck the King of a Hundred Knights so fiercely that the sword cleaved through the man and into the beast, felling both. Carados, who was of unusual stature and was sometimes called "the Giant," had seen the latter and charged to engage Arthur directly, but was swept away by the number of other combatants in the field. By the time he had fought his way clear, the tide had turned against the rebel forces, and his men were fleeing the field. That was when the armies of Kings Bran and Bors, ten thousand fresh, entered the field from concealment. King Lot of Orkney ordered a retreat, but also commanded that six of the lords, Carados being one of them, hold the pass and "do as much damage as possible."

Cowards! Carados swore. *Had we united forces, we could have stopped Arthur in the pass for we had the superior numbers. But Lot is too much a woman at heart and so ran like the bitch he is!*

So Carados and five other lords and their men turned back to wear the pursuing army down, and gave the main force a chance to escape. The fighting was fierce and bloody on both sides, and many a good warrior found his death that day. But that was the only good kind of death to find in Carados' way of thinking. He had heard of the Valhalla of the Viking raiders and found the idea appealed to him, for he was a man who took delight in killing and destruction. The battle raged on for most of the day, bodies of men and horses clogging the narrow canyons of the pass, giving neither side the advantage. Blood poured along the ground like a tiny river, so many had been killed or wounded. Finally, Arthur's forces turned back to pitch their pavilions and end the day's bloodletting. Carados heard later from one of his fellow lords that it was Merlin who called for the battle's end, but no matter. It had given them a chance to turn their men north toward home.

In their northward haste, Carados and his men burned the fields and villages along their way to prevent Arthur's host from finding forage and to burden the king with the dispossessed. Such was the way of the world, and such was the fate of commoners the realm over.

Poppa smelled the smoke before he heard the sounds of horses or felt the tramp of thousands of feet as they approached the farm. He dressed quickly, shouting for Michael and his sister to get up and grab their things.

"Hurry! Hurry!" he shouted at them as he pulled Michael, still bleary with sleep, down from the loft. Rose followed in her shift, holding hers and Michael's blankets in one hand while holding the ladder with the other.

"Poppa, what's the matter?" she asked.

"No time for that," Poppa hushed her. "Get out of the house. Now! Go down by the stream, and take your brother with you. Go to the spot where we find the best fishing, near the deep pool where the beavers have built their dam. You know the place?" He grabbed Rose by the shoulder and gripped her so tightly it hurt.

"You know the place?" he asked urgently. Fear was written on his face, and it made Rose afraid, too. She nodded dumbly as Michael began to whimper. Poppa had never behaved this way before, and it was terrifying.

"Good. Now go! *Run!*"

Rose grabbed Michael's hand and practically dragged him out the door and into the night. The southern horizon had a strange orange-red glow, and she could smell smoke as bits of ash fell on her face and stung her eyes.

She was already thirteen and had begun to grow as puberty began the process of transformation. She was still gangly and lean, but years of farm labor had made her strong, and she held Michael firmly as she led the way across the fields towards the apple trees her mother had planted long ago. Michael, though, struggled and fought against her.

"No! I want to stay! I want to help! Rose, let me go!" he shouted as he was pulled along.

Poppa ran across the yard to the barn and began to shoo the animals out. "Toothless Bill" their goat skipped away bleating loudly, followed by Brown Betty their cow. He had to lead their old workhorse, Gwynn, as it bucked and fought, frightened by the smell of smoke and the unaccustomed tone of its master.

Rose cast a quick glance back to watch Poppa, her heart hammering in her chest. *Hurry, Poppa!* she prayed. *Hurry!*

They had made it almost to the edge of the wheat field when they heard it – the jingle of armor and the tramping of men's feet. She saw torches appear just over the edge of the road and gasped at the sight of them. Dozens, then hundreds of them, coming at speed, many on foot but some on horseback. *These cannot be the knights we saw!* She thought to herself. These men were ragged and torn, covered in grime and filth, blood and mud, and looked more like beasts than men. And they were coming!

Michael's hand pulled free, and he ran back towards the farm.

"Michael!" she called after him. He disappeared into the high winter wheat, and she hesitated just a moment before heading after him, trying to follow the bent and broken stalks. "Michael!" she shouted again, but he didn't answer. She could hear him as he crashed his way across the field, but she lost sight of him, and panic began to set in. The ground was trembling beneath her; she could feel the vibration through the soles of her feet. She could hear the shouts and swearing of the men as they neared the field and heard one of them order "Burn it all! Kill anything that lives!" She peeped out from the cover of the stalks and saw a huge giant of a man pointing toward the farmhouse with a great axe and bellowing out orders to the ragged men around him.

Rose was terrified. She felt a sudden fear for both Michael and Poppa that overcame the fear she felt for herself, and she made a crouching run along the ditch that ran the length of the field back toward the barn. She heard a scream and turned to see Michael being seized by one of the men on horseback, his body hanging limply as it was thrown over the neck of the horse.

Oh my God! "Michael!" she screamed. Her feet seemed rooted all of a sudden, and the world seemed to slow down as in a dream. Sounds seemed both sharper than normal and muted at the same time. Her eyesight seemed as sharp as she imagined an eagle's would be, but also blurred along the edges. She saw Poppa come out of the barn, the long boar spear in his hand. She couldn't recall ever having seen Poppa stand so straight and tall as he did right now. His face looked almost calm, serene even, as he stopped midway between the barn and the approaching hoard. The giant on horseback roared something, but Rose couldn't make out what, and launched his horse toward Poppa, the great axe whirling in his hand. Two other men on horseback drew swords and charged after. She watched as Poppa stood his ground, the giant almost upon him, and then he planted the butt of the spear in the ground and leaned himself to the side as the tip entered the breast of the speeding horse. Poppa jumped aside as the great beast toppled, sending the giant of a man flying over the saddlebow and crashing into the earth. Rose watched, paralyzed, as the two other horsemen closed in on Poppa, who somehow managed to duck under the blow of the first, and coming up on his offhand side, reached up and pulled the man to the ground. The second kicked his horse so that it threatened Poppa with slashing hooves, but Poppa stayed out of the way. He kicked the horseman he had just unseated in the head, and Rose heard the snap of his neck quite clearly. She watched in disbelief as Poppa picked up the sword from the man's senseless hand and climbed into the saddle. He saluted the other swordsman and spurred the mount toward him. The other swordsman and he exchanged a furious round of blows, and she flinched as she saw Poppa's shoulder opened by a cut from the other man's blade. But Poppa didn't stop. He hardly seemed to react to the wound at all and parried the man's next blow, and the one after that, before catching the man in the throat with the tip of his borrowed blade.

The rabble of footmen had reached the farm by now, and Poppa turned with dead eyes to face hundreds of possible opponents. But a deep voice boomed across Rose's awareness: "Leave him to me!" it bellowed.

The giant had stood up, and he gestured for a horse with his free hand, his other holding tight to his great battle-axe.

"This one is mine," he said as he mounted his new horse and grinned like a wolf.

Poppa turned the horse he was on, and Rose saw the slightest trace of emotion cross his face as he looked upon the giant, and it made her blood turn icy cold. It was as if a ghostly face had lain superimposed on Poppa's for just a breath, and it made Rose's heart stand still.

Poppa raised his sword in salute, which the giant ignored. The giant snarled and kicked his horse into a gallop. Poppa did the same, and the two rode at breakneck speed toward each other. The giant whirled his axe, roaring as he struck, while Poppa tried to duck under the blow and catch the giant with a backhand slash at his side. But, the giant was too skilled and adjusted his swing so that it still managed to catch Poppa, and he was knocked from his horse with a terrible gash in his ribs. He coughed, and blood came out of his mouth as he tried to stand. The giant, however, took full advantage, and spun his mount around and brought his great axe down as Poppa struggled to rise. Rose watched in horror as she saw the blade bite deep into Poppa's skull, and she watched him topple forward into the mud.

"NO!" Rose heard a voice screaming, and it took her a moment to realize that it was her own.

The giant turned his horse, and pointed his great axe, still dripping with Poppa's blood and brains, right at Rose as he shouted, "Seize her!

Rose's feet came unfrozen, and she dashed away as a group of men came rushing toward her. She was quick and light and fueled by fear as it hammered through her veins. She also had the advantage of knowing the lay of the land, and she passed through field and brook like a fox, unmindful of the pull of briars and the catch of thorns that snatched at her clothes, skin, and feet. Rose stopped, seemingly coming out of a twilight dream and into painful awareness only when she had reached the stream that led to the place where Poppa had told her and Michael to hide.

Michael! The image tugged at her heart, making her want to cry. But the crash of the footmen hunting her spurred her into action. Rose stepped into the stream, the icy cold waters made doubly painful by the cuts and scrapes on her legs and feet, and made her way downstream to the deep pool Poppa had spoken of. At the southern end was a beaver dam, and further out was a little lodge made by the animals for shelter.

"Damn! When I catch tha' li'tle bitch, I'll make her sorry, tha's fer sure!" she heard a voice say.

Rose took a deep breath and plunged into the icy water. She swam towards the beaver lodge, hoping she might be able to squeeze inside as she used to when she was younger. She had managed to do it, but only once when she was pretty sure there were no beavers inside it. The trappers had taken them all one year for their furs. But, no, the entryways were too small for her now.

Rose came up for air, the cold chilling her rapidly, stealing her strength away like a bleeding wound. She knew she had to find shelter, and quickly, or she would die – from the cold if not from the men hunting her. *And I won't die!* Rose swore. *I won't die until I kill the man who killed Poppa!* The image came back, clear yet distant, the shock of it too fresh in Rose's mind for her to feel the emotions locked up with it. Her need to survive was too great.

Someone came crashing through the briar, and Rose ducked under the water, praying she wouldn't be spotted.

"C'mon, damn you! Where ye' at, ye' li'tle bitch?" a voice called out. The man poked about the edge of the briar. "I won' hurt ye'," he said. *Much*, he thought. He looked about the little pool and reached in with one hand to test the water. "Brr! If she wen' in there, I hope she drown'd. Serve her right, li'tle shrew!" The man watched the surface of the pond for a few breaths, then pushed back through the bracken and tramped away.

Rose came up with a gasp and swam to the shore no longer caring if she was found or not. The cold water was too painful to endure, and the cold air was enough to kill her anyway.

Better that than the death that awaits me at the hands of such beasts as those!

Rose shivered as she crouched beneath the barren tree that overhung the water. She pushed herself back against the bank of earth that lay exposed beneath the roots of the tree and kept herself out of the breeze and out of sight of casual seekers. Rose felt rather than heard the beat of hooves as they neared the place she crouched, and she held her breath for fear of being discovered. Another timeless stretch of terror seemed to go on forever before the hoof beats passed away, and she could breath again.

It started to rain, and Rose realized that she must find shelter or freeze to death. So, with slow and hobbling footsteps, she began to head west in hopes of finding one of the outlying farms unmolested. Tears streamed down her face and mingled with the rain, but Rose didn't care. She stubbornly put one foot in front of the other and kept on walking, unmindful of her bloody feet, stumbling blindly through the weather until at last she came upon a field of tilled earth. Rose didn't know how far she had come, nor was she sure which farmstead she may have found, only that arriving here gave her new hope. Food and a warm fire would do her good. Hopefully the people living here were still at home!

She pressed forward, squinting through the falling rain to see if she could catch sight of the stead, and nearly fainted with joy when she saw smoke coming out of the chimney.

Even if the owners have run off, at least their home is still standing, and there's a fire to dry myself!

Rose approached the wooden door carefully, suddenly fearing that someone less agreeable to chance upon may have lighted the fire. She placed one foot cautiously on the porch, which creaked causing Rose to stand still with her heart hammering in her throat. She heard a dog growl and begin to bark from inside the stead, and then the sudden thudding of several feet. Her hand was still stretched out in front of her, ready to push the door slowly open when it was suddenly wrenched open, and Rose found herself facing a red-faced old man waving a fire iron.

"Come nay further, ye' devils!" he shouted, brandishing the iron threateningly. "Ye'll have no sport here without a fight, an' tha's for sure!"

He stopped and gasped, gaping at Rose who couldn't help but laugh at the incongruity of the old man's appearance. Her fears had made her expect someone more dreadful than the thin, aged farmer standing in his nightshirt.

"Ay? What are ye' laughing at, girlie? Ye' daft or somethin'?" he asked.

A woman's voice came from behind the old man. "Who is it, 'arry?" she asked. "T'is no reaver, tha's for sure!" A large heavy-set woman appeared behind the old man and looked at Rose in surprise. "Why, lass! Ye' look quite a fright! Oh, let 'er in, 'arry!" she ordered as she pushed the old man aside and took Rose by the arm. "Why, lass, ye're near froze through an' through!" She tsked, tsked, tsked as she led Rose to the fire and sat her down.

The old man stood staring at Rose, still holding the iron as though he couldn't recall what it was for. The woman waved at him to put it away. "T'is al'right, 'arry. T'is clear she be no reaver. Now put the weapon down. *Put it down!*" she shouted the last part.

The old man seemed hard of hearing, but finally lowered the weapon, though he continued to stare at Rose in puzzlement.

Rose took in her surroundings – the simple homey furniture, sideboard, straw flooring. It all made her homesick, and she began to cry again. The memory of Poppa's death came flooding back, and her grief came pouring out.

Poppa! Michael! Whatever will I do? she wondered.

"Ah, now lass, lass, lass!" the large woman rushed back and threw a heavy blanket around Rose's shoulders. She hugged her in close and rocked her as Rose let out her grief. "Shh, shhh, shh … T'will be al'right, just ye' wait an' see." Rose let herself enjoy the woman's comfort, drinking it in.

Two small children came out from wherever they had been hiding, and watched Rose with wide, curious eyes. The old man came and sat opposite Rose, poking up the fire and seeming to dismiss the girl entirely.

Rose finally cried herself out, and the woman helped her to the loft and tucked her in. The familiarity of the act was comforting, and Rose fell quickly asleep.

Terrible nightmares awakened Rose, and she jerked awake with a start, scrambling back and waking the children sleeping with her. They began to scream, and it took Rose a moment to remember where she was. Candlelight appeared, followed by the concerned face of the woman as she climbed the ladder to see what was wrong.

Rose hugged herself, as she shook with fear that was slowly subsiding. She had had a horrible dream of a large wolf crashing through the doors of her homestead, and she was all alone. No Poppa, no Michael. She couldn't find any place to hide as the huge beast came lunging after her, saliva dropping from its cruel muzzle.

The woman managed to settle the children down, and she waved for Rose to follow her down below. The woman handed Rose a shawl and poked up the fire. She set a pot of herbal tea to heat, and sat with Rose while it heated.

"Bad dream?" she asked.

Rose nodded.

The woman shook her head slowly. "I'm not surprised, wha' with the soldiers passin' through, burnin' and pillagin' everything as they go. Were ye … did they *hurt* ye?" the woman asked with concern plain upon her face.

Rose shook her head. Tears came unbidden, but Rose choked them back. *Enough tears for one day!* She admonished herself. *Time for that later. After I have killed the giant!*

A scowl came over Rose's face, and the woman reached her hand out and touched Rose lightly on the back of her hand. "What 'as 'appened, me dearie?" she asked gently.

Rose looked at this kind woman who had taken her in, without question, and given her food, warmth, and comforting.

"Those – soldiers ..." Rose stopped, unable to speak, her throat taught with emotion. "Those *men*," she finally continued, "murdered my father, and my brother, Michael." She stared into the fire as if looking into the future. Her voice became cold and even. "They burned my farm. They would have killed me, too. And one day, I will kill them."

"Ach, lass!" The woman wagged her head in sympathy. "I'm right wise sorry for ye're loss. But, lass!" she pleaded, "Ye cannot mean that! Murderin' those men won't bring back those ye' 'ave lost. T'is somethin' for the King to attend to, metin' out justice an' all tha'."

Rose looked at the woman with dull eyes. "I will kill them. I will kill the man who killed my father. And I will kill the man who killed my brother." Her eyes were hard, and she spoke as if her words were being written in stone.

The woman felt a shiver go through her spine, and she crossed herself and made a sign against evil. *Can't be too careful!* the woman thought to herself. She stared at Rose sadly. "I know ye, don' I? Ye look familiar to me, some'ow." She tried to figure it out.

"I'm not sure," Rose said. "I helped Poppa at the market sometimes, but mostly he took Michael. He wanted to teach Michael how to help run things when he got bigger."

"Sure!" the woman snapped her fingers. "It come back to me, now! Ye're the child of tha' 'ansome young man. Oh, 'e was always so nice, I remember! An' yer' mother? Tha's why I remember ye – ye remind me of 'is wife. Pre'ty young thing, she was. Fiery red hair. Carried 'erself like a princess or somethin'. Wha' was it we called 'im? Ay, tha's right – 'The Squire' we used to call 'im. 'E weren't no run o' th' mill farmer, an' tha's fer sure!"

"My mother's been dead for several years, now," she told the woman. "Though my Poppa told me that I looked like her."

"Right pre'ty, she was! An 'im, so gen'lemanly. Ay, I'm sorry t'hear she's been gone some time, now." The woman wiped a tear from her own eyes with the corner of her shawl. "Ah, the tea's ready! Have a bit. T'will help ye t'sleep."

Rose took a mug and sipped on the hot tea. It was sharp, but soothing. "My name is Rose," she finally offered.

"Mine is Mary," she answered and smiled warmly. "My pa's name is 'arry. Well, truth be told, 'e's me poor, dead 'usbands pa, but I feel like 'e's me own!" She laughed at that. "An' me two youngun's are Bess an' Nathan."

"Thank you," Rose told Mary earnestly. "I ... I owe you more than I can ever repay. I owe you my Life!"

Mary drained her tea and gave Rose a warm hug. "Then ye' can pay me back by bein' sure ye' don't throw it away by lookin' for vengeance," she told Rose.

Rose hugged her back, but said nothing except, "Goodnight, Mary."

"Goodnight, child."

Rose woke late the next day. Mary had let the poor girl sleep, shushing her two children and making sure they did not disturb Rose's rest.

The freshness of Rose's loss came back to her as she awakened to familiar surroundings – the bed in the loft, and the smell of freshly baked bread and wood smoke. The sharpness of it clutched at her heart, and Rose wanted to stay in bed forever and escape into numbing slumber. But the low flame of vengeance burned inside, ready to be fanned into action, and Rose slipped out from under warm quilt and splashed cold water on her face before descending the ladder and joining Mary's household.

"Ah, I'm glad t'see ye're up!" the large woman said as she poured out hot herbal tea for Rose and set down a cup of honey and a small plate of bread and butter.

"Thank you," Rose said. The food was good, but Rose felt dull and heavy inside, and so ate very little.

Mary watched with sadness. *T'will take some time, poor child, afore this wound has healed.* "What more can we do for ye'?" she asked Rose. "Know ye' are welcome to stay as long as need be. Lord knows, I could use the 'elp, wha' with these two youngun's underfoot."

Rose was grateful for the offer, and part of her longed to say "Yes" and stay here in the comfort and coziness of a familiar setting. But the memory of Poppa's death, and of Michael – she feared the worst for her brother, and had to know for sure, or she could never know peace again – made her say, "I must go. I thank you from the bottom of my heart. And who knows? I may come back. But, for now, I must say no."

Mary understood, though it saddened her.

"Well, I have a few things, old clothes that might fit ye'," she told Rose. "They be boy's clothes, I'm afraid, but they'll keep ye' warm."

Rose was extremely grateful and felt that dressing as a boy might not be such a bad thing. It would help disguise her from the giant and his men, and she might be able to use that to her advantage in being revenged on them.

It was already past midday when Rose left Mary's cottage with a knapsack slung over her shoulder filled with what vittles Mary pressed upon Rose to take against Rose's protests.

Rose looked back and said a quick prayer to whatever gods might hear to bless the household, then took her bearings and headed off toward what remained of her homestead.

Rose came across other farmsteads that had been burned and destroyed, and it added fuel to her desire for vengeance. She hardened herself when she passed one steading where Rose heard women and children crying over the loss of their live-stock and household. Her own grief threatened to overwhelm her, and so she pressed on, determined to get back to the farm as quickly as possible before giving up in despair.

The sun was already nearing the horizon by the time Rose reached the edge of their property. The reek of wet, smoldering wood reached her, and she steeled herself for what she might find. Step by step, Rose neared the ruins of the cottage. She felt hot tears begin to flow down her cheeks as she approached the smoking ruin. The rain had kept the cottage from burning to the ground, and the skeleton of the barn was still standing in coal black, the remains still smoking. And there, in the middle of the yard, lay Poppa's body.

Rose went over and knelt over his remains. She felt suddenly cold inside. Numb. No amount of tears would bring Poppa back, she knew. And whatever had been Poppa was no longer here. What was left was just an empty vessel, one that deserved respect and a proper burial, but not tears. Rose stood up and approached the house. She stepped over what had been the entryway, and looked around to see what the fire had left. The hearth still stood, and the ironwork and pot for boiling water, as well as the cooking pot. The roof was completely destroyed, leaving the cottage open to the sky, and the loft had collapsed in ashes. Where Momma and Poppa's room had been there was only the remains of the bed frame – headboard and three of the four posts. The floorboards here were still relatively un-touched, saved by the rain which must have started not long after the cottage had been set aflame.

Rose crouched down and swept some of the ash away from the floor with her hand, and found the latch where her Poppa kept his "treasured things." Rose had been shown them before, the small wooden keepsake box that held something of her mother's – a silver filigree pendant – though Poppa hadn't told her what it meant, only that it had belonged to Momma and was significant to her before her passing. Poppa said that one day, when Rose was old enough, it was Momma's wish that she have it. *I guess I'm old enough, now,* Rose thought to herself remorse-fully. Rose took the pendant out of the box and looked at it. It was delicate with intricate, fine silver lacework that intertwined itself three times. She pulled the chain over her head and slid the pendant under her tunic to keep it safe. The feel of it on her chest was comforting, somehow, like the touch of her mother.

Rose reached down into the space to see if Poppa had left anything else, anything of his that might be buried with him, and Rose felt around in the space under the floorboards. Her hands felt a small bundle, wrapped in leather, and she pulled it out carefully. The bundle was tied tightly and was about a forearm in length. Rose pulled on the knot until the leather cord snapped, and it began to come open. Whatever was inside was wrapped in very old cotton cloth. Rose rolled it open and found an odd bronze rod topped with an eagle about a forearm in length. She examined the cloth more closely, noting the once rich but faded red color of it. It turned out to be a square cut tunic, edged with gold thread! Rose recognized it, but was confused by what she had found. *This is a Roman tunic! And the rod – that is a Roman eagle! Where did Poppa get these from?* she wondered. *Were they* his?

The light was fading quickly, and Rose did not want to spend the night in the ruins of her former homestead. She gathered up the tunic and the rod and carried them outside to her Poppa's remains.

"Poppa," she said to him, "Wherever your spirit may be, I promise you this - I will avenge your death. And I will find out what became of Michael, and I will avenge his spirit as well! I pray that the two of you are together, wherever you are. And that you are with Momma, now."

Rose was oddly calm. She went and found a shovel in the ruins of the barn, though the handle was burned almost entirely away. She gathered up what metal implements she could and laid them out next to her Poppa's corpse. Rose removed the small dirk she found in Poppa's belt, then she took her cloak, and rolled Poppa's body onto it, and dragged it out into the fields as dusk fell. It was too dark to see, so Rose resolved herself to sitting vigil over Poppa's body during the night to make sure no animals defiled it. She intended to bury him in the apple orchard next to Momma once daylight came.

And then I will find the giant, and I will kill him! She didn't know how, but Rose was sure that she would. And she would find out what had happened to her brother as well.

It was a lonely, cold vigil Rose kept. She dozed despite the chill, wrapped in the cloak Mary had given her. But she would wake with a start soon after slipping off, and struggled to keep herself alert and awake. Dawn was a long time in coming. The night was made more horrible by Rose's imagination, causing her to go still and hold her breath whenever she heard movement in the leaves – but no harm came to her. Rose longed to light a fire, but had neither tinderbox nor tools to do so, and feared the light might attract unwanted visitors, so she endured the cold.

When dawn came, it arrived wrapped in a dense, heavy fog. The moisture of it seeped through Rose's clothes, leaving her shivering despite her layers of protection. With stiff, cold fingers, Rose used the blade of the shovel to dig a shallow grave for Poppa, laying him next to where Momma had been put to rest. The soil was loose due to the recent rainfall, for which Rose was thankful, though the task still took her several hours. She worked without a break, not even pausing to nibble a biscuit, until the hole was deep enough to take Poppa's body. Carefully, she slid Poppa's remains into the shallow hole, placing the Roman tunic over him and the eagle in his hands. Then she reverently piled earth on top of him, repeating what prayers she could remember from Poppa and Momma – invoking both the Christian God and the Earth Mother in her blessings on Poppa's spirit. Rose said a prayer for Michael's spirit, too. Weary and cold, Rose gathered up her meager belongings and took one last look around. All she could see were the ghosts of the apple trees standing like silent sentinels in the mist. All the rest was just cold, grey emptiness.

Rose broke her fast, a light meal of dried apples, figs, and hard bread. She ate slowly, feeling no particular hurry to charge into the unknown. And the sense of her loneliness was profound. She was truly, for the first time in her life, all alone. No Poppa. No Michael. Momma had been gone for years now, and she had no other family that she knew of. No one to whom she felt she could turn, to ask for aid.

The mist had lifted slightly but showed no signs of clearing as Rose struck out for the main road. From there, she intended to follow it north, since that seemed to have been the general direction the giant and his men had been traveling.

Rose encountered refugees coming the opposite way, small pockets of women, children, and the aged. Rose asked of them from time to time if they had seen or heard of the hoard - if they, too, were victims of its rampage. And "Yes" she was told, as fingers pointed further northward, and sad, grim faces shook their heads in grief. She learned the giant's name from one of the dispossessed, a man who had lost everything – wife, children, farmstead – to the passing army.

"Carados, aye!" he spat and leaned upon his walking stick, gripping it tightly in leathery hands. "May all the gods curse him and his dogs!"

Rose thanked the man with a reassuring touch on his arm. "I promise you, old father, the gods intend to feast on Carados' soul as ravens feast on the fallen he has left in his passing."

The man looked at Rose closely, his eyes widening slightly, as he said, "Why, you be no lad! Why would you seek death, girl? Or worse, at the hands of Carados and his beasts? Come with me south. Let us petition the King, this Arthur, and let him seek retribution!"

Rose only shook her head. "The King may seek justice, but I seek vengeance. My own were taken from me, and it is my own that must have blood for blood."

The man seemed to shiver, and he made a sign against evil. "Then the gods watch over you, lassie! May your blade be true and swift!"

Rose picked up her pace. The stream of refugees had dwindled. Carados' army had stopped reaving the countryside once they had neared their own borders and slowed their march, either not fearing or not caring if pursuit was not far behind.

Rose began to try to formulate a plan, to think of some way to get close enough to Carados that she could kill him. She had no illusions that she would only get one chance. She had seen the giant's skill with that great battle-axe of his, and much as she desired to cleave Carados' skull with the same weapon that had slain her Poppa, Rose knew she could never wield so heavy a blade. No, she must use a dirk or dagger and slay the giant in his sleep if she could. Slit his throat and stare into his huge face as she watched his life drain out of him. *The same way we slaughter pigs!* she thought to herself with grim satisfaction.

It was still a couple of days before Rose heard signs of the army camped within the woods. Laying her hand on the dagger in her belt, Rose crept into the woods cautiously, crouching low to avoid being seen by any scouts or sentries. The men in the camp talked loudly, unafraid of being seen or heard in their own lands. It was still early morning when Rose found the camp, and she sneaked about looking for a place to hole up and wait until night. Hopefully she would be able to sneak into the camp and find Carados' tent without difficulty, assuming it would lie in the center of the camp. A host of concerns in Rose's mind clamored for attention, all the things that could go wrong. But Rose's determination was unwavering. The memories of that terrible night kept her focused on her goal. Michael's scream and the image of his limp body being pulled up by one of Carados' men. And the image of Poppa – Poppa as he stood there confronting Carados and his army, tall and proud, calm.

Poppa, lend me the courage of your spirit this night! Rose prayed. She found a little hollow screened by bushes that allowed her to spy into the camp, and she settled down to watch and wait. She knew she must eat in order to keep her strength up, but she felt no appetite and so ate very little.

The day wore on. At one point, Rose heard the clatter of hooves and peered out from her cover as Carados and some of his knights rode into camp. It took a great deal of self-control for Rose to remain where she was, but she knew that to expose herself now was certain death. And so, she gripped her dagger with white knuckles and stayed very still. She watched as the giant climbed down from his horse and greeted his captains with an embrace of forearms. Her heart leapt a little as she saw him enter a tent much closer to the edge of camp than she had imagined.

The gods must surely be with me!

If that was Carados' tent, it would be an easier matter to creep around the edge of the camp and slip in unseen!

But shortly after, Carados emerged from the tent, shouting something Rose couldn't understand from where she was, and climbed back onto his horse. Rose was startled as trumpets blared, rousing the camp into action.

What's this? Rose wondered.

Carados and his knights rode off, and the men began to strike camp.

No! Rose shouted inside. *No! Not when he was this close!*

Rose had nearly crawled out from under the cover of the brush when she heard footsteps crunching through the undergrowth around her. She scrambled back just in time to avoid being seen by two men, probably sentries, as they walked their patrol heading back to camp.

"The High King hasn't come any further is what I hear," said one to the other.

"Pah! Afraid to come any further is what you mean," said the second. "Arthur knows we outnumber him, despite the slaughter in Bedgrayn. King Lot and the kings of Scotland and Ireland have enough men here to beat him back to London should he follow."

"No, I don't doubt Arthur's courage. I saw him in the field, and so did you! It's the wizard who called him back. Told him he was doing too much killin'. Can you believe that? 'Too much killin'? And here I thought that was the whole idea of war."

"Aye, I do remember Arthur in the field. What a sight! You're right, he be no coward. But, still, I'm right when I tell you we outnumber him."

"All right, fine! You're right, so what? It was Lot who turned tail and ran when Carados wanted to stand and fight. Our own ally who left us to defend the passage, leaving us to face Arthur on our own!"

"Well, we did have help, of course," said the second.

"Help? It was us that did most of the fightin'! It was us that did most of the dyin', too! Pah!" spat the first.

The two men walked out of hearing as Rose pondered what she had heard.

Arthur isn't coming? So, what does that mean to someone like Carados?

The camp was quickly struck, and the army moved out well before sundown, following the road as it headed slightly north-east. The line proceeded without much hurry, though. Word of Arthur's forces having turned back spread quickly from man to man. Rose tailed them, staying far enough behind that she wouldn't be spotted. Or so she hoped.

The army neared a walled city, and Rose watched as the column of men broke as they approached, some entering the city while the main body began to pitch their tents outside the walls.

Great! Rose thought. *Carados must be inside somewhere. How on earth will I ever find him?*

Suddenly, Rose was grabbed from behind, a strong arm pressed across her throat strangling her as she was lifted off the ground and carried backwards.

"Hullo! What have we here?" said a smooth voice.

Rose felt the point of a dagger pressed under her chin, and she stopped struggling. She was turned around to face her captor.

"And what business do we have here, my young lad? Eh?" asked a slender young man. He stood more than a head taller than Rose and had a well-trimmed beard and moustache. His hood was thrown back revealing a head of reddish-gold hair, and his eyes were blue-grey and watched Rose with an energetic gleam. Rose saw that his buckle was made of gold, and that he had inlays of copper on the handle of the dagger he was using to control her.

"What's that? Cat got your tongue? Maybe I can help you find it," the man joked. He pulled the dagger from Rose's waist. "Hmm, a mouse with teeth. I suppose that makes you a *rat,*" he smirked.

Rose sensed that this man was incredibly dangerous. She had seen this look before, on a cat they used to have on the farm. "A mouser" Poppa had called it. It had gotten the same look one day when it had spotted a field mouse coming out of the barn.

Please, just get this over with! Rose prayed.

The man turned Rose back around and pressed the blade into her back. She could almost feel the point of it coming through her cloak and tunic next to her left shoulder blade, right where it could easily enter her heart.

"Off we go, my little mute! Let us go and see what my lord Carados has to say about my catching a spy right on his very doorstep."

Carados? Rose felt her heart leap into her throat. *Oh gods, but you do have an evil sense of humor! I wanted a way to find Carados, and here I am being brought right to him!*

Chapter 4

The young man escorted Rose through the throng of soldiers outside the walled city. He whistled to himself as he marched Rose up to the gates and kept the blade against her back to control her.

Apparently, the man was some kind of lord or officer as Rose noticed that the guards would salute him or make way for him as they approached.

"Evening, m'lord," said one of the gatehouse guards.

The man merely nodded, smiling, while he waited for the gates to be opened.

"Catch yourself a thief?" the guard asked as the heavy wooden doors swung wide.

"A mouse. Or a rat. Not sure which at the moment. I thought your lord might have some ideas of what we might do to find out," he replied lightly.

Rose's mind was in a whirl.

What do I do? Poppa, Michael – I have failed you!

Rose felt herself filling with dread the further they walked.

The man guided her through the streets, the alleyways light of traffic in the latening day.

"Ah, youth!" the man sighed. "Sweet innocence!"

Rose glanced at her captor, uncertain of his mood or meaning. He merely grinned at her, his eyes shining with an odd gleam.

"Treasured time, yes?" he asked Rose. "Over all too soon." His smile faded, replaced by a sudden sadness that washed over his features. Suddenly, his hand gripped Rose tightly by the nape of the neck and squeezed her painfully. The man pulled her close to him and thrust his face into hers, his eyes glaring. "Don't think I don't know what you're up to, little mouse! Spying! Watching! Who were you going to tell, eh? Poppa? *Daddy?* Well, Daddy isn't here, is he? No one to help. No one to tell." The youth began to sob, and his grip loosened on Rose's neck a bit.

The youth's mad! Rose thought to herself. She felt a twinge of fear go through her as she realized this. *He could kill me and not even know it! Not realize what he's done until it's too late.* She trembled.

The man appeared to feel her trembling, for the sadness left his face and his gay, playful look came back.

"Yes! That's it! You should be afraid, little mouse. Because you know what big, nasty cats do to poor, little, spying mice, don't you? We eat them up – gulp! All in one bite!" He smiled again, seeming to enjoy the idea of chewing her up and swallowing her down. He chewed his mouth, closed his eyes, and patted his stomach as though he had just finished a wonderful meal. His eyes snapped open, and Rose saw him suddenly very stern. His face betrayed a seething anger just under the surface, though at what or against whom she had no idea. The man quickened their pace, and he marched her through the corridors of the keep in silence, his whistling stopped.

They approached a pair of guards standing watch outside a pair of heavy, ornate wood doors. They snapped to attention, and one of them said, "Greetings, my lord!"

Rose was stopped as the young man acknowledged the greeting.

"I have business with your lord," he said. All lightness had vanished from his tone and he was suddenly very formal and businesslike.

47

The guard saluted him and entered the room. Rose heard a deep voice inquire, "What is it?" from within. She couldn't hear anything else, but then the voice said, "Very well, let him in!"

The guard reappeared and waved for the youth and Rose to enter.

Her legs were suddenly as heavy as lead weights as Rose was ushered into the ornate chamber. The room had a high, steepled ceiling hung with banners, and a long, dark wood table ran the length of it down the center. Torches were hung in sconces along the wall, and small, open windows allowed some of the fading daylight to fall in shafts. And there, at end of the great table, his face wrinkled in a deep frown as he studied something on the table, was the giant.

Rose felt her heart give one great beat within her chest, then felt herself go numb. The reality of him there suddenly made her feel like she was made of wood. Her mouth dried up, and she struggled to swallow. All the anger, pain, and frustration that had kept her going was gone like the morning mist in the sun. All she had left was this heaviness and dread.

The giant looked up from the map he had been studying and glanced over Rose before turning his gaze to the man behind her.

"Meraugis, what do you want?" his voiced rumbled with annoyance.

The youth behind her spoke, his voice smooth but firm, "*Lord* Meraugis, my lord Carados."

Rose saw the giant's eyes half-close in anger at the correction. Carados said nothing, but glared through slitted lids.

Meraugis continued unaffected, acting as though he was unaware of the giant's anger. "I caught this youth outside the city, spying on your men. I thought you might like to know that."

Carados' eyes swung back to Rose, and he studied her with intent.

"And you know this boy is a spy *how*, exactly?" he inquired. "I see a youth too young to even have fuzz upon his chin.

Hardly the kind of person I would use to spy in the heart of enemy lands. He'd be lucky to survive far from hearth and home. Look how spindly he is!" Carados' voice boomed in the hall. "He'd probably love to be home sucking on his mother's teat right now, wouldn't you boy?"

They think I'm a boy! Rose felt some relief at hearing that, and it gave her a little of her strength back. But not hope. Not yet, anyway.

Meraugis' hand twitched on the back of Rose's neck. He didn't like being disregarded by the giant, made fun of in this way.

"My lord Carados," he smiled sweetly, "I don't know yet if I am right or not, but this is exactly the kind of person I would choose to be my spy. Who would suspect a child, eh? With their sweet, innocent faces and bright, shining eyes? Watching. Always watching. Just waiting to *tattle*." Meraugis' tone turned sharp again. He grabbed Rose's cloak and shook her a little.

"And what would you have me do?" Carados asked him. "Torture a child for your amusement?"

Meraugis' eyes took on that hungry gleam again. "Oh ... oh, hardly for my ... *amusement*, my lord. No. But to know, that's all. To know what he's seen, what he might tell. Oh, he'd tell, I know he would. He'd tell, and tell, and tell ..." He turned Rose around to stare at her as he said this, while his eyes gazed right through her as if he could look into her soul.

I know what you think he'd tell, Carados thought to himself. *Believe me, I know all about your dirty little secret, my* lord *Meraugis.*

The giant studied the pair from where he sat. Arthur had turned back his forces, he knew, but that didn't mean he wouldn't have spies everywhere. *He did know we'd be coming*, Carados mused. *How else did he know to ambush us in Bedgrayn?* But it seemed too unreasonable, too unlike Arthur to employ children as spies. Carados just couldn't see it.

"How many children bear arms, my lord?" Meraugis asked and pulled out Rose's dagger. He tossed the weapon onto the table near Carados for the giant to examine.

49

Picking up the weapon, Carados noted its make and ran his thumb along its edge to test it. *Razor sharp!* He smiled. *I approve!*

"Most children near that age carry a knife, Lord Meraugis," Carados laughed as he stood. He walked down to Rose and Meraugis, turning the knife over and over, feeling its heft. "I myself was practically born with one in my hand!" he laughed.

The giant stared down at Rose, who glanced away lest he recognize her somehow.

Rose felt trapped between the two men – the giant who stood towering in front of her, and the madman who pressed against her back.

Carados reached down and grasped Rose's face in his huge, meaty hand, forcing her to look at him.

"And what were you going to do with this, boy?" Carados asked her.

Meraugis shook her from behind. "Answer him, my little fellow! Or else you'll come to know what nasty daggers can do!"

Rose felt angry and afraid, hopeless and strangely powerful at the same time. With nothing else to lose, she looked Carados in the eye and said, "I was going to slit your throat with it, *pig*!" She wanted to spit at him but her mouth was too dry. Her heart was hammering so loudly in her throat, she almost lost her awareness of anything else.

Get it over quickly! Rose prayed as she clenched her eyes waiting for the killing blow to come. What she heard instead was laughter! Great, deep, rumbling laughter.

Meraugis stood gaping at her like Rose had turned into a snake, his eyes wide and unbelieving. But Carados stood over her roaring with laughter!

"Oh, aha, ha, ha!" he bellowed with delight. The moment Rose had stared at him, he saw her look grow sharp and serious. When the words registered, the absolute conviction with which this youth had spoken them and the absurdity of the notion made Carados burst out with laughter. "Were you, now? And why would you do that, eh?" he asked with a chuckle.

"Because you killed my father and my brother," Rose said evenly. "Because you burned my farm." Rose felt strangely calm as she said this. "I swore an oath to avenge them."

Meraugis backed away a step or two, and looked up at the giant who was wiping tears from his eyes from his amusement.

"SO," Meraugis said, "I knew it! I knew he was a spy! Assassin! You see, my lord? I know what I am talking about. Send a child to do one's nasty work, yes?"

Carados leaned on the table, his laughter dying down a bit. He looked down at the dagger the child had had with him when Meraugis had caught him.

If this boy came for vengeance, then maybe Meraugis is right, he is a spy – an assassin. Of sorts, anyway. He may not be spying for the king, just out for blood to avenge blood. Carados could understand that kind of thinking. *And what did he say? Oh, yes – that he had come from where I had burned farms and killed those who defended them. That means he's from south of here, outside my lands.*

"Let me take him, my lord," wheedled Meraugis. "I know how to get the truth out of the likes of him."

Oh, I'm sure you do, Carados said to himself. *I'm sure you'd like to take this boy off somewhere by yourself and make him talk. Make him do other things, too, I'd wager. But this is my business. The boy was out for my blood, and for that he must answer to me.*

"Guards!" Carados shouted. "Come here!"

The two guards entered the room with weapons drawn, and stood ready.

"Please escort his lord Meraugis to his room. And close the doors after you! I need to speak with this child alone, and I do not wish to be disturbed. Understood?" Carados demanded.

"Aye, my lord!" they said and waited for Lord Meraugis to accompany them.

Meraugis' face turned a deep red as he stood staring at Carados, vexed.

"What do you mean 'alone' and 'undisturbed?' " he whined. "I found him! He's mine! I get to question him!"

51

Carados stood and glared down at the younger man.

"These are *my* walls, my *lord*," he bellowed. "The boy came here for my blood. And the army outside these walls is my army. That makes this my business, my *lord*."

Meraugis looked up at the giant with a poisonous look. "My father is King Mark, Lord Carados! When I tell him ..."

Carados cut him off. "I know who your father is, my lord Meraugis. But even he would agree that this is my affair. If you wish, you may return to Cornwall and ask him. Now leave me!"

Meraugis practically hissed as he took one last look at Rose, his eyes shooting daggers at her. Then with a huff, he turned his heels and left the room accompanied by the two guards.

Carados grabbed Rose by the front of her clothes and lifted her with one hand to look her in the eye.

"You will tell me everything I wish to know," he warned her, "or I will tear your limbs off one by one until you do. You understand me, boy?"

Rose stared mutely at the giant, and he shook her roughly.

"You know what I am capable of," he shouted at her. "I will put your feet into hot coals! I will break every bone in your body and turn you into jelly for my dinner unless you tell me what I want to know!"

Rose continued to stare at him mutely.

Just kill me and get this over with! she thought.

Carados shook her roughly with both hands, making Rose's neck snap painfully. "Answer me!" he roared at her. "Do you understand?"

When Rose did not answer, Carados struck her forcefully across the face with the back of his hand. The power of the blow nearly knocked Rose unconscious, and blood began to pour from her nose.

The giant seized Rose by the back of her skull and raised his fist again. Her vision blurred; Rose struggled to remain conscious. She tasted blood in her mouth and spat it out in

Carados' face. The next blow smashed Rose's cheek, and she blacked out, luckily for her.

Carados had begun to respect the courage of the child in refusing to answer him despite his size and strength. Grown men were known to balk and quake in the face of Carados' anger, but this boy held his own. However, when the boy spat in his face, his rage broke like a storm, and Carados vented it fully. The boy was knocked unconscious with his first punch, but Carados didn't care. He kept on pounding and pounding until the rage diminished, then hurled Rose's limp body across the room where it struck the wall and fell to the floor, unmoving.

He leaned on the table. The adrenalin in his system from venting his rage made him feel good. Powerful! The blood was coursing through his veins, and he felt hungry for battle.

Carados went over to Rose and checked to see if the boy still lived. He lifted Rose up, and slapped his face to see if he could rouse him. But Rose was too badly injured and remained unresponsive.

Carados growled, frustrated. He wanted more violence. He never felt so good as when he was in combat, be it in the field or in the exercise compound.

That's what I need! Carados thought to himself. *A good workout against some of the slaves. That'll do the trick!*

Dragging Rose's limp body in one hand, Carados seized his double-headed battle-axe and strode from the room. He found some more of his guards and turned Rose over to them.

"What would you like for us to do with him, my lord?" they asked.

Carados thought for a moment. The boy was no threat to him. But, if he were a spy, then it would be best to kill him and deprive Arthur of any further information.

"Take him out into the woods and kill him," Carados ordered. "Leave his body for the wolves." With that, he strode off to find some relaxation in the arena.

Meraugis was in a fit as he was escorted back to his chambers.

How dare he tell me what to do! He raged to himself. *How dare he deprive me of my catch! I know a spy when I see one. Filthy little child! All children are spying little sneaks. Everyone thinks they're so sweet and innocent, but I know better, don't I?*

"Here you are, my lord," one of the guards told him as he opened the door for Meraugis. "Is there anything else I can do for you, my lord?"

Meraugis studied the guard for a moment. *He's not an unhandsome young man,* Meraugis thought. *But, no, he works for that villain, that bully, Carados!*

"No, thank you," Meraugis smiled sweetly. "Very kind of you to ask. I will tell your master what excellent men he has in his household."

The guard smiled at that, saluted, and he and the other guard walked away.

Meraugis' smile quickly vanished, and his face became bitter and petty. He let out a howl of anger and collapsed, beating his palms against the stone floor.

"No! No! No! No! NO!" he shouted. Then he fell onto his back and began to kick and scream like a spoiled child deprived of its favorite toy.

A door opened, and Meraugis' manservant, dressed in the livery of Cornwall, entered the room. He bore a silver tray with a single goblet on it and stood silent and impassive as Meraugis finished his tantrum and lay panting and weeping on the floor. The man spoke not a word. He couldn't, even had he wanted to, for Meraugis had had his tongue cut out in a pique of rage a few years earlier, when he had first been sold into Meraugis' household. He knew too well the capricious and dangerous whims of his master and learned early on to stay still and invisible until his master wished to see him and be waited upon.

Meraugis sat up and noticed his servant waiting, attentive but still. It pleased him, and he felt a small thrill run through his body.

Ah, such faithfulness! he sighed.

"Come here," Meraugis said with a pleased smile on his face.

The servant moved instantly to his master, careful not to spill a single drop of the precious liquor in the cup.

Meraugis took the cup from the tray and took a sip of the wine it held, laced with herbs and honey. A special recipe prepared for him the first time by the King of Lot's beautiful wife, Morgawse. It was she who brought it to him, not so many years ago, and told him what a pretty youth he was. She had stroked his hair, and his face, and was delighted when he told her it was very good. And it was she, the wife of a king, and the daughter of the Duke of Cornwall, and of Ygraine, wife of the High King, that had made him a man that same night.

A princess! Meraugis mused. *And it was she who lifted me out of the shadows of my bastardy and made me a prince! For isn't that what she called me, over and over again that night? A prince?*

"Yes, I *am* a prince!" Meraugis exclaimed out loud. He giggled and sipped more of the special wine. "Prince among men." He giggled again and looked at his mute butler. The man kept his gaze far away, never looking directly at his master. "What is it you see, my sweet, when you look like that? Eh?" He got up on his knees and stared at the man's face. For a moment, he regretted having had his tongue cut out, wishing he could tell him what he sees. "Is it the future you see?" he asked quietly, almost reverently, and reached out to touch him gently. He sighed and dropped his hand. His butler remained as impassive as ever. A living statue.

Meraugis stood and set the goblet back on the tray. The wine always brought such a wonderful sense of relaxation, and Meraugis swayed just a bit unsteadily as he stood up. He straightened his clothes and looked at the open door the man-servant had come through.

"Well," he said, "let us see what fun I can have with my new page, yes?" He walked through the door and into the rest of his chambers. Soldiers in his livery snapped to attention, and he was pleased. Meraugis kept walking through the richly appointed rooms until he came upon a door set into the wall, almost blending into it. No guards stood here, outside this special door. He reached under his shirt, drew out a key hung from a slender gold chain, and set the key in the tiny keyhole, and turned. Behind him came the soft pad of his butler's feet, but Meraugis didn't turn around. The man knew his business and would be the only silent sentinel Meraugis needed here.

The door opened into a dark, windowless little room. Meraugis lit a candle and carried it with him into his "chamber of secrets," little more than a closet, really, intended for a servant to sleep close by to his master. The light revealed to him a young boy, about eleven years of age, bound and gagged and laying face down on a small cot. The boy's eyes shone with fear, and that pleased Meraugis. He sat on the edge of the cot and brushed the boy's hair away from his face. Bruises, some old and black, others still fresh, covered the boy's face, and he whimpered slightly at Meraugis' touch. That pleased Meraugis, too.

"There, there," he crooned to the boy. "Everything's all right. You see?" He pulled the boy to him in a tight hug, and rocked him slightly. "No harm, now. No. We've learned how to be kind, yes? And loving. Just like a daddy ought to be. Yes?" Meraugis looked into the child's haunted eyes, seeing his own reflection in their dark pupils. He stroked the boy's hair over and over again as though to sooth him. "My dear, sweet boy," he said. "My dear sweet ..." *What was it the child had told him his name was? Oh, yes – that's right!* "My dear, sweet *Michael*," he said and hugged the child tightly.

Rose became aware first of the sickening swaying as she was carried over someone's shoulder, then of the terrible pain in her head. Her face hurt, and she could tell she had swallowed some of her own blood from her battered mouth. She heard the jingle of the armor of the man carrying her, and smelled the oily smoke of torches. The light made her wince, and the pounding in her head worse.

"Far enough, d'ya think?" a voice asked.

"Yeah, I think we've come far enough," answered another.

"Phew! Good," said the man who had been carrying Rose. "This boy may look scrawny, but he's heavy as a deer, I can tell you! Must be all muscle."

Rose was dumped to the ground, and the impact sent pain flaring through her ribs and chest. She let out a small mewl and curled into a ball.

"Well, least he ain't already dead," said the second voice.

"Shame in a way," said the first. "Would've been easier on him if he had died from Carados' beating."

Rose heard the ring of steel as the man who had been carrying her drew his sword.

"Shut up, you two!" he ordered. "There may be someone about who wouldn't approve of our slaying a helpless child."

"Hey!" said the first. "Who says you get to do it?" he asked.

"Because I carried him," answered the third man.

"Why don't we dice for it?" asked the second. "He ain't going anywhere." A boot kicked Rose in the side. The pain of it made her vision dim, and she felt nauseous, gagging a bit.

"Why should I dice for what I have the right for?" asked the third man angrily. "I did all the heavy work, so I get to kill him."

Rose was rolled over onto her back by one of the men, who stood over her and drew a dagger from his belt.

"Well, whoever gets to kill him, he won't be needin' no clothes where he's goin', that's for sure," he said as he cut the laces from the front of her tunic. He picked her up by her shirt, and jerked it off over her head.

"Whew!" he whistled, and the other two men fell silent from their arguing. "This ain't no boy!" he exclaimed. He reached down and yanked the silver pendant of her mother's from her neck. "Lookie here!" he exclaimed, holding the prize over his head for the other two to see.

"Now you're gonna have to dice!" said the second man. "For who gets to have her first!" He wiped his beard and leered at her.

The first man, the one standing over Rose, sheathed his weapon and lowered himself down on top of her, bruising her lips as he crushed his mouth upon hers. The weight of him brought agony to Rose's injuries. She twisted this way and that struggling to get him off of her and fighting to breathe. Her struggles only seemed to excite the man on top of her all the more, and he pinned her arms up over her head with one hand while his other tore at her pants, trying to pull them down.

Suddenly the weight was gone from off of her, and Rose coughed up some blood and choked. The third man had pulled the first man off her and was keeping him away from her with his sword.

"Get back!" he commanded. "If anyone gets first takes, its me!" He undid his belt, dropped his pants, and kicked them off.

The first and second men drew their swords, and stood crouched, debating whether or not having first go at Rose was worth it. The second man still tried reasoning.

"C'mon," he said. "We'll all get a go at her. No need to spill anyone's blood but hers."

The third man had backed up until he was nearly straddling Rose, his sword pointed at the other two.

"I told you, I carried her, so I get first ... *gck*!" he was cut short as an arrow punched through his throat, the fletching standing out in front of him. He fell backward as the force of the arrow threw him back, toppling over Rose who lay there dazed and in pain. The ground hurt her exposed torso, and she couldn't find any way to hold herself that didn't bring pain somewhere inside her chest.

"What the ...?" said the second man as he was struck by several shafts. The first man spun around, only to be cut down by a final flight of arrows.

Dark figures emerged from the woods. They were cloaked and hooded with powerful hunting bows in their hands. One of them knelt down to check Rose's captors and slit their throats as good measure with a hunting knife.

Rose felt hands lift her gently to a sitting position, and a woman's voice spoke in an unfamiliar, musical tongue. Rose opened her eyes to see a stern faced, grey-haired woman holding her shoulders and looking at her with a concerned expression.

"Are you all right?" the woman asked. "Did they hurt you?"

Rose shook her head and retched.

One of the hooded figures handed the silver pendant to the woman.

The symbol of Avalon! She gasped slightly as she recognized it. *Is this girl an acolyte? She's far from the sacred isle if that's so. And why were these men going to kill her out here?* It was sacrilege to harm any of the followers of the Goddess. The woman couldn't fathom the mystery.

She squeezed Rose's shoulders gently in reassurance, then turned and spoke to several other shadowy figures in the odd language before turning back to Rose. Rose's shirt was handed to her, and the woman helped her put it back on, noticing the way Rose flinched and winced putting it on. "You'll be all right," she told her. "I have some skill as a chirurgeon," she said.

Rose didn't know what she meant, but nodded weakly.

"Can you stand?" the woman asked her.

Rose wasn't sure, but was determined to try. Arms helped lift her, but the movement brought fire to her lungs, and Rose struggled for breath.

"Ribs," the woman spoke to herself. She looked at Rose with concern plain on her face. "No help for it, now. *Whist!*" She made a circular motion in the air with her hand, and Rose was half helped, half carried forward at a rapid pace. They hadn't traveled more than a hundred yards before Rose's breathing became extremely labored, and she had to be put down.

This is it! Rose thought to herself. *This is how it ends for me.*

The woman and the strange men with whom she traveled had a whispered conference. Rose's head was held as a fiery liquid was forced down her throat. It made her sputter, and cough, which only made the pain in her lungs worse, but it also seemed to ease the hurt in other parts of her body. She felt suddenly very sleepy and mercifully passed out again.

Meg checked Rose carefully as the men with her rapidly built a stretcher out of evergreen branches swiftly chopped from nearby trees and lashed together with chords of leather. The men moved quickly and surely, never speaking a word unless it was absolutely necessary.

A young man in good, sturdy, well-made clothes stood watching, holding a light warhorse by the bridle. He was light haired, and waited with some impatience as Rose was taken care of.

"Not the adventure you were expecting," Meg spoke to the young man who simply shrugged his shoulders.

"I'm not sure what I expected," he answered her. His speech was refined, betraying a youth of some standing. "After all, I said I would follow you for a year, learning what you have to offer without question. So, I will not question you in this, either. You have the knowledge and wisdom that I seek, and I will abide by that."

Meg nodded. His answer was satisfactory and showed promise.

"Mercy," she said to him. "Succor to the weak. Protection to the defenseless. These are all the qualities of a good knight. Remember that, my lord. Knights are made to serve the people and not the other way around. In return, the people give aid and succor to the knight. It is they who provide his upkeep in exchange for his protection."

The young man nodded in understanding and smiled. "You see? Already you impart wisdom to me," he said and bowed to her in a courtly manner.

The hooded men spoke to Meg, letting her know they were ready to travel once again.

"If we may then, my lord," Meg said to him. "We will travel faster, and thus I can begin your training that much more quickly, if we may borrow your noble steed to pull this poor girl's sled?"

The young man's smile faded briefly. A warhorse was no common beast of burden! But, the girl did need help, and he had said that he would serve in whatever ways the old woman had asked when he had found her and her retinue in the wilds. He forced a smile back on his face as he said, "Of course, my lady Automne! As such is thy will, so even shall I do." He handed the reins to her and retreated with another bow.

Meg noted the moment of hesitation, but was pleased with the boy's decision. And she was amused by his calling her "Automne," or "autumn" – a jest about her age.

The men attached Rose's stretcher to the warhorse, and they passed swiftly toward the southwest, out of Carados' lands and into the borderlands of Wales, where Meg had her own lands and a small keep.

Chapter 5

Rose tossed in fretful delirium. Meg frowned, worried about the girl's condition. She reached down and felt Rose's forehead. *The child is burning up!* Meg had checked Rose as best she could and wrapped her ribs tightly in linen to help keep them from moving too much. *Lucky for her,* Meg thought, *that none of them had punctured her lungs or any of her vital organs!*

Rose moaned loudly, rolling back and forth under the blankets.

Meg spoke to one of her attendants. "Go and get me one of the healers from Holywell," she ordered the man. It would take a little over a day for the man to go and come back, but Meg feared that the girl's injuries were beyond her. With a touch of his hand to his brow, the dark-haired man silently left the room.

Meg looked once again at the medallion recovered from one of the thugs bent on killing the girl. *Maybe one of the priestesses should tend to the child?* Meg wondered. She placed the pendant in Rose's hands, closing her fists about it. The druids of Holywell had knowledge in the same vein as the priestesses of the Goddess. They would know what to do.

"*Poppa!*" Rose screamed, then fell back into deeper restlessness. "*Michael,*" she whispered, repeating the name silently over and over again to herself.

Poor child! Meg shook her head sadly. Whatever had befallen the girl, it hadn't been good.

"Will the girl live?" inquired a soft voice from behind Meg. She turned and looked at the young man who had become her pupil.

"I hope so," Meg said and ushered him out of the room. She closed the door softly behind her and nodded to one of the serving maids to watch over Rose as she walked with the youth downstairs and into the main hall.

The young man studied the older woman's face as they walked silently downstairs.

Face like an axe blade! he thought to himself. *I wonder if she was ever lovely, once?* Then, aloud, "I suppose I should be off seeking the man who would have such a thing done."

Meg came out of her thoughts. "Hm? Oh, yes ... well, of course it would be. 'To protect the weak and innocent,' remember?" The young man smiled at her knowingly. He was baiting her for some reason. "But, you know that already, my lord. What is it you wanted to ask, then?"

Gaheris paused, considering. "I beg your pardon, my lady Automne," he answered her. "But when I agreed to become your pupil, I rather thought my life would have greater adventures than playing nursemaid. I understand that part of my being a knight is to serve as protector and all that. It's just that ..."

Meg stared at the young man impassively as he sought for how to say what he wanted to say. "You thought it would have more to do with wielding your sword and fighting with lances?"

"Well, yes," Gaheris replied lamely.

"If I were to say to you, right now, 'Go forth and slay this villain for what he has done,' you'd be more than willing to leap on your charger and race off and kill him, wouldn't you?"

Gaheris felt his pulse quicken. "Yes! Of course I would! Now that's what I meant when I said 'adventures.' "

"Except, my lord Gaheris, while you possess great courage, you lack the skill to back it," Meg told him bluntly.

"B-but ...!" Gaheris sputtered in anger. *What does this crone know of my skills to lecture me?*

"Patience is a virtue, my lord," Meg continued, instructing him. "I guess I need to remind you that, though you are under no oath of service to me, you did agree to do as I asked in return for the instruction I have to give. A knight's word is his bond, my lord, especially when it is given to a lady." *Let him chew on that!* Meg thought. *A little shaming might be good for the lad. Bring him down to where I can work with him, at least.*

Gaheris' face turned dark red, and he clenched and unclenched his jaw as he fought to control his temper. He couldn't argue with Meg because she was right. He had agreed to do as she asked for one year. *God! One whole year of subservience to this woman?* Gaheris began to regret his hasty decision. *Damn this blood of mine!* For it was a trait of the Orkney breed towards impetuousness.

"I ... I ... forgive me, my lady," he said as he got control of himself. "I ... you are quite right. Patience is something I need to develop."

And badly! Meg thought. *But, he's not too proud to admit when he has made a mistake. That shows great promise.* And Meg told him so.

"Lord Gaheris," she said to him, "I promise you, if you do as I ask, you will be one of the greatest knights in the world. You have great abilities already and have even greater potential." The youth seemed to lighten at that. "Your brother's skill in arms is almost without equal, but I can teach you to be greater than he is."

Gaheris looked at Meg. "Greater than Gawaine?" he asked incredulously.

Meg nodded succinctly. "Strength is only one aspect of what makes for a great knight," she told him. "Wisdom is even better. Discretion. The ability to spot an opponent's weakness and turn that into your advantage – all these things I promised you when first we met, I offer them still. In exchange, you will serve as I bid. You will serve as protector to my people, in exchange for the knowledge I will impart to you." She raised an eyebrow in question.

Gaheris thought it over quickly. *To be able to best Gawaine? It might be worth it, just for that!*

"Very well, my lady," he replied. "I will do as you ask. I will serve your people as their knight. I will even fetch clothing, or food. Hell, I'll even cook the girl some of my mother's soup, if that is what you ask of me! In exchange, you will teach me to be the greatest knight the world has ever known?"

"Well, one of the greatest, my lord," Meg answered him. She smiled at the lad's impulsive yet generous nature. "Yes."

Gaheris gave Meg a sweeping bow, as if asking her to dance. "Then, my lady Automne, what is thy command?" His eyes sparkled as he stood waiting for her answer, and Meg couldn't help but laugh.

"You are quite the charmer with the ladies already, aren't you?" she asked him and gave him her hand. He took it in keeping with the charade. She motioned for him to continue onward, directing him down the long hall and into the kitchen. Meg watched Gaheris' face as he saw where she was taking him.

"The kitchens?" he dropped her hand and his playfulness deserted him. He looked at her, his eyes wide in disbelief. "You can't ... You don't mean? You aren't *serious*?" he asked with growing alarm.

Meg smiled sweetly at him. "I wasn't, until now," she told him. "Margaret?" Meg waved over her head cook. "I believe our young knight here has a special recipe for soup he would like to share with you. One that may be helpful to our young ward upstairs."

Gaheris stood with gaping mouth as the wiry old cooking woman came over and took him with a grip like iron and led him over to the chopping table and pots.

"Now, me young master, what is it ye needs?" she asked as he looked over his shoulder at Meg, his eyes pleading.

Meg merely shrugged and held her hands wide, as if to say, "What can I do?" The old cook tossed down some onions and set the youth to peeling and cleaning the vegetables for his stock. Gaheris, after a moment to collect himself, set to it with all the diligence and concentration at his command.

Fine! he told himself. *I can play this game as well as you! You just better deliver on your promise, old woman.*

Satisfied, Meg turned around and went back to attend to her other concerns about the keep. She prayed that help would be swift in coming for the young girl upstairs.

Rose was lost in nightmares, unable to wake. Again she dreamed of the enormous wolf, with its huge, slavering mouth, hunting her through uninhabited woodlands. She wanted to scream, to cry out, but no sounds would come. All Rose could do was run.

Poppa? Where are you? Michael?

There were no sounds of birds, no sign of any other living thing, as she ran and ran, pursued by the enormous beast. All she could hear was the panting of the huge animal's breath as it ran after her, and the pad of its heavy paws on the ground.

Meg was worried. The girl's color was fading to a deathly grey, and her skin was clammy.

I would that there was more I could do! Meg thought in frustration. All she knew were herbs and broth. The rest was practical knowledge: how to sew up wounds and set broken bones. Field medicine. She forced Rose to swallow a bitter tea boiled from the bark of a certain tree. It was helpful in case of a severe head injury, and Meg had reason to believe that a blow to Rose's head was the cause of her severe condition. She was pretty certain it wasn't from the fractured ribs, although Meg had known of men to die from internal bleeding if a rib had punctured the liver. Death was fairly rapid in such cases, and there were no earthly remedies for such an injury.

Meg felt a light touch upon her shoulder, and it startled her a bit. She turned and saw the young man holding a bowl of steaming broth in his hands. He had moved so silently, and his expression was all seriousness and concern, now.

"As promised, my lady," Gaheris said as he offered over the bowl. "My mother has some skill as a healer, what with a household of boys who know nothing but fighting and injury. This is one of her recipes, one she used quite often to tend to my brothers, my father, or myself when we were grievously hurt."

Meg took the bowl gently from the boy's hands. "Thank you," she said with all sincerity.

Gaheris came around the other side of Rose's bed and helped to sit her up so that Meg might force some of the broth into Rose's mouth without causing her to choke.

"In small amounts," he told her. "Just a few sips at a time is all."

Meg gave Rose a few sips, then set the bowl on a stand next to the bed. The aroma of the soup was strong but pleasant, and Meg realized that she had gone for some time without eating herself.

"It smells wonderful," she told the youth. "What is in it?"

Gaheris smiled shyly at the compliment. "Onions, garlic, some other herbs, and boiled beef. My mother felt it helped strengthen the body to drink the broth, sustaining the body so that it might have time to get over an illness or to heal."

Meg nodded. "I'll have to remember that. I have a similar concoction, but I must admit, mine does not smell nearly so nice as yours!"

"There's plenty more downstairs," Gaheris informed her. He felt a small twinge of pride at her compliment. He laughed. "Coming from a large household like mine, I made enough to feed an army!" He looked at Meg and said, "Go on down, my lady, and have some. It will do you good! And I will watch over the girl while you break your fast. It will be good practice for me."

Meg was appreciative and took Gaheris up on his offer. "There are servants right outside," she told him. "Inform me if there is any change – for better or worse. I want to know right away!"

She stood and walked back downstairs, her weariness catching up with her.

Getting too old for this, she thought to herself. Her knees felt stiff, and her back was tired from leaning over the bed so much. *Too bad no one has found a cure for age!*

Gaheris looked down at Rose. His expression was suddenly soft as he considered the pale face and red hair. Her face was horribly bruised and swollen, the eye sockets deep black, and her lips cracked and broken. At least she was resting peacefully for once.

She's not much older than my brother, Gareth, he reflected. He placed a damp cloth on her forehead, and was surprised by the heat pouring off the girl.

"You're a fighter," Gaheris said to her softly, not knowing whether Rose could hear him or not. "I admire your spirit." He saw Rose's face cloud over briefly as if she was haunted by some unpleasant dream, and he held her hands to comfort her. *Such tough hands on one so small!* He felt the calluses on Rose's hands and wondered what her background was.

Rose began to toss and mutter, her hands clutching at the bedding as though to draw the covers over her.

"Do you ...? What do you need?" Gaheris asked, wondering if the girl was getting worse or better.

"*Pa ... Poppa,*" she managed to whisper. Her face grew tense and tears slid from under her eyelids.

Gaheris saw something shimmer and recognized the silver pendant he had seen given to Meg by one of her attendants when they had first found the girl. It had fallen out of Rose's hands, and he retrieved it for her. Gaheris replaced the pendant, and her fist closed over it. Her restless rocking stopped immediately. She unknowingly drew her hands up to her breasts, clutching the pendant to her heart. Gaheris watched as the tension eased from Rose's face and she slipped once again into a deep slumber.

While he sat vigil over Rose, Gaheris thought about what had brought him here in the first place. Bored with sitting under his mother's watchful eyes at home, he longed for excitement. He had served as squire to his eldest brother, Gawaine, whom, while he loved his brother dearly, he found a bit boorish. How often had Gawaine impressed upon Gaheris just how strong he was, and how skilled he was, almost always seeking affirmation and compliments? His second oldest brother, Agravaine, was even worse!

God, please don't let me turn out to be like him! Gaheris prayed.

His mother had forbidden the boys to fight along with their father in his rebellion against the High King. Gawaine was livid and had ridden away from home, as had Agravaine, though his motives were more questionable. Gareth, being the baby of the family, and doted upon by their mother, had been kept close at home, and Gaheris felt a small shiver as he thought about how his mother seemed intent on keeping Gareth dependent on her for as long as possible.

Poor sod! he thought to himself. As for himself, he seemed almost invisible in his own household. Not as strong as Gawaine, nor as handsome as Agravaine, he was pretty much left to his own devices. He admired his eldest brother, and Gawaine was flattered when Gaheris insisted on serving as his squire for a twelvemonth. But that relationship was short-lived. By the end of the year, Gaheris couldn't wait to receive his own spurs and strike out on his own. He grew tired of always needing to compliment his brother, stoking his ego the way one might worry over a fire lest it go out.

Gaheris felt some guilt about his thoughts regarding his mother. Quite honestly, she made him uneasy, and he mistrusted her. She could be extremely sweet and giving on the outside, but she had a poisonous temper whenever she did not get her way. Manipulative. Cunning. His mother reminded him a bit of a serpent – one with beautiful scales but full of venom. It was his mother, the Queen, who was the more ambitious of his two parents. It was she who drove their father to challenge Arthur, always whispering into his ear how good a king he made, and how Arthur's bastardy made him unworthy of the High Kingship. She knew how to praise and how to cut someone with a word. Gaheris believed that to be the reason Gawaine was so in need of reassurance, and why Agravaine was so vain.

Gaheris had seen the High King once before, when he was younger. It was before the "rebel lords" had broken from Arthur, and he remembered him with affection. Arthur had a bright smile and a generous nature, and Gaheris took to him right away. As had Gawaine. Agravaine, though, was distant, and Gareth too young to recall him. Arthur just seemed full of sunlight, as though he was ringed in golden light, whenever Gaheris thought back on their encounter. It may just have been the excitement of the day, the thrill of meeting the son of the Pendragon, but Gaheris didn't care why – only that the High King had smiled at him and made him feel welcome.

And so, when he found himself unable to go with their father into the field to fight in open rebellion against Arthur, which he would have regretted doing anyway, Gaheris, like his older brothers, took his horse and armor and sought his own adventures. As he was out riding, out in the middle of the wilderness, he had come across this lady and her attendants. She had no great pavilion, but seemed content to camp in the open and to sleep on the ground, and this puzzled him. His own mother never went anywhere without twenty servants to attend her, and almost as many bags of clothes and whatnots. When he had inquired of her as to why she should be camping out in the rough, she had answered him, "Because I enjoy it!"

As he questioned her further, she found out from him who he was, and she made him the most incredible offer Gaheris had ever heard in his life!

"It is my calling to find young knights such as yourself and train them. I am very selective in whom I accept as my pupil, and my instincts tell me that you would make a very great knight."

"How do you know this?" Gaheris had asked her.

"From the way you sit your horse," she answered him. "And, if I am very much not mistaken, your right arm is just slightly longer than your left. This could be an advantage to you. Also, I can tell that your horse is well cared for. I suspect you take care of grooming it yourself, as I see no squire or page attends you."

Her perceptiveness and matter-of-fact manner captured Gaheris, and he felt this wild impulse to say, "Yes." And so he had!

I pray I don't regret my decision! he told himself, though he felt sure that the old woman, however odd her requests may be at times, would be able to deliver on her promises. He noted the manner in which she carried herself, her long gait and almost mannish gestures. She was clearly able to keep up with the men who attended her, these Welsh hunters of hers. *But, can she really fight as well as a man?* Gaheris had his doubts.

Meg returned, pleased to find Gaheris still watching over the girl.

Gaheris stood as she entered the room and offered her the stool he had been sitting on.

"She's been sleeping peacefully for quite a while, now," he informed her.

Meg checked the girl's condition. She was still warm, not burning up like before. But, her color showed no improvement, and her breathing was shallow. Hopefully, her man would return with the healer by morning.

If we can get her through the night, Meg thought to herself, *she just might make it.*

Meg patted the youth's hand, thanking him, and indicated he should go while she took over for him. Gaheris wanted to stay, as much to prove himself as out of concern for the child. But he realized it was probably best not to argue with the woman, and so he took his leave.

"Call me if you have any need of my services," he told Meg quietly, then left, closing the door behind him.

I pray we won't, thought Meg.

It was a long night. Meg kept herself awake, catching herself nearly dozing off every time Rose murmured or tossed fitfully during the night. Finally, as the window slits lightened with the coming of morning, Meg heard the tromping of boots coming up the stairs. The men were speaking in their lyrical tongue, and Meg knew the healer had arrived. She turned as her servant and a brown-robed man bearing a yew staff entered the room.

The man had long, grey hair and a beard that hung nearly to his waist. His eyes were steel grey, and his face was tanned and lined with age.

"Cyfarchion," he said as he approached the bed. "Bendith oddi duwdod ar warthaf chi."

Meg bowed her head reverently and stood. "Thank you, wise father, for coming." Meg stepped back as the aged man bent down to examine Rose. He looked up questioning as he saw the medallion hanging limply in Rose's hand.

Meg told him, "It was found on one of those who were going to do the child harm, though whether it is hers or not, we are not certain."

The old man made a sign over the girl, a gesture of blessing from the Goddess, and he touched her brow with his brown fingers.

"May the Goddess bring blessings and healing upon this child," he intoned. "May she be brought forth from the Darkness and return to the Light if that be Thy will, in order that she fulfill Thy great purposes, O' great Mother, O' great Father! By Ash and Oak, let Thy will be done!"

The man sat down upon the edge of the bed, keeping his eyes closed and his hand upon Rose's brow, waiting.

"What is he doing?" Gaheris asked softly. He had seen the servant returning, and had followed them upstairs to see how Rose was doing, silently entering the room so as not to disturb the proceedings.

Meg turned and saw the lad and stepped away to whisper to Gaheris, "He's invoking the powers of the God and Goddess to heal the child, if that is for the highest good."

Gaheris furrowed his brow. "How could it not be for the best to heal the child?" he asked. "How could that not be a good thing?"

Meg glanced quickly at him before turning her attention back to the girl. "Are you so sure of that?" she asked him. "Do you know this child's future so well that you can claim it is better for her to live than to die? We do not know what role Destiny has in store for us. Maybe her purpose will be served by her passing and not by her living." Meg shrugged. "I know it isn't in my power to determine. Is it in yours?"

Gaheris wanted to defend his position, but saw that Meg was not trying to shame him. He paused, considering. "Are you saying, then, that maybe we should do nothing, because to take any action might be to interfere with God's purposes for us?" He couldn't puzzle it out. If one had the power to help, wasn't one supposed to? Why else were knights bound to right wrongs and protect the innocent, if not because they were meant to do so?

"No, of course not. I'm not saying that one should do nothing if one has the means to help, to give assistance. Never. But one must do so without attachment to whether their actions are 'right' or 'wrong' because we simply can't determine that. Am I doing right by teaching you to be a more skilled swordsman? I do it because that is my calling. I can improve your skills, in horsemanship and in battle. But is it right for me to do so? I don't know. I have to trust that it serves a higher purpose than that of my own pride, or else we would never have met."

"But how am I to know if what I am doing is out of choice or design?" Gaheris asked her. His voice carried in his earnestness, and the old man opened his eyes to look at him disapprovingly before returning to his meditation.

Meg looked at the youth. She could see him struggling with the question, and she empathized with him. "It isn't easy, I know. It requires trust. Faith in a will bigger than your own. You follow the Christian God, do you not?" Gaheris nodded. "Then trust that your God has a design for you, but that it is still within your power to choose whether you will act in accord with that design, or against it. Both have consequences, neither is particularly 'right' or 'wrong.' If I move with the current, or against the current, I am still in the water. One way takes less effort is all. Chances are if I fight the current too long, I'd drown. But I still exercised my free will in choosing to fight the flow, and I think your God respects that. Why else would He have given us free will?"

Gaheris thought this line of reasoning over. "But, you still haven't answered my question. How do I know if I am moving with the stream or against it?"

Meg placed her hand over the boy's chest. "You know," she said, "in here. It may take some time. I know I haven't perfected my ability to always know, I must admit. But, you can begin to pay attention to your inner calling. Some things you simply know are right; the others, as I said, you have to take on trust. If you do something that is not in accord with your God's higher will, believe me, one way or another you will find out!"

The old man opened his eyes, and he seemed very weary even though, to Gaheris' eyes, he had done nothing but pray over the girl. Meg moved to him, and he spoke in a dry whisper. "Have you any ale?" he asked.

Meg nodded and waved for her serving man to fetch some.

"For the girl?" Gaheris asked. "Should she be drinking ale in her condition?"

The old man raised an eyebrow at the lad and said, "Who said the ale was for the girl?" He watched as his question registered with the boy. "I have traveled many miles, at speed, and have not stopped to have either food or drink for some time, now. And I'm an old man!"

Meg laughed, and so did the healer. Gaheris blushed, ashamed and angry at being made fun of.

"'Tis all right, lad," said the old healer. "No harm done. I know you are worried about the girl, too, as is Megan here," he indicated Meg. Then, to Meg, he said, "She's in a dark place. Something haunts her in her sleep, and her spirit shrinks from it. Some memory stands between her and the Light." He chewed his lower lip as he thought.

"Can you reach her?" Meg asked and looked down at the pale face with its bruises and wounds.

"I can only try," the old man said. "I'll keep on as I've been. Her spirit is bright and strong, that one! But confused, and angry. Lost. I think, once I get her pointed in the right direction, she'll find her way back out." He gave Meg a reassuring squeeze.

A mug of ale and a plate of bread, fruit, and cheese were handed to the old man and he wolfed them down gratefully.

Meg indicated to Gaheris that he should follow her, and they left the room together.

"We'll leave him to his craft," she said as they walked down the stairs. "As for you, I think it is time to start your training."

Gaheris had mixed feelings. "But what about the girl?"

"If Gleinguin can't help her, then perhaps it was her destiny to die here – for what purpose, I do not know," Meg answered him. "But our worrying won't change the outcome. So, I think it would be good to focus our attention on something we know we can make a difference in!" *I know I need the exercise*, Meg added to herself. Physical workouts, she had learned, seemed to focus her, relax her, and leave her feeling more centered. It gave her something she was familiar with to do whenever she felt frustrated or helpless. At least a lance was a tangible thing, and a sword aimed at one's self was a tangible threat that could be dealt with!

Gaheris walked with her, his mind on the girl, and he said a silent prayer for her.

Gleinguin took the pendant from Rose's hand, wrapping the chain about her palm but laying the medallion where he could see it. *Let me see, then, my little mystery*, he pondered. *Mayhap this shall be the key to bring you home.* He began to follow the maze of silver wire with his eyes, tracing the winding path the filigree followed. *Three times three*, Gleinguin told himself as he sunk deeper into trance.

Rose ran and ran, it seemed forever, and the wolf continued to pursue her. She ran through silent woods, and thought she may have lost the beast, but she could hear its breath and feel the heavy footfalls through the earth. At one point she seemed to recall passing a ruined field, a cottage in smoking ruins, and a circle of ravens flew about the sky. But the wolf kept up its pursuit, and she ran on. She never seemed to tire, though – only the endless flight. Deeper into the woodlands she ran, where the trees grew thicker and heavier, and the light became dimmer and the silence deeper.

Poppa?! Michael? Momma? Where are you?

Rose ran through a thicket and found herself in a hollow ringed with dark oak. There was a stillness here unlike any she had ever encountered and a feeling of security.

Gleinguin's brow was furrowed in concentration. *The girl's spirit wanders far!* He felt a sense of the energy that pursued her – an impression of destructive hunger, devouring every living thing it finds. *A dark memory*, he mused. *One she seeks to flee.* He was in her world, now. He saw images of burned and ruined farmsteads, bodies lying on the ground, carrion for birds. Like an expert tracker, Gleinguin hunted the girl's spirit as it fled through the borderlands of the dead. If he did not find her soon, she may wander too far, crossing over never to return. But there were also places of power, here in the borderlands, places he was practiced in finding, and powers he was familiar with using. The girl, knowingly or intuitively, had found such a place and was using it for refuge. *Stay still, young one!* he willed as he followed and moved over the landscape like flowing mist.

Rose felt a presence in the grove and became momentarily afraid that the great wolf had somehow found her. Instead, it was only the shadow of an old man who moved like a wraith, and spoke with the whispered breath of a breeze through the branches of the trees. "You must go back," he said to her. But Rose didn't want to go. It was peaceful here. More peace than she had known her whole life. It would be so easy to just stay here and forget.

"That which you flee, it is but a shadow – a dream, or nightmare. It has no power save that which you lend it with your fear," said the wraith.

Why must I go back? Rose demanded. *What is there for me there?*

The shadow moved to Rose, and it held something that glittered in its hand. Rose recognized it. It was her mother's pendant! What did this mean?

Gleinguin's shadow placed the pendant into Rose's hands. The girl stood as if entranced by it. "Follow," was all he said. He had reached out with his feelings to the powers of the grove, willing for it to lend him its strength. *Help this child to make the right choice! Help her to fulfill her that which you have intended for her.*

For Rose, it appeared that a path had opened through the trees – a trail that led through deeper shadows and away from the safety of the grove. The wolf, she knew, was still out there somewhere. But the silver pendant gave her a small sense of comfort, and she took a faltering step, then another, until she had passed out of the grove.

Gleinguin was exhausted as he came out of his trance. The girl's color had improved slightly, which was a good sign.

Whether she would follow the path into the Light or cross over into shadow, he did not know. Only time would tell. Wearily, he got up from Rose's bed and knocked for a servant. He leaned on his staff as he walked back downstairs. Meg had prepared a room for him to rest himself, and he settled down gratefully and slept.

Rose was aware of the ring of steel against steel as she awoke. A candle stump burned near her bed, and a plate with the remains of a meal sat upon a stand. Daylight slipped past closed curtains at the windows. She was in a soft bed with no knowledge of how she got there, or of where she might be. In her hands was her mother's pendant. *How did I ... ?* she wondered.

Her face hurt, and she ached all over. As she tried to sit up, Rose gasped in pain. Stiffly, Rose lifted off the blankets and swung her legs over the edge of the bed. She stood unsteadily and hobbled over to look out the window. The bright sunlight blinded her for a moment, and she gazed down into a long yard from the second story. Below, she saw several dark-haired men going about various chores, and she saw a handsome young man dressed in armor practicing swordplay against a similarly clad older man, while a grey-haired woman sat by, watching. Rose didn't recognize the youth, but the older woman looked familiar. It took Rose a while to recall the night in the forest, and the sudden appearance of this woman and hooded figures that somehow had saved her. The memory was dim, and it made Rose dizzy as she stood there trying to remember.

"Not bad!" Rose heard the woman say. She looked down and saw the woman rise from her chair. She appeared to be instructing the young man in something, pointing at his weapon and making slashing motions with her hand as though showing him how to swing.

The door behind her creaked open, and Rose swayed from turning too fast to see who had entered.

A serving woman had come in, and she spoke to Rose in an unfamiliar language, but she seemed pleased to see that Rose was up. Rose held onto the curtains to steady herself, and the woman came over and helped her back to the bed. She spoke again to Rose, who merely shook her head indicating she did not understand, and the woman patted her on the shoulder gently and motioned that she would be right back.

Rose lay back down. She couldn't believe how tired she felt! Every part of her seemed to hurt.

It wasn't long before the grey-haired woman, the fair young man, and a leathery old man in brown garb came into Rose's room. They all looked relieved to see her, pleased that she was awake.

"Our traveler returns!" said the brown-skinned older man. He leaned on his yew staff and smiled warmly at Rose. He winked at her, and Rose found she liked him right away. She gave him a smile in return, though it hurt her mouth to do so.

The young man stood and watched her with bright, caring eyes, though he stayed silent and remained near the door.

Is he the son of the master here? Rose wondered.

Meg sat on Rose's bed and checked the bandages wrapped around her chest. "How are you doing? Do you have any appetite?" she asked the girl.

Rose went to speak, but only a croak came out. "I ... I'm very sore," she answered. "And terribly thirsty."

"Of course," Meg said and frowned as she admonished herself for not thinking. She spoke to the serving woman in the musical speech Rose had heard the other night, then turned back to the girl.

"You had us quite concerned," Meg told her. "But, thanks to some help from my Lord Gaheris here, and Master Gleinguin, you can consider yourself lucky to be among the living!" She wanted to ask about the men who were bent on harming her, but Meg felt it might be too soon to press for answers.

Rose looked down at the pendant in her hands and felt tears well up. "Thank you for saving me," she said. "And thank you for saving this for me." She held up the pendant, and Meg nodded.

"Time enough for talk, later," Meg said to Rose. "For now, lie back and rest. It will be some time before you are back on your feet again! We'll have plenty of time to talk, and get to know each other better." She stood as the serving woman entered bearing a tray with something to drink and a bowl of broth. Rose would have loved to have something solid to eat, but felt that her mouth might be too sore to chew, and so she was thankful for what she was offered.

The handsome young man bowed shyly and exited the room accompanied by the old woman and the old man.

Rose sighed as the serving woman once again asked her something indecipherable, but helped Rose to take a sip of the bitter tea.

Lord Gaheris? Rose reflected on the youth as she lay back, and the serving woman spooned broth into her mouth for her. *Why does that name sound familiar?* She felt a sharp pang as she wished that Michael were here. He'd know. *Michael!* Suddenly she didn't feel like eating.

As Meg had told her, Rose was a long time on the mend. Her face was swollen for several days, and the bruising lasted for several weeks. Her ribs gradually caused her less and less discomfort, though she still felt pain whenever she got out of bed or twisted too much moving about. And she was horribly tired despite the fact that she did almost nothing but sleep all day! Rose was unaccustomed to such prolonged inactivity, and she chafed to get up and do something by the end of the first week. So, to challenge herself, Rose took to walking the circuit of her room at least once per day with no assistance. The stairs outside would be too much for her so soon, but this much exercise Rose was determined to have.

And many were the mornings she would wake to the clash of metal and struggle to get out of bed and hobble to the window to watch the young lord at his practice. Rose felt a strange fascination with the youth, and she felt oddly pleased just to gaze at him day after day from her bedroom window. She thrilled at his progress, and shared in his frustrations, as she watched his training. Rose was surprised at first, then deeply curious as she realized that it was the old woman, Meg, who was instructing the boy. On rare occasions, Meg would actually take up the young lord's weapon and demonstrate to him a new move, or an improvement to what he was doing. She moved with such smoothness and speed, Rose felt it was like watching a dancer – such fluidity and grace. And she began to wonder: *Why is it that Meg isn't a knight? She could easily fight as well as most men. So why wasn't she in service to some king or lord as his champion?*

And, being Rose, she asked her one evening when Meg had come to visit after a long day instructing Lord Gaheris.

"Why am I not in service to some great lord?" Meg asked in surprise. "Lord, why should I be? And besides, most men being what they are, who would have me as his champion? Their pride would never stand for it. Ha!"

"But you could have done it!" Rose insisted. "You could do it still, you move with such ... such skill and grace. It's beautiful!"

Meg felt strangely embarrassed by the girl's insistence. She had never heard anyone describe what she did as "beautiful" before, and it struck a chord within her. *That was exactly how I felt about it when I was younger!* Meg thought. *There is a certain martial beauty about it, isn't there?* Meg thought about how rare it was to find someone, anyone, who could appreciate it in such a manner.

"Whist, now! Enough," she said to Rose. "Strange thing to find beautiful, don't you think, teaching men how to kill each other?"

Rose disagreed. "No, not that. Not the killing. But, just the ... the way in which you move ..." She couldn't describe it. It *pulled* at her, making her long to do the same thing. Rose stopped. "Yet you do it," she said to Meg.

"Do what?"

"You teach men how to kill each other. Why?"

Why indeed? thought Meg. *I have never really asked myself that before. At least, not in such a blunt fashion. And yet, I have done exactly that, haven't I?*

"I didn't realize I was housing such a philosopher under my roof!" she said to Rose. Meg shook her head. "My dear child," she explained, "I have lived my life in this fashion since long before you were ever born, and I am answerable to powers other than thee. If I am leading my life falsely, it will be myself that's to blame and no one else. I accept that, and so shall *you*," she said before Rose could interrupt her.

Rose scowled slightly at Meg's reluctance to talk. "I'm sorry, my lady," she said softly. "I didn't mean to offend you. I … I was only curious, that's all."

Meg softened. "It's all right, my child. I, however, am more concerned with matters concerning you," she said.

Rose felt a darkness begin to fill her, and she grew quiet, dreading the questions she felt were coming.

"You want to know how I came to be … where I am?" she asked reluctantly, her face downcast to avoid looking Meg in the eye.

"Among other things, yes," Meg responded honestly. "But, it can wait, child. It can wait. When you are ready, you'll tell me. I am a pretty good judge of character, and I can see that honesty is important to you. You've a good heart."

Rose felt relieved, and the darkness receded. "Thank you, my lady," Rose told her. "I … I am very grateful. For all that you have done for me …" Rose couldn't continue.

"Well, like I said," replied Meg, "All in good time."

There was a long pause where neither of them spoke, and Meg felt suddenly uncomfortable. She turned to leave when she heard Rose speak behind her.

"He had killed my father," she said softly, almost without emotion. "And my brother. And I wanted revenge."

Deep inside Rose, a small flame rekindled. It was tiny, but it was still there, and it helped give her strength.

"Who did this?" Meg asked Rose gently. "Who was the man who did this to you? To your family?"

Rose looked up at Meg with haunted eyes. "Carados. That was his name. Lord Carados."

Carados? Meg knew of the man's reputation for ruthlessness and ferocity – *but that he would do this to a child? A young girl? What kind of threat did she represent to him that he would have her killed?*

Rose bit her lip to keep from crying again. *No! No more tears! I will not shed any more tears until the giant is dead!*

Meg approached the girl, wanting to touch her, but she held herself back. She could see that the girl was fighting to hold herself together, and Meg respected that.

"Thank you," was all she could think to say. "For being so honest with me." She paused, considering. "If you like, I will send word to the King of Gwynedd? He has ... dealings ... with the men Carados serves, the King of Orkney and Lothian, and the kings of Scotland and Northumberland." *And I have the son of King Lot here, as well! I think it would be very interesting for young Gaheris to learn of the kinds of men his father has in service.*

Rose was grateful for the offer, but she couldn't speak. The darkness had welled up again, and she was afraid that if she spoke, it would swallow her whole.

Meg took Rose's silence as a need to consider. "Very well, then. You let me know. And, if I heard you correctly, I understand you have no family, no relatives to whom you may go?"

Rose shook her head in the negative.

"Not even ...?" Meg paused. She wanted to ask about the pendant, but felt that perhaps it was pressing at a time when the girl needed simply to grieve, and recuperate. "I welcome you to stay for as long as you like. Certainly until you regain your strength."

"Thank you. I will," Rose answered feeling very drained.

I will, however, have a word with my young pupil. And it wouldn't hurt to send a messenger to the sacred isle, to see if they are missing any novices, Meg determined as she left the girl to rest.

Chapter 6

Gaheris was outraged and demanded his horse and armor as soon as Meg told him about Carados.

"Peace, my lord! Peace!" Meg tried to calm the youth. "I don't yet know all the circumstances involving Carados and the girl's father."

Gaheris paced in anger as he vented his frustration. "What more do we need to know? We've seen the evidence of his handiwork on the girl's body! Or do you forget, my lady, the manner in which we found her? If it hadn't been for us, the girl would have been ill-used by those foul men before they butchered her!" The thought disgusted Gaheris, and he longed for a sword to make Carados answer for ordering such a thing. *To butcher a child?*

"I agree, Lord Gaheris," Meg placated him. "But the slaughter of innocents is hardly a new crime in this world. It is common practice for warlords to burn and pillage, reaving the countryside, to delay a pursuing army. One that, I am sure, your own father has participated in from time to time ..."

Gaheris strode up to Meg and put his face into hers. "Do not ever accuse my father of using such tactics as this ... this beast, Carados!" he raged.

Meg held up her hands in a gesture of apology. "Forgive me, my lord. Perhaps your father is one of the few who have not done such things. But what I say is true. The Romans have done it for centuries. 'Scorched earth' they call it – leaving nothing behind for an army to use. They would even go so far as to salt the fields of abandoned lands so that nothing would grow there for years to come! And it has always been the peasants, the serfs, and the lowly farmers who suffer the most from the decisions of 'great men.' "

Gaheris calmed himself a bit. "Excuse me, my lady. It's just that … it makes me so …!" Gaheris choked on his frustration. "The innocent should never suffer from the hands of men such as these," he said.

"And yet, my lord, such has always been the case," Meg replied with a sad shake of her head. "It is men like this new King who have sought to change all that. Arthur seeks to inspire knights to fight as protectors of the weak and as servants of the people. He appeals to that which is the greatest that men may aspire to become, not to dominate and impose their will on others."

"Then what would you have me do?" Gaheris asked her. "Why am I learning skill at arms if I am not to use them?"

Meg laid her hand on the boy's arm and said, "To fight against those who would. Those who would impose their will through force of arms, regardless of the cost to foe and commoners alike."

"Isn't that what I am trying to do?" he asked. "Why do you stop me, then, from challenging this Carados and bringing him to justice?"

"Because you wouldn't win, my lord," she told him honestly, knowing the truth would hurt his pride. She watched as his face clouded over. "Not because you lack in courage," she soothed, "nor from greatness of heart. But I know this Carados, and you are not ready to face him." She watched as Gaheris struggled with this. "Lord Gaheris," she said, "I could order you not to go, according to the conditions under which I accepted you as my pupil. But, I will not, out of respect for you, and the greatness I see in you. I only ask that you take word to your father on the girl's behalf."

Gaheris glanced up to Rose's window, where she had watched for several weeks the training he received from Meg.

"It serves your father as well," Meg encouraged him. "If your father does not wish for such men to be associated with his name."

Gaheris' horse was brought to him, and he was helped into the saddle. He raised his arm in salute, and said, "Lady Automne, in accordance to our agreement, I will do as you have asked. Though I long to smite this villain, Carados, and bring him to justice, I will go to my father and seek his counsel. For the moment, I will not challenge this Carados. But, I do not fear him. God is on the side of the righteous, and I do not doubt but that I would prevail!" So saying, he spurred his horse and rode away from the compound.

Rose stepped back from the window. She had overheard the argument between Gaheris and Meg and was touched that she was so important to them. But she didn't want Gaheris to avenge her – that was something she felt she had to do. It was something she *wanted* to do! And now, she felt she might have a way to do so.

"Teach me how to fight!" Rose demanded.

Meg looked the girl over. She was healing, though the remains of bruises still lingered on her face in sickly greens and yellows – much improved from the deep black and purples she originally had. She was tall for her age, and likely would grow to be as tall as a man when full grown.

"And why would you be wanting that?" Meg asked.

"Revenge!" Rose answered. Her green eyes burned fiercely.

"Death," Meg retorted. "That's all you would find if revenge is all you seek."

Meg turned her back on the girl and went back to issuing her orders to the dark-haired retainers in their musical, unfamiliar language. A handful carrying long, unstrung bows and quivers touched hands to eyebrows and silently slipped off across the exercise yard and into the woods.

"Then death is an acceptable price if only to have the chance to be revenged on the man who ... who..." Rose choked back the emotions surging up within her.

Meg turned back to the girl. *Ah, child! Do you know what you're asking?* "No."

Rose was nearly shaking, fighting to keep herself from breaking down in both tears of anger and of frustration. "You have to teach me!"

"And why *must* I, child? I am mistress of this manor, or has that changed? Have I brought a cuckoo into my nest, seeking to displace those who rightfully belong here?"

"Because you know how," was all Rose could say.

Meg sighed. She couldn't argue that point, at least. *If anyone could, child, yes, it would be me. But should I?*

"I watched you train that young man to fight. You said that you could teach him to be the greatest knight in the world, if only he would heed what you would tell him! All I ask is that you give me the same chance."

I could have been the greatest knight in the world, Meg thought to herself with some bitterness. *If only I had been born a man instead of a woman!*

She looked at Rose with narrowed eyes. "And you will do exactly as I tell you? Without question? You will do everything I say?"

"Yes," Rose answered. Hope began to flicker in her eyes. "Yes!"

"You will sleep in the cold, sharing the pens with the swine, and eat meager fare, and wake before dawn, and do everything I ask exactly as I ask you?"

Rose felt a renewed energy fill her. "Yes! Yes I will! I will do everything you ask, and more!"

Meg smiled grimly. "That we'll see."

She beckoned for Rose to follow her into the middle of the muddy expanse that made up the practice field where Meg had her quintains and practice posts. What men there were in the yard began to gather around to see what was happening.

"Well, and I'm sure you've hefted a spear before?" Meg asked with a cynical bite.

"Of course," answered Rose defiantly.

Meg nodded curtly, and one of her dark-haired followers tossed a long, heavy hunting spear to Rose, who grunted with the weight of it as she caught it.

"Show me," commanded Meg.

Rose shifted the awkward weight of the spear and braced the end of it against the ground, her foot backing the end, and the point up and outward against an imaginary foe or animal. Her lower arm held the spear firmly, while her upper arm gripped it tightly, palm down, forearm and wrist turned away from her body. It was how her father had shown Michael when he was teaching the boy how to hunt. *Michael!* The thought of her brother brought hot, angry tears to her eyes.

A look of satisfaction flashed over Meg's face briefly before being replaced by her stern, critical countenance. "Not bad," she said. "And it might work against a dumb animal rushing blindly into you. But not against a man, unless he's blind *and* a fool!"

Rose felt a flush heat her face. She held her tongue, though, as tightly as she did the weapon. Her upper arm was beginning to tire, and it took all her concentration to keep the tip from dipping. Rose was determined not to allow Meg to deter her.

Meg spoke again in the musical language of these dark men, and another spear was cast out to her. Meg caught the spear by the haft, and rapidly brought the tip up under Rose's chin. She stared Rose intently in the eye, gauging, before sweeping the long blade of the weapon away and to the side. Her hands moved fluidly, and the spear seemed an extension of her body – a long deadly limb that moved with ease and grace. Meg twirled the weapon with both hands and executed a series of thrusts, side-sweeps, and slashes almost too quickly for Rose to follow. The tip of the spear whistled as it cut the air in a figure eight, then froze in position as Meg maneuvered herself into a new stance, the blade moving again in arcs and circles. Sometimes she used the haft of the weapon like a quarterstaff, parrying, or the blunt end of the weapon would thrust out in a quick stabbing motion.

Rose felt herself trying to imitate the movements, picturing them in her mind as her body longed to copy them in life. She could almost sense the flow of the movements, as if they were part of a dance she knew but could not recall. And she surrendered to the pull of it, allowing her body to move with the heavy spear as it seemed to want to do. The spear's weight caused her to feel clumsy and self-conscious. But she set aside her feelings and let her body continue to imitate, if not the exact movements, then at least the general pattern of Meg's.

Meg watched Rose's actions out of the corner of her eye, and she began to repeat the routine of slash, cut, thrust, and parry with the spear. A wave of admiration welled up inside of her, which she quickly quelled and focused even more determinedly on her sequences of moves. *The girl has spirit, that's for sure!* But she had to learn patience and how to pace herself, so Meg hardened her feelings, determined to wear Rose out.

It seemed like no time at all before Rose found herself panting for breath, her arms burning and shoulders aching from exertion. But she kept on, channeling her anger, first at herself, then at Meg, into one more thrust, one more sweep of the spear, one more – *just one more, dammit!* Finally, she could take no more and fell to the ground, the spear slipping from nearly nerveless fingers. Exhausted, Rose was unable to push herself over and instead lay face down in the mud of the exercise yard, weeping.

Meg stopped her routine and looked down at the girl with mixed emotions. She wanted both to comfort the girl and to yell at her to stop crying. The world was a hard place, and there was little room for comfort if one wanted to be strong in it. And she felt incredible admiration for the girl's resolve and determination. *She lasted far longer than I'd expected*, Meg thought. Lastly, Meg felt fear. Fear both for the girl and what harm the future might hold for her, and fear of the girl because of the way she touched on Meg's own deep feelings – feelings she thought she was done with long ago. *No time to go soft!* she told herself. Meg spoke again, and one of the dark-haired men came and gently lifted Rose onto his shoulder and carried her back to the pens where Meg had determined she would sleep.

A hard blow across the bottom of her foot awakened Rose. It was dark, and she had no idea what time it was. She had slept deeply, but now felt incredible pain and stiffness throughout her body. Her arms felt like leaden weights, unresponsive. Her shoulders ached, both from the unaccustomed exercise she had done the afternoon before and from sleeping on a cold, hard surface with only a little straw matting to insulate her from the floor. And she was hungry.

"You come now," said a black shadow of a man holding a stick. He had the odd accent of the lady's retainers. He carried an axe over his one shoulder, and the stick and a lantern over the other.

Rose groaned as she stood and forced herself to put one foot in front of the other as she followed the man out into the exercise yard. There was no moon out, so Rose did not know if it was morning or night, but she stood where the strange man pointed.

"You take," he grunted as he placed the heavy axe into her hands. He pointed out into the dark woods that bordered the manor and said, "Chop wood. Now." With that, he handed the lantern to her and nudged Rose towards the woods.

Rose was about to protest, asking what this had to do with learning to fight, but she recalled her promise to do everything asked of her – *and more*, she thought with a groan – and slowly made her way to the edge of the property.

Chopping wood was a familiar exercise for Rose, but her muscles burned and her back ached terribly from yesterday's unaccustomed exercise. Hunger gnawed at her belly. Her first swing almost caused Rose to fall over. But she held the image of her father's slain body lying in the field, and of the men who had burned their cottage, killing livestock, and driving her and her brother out into the wilds. And she recalled the *man*. Carados, his features forever imprinted upon her mind. *Whack!* The axe bit deeply into the fallen carcass of a tree. Pain flared across her shoulders, but with it came more memories. *Whack, whack!* Carados in his rage, holding her like a limp doll as he beat her with his fists until Rose was half-dead. *Whack!!* The axe stuck, and Rose had to plant her feet on each side of the blade and pull with both arms to free it. The pain in her arms was lessening with each stroke while her anger grew, making her forget her hunger and warming her stiff and cold body. Carados as he brought his axe down into Poppa's skull. *Crack!* The log split in two, and the pieces went flying. The axe bit into the ground between her feet.

"Remember that," said a voice behind her.

Rose looked behind her and saw Meg standing watching her with a small lidded pot in her hand.

"Anger can be useful, but make sure it doesn't make you careless," Meg instructed her without emotion.

Rose wanted to ask Meg how she knew what she had been thinking, but remained silent. She had worked up a sweat, which the cold air was beginning to chill, and shivered slightly.

"Good!" said Meg. "You understood me when I told you not to question what I told you. You learn quickly."

"Thank you," Rose replied. "I'm cold," she added.

"Exercise will cure that," Meg responded. She watched as Rose sighed inwardly. "But, come, a little food will do your body good as well."

Grateful, Rose set the axe down and approached this strange, hard woman.

"You must make your feelings your ally," Meg instructed. She gave Rose the pot of gruel she had brought with her. "Anger is a great motivator, but a terrible master. It turns men into beasts, blindly striking at whatever is in their way. But the one who masters his emotions, who learns to use the impetus they provide – ah, now that is a man to follow!"

"Did that young knight learn to do that?" Rose inquired. The gruel was warm, but cooling rapidly, and Rose shivered a little sitting in the cold. Her pride refused to ask for a blanket, however, and she recalled her promise to Meg the day before.

"Lord, no," Meg answered regretfully. She stared off into the East where the horizon was beginning to lighten heralding a new day.

Rose studied the old woman carefully while Meg mused, her guard down for the moment. Or so it appeared.

"Why do you do what you do?" Rose asked.

Meg's reverie was broken by the girl's question. Her first impulse was to chide the girl, but the sincerity in Rose's eyes calmed her.

Meg laughed. "Pah! In all my years I have been teaching boys to become men, and men to become knights, I have never met anyone who would understand my answer. Until now, that is." She glanced at the girl. "When I was about your age, I came to the realization that I was no great physical beauty."

Rose went to say something but Meg stopped her with a wave of her hand.

"Tut, tut, tut! I know it was true – at least for what most men considered beautiful, though I have had my share of lovers in my day. Some men see beyond the surface and recognize a beauty underneath. But, that's not why I do what I do. To answer your question, I do what I do because … well, quite simply, I must. It is my calling, if you will. God, or the gods, knows what purpose it serves. But, I know it down to the very marrow of my bones.

"I used to go to the great tourneys with my father when I was a child. And I thrilled to them! Oh, I remember how I longed to be out there doing what the men were doing! And I knew that I could do it, too. I saw how this one leaned too far forward before the moment of impact, or how another tended to shy away as his lance readied to make contact. I could see the way most men fought with their weapons, resisted the natural flow and rhythm of the way a sword swings through the air, or a mace carries its momentum around in an arc. I knew, but no one would listen. No one heeded a small girl, for what did girls know of men's work? Pah!" Meg spat. "It was a long, hard time before I accepted that I would never be given the chance to prove myself in the field, so I decided to share my insights with those I thought showed promise. Men who seemed to have potential, and who were of more receptive and open minds. My first lover was such a man. He appreciated me the way he appreciated a fine sword or piece of armor. So long as I served him and his ambitions, great!" Here she paused as the memory brought with it some bitterness. "But, once he had won a few tournaments using the skills I taught him – well, he had no more need of me! And off he went to prove himself of greater worth to the world."

Meg fell silent, and Rose felt uneasy with the pause.

"Did he?" she asked.

"Mmm? Oh … yes. Yes, he did. He went on to be a very loyal and excellent knight for the late High King, the Pendragon. When I heard, I felt some small satisfaction, which helped take the sting out of his rejection of me as a woman. And so I started teaching. Secretly, at first. Just local boys, then men who did not know me. Strange, but the people who think they know us best are the first ones that seem to reject us if we stray from what they think of as 'right' for us!

"Later, as boy after boy, and knight after knight, went off, improved by my tutorship, I began to desire to see the world. And so I would go off by myself into the wilds and sit beside a crossroad and wait for errant knights to come by and inquire why I was out there. Those who asked received an answer, and those who believed received instruction. Those who did not, well, they were not the kind worthy of it because their minds were too small, imprisoned by their prejudice as their bodies were imprisoned in their armor.

"When my father died, I inherited this small manor and began to teach here. Part of the price for my instruction was that the men or boys would serve as protector for the local inhabitants, and so a fair exchange was created. My people gained security for free and the knight gained in skill. They have come to regard me as highly as they would a real lord, and so I have my retainers and household servants. However, my servants are free men all, and serve me out of gratitude and not out of fear and indebtedness. Ah, I could teach a thing or two to men who think themselves 'great lords' as well as I teach men skill in arms!" Meg shook her head ruefully.

Rose had finished the gruel, and the cold had begun to stiffen her sore muscles.

Meg saw the girl shiver and said, "Well, enough about me. Back to work, my lass! The exercise will help, believe me. Not only to keep you warm, but also to ease the pain in your muscles, though it may not seem that way at first. Indeed, it may not seem that way at all for the first few days!" She laughed.

The first rays of the sun crept over the horizon and brought with it the promise of a clear though crisp day. Meg picked up the lantern and blew it out, and carried it away with her as she took away the pottage.

Rose stretched, picked up the heavy axe, and once again began to chop at the fallen, dead trees that littered the border of Meg's manor. She blew on her hands to warm them a bit and rubbed them. She found, as Meg had said, that the exercise not only kept her warm while the sun slowly climbed into the sky but that it eased the aches and pains in her back and limbs as well. And her anger was subsiding, vented as soon as it surfaced and channeled into the work at hand. By midday, Rose was feeling pleasantly tired physically, and very much lighter emotionally than she had recalled feeling in a long while.

Meg sent out a light snack of bread and cheese, along with a few apples, for Rose's midday break. The strange dark man who sat with her did not speak with her, however, and so Rose ate in silence, pondering. Meg was a strange mix of both reassurance and fear for Rose, comforting and threatening at the same time. Rose felt a very deep gratitude toward Meg.

Rose chopped wood all day, from sunrise until sunset when another of the dark retainers came to fetch her in. He brought with him a meal of dried meat and hard tack and a cup of goat's milk to wash it all down. Rose took the food gladly, famished from her day's labor, and crept off to sleep immediately after.

And so it went for several weeks. Rose would be awakened before dawn, and set to work, chopping wood, pulling away brush, or milking and feeding the goats, and tending to the swine – tasks that were already familiar to her and brought back to her a sense of home and belonging.

As Meg had said, the first few days were agony. But the pain faded quickly and was replaced by familiarity and a sense of security. Rose took to her tasks readily and proved herself useful and capable. She churned butter. She helped with the foddering. She made herself as much a member of Meg's household as any there. And Rose began to feel happy again. The wounds to her body had healed, and now, so too, were the wounds to her spirit. She would hum or sing to herself while she did her chores, though it was often that doing so would bring back painful recollections of happier days spent with Poppa and Michael. Then tears would come, and Rose would let them fall, freely. The labor brought comfort eventually. And labor brought rest when the day was through.

And Meg watched all this carefully. Rose was something she wanted to craft with every skill Meg had at her command. She already began to look for tutors to teach Rose Latin and grammar, as well as ladies to teach her dancing, music, and needlepoint. The "feminine arts" which she, herself, was little skilled at. She couldn't say exactly why, only that it felt important to her that Rose be taught these things – "men's" skills and "women's" skills – to keep her balanced. Maybe it was that Meg saw in Rose the potential to have the best of both worlds. She saw in Rose a developing beauty that men would find attractive, though a bit leaner and more muscled than some might find desirable. But, beauty nonetheless.

And Rose complained bitterly that Meg was "not keeping her promise to her" by being taught these things instead of the arts of war. But Meg insisted, saying, "Discipline is a skill that serves you in both love and war. What is a battle between two knights but a form of dance? Go to! Go to!" That argument wouldn't have worked on Meg when she was younger, but Rose accepted it dutifully and went to her lessons. Her days were more full than those of the young men Meg trained, for they were only taught the physical skills which suited their profession – sword and shield, lance and mace. But Meg kept this from Rose, feeding instead Rose's stubborn insistence on mastering everything Meg set to her.

Weeks became months, and Rose was blossoming into womanhood. She carried herself with a feline gracefulness, the product of both her physical exercise and the dance lessons. Her hair had grown a richer shade of red, and her complexion was pale and clear. Her arms and legs were long and well-proportioned, toned like a mountain lion's. Her green eyes were bright and sharp. And Rose topped all but the tallest of Meg's retainers, standing almost a head taller than Meg herself.

And Meg noticed the way that the men in her manor began to look at Rose, the lingering gazes when they thought Rose wasn't aware.

"Time," Meg told herself. It was time to take the rich, raw material Rose possessed and begin to hammer it into shape. *I wonder,* thought Meg, *does the sword question why it must be continually thrust into the fire then pounded by the smithy's hammer? Or does it simply accept the beatings and firings as part of the process of coming into being? I wonder, is this what motherhood is like? This fear and apprehension as well as the desire to see what the child will be like?*

Rose was pulled from her bed roughly, and she felt a moment of panic before she began to fight back against her unknown assailants. For a brief moment, she re-experienced the violence of her beating, and anger flared up within her, driving out the paralysis of fear and confusion. Rose struggled mightily, landing a blow or two against the men who dragged her, struggling, out of the pens before throwing her roughly into the snows of the frozen exercise yard.

Rose jumped to her feet and adopted a defensive posture as she looked around at the group of men standing in a circle about her. The snow bit into her bare feet with cold, sharp teeth. Her woolen gown hung loosely from her tall, lean frame, and flapped in the chill breeze.

It was dark, and a sliver of moon revealed itself in mid-sky.

"What is the meaning of this?" Rose demanded. "What do you want from me?" The circle of men stood still and silent. Suddenly, Rose was grabbed from behind, a heavy arm locking across her throat while the other twisted her right arm up and behind her back. *Oh, God!* thought Rose. *Not again!*

"No!" she choked out as she pulled on the man's arm across her throat with her left hand. "NO!" He had lifted her off the ground in the deadly embrace, and her legs kicked wildly. "NO!" she cried as she kicked her captor in the groin. Rose heard a satisfying grunt of pain, and the man's grip loosened enough for her to break free. She spun quickly and hit him across the face with the back of her hand, though the blow hurt her cold hand probably as much as it did her attacker.

The circle of men continued to stand still, saying not a word. Her assailant backed away a few paces, warding his face with his hands in a practiced manner.

What was going on here?! Rose wondered wildly. She turned about the circle and held her gown tightly both against the cold and to keep it from hindering her movements.

Her eyes adjusted to the twilight, and she recognized these men as Meg's retainers and field hands.

Another of the circle stepped forward, swinging his fist at Rose's head, and she quickly ducked under the blow and struck her right fist into his stomach. The man let out an "oof!" and stepped back to his place in the circle as another man came forward from Rose's left, his arms wide in an attempt to tackle her. Rose ducked and rolled into his legs, forcing the man to topple over her. She ended in a crouch on the edge of the circle, just about in the place where that man had been standing. The men to either side of her grabbed for Rose's arms. The one to her right caught her, but the man to her left was just a bit too slow, and his grip slipped off of Rose's left arm. The man to her right pulled her forcefully, and Rose slipped in the snow and was dragged a few feet before the man stopped, releasing Rose unexpectedly. He stood ready but did not attempt to reach her again.

Rose was horribly confused. *What is going on here?* The men she had struggled with earlier had rejoined the circle and stood waiting, still and silent. None of them spoke, not even to each other. *Is this some bizarre custom of theirs? Some strange ritual?*

The man who had just released her touched his hand to his eyebrow and walked back toward the circle. When he got back into position, he turned, making an opening toward the center as if inviting Rose to step back into the ring. It was then that Rose caught site of Meg watching from an upper window of the manor.

So, this is some part of my training? The realization began to dawn on her.

The man motioned for Rose, waving to her silently to enter the circle. With a shrug, Rose went.

There were a dozen men standing there. Some of them Rose even knew, some of them had been the ones that she had hunted with, others she had done chores with. It became clear that these men meant her no real harm. They were here to help with her training! *At last!* she thought to herself. *Finally I get to learn how to fight!*

Rose adopted a stance she had seen the men take when they had gotten into fistfights. She kept her legs slightly apart and kept herself low for balance.

The men, upon seeing this, seemed to relax a little. Unspoken, an agreement seemed to pass from man to man, and they took turns, somehow determined without speaking, to come into the center and spar with Rose. The first man came up to Rose and said, "Like this. Hands." He indicated a new way to hold her hands in front of her. "Roman way," he said. "Gladiator way." He took a swing at her that Rose blocked. Then another. Then another, faster. Each time Rose blocked it. If she went to counter, however, he slipped back out of range. *I guess I'm supposed to just learn defense,* Rose thought to herself.

He sparred with Rose for several minutes, throwing punches and landing a few on Rose's body, though he pulled them whenever he might have caught her on her face. And if she made any move to retaliate, he stepped back. *Focus on defense,* she reminded herself. The cold was hurting her feet even though the exercise was warming the rest of her. Thankfully, some low soft leather shoes were handed to her when the first man had finished, the bottom covered with a sticky sap for traction. The cold from the snows melted through the soles of her shoes, but it was better than nothing. A wool cloak was thrown around her shoulders by one of the others with a reassuring squeeze of her shoulder. The cloak might prove a hindrance, but Rose was thankful for the gesture.

So it went for some time. Rose lost track of the time, hardly realizing the lightening of the cloud-filled sky. She had become so focused on the training, how to duck and weave, how to block, and so on, that she hardly even felt the cold anymore. Or how hungry she had become! Man after man stepped forward, teaching some new trick or variation to Rose and keeping her on her feet. Rose thought back to her wilder days as a child, when she got into fights with her brother, Michael, and it brought a small pang of remembrance.

"Enough!" came Meg's command. She regarded the girl with masked approval. The men in the circle nodded, indicating to Rose she had their respect as well.

Meg had come down once the sky had lightened, and warm food was set out for the men to refresh themselves.

"Go and put some clothes on," Meg told Rose. "Your day has only just begun!"

Thankful, Rose went back and dressed as the men ate. A fire was started in the exercise yard, a great pyre that melted the snow for several feet around it. Meg gestured for Rose to partake of the meal as well, but warned her not to eat too much. "Too much food can make you sluggish. It would do you little good to have a full belly before a fight only to die because of a sudden cramp."

"I don't know what to make of you, Rose," Meg confessed as the girl ate. "You take to these skills like you were born to them, far more than seems natural to me. If I didn't know better, I'd say you had faerie blood in you." She laughed at that.

Rose responded, "My little brother once accused me of being a changeling. He got a bloody nose for it." The memory was bittersweet.

"I don't doubt it," Meg replied. "And what did your parents do? Who taught you how to fight? Your father? Or was your mother, perhaps, an Amazon?" She laughed again.

"I hardly knew my mother," Rose told her. "She died when Michael and I were very young. Michael was maybe five, and I was seven. I missed her at first, but Poppa ..." Rose felt herself choke as tears came forth. "Poppa was the most affected by it. He missed her very much and kept her things. I found some of them in the ruins of our home after the soldiers had burned it down." Her tone became colder and more controlled.

So that explains the pendant! Meg realized. *Was Rose's mother an acolyte of Avalon?*

The girl had become silent, brooding, and Meg wondered just how much she had healed inside for she knew that the deadliest wounds were those to the soul. Wound a man's body, and he might continue to fight. But wound his soul and men were known to lay down their arms and welcome Death. Meg felt a sudden tenderness for the girl, and felt angry with herself for feeling it. *I am not the girl's mother!* Meg told herself sternly. *I have no time to waste on such soft indulgences as tenderness!*

"Armor, next!" Meg shouted as she stood from where she and Rose were sitting. Attendants rushed to fetch the equipment as Meg motioned for Rose to finish her last bite and get back to the training.

"Armor?" Rose asked. "Shouldn't I be learning something like the lance or sword?"

Without warning, Meg gave Rose a swift backhand across the face that sent the girl sprawling into the snow. A stunned silence swept the yard as the men stopped what they were doing, as surprised as Rose at the unaccustomed outbreak.

"I told you, you were not to question me – on anything!" Meg shouted at the girl.

Rose stared up at Meg in disbelief and horror. The blow felt like it had struck her feelings as much as it had bruised her cheek!

"I ... I'm sorry," Rose said weakly as she got up from the ground. "It ... won't happen again," she said.

Meg felt regret for having lost her temper, but stuffed it down and stiffened her resolve. Control was what was needed here, and she felt it slipping away whenever she dealt with Rose. *It will serve the girl no good for me to be soft with her! She may find mercy and tenderness from others out there in the world, but she would find harshness and cruelty as well. And it is far better that she learn how to deal with the latter now, where I have some chance to help her, than later when she would be on her own. Tenderness could get the girl killed!*

The men brought in a set of heavy plate armor and assisted Rose in getting into it. They worked swiftly and efficiently, and soon Rose was standing fully outfitted and almost too weighted down for her to move.

How am I supposed to fight in this? she wondered. *I can barely stand up, let alone move with all this metal on me!*

Meg sat near the fire in a great, carved wooden chair the men set out for her. She spoke to the men in their musical tongue, and they helped Rose make her way slowly out into the midst of the exercise yard. Then, with a sharp command, Meg had the men topple Rose over onto her back unexpectedly.

With a loud crash, Rose fell down, all in a clatter. Her helmet, which must have weighed twenty-five pounds alone, kept her from hurting herself on the frozen ground, but the weight of it made it difficult to lift her head and see what had happened. The heavy breastplate held her torso down, and Rose found that her arms were too restricted to help roll her over onto her face or side. She lay helplessly flailing on her back like an overturned tortoise.

Why is she doing this to me? Rose asked herself in frustration. *Does she simply want to embarrass me? Does she want me to give up? Why, after all this time, is she suddenly being so cruel?*

"Lesson the first!" came Meg's voice from the far end of the yard. "If a knight is knocked from his horse, how does he get up? Eh?" Meg watched as Rose tried to twist and squirm, a metal beetle on its back. "And you wanted to know *why* I said 'Armor' first?" Her voice held sarcasm. "A knight might have a squire nearby to help him to his feet, but that's hardly practical, now, is it? Can you imagine two knights going at each other, and every time one of them falls down his poor squire has to rush out into the field and help him up? I'll tell you this – many a knight has met his doom because he had been knocked flat and couldn't get up. Then any sod can come along and kill him at their leisure!"

Rose was getting angrier and angrier and hoped that her rage would give her the strength to push herself up, or at least over. But all it did was fuel her frustration in her useless struggle. Finally, she gave up, and lay panting on the cold ground. Icy water was flowing in along her back as the heat of her body melted the snow under her.

I refuse to give up! Rose told herself. *There has got to be a way!*

"I have told my men not to assist you in any way," came Meg's voice. "You can lie there until you freeze to death, or

102

until you give up this quest of yours to become a knight." Her tone betrayed no emotion, no concern over one outcome or the other.

How do I do this? Rose furrowed her brows in concentration. *If I could just get myself to roll over, I might ...* A thought came to her. *Maybe!*

Rose began to work her legs, bending her left leg as much as the greaves allowed until she could push against the ground with her foot, and she tipped herself over onto her face.

Great! she thought. *Now if I can just use my arms ...* But her arms were simply too weak to push herself up. *But what if I ...?* Again, Rose used her legs, bending them and getting them into position for her to push herself back onto them into a sitting crouch. It took a few tries, but she finally managed to push the weight of herself back, and pivoted the weight with her legs and hips until she was sitting in a crouch. Then, with a huge effort, she began to stand. She was unsteady, and the armor's weight and awkwardness made standing difficult. But at least her legs and hips had some flexibility, and she eventually stood up.

Meg stared at Rose, her face unreadable. Inside she felt a sense of pride, more than she had ever felt when a young man had discovered a solution to the problem. But the very strength of her feelings was used to maintain the mask of unemotional resolve.

"I did it!" Rose shouted and glared across the yard at Meg. The men who had watched let out a small cheer of support.

"Now do it again!" Meg yelled back at her. Another sharp command, and a pair of men came out to Rose and pushed her over again.

Rose groaned loudly. The first time had taken nearly all she had, and now to do it again?! She took her time, but eventually she stood facing Meg once more. She waved her fist in triumphant defiance before being knocked down yet again. This time, she lay in the snow and cried. She simply didn't have the strength left to go through the whole process once more.

"Do you yield?" asked Meg, standing from her chair.

"Never!" shouted Rose, and her voice echoed inside her helm. "I'd rather die first!"

Meg shook her head sadly, knowing Rose could not see her. *Such Pride in this one! It could be her undoing.* "If that is your wish." Meg sat down again. The men retreated to the side, watching. Meg could tell from their whispered conversations and the few words she could catch that they were worried for Rose. It was as if Rose had become one of their own, and they wished for her to succeed. *They have never felt any attachment to any of the others I have trained. But this girl … There is something about her that seems to have touched them as much as it has touched me. What is it about this Rose?*

Rose lay face down, feeling the cold ground draining her strength and warmth. She felt a despair she had never known before. Her spirit was becoming as cold as her body. And she felt so very tired. So tired of her own anger; tired of her frustration; tired of fighting! It would be so nice to just let it all go and go to sleep, never to have to wake – never to have to deal with the pain of Poppa's death, and the loss of Michael. *Michael, what happened to you?* she cried within.

Cold. So cold. A sudden thought came to Rose, and it brought a brief flush of warmth as she became angry with herself. *What am I doing?* she thought. *I am surrendering by just lying here! This isn't going to do me any good! This isn't going to avenge Poppa and Michael! This lets Carados win! Never! Never!!*

"All right!" Rose shouted. "I *yield!*" she spat out the words. "I yield."

Meg smiled faintly to herself. *So, there's hope yet for the child!*

"I accept your surrender. Gladly!" she said as she waved for her attendants to lift Rose up from the ground. They quickly stripped her from her armor, their hands firm and reassuring as they worked, and a fresh blanket was brought as well as warmed ale, and they placed her near the fire. *Their own fire,* Meg noted. *Not the one near me.*

Rose was the most exhausted she had ever been in her life. She could barely hold herself up as she sipped the warm mug and warm herself by the fire. Meg sat staring at her, again her eyes and face unreadable. Rose stared back, feeling a mixture of sadness and confusion. She had the feeling something profound had happened today, though she had no idea what it may be. A test had been passed, perhaps, but it felt more like a loss than a victory. The feeling filled Rose with a sense of heaviness and the desire to sleep. The mug was heavy in her hand, and her eyes felt heavy in her head. The men kept patting her on the back, or touching her shoulder supportively, and expressing their pride in her achievement for the day. But Rose simply felt too tired to care. She drained her mug, glanced once more at the strange, hard lady who had taken her in, and dragged herself off to bed.

Chapter 7

Rose was awakened the next morning, gently shaken by the serving man – a nice change from the past. He stood waiting for her, keeping his gaze respectfully diverted as Rose dressed in the quilted leggings and tunic he had brought. They were heavy, but nothing compared to the plate armor Rose had worn the day before, and allowed her far more flexibility.

When she was done, he led her out to the exercise yard where a long table had been set up with various weapons upon it.

Finally! Rose thought with excitement.

Meg came outside and sat in the great chair her men always set out for her. The day was grey and overcast and bitterly cold, so she was wrapped in a heavy wool shawl, and steam misted from her mouth like a dragon when she spoke. "Today, yes – weapons. But don't get too excited, my dear! Weapons training takes several years to master, if one ever does master anything. And there are certain weapons you will probably never be taught," Meg indicated a row of long pole-arm weapons. "These, for instance, while similar to the spear are too unwieldy unless one wishes to specialize in them, at the cost of learning other weapons available and more useful to you."

Rose looked them over, and she agreed. A spear she might use, much as Meg had done that first day. But these were heavier, and their odd shaped blades and points and hooks confused her.

"What weapons would you like to learn?" Meg asked.

There was a strange glint in her eye, and Rose knew she was being set up for some kind of a "mistake" no matter what she answered. And that annoyed her, this constant testing and probing and trying to discourage her, so she said, "The sword!"

Meg smiled as though she already had known the girl's answer. "Of course," she said. "A knightly weapon, and a good choice. Practical. There are many types to choose from – the battle sword, cut-and-thrust, the falchion – a little awkward at first, but an effective weapon and one favored by many knights."

Rose looked at Meg. "No criticism?" she asked a bit surprised. "No 'That's not for you! Guess again'? " Rose was almost disappointed that this was not a trick question.

"No, no tricks," Meg answered, though she still looked like she had something up her sleeve. "I had asked you a question, and you answered it fairly. It is the choice made by almost every boy I have ever instructed." Meg stood, walked over to the table, and picked up a heavy flanged mace. "This would be a better choice, and I'll show you why, though, again, for you this may not be the best choice of weapons."

One of the mannequins was outfitted with a suit of heavy plate armor much like the one Rose had been forced to wear the day before. Meg walked out towards it, and indicated to Rose she should follow.

"Take up a sword, any one that appeals to you, and come with me," she ordered.

Rose looked them over, amazed at all the different styles of blades and cross-guards. Some were quite broad while others tapered to a narrow point. Some had broader heads than the main body of the blade, while others had deep grooves running the length of them.

Which one do I choose? Rose wondered sensing that this may be where the trap lay. *Which one is the right one for me?* Finally, Rose settled on a blade with a very broad base, of average length, set with deep grooves. It was heavier than she expected, and the balance was more toward the hilt than the blade, but she picked it up and strode out to the mannequin with Meg.

Meg glanced at the weapon Rose had chosen, noting it critically but saying nothing. Rose could tell she had chosen wrongly, but stuck out her chin and waited for the remark to come.

Let her tell me! I don't need this game – I want to learn.

They stood in front of the man-sized dummy, and Meg said to Rose, "I want you to take a swing at his breast plate with the sword you have chosen. It's the biggest and easiest target, and thus is the one most protected. It is also, therefore, the least vulnerable."

Rose tested the sword, hefting it to get a better grip and sense of its weight, then swung with all her strength at the mannequin. There was a loud ring as the blade rebounded off the thick breastplate. It dented only very slightly, and Rose's hand stung with the shock as it hit, the cold making it even worse. She nearly dropped the heavy weapon, but managed to save herself that embarrassment.

Meg nodded as though satisfied, then spun quickly and struck the armor with the heavy mace she carried. The results were devastating! The armor crumpled under the force of the blow, the thick flanges puncturing through the steel. Meg had to tug a few times to free the weapon from the dummy, which leaned a little askew from the blow.

"This is a much better choice against an armored opponent than a sword," she said as she walked away.

Rose looked at the damage with amazement. Where her sword had left a dent, the mace had staved in the breastplate. The metal would have crushed the chest of whomever was wearing it, or at the very least have left them badly injured and unable to get out of their damaged armor without help. Rose ran her hand over the cold metal as though she couldn't believe what she saw, then looked down at the heavy sword she had chosen.

"You'll learn the sword," Meg called to her from her chair where she sat bundled up against the cold. "But, you will also learn the mace so far as you can. And the lance and shield. The spear, too, would make a good weapon for you. It requires great agility, and that is where your strength lies."

Rose walked back. She gazed at Meg with renewed respect. "Why teach me the sword when I barely scratched the dummy?" she asked. Rose replaced the heavy sword with the others and picked up the mace Meg had just used. "You just proved to me that this would be a better choice."

"I said it was a better choice against an armored opponent," Meg reminded her. "And I also said it was a better choice for most, but not necessarily for you."

Rose looked at her with confusion.

Meg went on, "You have great agility. An amazing agility the likes of which I have never seen before in any knight or boy I have ever trained. But, you are also physically never going to be a match for most men you would need to fight." *Especially Carados*, she wanted to add. "You must rely on speed and agility, not on strength. The mace is more a weapon of brute force, like the axe. Even an axe would have done more damage than a sword! But the sword can be used to more easily penetrate the finer points in an armor's defense – the vulnerable spots under the armpits, or throat, or groin. Used against an unarmored opponent it can be deadly, of course, much like any other weapon. But against heavy plate, it requires skill and intelligence. Both of which you possess, Rose – never doubt it."

Rose flushed with the unexpected compliment. The mace in her hand was heavier than the sword she had chosen, its weight at its tip. It could be an unwieldy thing unless she practiced a great deal with it, learning its flow. And she would need to build up her arm's strength to use it properly, that she could feel as well.

"Yes," Meg said as though she could read Rose's thoughts. "You will indeed need to build up your strength and endurance! This will be no farm chore. This will be about saving your life!" Meg smiled her wicked smile whenever she was about to give Rose some particularly tiring chore to do. "For that, we use this!"

A heavy wooden practice sword was handed to Rose. The weight of it was easily twice what she had hefted and more than that of the mace. It must have been filled with lead it was so heavy!

"You will practice with that upon the practice posts until you can swing it no longer. Then, you will help the men carry sacks of grain until the midday meal. After the meal ..."

Rose felt like groaning. "I know! More practice."

Meg leaned back in her chair. "Not so glorious anymore, is it?"

Rose shook her head. "It's not that. It's just ... I never knew how much work went in to becoming a knight before. It ... I have a new respect for those who undergo the journey!"

"But you understand the need, yes?" Meg asked rhetorically. She could see that Rose was accepting of the situation. Everything she had been asked to do, all of it was coming together now. The physical exercise with the heavy chores, the chopping wood and so on. Even the dance lessons would come in useful here. The weapons Rose would learn required grace and fluidity in order to be used to greatest effect, qualities Rose possessed in great measure.

"Once you have eaten, take the afternoon to rest lightly. Let your meal digest. It's the same way for the farmer and the field hand as it is for the knight in training – a short break before one returns to the toil of the day."

If you think you were doing a lot before, Meg thought to herself, *just wait until we add some armor!* She couldn't pity Rose, however. Everything had its purpose. And everything she was asking Rose to do was to help ensure that Rose survive.

Rose worked with the weighted practice sword until she simply couldn't lift her arms any more. Meg instructed her in both one-handed and two-handed blows, and instructed Rose to work as often with her off-hand as she did with her main one.

"This will not only balance you physically," Meg told her, "but it can give you an advantage to fight with your left hand as most men are accustomed to fighting with their right. It puts your weapon on their offensive side and forces them to adjust their defense."

With heavy steps and arms that felt like they were dead, Rose then went to work with the men as they carried sacks of grain into the storehouse. Rose was unable to lift the sacks with her numb arms, and one of the men lifted them onto her back, securing it with a sling of belt leather that looped around Rose's forehead so that her arms were free.

"Easier to balance," he told her in Welsh. Rose had begun to pick up the language after her months living here. He smiled in sympathy at her struggle, and waved as she plodded with the grain to the granary.

Gods! thought Rose. *Will I even make it to the midday meal?*

But Rose kept on carrying sack after sack, dreading as each one was loaded onto her and grateful as each one was lifted from her. The men worked cheerfully, singing as they went, while Rose trudged back and forth until the midday meal was rung. Rose had lost track of time moving like a sleepwalker, and it was one of the workers who told her it was time to eat.

Rose was treated as one of their own by the men seated at the long table, and their acceptance helped make her feel better. They joked with her, though Rose only understood about half of what they were saying. And several of them patted her on the back as they walked by, or squeezed her shoulder as they sat down or got up from the places next to her. It was a familiarity Rose had seen the men exhibit with one another, and it pleased her.

When she first sat down to eat, Rose felt wooden, with no appetite. But after she had a few sips of warm cider and a few bites of food, her stomach growled, and Rose ate with enthusiasm. Her arms still shook from the exercises with the practice sword, and they felt like they might fall off at any moment. Rose was sure she'd be sore the next day or two, but she had learned that it passed. She wouldn't feel like this forever.

Meg observed all this with quiet wonder. Never before had any of her students been so accepted by her people. The serving women had accepted Rose early on when Rose would help with the chores. And the men had not only come to respect the girl, but to see her as some kind of totem, a sign of good luck and the favor of the Great Mother upon them.

Rose ate and slept and returned to work like the rest of the men. That night, she fell into a heavy slumber, glad that the day's work was finally ended.

This became Rose's routine for the next few weeks: exercises in the morning, followed by heavy labor the rest of the day. It wasn't long, however, before she noticed she wasn't getting nearly as tired or as quickly as before.

"I think you're ready for more," Meg said unsympathetically one morning. Rose sighed inwardly as two men brought out a steel breastplate and helped her put it on.

"I had to have this … adjusted … in order to accommodate your, shall I say, unique build," Meg informed her with half a smile. Her smith had looked at her as though Meg had lost her mind, but she paid him handsomely and also commissioned an even more unique suit of armor – one that would be tailor-made to Rose's physique and talents. One the likes of which few had ever seen, let alone worn.

Rose grunted with the unaccustomed weight and bulk as she went through her morning sword practice. The edge of the armor chafed her armpits and shoulders despite the heavy padding of the quilted arming doublet she wore underneath. She had to redouble her efforts to accommodate the awkward metal, glad that Meg hadn't ordered her to wear the entire suit, greaves and all.

Meg had another change in Rose's routine. Rather than just swinging at the practice post until her arms grew weary, Meg had one of her sergeants-at-arms work with Rose practicing various kinds of blows and parries.

"Block with the flat of the blade when you can!" she shouted to Rose. "To save the edge as much as possible. A blade is strongest in cross section, but you'll dull it that much faster if you think to strike with only the edge – in which case a metal bar would do you as much good!"

Parry with the flat, not the edge – right! Rose tried to remember. It was hard because her natural inclination was to meet edge to edge rather than to turn the wrist and deflect the blow, letting it slide down and be pushed away from her body.

"That's it!" Meg encouraged. "Yes! Remember, don't try to meet strength with strength. That isn't the way for you to fight! Rely on speed and agility. Think!" Meg watched as Rose dodged away from another blow, sidestepping it quickly. *Ah! She's still letting him stay on her weaker side. Move the other way next time! Get him on your weapon side so that you can protect yourself with the blade as well as attack!* There was so much to teach the girl!

Rose panted as she dodged and struck, parried and retreated. Her awareness began to narrow, and a sudden lightness came over her as though she were no longer aware of her body, no longer weighted down and fatigued. She laughed, which brought a confused expression on the face of the sergeant. To Rose, this felt like one great dance, and she flowed into the open spaces, stepping lightly this way and that, stepping in when there was an opening, and stepping back when there wasn't. In the middle of one pass, Rose shifted the blade unexpectedly from her right hand to her left and brought it smashing into her partner's helmet. The blow stunned the man both from the shock and from the unorthodox manner in which it had been delivered.

Rose looked over at Meg who stood with her mouth slightly agape, and the magic seemed to vanish like a burst soap bubble.

"What?" Rose asked as both sergeant and Meg stared at her. "Did I ... did I do something wrong?" She suddenly felt very self-conscious.

"How did you do that?" Meg asked.

Rose did not know how to respond. "I ... I just, uh... did."

The sergeant spoke to Meg rapidly, but Rose caught the words for "dishonorable" and "unkindly" among them.

Meg listened, then thanked the man and dismissed him. The sergeant gave Rose a dark glance, saluted, and stalked away. Meg began to laugh.

"Oh, my!" she wheezed. "I have never in my life before, and doubt I shall ever see again, anyone catch Sion ap Gwdion off-guard like that!" Meg shook her head. Then, more seriously to Rose she said, "Rose, where did you learn to do that? Did you see someone change their weapon like that before?"

Rose shook her head. "No, never. I just ... it just came to me. It was like we were dancing, and it kind of happened." She shrugged. "Did I do something wrong?"

"Well, no, not wrong really. Nor something especially inventive. In battle, one must do whatever one can in order to survive, let alone be victorious," Meg answered. "But, something I neglected to teach you, and something that is drilled into the skull of every young page, squire, knight, and soldier, is that there are certain rules of conduct – certain modes of behavior that are considered acceptable, if you will."

Rose suddenly felt downcast. "So I did do something wrong."

"No, of course not. More, well, unexpected and not in keeping with tradition I'd say. Sion might say otherwise," she laughed again. "Ah, Rose!" she leaned on the girl's arm as she spoke, "You bring a whole new light to something I thought I knew so well."

Rose smiled at the praise she sensed hidden in the comment.

"Knightly conduct is something I never realized before as such a limitation," Meg said half to herself. "You just taught me something, something I might have recognized before but never did. Ha!"

"Are you going to share, or must I figure it out as part of my training?" Rose asked.

"Hmm? Oh, yes ... of course, of course. I told you before how I never trained a knight who wasn't open to the idea of a woman instructing him in the arts of war, despite the fact that we Celts have had a long tradition of queens and female warriors who do so. I said something to the effect of how their minds were imprisoned by their prejudice like their bodies are in the armor that they wear."

Rose nodded that she remembered Meg saying so.

"Well, what I just now realized is that the whole 'Rules of Conduct' is just as imprisoning, to the point where men don't even think beyond them. Part of Sion's mistake was to assume that you would fight what he considers 'fairly.' Am I making sense to you?"

"So, what you're saying is that by not being trained in the 'proper' ways of fighting, I have a ... slight advantage?" Rose asked trying to work it out. The implication was interesting!

"Yes. Exactly. Now some men would say that what you are doing is simply fighting dirty, and, of course, that isn't the way to win great fame and be popular with the people. And there are plenty of rogue knights who are little more than brigands who use every evil trick at their disposal, little caring how that might sully their reputation. But, that's not what we're talking about here. You didn't do anything dishonorable. You simply acted outside the convention. And that could be an advantage to you against men who fight 'by the book' as they say."

Rose was a bit confused. "So, simply by changing sword hands in the midst of a fight, I somehow broke the rules?"

"No. That was something unexpected by one who is so unpracticed at swordplay, a very advanced maneuver, and so it surprised me that you would 'instinctively' arrive at it. But, in practice, it is dangerous to aim a blow at the head when using a weighted sword. If not for Sion wearing a helm, he might be dead right now."

Rose suddenly felt extremely guilty. "Oh my! I ... I am so sorry! I didn't realize ... of course!" She felt so stupid!

"No harm done," Meg comforted her. "Except to Sion's pride. But that will heal, especially once he gives you a good thrashing!" She smiled while Rose frowned. "My fault as well. Getting old, I suppose. And, like Sion, I assumed you already knew. Of course you didn't, how could you? But, you see, my assumptions led me to a certain course of action – they limited my own thinking. Quite an eye opener, that!" Meg looked at Rose. She suddenly felt twenty years younger as a whole new way of thinking opened up to her! "Tomorrow, my girl, you'll use simple wooden practice swords. They still can hurt, but are less likely to be lethal. Just ..." she paused. "Just be ready for a good beating is all." Meg pat Rose's arm, then let her go to continue with the day's labors.

The next day Rose was surprised as the practice yard looked like it was being readied for a tournament. Several of the workmen and servants loitered about the yard, nibbling on their morning biscuits and sipping drinks.

Is today some sort of holiday? Rose wondered. She was dressed as she had been the day before – quilted shirt under the breastplate of thick steel.

The yard had been cleared except for the practice posts, which were buried too deeply to be moved, and rope barriers set up to form a ring around the yard. Rose felt a sudden apprehension in her stomach as she slipped under the ropes and walked into the ring. Sion ap Gwdion strode from the barracks, slipped under the rope, and approached her. His face was tense, and he looked at her with stern regard as he handed her the new weapons – wooden practice swords, a little longer than the one Rose had been using but much, much lighter. The blades had been covered with black pitch, for what purpose Rose could not fathom. Sion handed Rose a light helm to put on, much like a simple cap rather than the great tourney helms and visors of a knight. Rose put it on and adjusted the padding inside so that it settled more firmly on her head and wouldn't slip down into her eyes.

Meg came out and sat down in her chair as usual, silently watching.

Sion stepped back a few paces, and turned, saluted Rose, and readied his weapon.

I guess I'm the great attraction today, Rose realized as she took up her stance and readied the sword as she had been shown. *Great!*

"To settle a matter of honor, Sion ap Gwdion challenges Rose to a duel – a contest of skill," announced Meg's steward. "Points will be counted, with three points determining a winner. A single point will be awarded for a strike to a hand, foot, forearm, or lower leg; two points for blows to the thigh or upper arm; and three for a blow to the chest or head. Will quarter be given?" he asked out of tradition, though no one expected a contest of this sort to require it.

Sion nodded his head, and so Rose did the same.

"Then, combatants, ready. Begin!"

Sion came at Rose immediately, raining blows at Rose's left side and head.

He's not wasting any time! Rose thought as she parried blow after blow and sought either an opening or an escape. Wham! A blow landed painfully on Rose's left leg, below the knee causing her to stumble slightly. Sion backed off as the judges noted where the pitch had marked Rose's leg, and Rose was glad for the sudden reprieve.

"Lower leg – one point," came the tally. Men along the perimeter began to exchange hurried banter as they made bets on who would score next, and on who the ultimate winner would be.

"Resume!" came the command, and again Sion charged Rose, batted her sword aside, and caused her to leap back, narrowly avoiding being hit in the chest. He followed her, and Rose fell backward overbalancing. Sion pounced, and Rose thrust her sword at him as she rolled out of the way. She felt it make contact, and a roar of surprise went up from the spectators. Sion cursed and stepped back, looking down at his right thigh where there was a clear black smudge of pitch.

"Right thigh – two points, Rose!" came the judgment.

Lucky blow! Rose thought as she stood and readied herself for the next onslaught.

Many of the men gathered to watch began to cheer on the combatants, and Rose heard more chants of "Gwdion!" than she did of her own name, and figured she was not the favorite.

"Resume!" again came the command. This time Rose was prepared, and she gave ground as Sion charged once more. She tried to remember everything she had been taught by Meg so far.

"Watch an opponent's style of fight," Meg had told her. *"Be aware of a rhythm in your opponent's fighting. A common mistake is to be lured in by an opponent repeating a certain sequence of moves, then changing it abruptly to catch one off-guard. Be ready to use that tactic yourself, but always be looking for something new – something unexpected."*

Sion backed off, his sword testing Rose's defenses. Rose stopped trying to parry every feint and blow, only those that looked like they might land, keeping her defenses tight. Sion again charged, raining a series of blows at Rose's head as though he might land one out of such an unrelenting attack at one area. But Rose sensed that he was pulling his blows and conserving his strength.

What are you up to? she wondered. Then she realized, almost too late, that Sion had succeeded in getting Rose to continue raising her sword higher and higher, exposing her torso and lower body to attack. She swiftly parried Sion's sudden cut which, had they been using real weapons, might have gutted her. She countered, using her left hand to push Sion back as she brought her sword around and down at an angle, attacking him where his shoulder met his neck on his left side. Sion parried, but Rose followed up with a sweeping belly cut of her

118

own, stepping in to keep him on the defensive for a moment. He blocked that as well and gave ground slightly looking for a means to counter. Locking his blade against hers, Sion used his greater strength to push Rose forcibly away from him, and swept his blade at her legs. Another shock of pain as his sword connected with Rose's right shin. There was a roar as many of the spectators cheered for the success of the sergeant, but Sion stepped away and shook his head.

"Right lower leg – one point!" the judges decreed. "The match is even, two points apiece. Resume!"

Rose watched as the sergeant-at-arms circled her, watching her as she favored her weight on her left side because of the blow he had struck on her right. Sweat dripped down into her eye, and she blew to clear it away. The moment she diverted her attention, Sion struck at her – a quick two-handed thrust followed by a spinning cut at her right side. Rose leapt backwards, avoiding the thrust, and barely managed to block the cut at her shoulder.

Close! she told herself. *Keep your eyes on your opponent at all times. It's basic!*

Rose noticed that Sion was panting a bit as well, glad that she wasn't the only one feeling fatigued. He paced back and forth in front of her, looking for an opening. Rose had an idea.

It worked once before, it might work again.

Rose took a feigning step backward, then suddenly stepped inside Sion's guard, shifting the wood sword from her right hand to her left and spinning to strike at him. But Sion was ready for her this time. As Rose swung her blade backhand at his left upper arm, he stepped inside her blow and caught her wrist with his left hand, stopping her swing. Sion had her sword arm trapped in his firm grip, and Rose's back was exposed completely.

Oh, gods! What have I done to myself? Rose wondered, her mind racing to think of a way out.

Rose continued her spin, twisting in his grip, and swept her right leg into Sion's left knee then kicked backward against him.

119

This caused both of them to topple to the ground, Sion falling on Rose's legs. Rose felt a sharp pain in her ankle as his weight landed on her, but she saw an opening and took it. Rose lifted her sword and brought it down right on top of Sion's head. He grunted, dazed by the blow, and Rose scrambled out from under him.

"Blow to the head – three points! Rose is the winner!"

Men leapt over the ropes and lifted Rose onto their shoulders to parade her around the compound. Her ankle throbbed, but Rose felt elated by the cheering of "Rose! Rose! Rose!" by the men who had picked her up. Others came into the ring and helped Sion to his feet. He shook his head and removed the protective helm, dropping it to the ground where he stared at it for a moment.

Rose felt sorry for him, suddenly. She had nothing against him, and now she had shamed him a second time without meaning to. She wanted to say, "I'm sorry!" to the man, but she was surprised when he looked up at her and then he, too, began to cheer "Rose! Rose! Rose!" with the others!

Meg was pleased and very proud of herself right then. Rose had acquitted herself fairly, and Sion's sense of honor was placated. He was not so proud he couldn't acknowledge when he had been beaten. And he had been reminded not to let his pride get in the way of his judgment – something Meg tried to impress upon all her students.

The men finally set Rose down and realized that she had been injured. She leaned on one of them as she hopped to the sidelines, and they helped her under the ropes and to a bench. They had to slit her boot to get it off her right foot and could see how black and swollen it already had become. It throbbed terribly, but Rose grit her teeth as Meg came over and probed it to see if it was broken.

"Just a good sprain is all," was Meg's diagnosis. "You'll need to stay off of it for a couple of days. But don't think that gets you out of doing any work!"

Rose nodded and winced. "I won't," she said. One of the men handed her a cup of spiced wine. Meg gave instructions for how to bandage Rose's ankle, and went to see how her drill-master was doing.

The girl is creative, I'll give her that! Meg thought. *She thinks on her feet, always finding some way to turn things to her advantage. Spontaneous and inventive … remarkable!*

She checked Sion, who nodded he was fine and made his way to Rose. When he had Rose's attention, he snapped to attention and saluted her.

"A good fight!" he said to her in his language. "Next time, maybe you won't be so lucky!" he said with a smile. With a touch of his hand to his brow, a sign of respect between the men here, he turned and walked away, waving off the men who were angry with him for losing to the girl because they bet against her.

Rose felt herself blush. She was glad that things were all right between them, that he wouldn't be holding a grudge. And she felt flushed with pride, basking in the admiration of these men. The throb in her ankle, however, put a damper on it, and she wondered what Meg had in mind as "work" while her ankle mended. *Whatever it is, I'm sure it won't be pleasant.*

Her ankle was better the next morning. Still quite sore, but the swelling had gone down considerably. Rose still couldn't put weight on it, however, so she kept it wrapped and hobbled out to the yard to see what Meg had in store for her. Rose's heart leapt when she saw a horse saddled and waiting. Meg was standing beside it looking it over one more time while she waited for the girl.

"As you cannot use your own legs today," Meg said, "you will need to rely on these. This is Seren Llwyd, that means 'Grey Star' – one of my own. He is very well trained and knows his business. See to it that you know yours," she said to Rose who came up and stroked the great beast on the nose.

"He's very beautiful," Rose said as she rubbed him.

Meg nodded, but said, "Beauty aside, he's not just a tool. He is an extension of yourself when you ride him. As you will note, there is no bit on his bridle to control him. A knight guides his horse through the use of his knees and legs. You can't hold the reins while you fight from horseback with sword and shield very well, now can you?"

Rose was helped into the saddle. This wasn't her first time on a horse – Poppa had let her ride bareback on old Gwynn occasionally. But Rose had never sat in a saddle before, and it caused her to rock with every movement the horse made.

"You don't really *sit* in a saddle," Meg instructed. "You more stand in the stirrups, though you don't want to stand too high off the saddle. It's a mistake many novices make, and leaves a knight off balance. Such knights are more easily unhorsed. Remember that! Study an enemy to see how he rides, how he sits his horse. A good knight will barely clear the saddle when he stands in the stirrups."

Rose guided Grey Star out into the exercise yard where Meg instructed her to walk him gently until he's warm, and then to practice guiding him in a figure eight around the deep practice posts at either end of the compound without using her hands. Standing in the stirrups caused Rose considerable pain as she tried to do as Meg instructed, but she grit her teeth and bore it. Grey Star was intuitive, taking to guidance quickly with a slight shift in her knees or a squeeze from her legs. Rose had him cantering in a figure eight in no time!

"Excellent, Rose!" Meg called to her. "Remember, your mount is a part of you when you ride. Horse and rider are one! Treat him with dignity and care and he will do the same for you."

"Oh, he's wonderful!" Rose exclaimed as she was helped out of the saddle after having ridden for a while. Her legs felt wobbly and tired from the unaccustomed usage. "He does half the work for me!" she said. Despite the pain, the day was incredible!

"He will be both instrument and companion to you in your questing," Meg said. "He's worth more than any armor or weapon you will ever own."

Rose and Meg ate while men set up the tilting quintains and practice rings hung from ropes.

"For the lance, it, too, can be a weapon of finesse like the sword and spear. There are plenty of knights in the world who use it like a long battering ram, an item of brute force and no subtlety. Some men will try to unhorse you by batting you with it sideways at the last second, like a club. Others will hit you square, and the shock is like nothing else in this world! Remember – never take a blow square on! Deflect and divert, that's your strategy. Even your shield should be used to deflect, not take the full brunt of the blow. Too many knights get in that habit! I guess it seems manlier, somehow. Fools," Meg shook her head sadly. "Lean forward but don't overbalance. You want to try to meet your opponent first with your lance before he hits you with his. This will steal some of the force of his blow. And by leaning forward, you present a smaller target for him to hit."

Rose felt a little overwhelmed by all the information Meg relayed to her. There was so much to try to remember! The rest of the day was fraught with frustrations. While Rose quickly learned to guide her mount, getting a lance to balance while in the saddle was much harder than it looked. The tip wavered all over the place, and she kept missing the practice rings, which were probably little more than a hand's span in width! Until she could ride the circuit of the yard and catch at least eight of the dozen or so rings, Meg did not feel Rose was ready to face the quintain with its pivoting mannequin. The counter weight was a heavy bag of sand that could knock a man from his horse if he wasn't careful.

Meg was surprised by the change in Rose's progress. Until now, she had mastered everything rather quickly. This was the first time Meg could ever recall the girl becoming frustrated.

"What's the matter?" she shouted at Rose. "Focus!"

"I am trying!" Rose shouted back at her.

"Then stop," Meg answered back.

"What?" Rose was confused.

"Stop *trying*. You've never had such a hard time with anything before. Why now?"

Rose wanted to cast the lance to the ground and ride away. *Maybe this is one thing I'll never learn!* "I'm making progress with the sword, and getting better with the mace! Maybe I should stick to those," she shouted.

Meg wanted to slap the girl. "You'll never be a knight with an attitude like that."

The words stung Rose.

"If you want to give up, very well then. Get down from that horse, pack your things, and go! I won't have such an ignoble creature on the back of one of my horses. Now go!"

Rose stopped. She could tell that Meg was serious. *Would she really ask me to leave?* Rose asked herself.

Meg walked over to Rose purposefully, limping a little as her arthritis pained her hips and knees. "Welcome to the world of we mortals," Meg spoke to her pointedly. "Dealing with you I had forgotten how to deal with a real knight, one who errs and needs correcting." Her voice dripped with sarcasm. "But down here, Rose, things take time to learn, time to master. It is a process of mistakes and learning from those mistakes that we lesser beings have to go through. But one like yourself," she gestured at Rose, "blessed by the gods, bound on vengeance – I suppose you don't need to endure any of this. So, please, your grace, go. By all means, leave!" Meg waved her hand dismissively at Rose.

Rose swallowed. The thought of leaving – it brought up all kinds of emotions. Meg's keep had become a second home! She had friends, shelter, a purpose. Training had occupied so much of her time; Rose felt it helped her grieve. But she recognized that instead, it had diverted her from grieving, diverted her from healing fully. Her anger had fueled her in the beginning, but that too had kept her from feeling the full pain of her loss. And now, Rose stood to lose everything once more.

To Meg's surprise, Rose hung her head and began to weep. Her heart went out to the girl, and she once again felt the urge to hold her, soothe her, and make it all okay. But she stood firm, looking up as the tears rolled down Rose's cheeks. "Rose," she said gently. "Everything takes time. You may not be able to master everything in an instant. Even your feelings." *Especially your feelings.* Meg was surprised at her own sudden softness. She melted even further when Rose looked down at her with wide, sorrowful eyes.

"I ... have nowhere else ... to go ..." she sobbed, and held her arms out to the old woman.

Meg's servant helped the girl down from the horse.

How tiny and frail she looks suddenly, Meg thought to herself.

Rose stumbled toward her and wrapped her arms around Meg as the tears poured down. Meg found herself returning the embrace and ran her hand over Rose's head, stroking her gently.

"Shh ... there, there," she said. It seemed perfectly natural to be doing this, and Meg let herself go with it. *So, this is what it's like to have a child*!

Chapter 8

"Rose!" Michael jerked awake in fear, as he had so often for the past several months. His nights were marred by horrible dreams, and his days by the alternating whims of his master.

Michael scrambled back to the corner of the room and sat in the darkness, shaking. He thought back to that night, it seemed so long ago, when he had run back to help Poppa. The dash through the wheat, losing touch with Rose. Michael felt tears slide down his cheeks as it all came back to him. He had been seized by one of the reavers on horseback and had fainted in terror, certain that he was about to be slain. Instead, he had been taken north with the vanguard, sold by the man who had captured him to one of the noblemen fighting alongside Carados. Michael knew him to be from King Mark's household by his crest – three lion heads in gold upon a field of red. He knew much of this from the lessons Poppa had given him, showing the boy the lineages of the great families.

After that, his world became one great nightmare of darkness, pain, and terror. Meraugis, Michael realized quickly, was quite insane. His mood swings and outbreaks of violence were abrupt and unpredictable. Michael learned never to speak unless told to do so, and to stay within arm's reach of his master, never to stray more than two strides away from him.

Meraugis seemed to respond favorably whenever Michael complied instantly, and to flattery. So Michael learned to gauge his master's moods as best he could and offered up information in order to impress Meraugis with his quick mind and sharp eyes.

"Yes," Meraugis had told him. "You see? I always knew children were such expert little spies. Always watching. Always telling. Never keeping secret what should be kept secret."

It was a tricky thing to deal with his master, but Michael learned swiftly, and he agreed with the madman.

"Yes, master," he said. "Except I will only tell you. I will only tell you what secrets I see. Is that all right, my lord?"

And Meraugis was greatly pleased by that and hugged the boy and kissed him as though he were his own.

"Oh, my, yes!" the man responded with an unnatural glee. "Yes! Only to me! To me! I'll be the only one who knows, then, won't I? The only one ..."

And so Meraugis had begun to train Michael as his page and had Michael tutored in Latin, Greek, and several other languages besides. Here Michael impressed him even further by how rapidly he memorized everything, and was tickled by Michael's ability to repeat back word for word orders given verbally only once.

"Ah, but you are a treasure!" Meraugis would say to him with bright, shiny eyes.

Michael learned other things as well, to please his lord: Music and singing, poetry, history. It became Michael's duty to sing his master to sleep whenever he felt restless, which was often.

But Meraugis kept Michael like a prized possession, jealously hidden when it was not on display. So he would be locked away in the servant's chambers, with no light, until such time as his master needed him.

Meraugis had left Carados' fortress and traveled north to Scotland where they visited the king there, and Meraugis had Michael go with him everywhere and tell him what he had seen. Michael played a dangerous game for he realized that his master, as unstable as he could be, was very perceptive himself and suspected plots everywhere, always on the lookout for deception. So, Michael would tell him what he felt Meraugis wanted to hear, or expected to hear. And his master began to trust him more and more, sending him off on his own "to explore" and then report back to him what he saw.

By the time they left Scotland and headed east to the lands of Lothian and Orkney, Michael had convinced his lord that the King of Scotland was not to be trusted. He kept a large army in the field and had many secrets. And Meraugis promoted him to squire. The truth, however, was that Michael had no idea if the King of Scotland was true or not. But, it served his personal vengeance to convince his master it was so, for Michael had a plan. One that he kept in the deepest fastness of his own mind.

"I knew it!" Meraugis would say. "I'll let my father know immediately. Good boy! That's my precious Michael!"

In his heart, Michael despised the man. But he never let it show on his face, or even in his eyes. He learned deceit, Michael did, in the household of Meraugis, bastard son of the King of Cornwall. And he learned about power.

In secret, Michael grieved the loss of Poppa and of Rose. He assumed they had been killed or captured and sold into slavery as he had been. In any case, Michael feared the worst and figured that he was alone in the world, now, and had to do his best to survive in any way he could manage.

Meraugis' household was rife with tensions and petty ambitions. Every page and squire had his secret ambition, and could be manipulated by one shrewd enough to pit one against another. And so Michael did. His own rapid advancement and favored status with their lord made him the object of lies and jealousies, and so Michael felt he did what he had to do in order to secure his position and power. Since he had Meraugis' ear, he would tell him lies and get this one beaten or that one demoted, until the others learned not to cross him. Soon, the more clever ones sought Michael's influence in order to further their own, and Michael ran a "shadow" society behind the fa-cade of Meraugis' household.

The mistress of the manor, the Queen of Lothian and Orkney, Morgawse, welcomed Meraugis and his entourage. She was a beautiful woman, voluptuous and sensual, dressed in rich, black velvet and a circlet of gold upon hair that shone like burnished ebony. Her lips were rouged, and her eyes kohled, and her skin was powdered to look pale and even. Tiny crows feet hinted at the corners of her eyes, which were large, beauti-ful, and dark.

Michael was struck by the queen's beauty and felt something odd at the sight of her. His master, too, seemed strangely af-fected by this beautiful woman, and he kissed her on the lips in greeting and laid his head against her breast. She leaned over him and brushed his hair, smiling.

"Welcome to Lothian, my lord Meraugis," she said in a voice rich and sensuous, like honey. "Alas, my lord cannot greet you himself as he still recovers from his wounds. But he sends you his love and welcome, and bids you enter and refresh your-self."

"Ah, mistress," Meraugis sighed. "It seems like forever since I have seen thy beauty."

Morgawse smiled and glanced around, as she hushed him. "Silence, my lord. My *prince*," she said quietly to him. "My hus-band may be bed-ridden, but he is no fool."

Michael caught all this and set it down in his memory, as he had been trained to do. *Oh, I do remember, my* lord, he thought with grim satisfaction. *I watch and I see and I hear ...*

And so, Meraugis and his company were welcomed to the castle, and Michael gave orders to the pages and squires and serving men to do their various tasks and noted who obeyed immediately and who hesitated.

The castle of King Lot was a hard place, heavily fortified and circled with moats and ring walls. Facing the North Sea as it did, the place made an inhospitable but convenient landing place for Viking and Saxon longboats. King Lot and his sons knew much of battle, having to defend their shores so frequently.

Michael saw the standards of Lot hung everywhere, a shield of silver with a small square of red in the upper right corner. The King, he knew, was older than the Queen by several years, married to the daughter of Ygraine at the same time Uther Pendragon had married her mother. He recalled that her sister Elaine had been married to King Nentres as well, while her youngest sister, Morgana, had been sent to live in a nunnery.

And what became of her? Michael wondered as he explored the great keep. He made mental notes of how many guards Lot kept on duty, and where. He noted doorways and hallways, and would reproduce a ground plan for his master later that evening. Rumor had it that Morgana had become schooled in necromancy, though Michael doubted it was true. He did not believe magic existed, and thought that those who practiced it were all charlatans and cons duping people with sleight of hand and misdirection. He had mastered some small sleights of his own, though he was careful not to display them lest he be accused of sorcery. Morgawse, too, had a reputation as something of a sorceress, and Michael gave her some credit as an enchantress of sorts. She certainly seemed to have some kind of sway over his master. The thought of the queen made Michael's pulse quicken, and his mind wandered.

Even myself! He blew hard as though to expel the images that had begun to come to him. *I may have to look into that*, he thought to himself as he continued his tour.

"Here, now! What are ye doin'?" came a great voice as Michael entered a chamber off the main passage. Michael heard a woman's squeal and the rustle of sheets as he popped his head around the door. A large, burly man stood over a rumpled form hidden by the bedding, his face flushed red in agitation at the unexpected interruption. He had a large mane of dark, auburn hair, and a beard to match. His body was naked and covered by a heavy matting of hair the same color as his beard. "Ach, man! Do ye not knock before ye enter a room?" the man demanded.

"I beg pardon, my lord," Michael said. "I didn't realize it was occupied."

"Well it is, ye great git! Ye would've known that had ye knocked!"

"I am sorry, my lord. It won't happen again," Michael soothed. "I am new here and unfamiliar with your castle."

The huge man seemed placated by Michael's tone and jumped down from the bed, unashamed by his nakedness. "New, eh? Well, why didn't ye say so?" he said as he looked Michael over. "From Cornwall, are ye?" he asked.

Michael kept his eyes averted, though he did see a naked girl slip out from under the covers and sneak into the adjoining chamber out of the corner of his eye.

"No, my lord. My master is, yes. But myself, no. I am from …" Michael paused, uncomfortable with relaying too much about himself. "I am from further north. A small village, one of many."

The burly man hardly paid attention as he clapped a meaty hand on Michael's shoulder in a familiar manner. "Well, between yerself and me," he said conspiratorially, "I always thought the men of Cornwall t'be a bit womanly. A wee bit thin, ye know?"

Michael nearly laughed, but controlled himself, allowing only a light smile. The man clapped him roughly on the back before he could answer.

"Ach! I see ye do!" he said. "Ah, where'd she get to?" he strode back to the bed, noting the missing girl. "Snuck off like a mouse, eh?"

Michael indicated the adjoining chamber door. "In the closet, my lord," he said.

The big man raised an eyebrow and grinned, "Sharp eyes ye've got there, master …?"

131

"Squire, my lord. Michael," he answered. Despite his general mistrust, Michael couldn't help but like this man with his open and gregarious nature.

"Master Michael," the man went on, ignoring the correction of title. "Gawaine hight," the man said with a sweeping mock bow. "Now, if ye'd excuse me, Master Michael, I have a wee mouse to catch," he said with a wink and gestured out the door.

Michael bowed formally. "Of course, my lord Gawaine," he said as he stepped back and closed the door behind him.

"Ahhh ..." Meraugis sighed deeply and rolled over to lie on his back. He enjoyed the sensation of Morgawse's long hair as it brushed over him while she laid her body on top of his. It hadn't taken long before she had come to him bearing a cup of "nectar" as she called it.

"*Ambrosia*," she said to him as she offered it to him. "The drink of the gods."

She had come alone, sending away the serving men and women who would normally attend guests of the castle. Meraugis took this as a sign of high favor, whereas Morgawse did it out of necessity and secrecy.

The drink was sweet and thick like honey, and it brought a delicious sensation shortly after Meraugis drank it. Morgawse watched him with hungry eyes, like a cat after it has spotted a mouse or bird.

Once he had finished, she disrobed and came to him. And to Meraugis, she was no longer just a mortal woman, but a goddess. One that had come to bestow her great gifts upon him – earthy and sensual delights, and soothing caresses; hungry kisses and passionate embraces. Venus made manifest she seemed to him. And she loved him, or so he felt, though she never spoke the words.

"You like, yes, my prince?" she stroked his face as she said this, looking down on him.

Meraugis could only nod dumbly. He longed for each caress, yearned for each touch. It was as though his entire body hungered for her like a man gone too long without food or drink.

"I cannot remain long, my prince," Morgawse told him. Meraugis' face betrayed his pain. "Shh ... hush," she whispered to him. It pleased her that the thought of being separated from her caused Meraugis' eyes to tear up. She leaned down and kissed the tears off the corners of his eyes and followed one as it rolled down his cheek, licking up the salty wetness, until her mouth met his. "My husband heals from his wounds and will be wondering where I am if I tarry too long. I am his nurse as well as his queen."

Morgawse slid from the bed, letting Meraugis drink her in as he gazed at her nakedness. She dressed more slowly than she had need, teasing him and feeding his hunger for more.

"I wish he had died in that battle!" Meraugis said petulantly. "Surely he doesn't satisfy you like I can! You deserve someone younger, someone better."

The "younger" statement struck at Morgawse's vanity, and she flinched slightly at it. But she forced a smile onto her face as she turned around and looked at Meraugis as he lay leaning on one arm, the sheets fallen and exposing his bare chest.

He is a handsome youth, Morgawse thought. *What though he's about the same age as my oldest son? It is his youthful vitality which keeps me young!* And she thought about Lot and how close she had come to losing him, for Kay had injured him grievously. *Not yet! I still have need of him if I am to become Queen of more than this rocky shore!*

"I'm sure you don't mean that," she said coyly and sat on the bed next to him. "It hurts me deeply that your love for me does not extend to my husband."

Meraugis took a strand of her hair and smelled it. His pupils were wide and his eyes glassy, affected by the drugs Morgawse infused into the mead.

"I apologize, my Queen," he said distantly, a lethargy creeping over him. "I do love you, you know, and would never wish harm to anyone you did not wish it to ..." He lay back as the peaceful feeling stole through his body.

"That's my good boy," she said as she kissed his eyelids as he slid off to sleep. "That's my lovely prince."

Meraugis was fast asleep by the time she stood up and blew out the candle.

How easy it would be to kill him, Morgawse thought as the candle went out and the room became dark. *Men's blood has power in certain spells and incantations, as does his seed.* She thought about their prior lovemaking. *But, he is still useful to me, like Lot. I won't sacrifice this pawn just because I feel like it. If he loses his usefulness, then we shall see.*

Morgawse made her way to the chamber door. As she exited, she was surprised by the sight of a young thirteen-year old boy with blonde hair waiting silently and still in the antechamber. She could see that he wore the livery of King Mark, and was, therefore, part of Meraugis' retinue. But it disturbed her to be seen leaving Meraugis' chambers.

"What are you doing here?" she demanded with all the majesty and intimidation at her command.

Michael looked up at the Queen and very simply said, "I attend my lord, and am privy to all his secrets, your majesty."

Morgawse exuded a musky scent that made Michael's heart beat faster, but he stood his ground and kept his eyes looking slightly beyond Morgawse's. It was a look he had found calmed many potential antagonists, as though he had some special power to "see beyond," as though he could look into their souls and read their spirits.

Morgawse was strangely taken aback by the lad. He demonstrated no fear of her and yet openly acknowledged that he knew their secret, for which she ought to have him killed. *What odd courage this boy has!*

"You know who I am?" she inquired of him. "You know that I could have your tongue cut out, or your eyes blinded, just for admitting what you have?"

"But you won't," Michael answered back calmly and shifted his focus more directly into Morgawse's own.

"And why won't I?" Morgawse demanded, intrigued despite her irritation.

"Because I am also at thy service, my Queen," Michael replied and bowed deeply before her. "Wholly," he added and kept his head bowed.

Ah! thought Morgawse. *So the mouser has a serpent in his midst. Does he know, I wonder?* "And what services will you perform for me?" she asked.

Michael straightened slightly, still demurring to Morgawse, though he met her gaze as he answered, "Even what you ask, even so shall I endeavor to perform. Save that it put my own life in danger, of course." With that, he smiled.

Is this a child or a devil? Morgawse wondered, slightly impressed by the boy's bravado.

"I will ... keep that in mind," she responded and felt a strange tickle of pleasure at the thoughts that came to her regarding the child and his usefulness to her. "Very well ... you are safe. For now," she said as she swept past him, deliberately brushing his shoulder with her hand.

Michael felt a shock go through him as the queen touched his shoulder, and a wave of her musky scent rocked him. He gathered himself quickly to bow as she went by, and had to take a few deep breaths to calm himself once she was gone.

So, that is the Queen of Lothian and Orkney! Michael thought to himself. *If I can gain her favor ...* Michael mused on the whole realm of new possibilities that would open up to him if he could form an alliance or association with this woman. The ambition she radiated pulled at him more strongly than her sexuality, which feelings had only newly begun to form in him.

He went in and checked on Meraugis only to find him sleeping peacefully, and unusually deeply. Michael dipped a finger into the cup beside the bed, and tasted the drugged mead off his fingertip.

Sweet, but something lingers ... I must beware of taking any drink offered by my lady! Perhaps this is where part of her "magic" lies – in potions and herbs.

Michael went out and called for the servants who should have stayed behind to attend their master if he had need. He knew full well that they had only left because the Queen had ordered it.

But, thought Michael, *it does give me a convenient excuse to punish some of those who need to be put in line! Let them hate me, so long as they learn their place!*

"Father, we do not need such men in your service!" Gaheris argued hotly.

Lot tried to rise, but the room spun too much whenever he did so, and he lay back while his third youngest son paced the room and made his arguments known. Lot was an otherwise fit man for his early forties, graying at the temples and still possessing a full head of gold hair fading to a dull sheen as more grey grew into it. His face was broad, and generous. His eyes were the grey of the North Sea, which lay just off their shore.

"Gaheris!" he cut in weakly.

"No, father, I mean it!" Gaheris went on. "This girl I spoke of … she was nearly raped by the thugs that serve Carados, and he beat her half to death! I tell you, it took all I had not to charge into his keep and kill him myself!"

"My boy," Lot managed to say, "I understand you're upset. And it heartens me to see how much this matters to you." Lot coughed a bit, and Gaheris brought him a cup of spiced wine, which he sipped before he continued, "But, my boy … such things happen in war. The innocent …"

"Are the ones who suffer!"

Lot reached out and laid a hand on Gaheris' arm. The sight of how thin his hands had become surprised him. *How much of me has wasted away lying here!*

"Gaheris … lad … This is the fate of those who are not born to power," Lot tried to explain. "It is a hard lesson, I know. One of the hardest. It is what makes being a king such a responsibility, for it is we who must answer for the blood shed in the end."

Gaheris stared at the wall, unable to believe that his father – *his father* – could condone such a thing!

"Arthur would never do such a thing!" Gaheris said. "I have never heard of the High King ordering the slaughter of innocents."

Lot felt as though the boy had struck him across the face, and his blood rushed up hot and angry.

"How dare you ...?" he choked on his outrage. "Don't you ever throw that bastard's name in my face again, do you hear?" Lot gripped Gaheris' arm as tightly as he could. He wanted to strike the boy and teach him some respect, but his head began to pound, and his vision dimmed as the blood rushed into his head.

Gaheris shook off his father's grip, but his anger faded and was replaced by worry as he saw his father's face become ashen.

"Father?" Gaheris asked in concern. "Father? I ... I'm sorry! I didn't mean to ... I don't mean to upset you. It's just ..."

"What are you doing!" a woman's voice exclaimed. "Are you trying to kill your father?" Morgawse pushed Gaheris away as she checked on her husband.

"Mother," Gaheris acknowledged her coldly.

"Whatever you have come for, get it and go!" Morgawse ordered him. "But leave your father alone. He's too weak to deal with your petty complaints."

Gaheris watched as Morgawse dipped a cloth in water and laid it over his father's forehead. *The very image of loving concern*, he mused. *To all the world, she appears a doting wife. Why do I mistrust her so? Why is there no love lost between us?*

"Forgive me, my lady," Gaheris answered her, though he couldn't mask his contempt. "But what I have to discuss is between myself and my father, the King of Lothian. It is of concern to our kingdom and is hardly 'petty.' "

Morgawse waited until Lot's color had returned to normal before saying to her son, "If it is a matter of concern for the King of Lothian, then it is a matter of concern for the Queen, your mother, as well." She shot Gaheris a venomous glance. Gaheris stood silently brooding, so she prompted him. "Well, what is it then, my son? What is so important that you would risk your father's health by arguing with him while he lies sick and injured in bed?"

Gaheris flushed as Morgawse's question goaded him.

"If you will excuse me, your majesty," Gaheris bowed and strode out of the room brusquely.

What was that all about? Morgawse wondered. She had overheard only the end of the discussion and had perked her ears up at hearing the name of her half-brother, Arthur. *Arthur? Hmm … Perhaps it would be a good idea if we made a "conciliatory" visit to my half-brother, the High King. Maybe I can cool his anger at my husband and convince him that it was the doing of King Mark, and not of Lot, that led to this latest rebellion?*

Lot muttered something under his breath, breaking Morgawse from her reverie. He opened his eyes and looked at his wife as though she were a stranger. But, his expression softened as he recognized her.

"Ah, my Queen …" he said softly, wheezing a bit. "Where … where is my son? I … I thought … Gaheris was here, was he not?"

"Shh, my husband. You dreamed, that is all. Gaheris is adventuring, is he not? He left us when you went off bravely to fight my brother. Don't you recall?" Morgawse spoke smoothly, feeding Lot's uncertainty while playing on his pride.

Lot took her hand in his. "I … I miss you, my … my bride," he said as he looked at his wife. "It has been … so long … since we have … have made ourselves another child." Lot smiled weakly, remembering with fondness their passionate love play from their earlier years. "We have made some … fine sons … have we not?"

Morgawse felt a surge of old anger come up, which she quickly covered with a smile and a sensuous look, laying her head on her husband's chest. Lot had been forced upon her when she was still young, though he had been a strong and attractive man. But he took her like a prize that first night, hurting her, and not caring until he had satisfied his own lust. Morgawse had dreamed of something more mutual than the marriage she found herself in, but she learned that Lot was actually quite soft-hearted and generous and genuinely loved her, and that she could use his feelings to get him to do what she wanted. It was then she learned about the power of her sex and began to flirt with guardsmen and servants whenever Lot was not around. She began to learn about the use of herbs and potions, scents and looks, delving deeper into magic and pacts with powers in order to further her own influence and command. She found it quite thrilling to get a man to want her, desire her, to the point that they lost all sense of reason and were willing to do anything for her. Her greatest triumph was the time she caused two guards to fight each other to the death because she had played them off one against the other, both hoping to win her favor by killing the other, each accused of "slighting" her. Morgawse smiled, and the memory of that victory over men caused her to feel warm and aroused, and she said to Lot, "Yes, my lord … fine sons! Fine sons indeed."

Against her better judgment, for the strain might kill her husband, Morgawse gave in to Lot's invitation, though this time it was she who did not stop until she had satisfied her lust. The thought that Lot might actually expire while inside her thrilled her slightly, and she rode him long after he had finished in the hope that it might actually happen.

Queen of Lothian and Orkney! Morgawse thought as she climaxed. *Make me High Queen as well!*

All the Orkney sons were present at the dinner table and were supping while they awaited their mother who had sent word she wanted to see them.

"Well, we're a fine lot, aren't we?" Gawaine jested as he quaffed down yet another mug of bitter northern ale. "It's been a while, hasn't it?"

Agravaine, who sat opposite him, snorted his disdain at his brother's behavior and remained silent. Gaheris sat playing with his food, hardly eating, while he thought about his last encounter with their mother and of the reaction his father had displayed concerning the news he brought. Gareth, however, was delighted to see his older brothers home for once, and could hardly contain himself as he asked about their adventures. Gawaine, of course, never tired of telling his tales of how he slew this miscreant or that villain, or how he rescued ten, a dozen, or more virgins somehow or other. Gareth listened with wide-eyed wonder, while Agravaine rolled his eyes, and Gaheris felt the same anger and sadness over his oldest brother's need to be bigger than life that had caused a rift in their relationship to begin with.

"And so," Gawaine went on with his slightly drunken enthusiasm, sloshing a little as he waved his mug about while he parried and plundered, "I gave the wee ogre a terrible chop with me sword, and down he crashed like a fallen oak!"

"How can you fight an ogre that's 'wee?' " Agravaine asked in annoyance. "Please, Gawaine, must you keep on like that? Gareth doesn't need to hear any more of your fanciful exploits any longer. He's not a *bairn* anymore."

"Do ye accuse me of lyin'?" asked Gawaine. "Me own flesh and blood calling me a liar? Why I ought to ..." He went to stand but ended up knocking over his chair and nearly fell over it himself.

"You'll do nothing," came the commanding voice of their mother as she entered the hall. Agravaine stood and bowed to her, a slight smirk on his face. Morgawse nodded to him as she passed him. She swept her gaze past Gaheris as he looked up from his plate, noting that he did not stand like his brother. "Please, Gawaine, you're an embarrassment to this household. Don't sulk! Pick up your chair and sit down. I have something to tell you all."

Morgawse sat down and held out her arms to Gareth, indicating that she wanted him to join her. Sullenly, Gareth did so, ashamed of the way his mother drew him into her in front of his brothers as though he were still a little child.

"Your father is still too ill to travel, but it is our desire that we reconcile with the High King."

"King Arthur?" asked Gawaine. "Da wants to make peace with the man he just went to battle with? I heard him call Arthur all sorts of nasty things besides that of 'bastard' last time I spoke to him."

Agravaine narrowed his eyes, thinking. "Seriously, mother? Isn't it a little dangerous to see our ... rival ... quite so soon?" He couldn't bring himself to call Arthur "king," and knew that Gawaine was right. Their father would never sue for peace with the bastard heir. His pride and ambition wouldn't allow it! *What is she up to?*

Gaheris stood and asked, "Really? All of us? We'll be seeing the High King?"

"Yes, all of us. Of course!" Morgawse replied, and laughed as though this was to be some family outing or a picnic. "As for your father ... Well, he does have some very strong feelings about the High King, I'll admit. But, he's also shrewd enough to know when it is wiser to bide one's time, waiting for the right moment to attack. Like you, Agravaine, he thinks ahead, your father."

Gawaine frowned even as his brother smiled at the praise. "Humph!" he sat down.

Morgawse noted her son's reaction and waited just a moment before soothing him with, "And I know you inherited your father's great strength, Gawaine, as well as his passionate nature. You are so like him, when he was younger."

Gawaine perked up a bit, but still felt a little put out by her compliment to his brother.

Agravaine sat down. He had a knowing look on his face as he looked first at his brother, then at his mother.

Gaheris was disgusted with the way his mother did this, playing his two older brothers off against each other. Agravaine was cold and calculating, and terribly vain – *like Mother* – he thought; and Gawaine, he was too much like their father – volatile and passionate, and easily swayed by his mother.

"And what of the other rebels, mother?" Gaheris asked. "Do we seek pardon for all of them?"

Morgawse looked curiously at her second youngest son, trying to read him. "Don't be silly! Of course not. We can't speak on behalf of any of the other kings who have rejected Arthur's claim to the throne. We only seek to make peace between our two great families."

Gaheris pressed further, "What about those who followed our standard, mother? Do we ask the King's forgiveness for all those who followed father in raising arms against the High King?"

Morgawse disliked this line of questioning and stared coldly at Gaheris. "I have already told you, my *son*," she said, "that we only seek peace for our own household. Those petty lords who agreed with your father … well, they must make their own peace with the High King." She watched him closely as he mulled over her answer.

Gaheris seemed satisfied for the moment and sat down, his mind working on – Morgawse knew not what. And it irked her. Gaheris was always the odd one, silent and aloof. Agravaine she knew, or thought she knew as well as anyone could. Play on his vanity and intelligence, and one could fairly well predict his behavior. And Gawaine! Well, he was like a great mastiff or tame bear – predictable within his nature, but fairly simple and trusting. And as for Gareth, he was her baby. He needed her, and she enjoyed the one true pleasure of feeling motherly that he provided. Gareth was amicable and open, beloved by all the servants, pages, and squires. It was in Gareth Morgawse placed the greatest hope for the future of their bloodline.

"Well, then, as soon as we can gather our belongings, we travel south to see the King," Morgawse informed them. With that, she kissed Gareth who squirmed and blushed to be treated that way in front of his brothers, which only made Morgawse laugh. "Oh, don't be that way," she told him playfully. "All too soon you'll be wanting kisses from pretty maids, and then what will you do?"

Gareth wiped his mother's kiss from his cheek, and replied, "Never! I'll never kiss a girl as long as I live! I intend to be the greatest knight the world has ever seen, and I won't have time for such things."

"Ach, now, laddie!" Gawaine laughed as he rose from the table and reached down to rumple Gareth's hair. "Don't be too quick to judge the fairer sex! Why, what's the good of being a knight if one can't win a kiss or two from some bonnie lass, eh?"

Morgawse spoke up before she left the room using her "and don't argue with me" voice, "Gaheris? I would like it if you served as your brother's squire once more. I won't have him enter Camelot unattended, and it would mean much for him to be waited on by one of his own blood. That's what this trip is about – family!" So saying, she left them for she had many things to pack, and certain books and scrolls she wished to consult before they departed.

Gawaine smiled broadly while Gaheris slumped in his chair wishing he could slip out unseen and return to his "Lady Automne" and her training.

"I see she is never quite so concerned for my well-being," Agravaine said resentfully. Then, with a sidelong glance at Gaheris, he said, "However, considering who is to be your squire ..." and smirked.

"Sod off," Gaheris mumbled.

"Tut! Such language!" Agravaine goaded. He made a mock bow to Gawaine, and took his leave as well.

"Phew!" said Gawaine. "We're better off without the likes of him," and made a rude gesture after his brother's back. "As for you, me boyo, ye remember where the armory is, eh? I have a few knocks and dents I need banged out of me armor before we leave. And I want it bright and shining like the glorious midday sun by the time we reach Camelot!" He laughed and threw a few practice punches in Gaheris' direction, then left the hall as well.

"You don't look very happy," came Gareth's voice from next to Gaheris.

Gaheris looked at his younger brother. "You're, what now ... twelve?"

"Eleven," Gareth said and hopped up onto the long dining table and began to walk up and down on the benches.

"Why do you let mother treat you like a wee bairn still, then?"

Gareth shrugged, "I don't know ... She seems to like it."

"But, what about you? Isn't it time for you to start serving as a page, and learning about becoming a knight and all that?"

"I get tutored," Gareth said in his defense and sat down to finish his trencher of food. "Momma wants me to learn all I can about being a lord, so I have teachers instruct me in all sorts of things. It's boring sometimes, but ... well, you know how she is."

I do indeed! Gaheris thought to himself.

"At least this time, I get to go along, too!" Gareth said brightly.

Gaheris smiled at his younger brother's enthusiasm, and he lightened up a bit as well. "Yeah, you do get that, don't you? Which reminds me, I need to get Gawaine's armor cleaned up. And, knowing him, his sword is probably as dull ..."

"As Agravaine?" Gareth giggled at his own joke.

Gaheris smiled. "No, git ... though that's not bad!" The brothers looked at each other with mutual enjoyment. It would be their shared secret behind their brother's back. Gaheris rose and took his brother by the shoulder, "It's good to see you again, newt."

Gareth smiled back, "And you, too, sod."

"What's going on out there?" Meraugis complained as he roamed about his chambers. "Brrr! I hate the bloody weather in this place."

"It appears that the family, or most of them, are getting ready to depart, my lord," Michael informed him. "I understand that the King is too ill to go with them, but from the amount of baggage I see being packed, I can pretty well assume that the Queen is going with them."

Meraugis' face turned nasty, tight and angry. "And *where* are they going, you little shit?" he hissed as he grabbed Michael by the back of his neck and thrust his face into Michael's.

"Camelot," Michael said calmly. He found that he could seemingly detach himself while Meraugis raged, and become like a puppet, imitating the silent countenance of Meraugis' mute bodyguard.

The word struck Meraugis like acid, and his face writhed with suspicion and doubt. He began to pace back and forth very quickly as he spoke to himself. "No. No. No. She'd never betray us! What does it mean? What can it mean? She would never leave without telling me. Me! I ... I must tell ... no! I can't tell father. Mustn't tell father." He strode over to Michael and grabbed him by the front of his tunic and screamed into his face, "*Daddy mustn't know!*"

Michael felt the spittle from Meraugis' mouth spray all over him, but he kept it aside, shutting out everything but one thought which he repeated to himself over and over again, *I am Michael, son of Lucas, son of Branwen, brother of Rose, and I will survive!*

"You ... you won't tell him, will you?" Meraugis was suddenly pleading, but Michael had learned not to trust him when he seemed weak and vulnerable, and remained impassive as ever. Meraugis drew his dagger and threatened Michael with it. "I ... can make sure ... you *never* tell!" But Michael did not reply. Meraugis held the dagger in front of Michael's face, the point only inches from his right eye. Michael continued to repeat his mantra over and over again, silently, watching Meraugis' trembling hand.

Ah, God! He means to do it this time, the sick bastard!

Finally, Meraugis let out a wounded howl and dropped the dagger to the ground. He lowered his head and went into his bedchamber weeping.

Michael took a breath, letting himself come back into his body, then stooped and picked up the dagger. Under his breath, he said, "I am Michael, son of Lucas, son of Branwen, brother of Rose ... and one day, I will kill you."

He glanced at the mute, who gave no sign whether or not he had heard Michael's utterance ... or cared. He placed the knife on a table and poured a drought of the sleeping potion Morgawse prepared for his master.

"Give him this," Morgawse had instructed him, all smiles and perfumes and heavy musk, "when he is restless and desires sleep. It will soothe your lord. And leave you free for ... other duties ..." She had smiled at him as she said this, his hand touching hers accidentally as he accepted the vial. "I understand you have a sweet and soothing voice, and I am sure it has helped your master to find sleep in the past. Perhaps I will ask you to come and sing me to sleep one night?"

Michael put on his best smile and bowed, "Even as you desire, your majesty." It seemed to satisfy her, though Michael mistrusted that this woman would be so easily fooled. *As soon trust a spider!*

But the potion worked, and Meraugis was soon deeply asleep. Michael gave orders for the servants to gather up Meraugis' belongings, for they would be leaving as well. Their party would journey with that of the Orkney brood most of the way, then separate to return to Meraugis' father's lands in Cornwall, far to the southwest. Michael took the opportunity to go over the notes he had gathered, his mind turning to see if there was any way to create an opportunity to join the Queen and her retinue as they went to see the High King.

The High King! Michael thought with regret. *Oh, how Rose would have loved that. Wherever you are, Rose, I hope you are in a happier place than I!*

Chapter 9

Rose was miserable. She was cold, and her clothing was pretty well soaked through by the freezing slush that fell like rain. Her boots were wet and covered with slush and mud. Her one saving grace was the cloak lined with beaver fur to help hold in some of her body's warmth.

"The scouts say we are a day, maybe less, behind him," Sion said to her as he squatted down and handed Rose a wineskin.

Rose accepted the skin and took a sip of the warming brandy within. "Thank you," she replied.

Sion looked at her, "You wish we were still back at the keep practicing against wooden dummies, don't you?" He gave a wry smile. "I thought it was you who said, 'Can't I do something a little more exciting for a change?'"

"I didn't expect Meg to say, 'Yes, by all means! Go out into the freezing countryside and kill this beast who has been terrorizing my farms, stealing sheep and goats.'" Rose answered back. She paused to blow on her hands to warm them even if for only a second or two.

"In order to keep warm, it is better to keep moving," Sion said. Then, with an odd look in his eye, he added, "There are other ways of keeping warm out here, of course ..." and raised an eyebrow.

Rose felt a flush of embarrassment as she thought she understood what he was suggesting. *Does he ... ? Is Sion attracted to me?*

Sion stood up to break the uncomfortable silence and smiled weakly. "I mean no offense, Rose. Nothing like ... what you might have been thinking. It's just that ... Sometimes, to survive in the cold like this, it is best to wrap up with another person, to share each other's warmth and conserve your strength. We do it all the time, although, in your case, I can see how that might be a bit ... uncomfortable?"

Rose looked at Sion in a new way, suddenly seeing him not only as her drill instructor, but also as a man, and felt a strange shift inside. He wasn't unhandsome, and he was actually kind of attractive even if he was about twenty years her elder. But it seemed somehow wrong, and both of them knew it. *At least he isn't after me like I have seen some of the younger men go after the maids at the keep,* Rose thought with a mixture of relief and disappointment. *Why haven't any of the others made any attempt to woo me?* she wondered. *Am I that uncomely?*

A horn blew in the distance.

"Ah," said Sion as he offered Rose a hand to help her up. He took back the wineskin, and slung it over his chest, keeping it beneath his cloak to ward it from the elements. "We may be in luck. The beast may have turned back this way, again."

"Wonderful," sighed Rose and checked her gear to make sure everything was secure. She pulled back on the woolen gloves and grasped her spear firmly. "Let's go hunt us an ogre," she said.

When Meg had first told her what it was she wanted Rose to hunt, Rose thought she was kidding.

"An ogre?" Rose asked incredulously. "I thought they only existed in tales told to frighten children."

"Oh, no," Meg told her, "They're quite real. Giants, now ... those I have never seen. At least none so big as a mountain, or with footsteps as wide as this keep. But ogres, trolls, goblins … yes, they exist. They have been driven deeper and deeper into the wilds, and seldom venture forth to be pursued by man. But, occasionally, it does happen. Or some fool goes off adventuring and disturbs them from their habitat."

"How do you expect me to fight an ogre?" Rose asked.

Meg gave her a disapproving look. "What have you been studying for the past several months? Besides needlepoint and dance, I mean." She slapped Rose's hip where her sword usually hung. "It seems a good test of whether or not you're ready to go back out into the world."

Back into the world? The words echoed in Rose's mind making her aware that her training here was nearing an end. *And then what? What will I do once this is over?* "Kill Carados," came an answer from deep in her mind. "Isn't that what this was all about? To find out what happened to Michael, to know for sure if he is dead or alive? And to kill the man who murdered your father and destroyed the life you had?" *But is that all this is for?* Rose wondered. In her time at the keep, Rose had formed friendships, and indeed felt like part of one huge family with Meg as a surrogate mother. Finishing her training was bittersweet, especially if it meant an end to the peace and happiness she had found here.

"Suppose I fail?"

Meg raised an eyebrow in disbelief, "Hardly likely, my dear. I wouldn't send you if I thought it beyond your abilities, believe me. But in this profession, there is never any certainty, never any way to know until one tries. Like so much of life …" Meg trailed off, and her attention seemed to drift away for a moment.

Rose noted a look of sadness pass over the older woman's features, and wondered if Meg was feeling the same thing she was.

"Any suggestions on how to approach this?" Rose inquired. *If I might get myself killed, I'd certainly like to know it wasn't because I was too stupid to do this right.*

"Hm? Oh, sorry ... Well, one thing that might work is to stick the poor creature full of arrows. Our Welsh archers are a force to be reckoned with, though I've only ever used them to skirmish with when need arose. I'd avoid wearing any heavy armor, that's for sure. Ogres tend to be slow moving creatures anyways and speed is your ally there. But, if this is more of a troll, then arrows might not work. Indeed, they might only enrage the creature further! If it's a troll, then I'd use fire. Take along some flasks of oil, and I'll have some of the better archers carry some fire arrows they can use to light it from a safe distance. Of course, in the weather you're likely to be traveling in, I wouldn't count on fire as my only weapon. Better wait and see. I'm sure you'll come up with something. You're a bright girl, and it's time for you to begin to develop a sense of strategy and tactics. Trust Sion, he has some experience."

Well, I'm certainly trusting his experience now, Rose thought as they traveled as fast as the slippery, mud-holed ground allowed.

"There!" shouted one of the huntsmen and pointed.

Rose squinted her eyes as she looked out onto the moors where the man pointed. She could just barely make out a dark bulk of a figure as it moved slowly through the bogs and fens.

"What's your plan, my lady?" Sion asked, and Rose took a moment before she realized that "my lady" referred to her!

"Ah, my plan ..." Rose said, "Well, first, I'd like to know what you would suggest?"

Sion shook his head. "Rose, men will follow a leader who appears decisive, even if that decision is wrong. Men will follow a good leader to the death because they trust that he knew what he was doing, that they might at least have a chance, no matter how slim, of surviving. I have ideas, yes. But Meg wants the decision to be yours. It is up to you to make sure that this beast is taken down. Or ..." Sion paused.

" *Or* what? What other alternative is there?" Rose wanted to know.

"It is very unlikely, but ... sometimes these beasts are, well ... simply lost and confused. Possibly even injured, which can make them dangerous. But, if it were me, I might simply want ..."

"To go home," Rose finished for him.

Sion nodded.

Would it be possible to drive the creature back home – wherever "home" was? Rose considered. *The weather is too wet, and too windy, for the archers to be of much use, so I guess it would be up to me to take on this beast hand-to-hand. And I somehow feel that should be my* last *choice, no matter how much faith Meg has in my abilities! So, what do I do ...?*

A hand touched Rose's shoulder, and she looked up at Sion who motioned for her to stay silent. He pointed, and Rose saw that the creature – ogre or troll – had come closer to where they lay hidden. She got a much better look at the beast – massive chest and short, squat legs; thighs that appeared as big around as Rose's waist; and arms that reached nearly to the ground. On top of a nearly neckless shoulder sat an enormous head with low, sloping forehead – the face of an idiot child, though mottled and much larger than any human head. It stopped and sniffed the air, and let out a sorrowful bellow, grunting and chuffing to itself as it wavered on the edge of the moor as though sensing danger waiting for it in the nearby woods.

Troll, Sion mouthed silently to Rose, and shook his head indicating that this was not what he was hoping they would encounter.

Great! thought Rose. *What am I supposed to do?* An idea came to her, but she wasn't sure if it would work. So she crawled over to Sion's position and whispered to him, "Would the creature be attracted to meat, do you think?"

Sion nodded, "Of course. Fresh meat, or even cooked meat, if it caught the scent. Why? What are you thinking?"

"Are there any farmsteads nearby where we might borrow a sheep or two?"

"Yes … I think there's one maybe a few miles back and to the north of us. Why?"

"I think we ought to have a feast," Rose said with a smile. "Doesn't a nice fire and fresh lamb sound good to you?"

Sion looked at her for a moment, then smiled and said, "Yes. Yes, I think it does."

Taulurd caught the scent of roasting lamb and wood smoke not long after it left the relative safety of the moor. It had stayed there because the "little creatures" – men - seemed reluctant to follow it out there. It had managed to catch one or two who had gotten lost among the archipelago of firm islands amidst the sucking mud and bogs, and they had tasted good! But nice mutton – mmmm! Fresh mutton, or even cooked, mutton was such a nice juicy meat.

The smell of the cooking meat overrode the creature's sense of safety, and it hobbled its way directly toward the smells.

A chirrup signaled to Rose that the troll was coming, and she said a quick prayer to any gods that might listen that her plan would work, and she and the men could return home themselves. She took a quick glance at the large campfire they had started, nearly a bonfire, hoping that the light of the fire would also bring the beast directly into her trap. She held a torch carefully wrapped with oil-soaked rags in one hand, and an oilskin, which had been scored by her dagger to break open more easily, in the other. Sion readied his broadsword, though he knew how difficult a foe a troll could be in direct combat. Over the fire on a huge, makeshift spit roasted a whole sheep carcass. She prayed that her scent, and that of the other hunters hidden here, would be masked by the smoke and overpowering smell of cooking flesh.

The troll came to the edge of the clearing they had laid their trap in, and it hesitated.

Something was wrong here. Never before had Taulurd seen a fire and meat with no "little creatures" around. And ... was that the scent of man, or not? Taulurd suddenly became alert for danger. But the smell of the meat, and the sight of a whole carcass just sitting there unattended drove the troll nearly mad with hunger, and it finally broke into the clearing with a speed that belied its bulk and went right for the roasting meal.

"Now!" shouted Rose as she and the hunters sprang from their hiding places on all sides. Sion and one other moved to cut the troll off from retreating the way it had come. She threw her oilskin at the troll, who roared in surprise and anger as it ripped the carcass from off the spit, then grabbed the spit to use in its huge fist as a weapon. It looked down in surprise as the oilskin struck and broke open, covering part of its side and leg in oil. Two other skins hit it, one in the middle of his back where the oil ran down its whole spine, and the other on the side of its face, spraying the troll's shoulder.

The troll, however, flailed about it, swinging the carcass in one hand and the spit in the other. It bellowed with pain as the spit burned its hand but refused to let go of either the spit or the carcass. One of the huntsmen who had thrown his flask headed nearer the fire to light his torch, but the troll caught him with a powerful sweep of the cooked carcass, and he was knocked back several feet and lay still. Rose charged in and got her torch lit, narrowly dodging a wild swing of the spit, and rolling aside as the carcass came crashing down where her body had been.

The beast fights brutally, with no method or style – blindly, Rose noted as she looked for a chance to light one of the oil stains on the creature's body. But the troll kept coming after her, keeping her dodging its wild swings that crashed and thudded into trees or the ground, making it very clear to Rose she had better not be struck by even a passing blow.

Out of the corner of her eye, she saw the other huntsmen rush in and light their torches and Sion trying to taunt the creature with both sword and torch in his direction. But, unfortunately for Rose, the beast stayed on her, trying to smash her with its clumsy weapons. She nearly tripped over the body of Ellis, the huntsman who had been hit first, and dove over him instead. The troll closed in on her, then let out a bellow as flames leapt up its back, lit by one of the other hunters. It swept its arm back and batted the man who had lit it into the trees where he struck with a sickening crunch and fell to the ground, clearly dead. Rose took her chances and rushed past the beast as it dropped the spit and tried to beat at the flame on its back with the sheep carcass that still remained in its hand, gripped with a death grip. She touched the oil on the creature's thigh, and the flames rushed up its front, lighting the oil on its shoulder and face. The troll screamed and crashed through the line knocking down Sion as he swung his sword at its belly to no effect, the blade barely biting into the blubbery flesh. It ran back toward the moor, back to safety, all the while beating at the flames that tortured and devoured it even as it ran.

Rose hesitated, checking on Sion, who only croaked, "Hurry, Rose … before it can get to water …"

Rose called the other hunters to her, and they raced after the beast. The others strung their bows, and ran and fired, ran and fired, as they had learned to do after years of skirmishing. But the arrows hardly seemed to faze the troll at all, and Rose realized it might be up to her and the great spear she carried. Rose made a sweeping cut at the back of the troll's legs, hoping to cut its tendons, if trolls had any, and slow it down. The blade did cut the flesh of the creature, and it slowed only a little, but enough for the others to catch up and begin to pepper it with arrows to the back and head. The arrows that hit the skull, however, seemed to glance away harmlessly, while the rest hit it in the back and thighs, and eventually, the troll was down to a crawl.

When the huge beast fell, it landed face down which extinguished most of the flame, though its back still burned with choking, greasy roils of smoke. It alternately bellowed and whimpered in pain, and Rose felt her heart go out to the creature in its agony. She wanted to just put it out of its misery, and began to cry as the beast continued to crawl while the men shot at it until they ran out of arrows.

What does it take to kill this thing? Rose wondered. She had stopped stabbing after having thrust about a dozen times once it had fallen and started to crawl, until she couldn't stand to see or hear the creature's agony. And the stench! Rose was sure she would never get the stench of its burning flesh out of her nostrils. Finally, the troll couldn't drag itself any further and lay whimpering and crying, the remnants of the carcass still gripped in its left hand.

Rose cautiously approached the beast. Her spear was ready to deliver what she hoped would be the killing stroke. It looked up at her with glazed, pitiful eyes, almost human, and Rose felt ill and ashamed. *Surely there must have been another way!* she thought.

The troll lifted the mutton in its left hand as though offering it to Rose. "Please," it managed to say in a weak, earthy voice. That one word shook Rose, and as it looked Rose in the eye, she felt that it was a stranger who thrust the spear into the troll's back, the tip coming out through its chest and into the ground. With a last grunt and a trickle of black blood from out if its mouth, Taulurd died. Rose felt that the blow only managed to end the creature's life because it had given up and wanted to die. And she was sad that she was the one who had killed it.

"You mustn't regret what you have done, Rose," Sion said weakly as they strapped him into a litter to carry him home, Rose and the others pulling it along. "You won a great victory."

But Rose didn't want to hear any of it. She felt disgusted with herself, and with the whole business of killing.

Is this how I would feel if I had killed Carados? When *I kill Carados?*

"We lost two men against a troll. That's a remarkable feat!" he continued. "I have seen trolls take out twenty men with their terrible strength."

"That's two families whose poppa won't be coming home," Rose said. "Two families who will be in pain and mourning because of my plan. Some plan."

"Two men who knew the risk they were taking, and have taken each and every time they come out here. Two men who had faith in you, Rose ... and in your plan."

Sion was right, but Rose didn't want to argue. She just wanted to get back to the keep and bury herself in her blankets and wait for the world to go away. She felt like she carried a lead weight inside, in her stomach or her heart. She wasn't sure which.

The other men respected her mood, only speaking when they let her know it was time to stop for a brief rest, or to rotate who carried the injured and fallen. It was considered a privilege to carry one of the fallen, and only those deemed most worthy were offered the chance. Rose declined when they asked her to take one end of the carriage for Ellis, but the men became very angry when she did so.

"Do not dishonor the deeds of these men," she was told, "in self-pity and regret. These men are champions! They deserve the respect that is their due. And they honored you with the sacrifice of their lives. Do not diminish them!" So Rose helped carry the dead back to the living who awaited them.

Meg listened to the report gravely, saddened by the loss of two good huntsmen, and made assurance that their families would be provided for. But it was Rose she was worried about most. The usually defiant, strong-willed Rose who had left was not the same Rose who stayed in bed and refused to exercise that had come back.

Sion leaned on a wooden crutch, his head bandaged, and held himself stiffly due to the wrappings around his sides beneath his shirt. His sword arm was also wrapped lightly. It had been slightly burned in his cut at the beast's belly. Meg had put a special salve on it, but the wound was light, and she didn't fear that it would become inflamed or turn gangrenous. He gave Meg the news of the creature's death and the means by which it had come about. When he had finished, Meg thanked him and dismissed him, telling Sion to take some rest for a couple of days before returning to his duties.

Gleinguin had been at the keep as well when the men arrived, and he offered to help escort the spirits of the dead through the Borderlands to see to it that they could go to the Resting Grounds before embarking on a new cycle of the spirit. Meg was thankful to him for his assistance.

"You're worried about the girl, aren't you?" he asked Meg as they sat near the fire one evening, two days after the men had returned.

Meg stared into the fire. "It is always a question of readiness, isn't it? How does one know when the sword is ready? How does the smith know that the blade is properly tempered, ready to take an edge and be used?"

"Through lots of experience," Gleinguin answered her, "That is always the only way. Time and trial."

"I ask myself, 'Did I do right to send this girl, this child, out into the wilds like that? Was it too soon?' And I don't know what the answer is," Meg frowned with self-doubt.

"This child is ... special. She means more to you than the dozens of men and boys whom you have trained in the past. Not that any of those never meant anything to you – I'm not saying that," Gleinguin said. "But this Rose, now ... she is more important to you because, if I may be so presumptuous, she reflects so much of you when you were her age, yes?"

Meg glanced at the wise old man, and said, "She is more like the child I never had. But, yes, she does remind me of my-self, though I think Rose far surpasses what I ever could have accomplished."

"How so?" asked Gleinguin.

"Look at how far she has come in so short a time! She han-dles a sword like it was an extension of her arm, her hand - like the point is a fingertip with which she can just reach out and touch an opponent. She rides well ..."

"But still has difficulty with the lance," Gleinguin reminded Meg.

"Indeed ... I don't understand it. She excels at everything else – dance, the spear, even her skill with the mace has gone much better than I had ever dreamed. But the lance, it still eludes her. Grey Star does his best, but Rose resists flowing with him. It's almost as if she is afraid to let go of control, trust-ing ..." A new thought came to Meg. "Trusting doesn't come easily to her."

Gleinguin nodded. "But who doesn't she trust, Meg? The horse? You? Or herself?"

Meg knew the answer, of course. "Herself, obviously. How do I teach her to trust in herself?"

"How did you learn to trust in yourself?" Gleinguin re-turned.

Meg thought about it. It wasn't a question she ever had to answer before. *How did I learn to trust in myself?*

Gleinguin rose and placed a comforting hand on Meg's shoulder. "When you have the answer to that, you will have your answer to the other," he said gently.

Meg patted his hand in appreciation, and Gleinguin left her to ponder while she gazed into the fire.

A knock came on Rose's door.

"Go away!" she yelled and buried herself under her blankets and pillow. She had refused to eat, and remains of old meals lingered on the floor, left by the servants whom Meg sent to check on the girl from time to time.

"Rose? It is I. I've come to speak with you, if you will," came a warm, concerned voice.

Rose recognized it, but was surprised that the old healer would come to see her at this late hour.

"I'm not ill," she said aloud.

"Not in body, no," came Gleinguin's reply through the door. "But in spirit – that may be another matter."

"What do you want?" demanded Rose when she opened the door.

Gleinguin leaned on his yew staff and looked with his deep eyes into Rose's. "I come where there is need," he answered. "Blame the gods, for I do their bidding, not my own," he said with his warm smile.

Rose let him in, but went right back under the covers, not only to escape her visitor but because it was cold.

Gleinguin took a seat by her bed, laying his staff across his knees. "You must eat, dear girl," he said to her.

"I'm not hungry," Rose answered from under her pillow.

Gleinguin reached down and pushed the pillow harder onto Rose's face. Rose immediately began to struggle and threw the pillow off and jumped up from the bed.

"What are you doing? Are you crazy?" she demanded.

Gleinguin smiled disarmingly. "Well, I see that you do have some spirit left, after all! And recognize the need for air, at least."

Rose sat on the bed, curled her legs under her, and crossed her arms across her chest. "Okay, so I have spirit, so what?" she asked. She looked at the old man, who merely gazed at her gently and lovingly. "What are you looking at?"

"I've never realized just how beautiful you are when you get angry," Gleinguin said half-jokingly. "Your eyes flash like green lightning! It truly is remarkable."

The compliment disarmed Rose, and some of her annoyance subsided.

"Do people have a hard time staying mad at you?" she asked Gleinguin.

"Most, but not all," he replied. "I hope you are one of those who can't." He paused as he looked at her. "It might be a good idea to pull on a shawl, don't you think? Meg seems to have given you one of the coldest rooms in the keep."

"She did it on purpose, I'm sure," Rose said as she did as the old man suggested. "Part of teaching me a knight's humility, or something. Or maybe just because she finds it fun to torment me, I don't know." Rose began to pace around the room.

"Do you think she enjoys tormenting you?" Gleinguin asked.

Rose stopped, "No, not really. I think … I mean, I know she cares about me, and all that. But she does like to get my goat, sometimes."

Gleinguin had to agree. "So, is it possible that Meg has your best interests in mind when she asks you to learn something? Or to, say, *eat*, perhaps?" he asked with a glance at the untouched food.

Rose sat back down on the bed and slumped her shoulders. "I know. I know! It's just that … I don't much feel like eating, is all."

Gleinguin was pleased by Rose's honesty. He leaned forward a little and spoke as though someone might be listening, "I'll let you in on a little secret. Meg does enjoy tormenting you."

Rose had to laugh. The old man had completely drawn her in, and she was expecting some deep secret to be imparted.

The old man leaned back in his chair with satisfaction. "Now, that's more like the Rose I know!" he said.

Rose got up and hugged Gleinguin, who was surprised by the sudden emotion. "Thank you!" Rose said as she hugged him, and kissed the old man on the cheek. "And thank you for caring enough to see me like this."

"You're welcome, my dear," he said.

Rose sat back down on the bed, and her lightness began to sink a little.

"Gleinguin? Have you ever ... killed anyone before?"

Gleinguin nodded, and his face became more serious. "Yes, my child. I have, indeed, when the need was great. It is never something to do lightly. The taking of a life, well, it creates an imbalance in the world that must be paid, somehow."

Rose looked down at her blanket and began to knot and unknot the twill as she spoke, "I ... this was not what I thought it would be like," she said with difficulty. Strong emotions fought to get out at the same time, and Rose tried to keep them in order.

Gleinguin leaned forward and touched Rose's arm gently. "It never is, my dear. Life never is what we expect. It only is what it is – no more and no less. The rest is merely our expectations or demands of what it *should* be, that's all. Just thoughts."

Rose suddenly felt such love for this kindly old healer, for she felt truly listened to by him, truly heard. "When I ..." she choked as the memory came back, fresh and powerful. "When I saw the creature ..."

"Taulurd," Gleinguin offered. "The creature had a name, and that was 'Taulurd.'"

Rose looked at Gleinguin quizzically. "How do you know this? Why are you telling me the creature had a name?"

"Because," Gleinguin answered her, "it is important to realize that this creature was a being, like yourself. One that had its part to play in the great web of Creation, in Destiny, no more or less than you. Far too often those who become cold and uncaring find it easier to kill other beings because they lose their respect for the lives they take. Those are the real monsters in this world. I would not see such a fate befall you."

Rose began to sob. "Then I have done something awful, haven't I?" she asked in tears. "I killed a creature that simply wanted to live, and caused the death of ... of two men ... two friends ..."

Gleinguin wanted to hold Rose and comfort her, but Rose stayed where she was, wrapped in on herself, holding herself and rocking as she sat on the bed. "Rose, what you did ... may have been fated to happen. Taulurd killed men, women, children, animals. All were the same to him, something to feed upon. He killed without regard, without respect for the sanctity of life. You … you care! It matters to you. You feel regret and remorse because Life is important to you! I can't think of a better instrument to correct the balance of Nature than you with your great heart."

Rose looked up at the old man with sorrowful eyes. "I am … so sorry!" she sniffled and wiped her nose with her sleeve. "It hurts. It feels so *bad* …" She came to the healer and let him hold her while she cried. "I wanted … so many things! I wanted Meg to be proud of me. I wanted Sion and the others to respect me, and like me, and … and …" she sobbed hard for a while. "I thought I was being so clever, the way I had planned to trap the … to trap Taulurd," she went on. "I was only thinking of him as a beast. But … it took so long to … to finish him … I just wanted it to stop. I was sick of all the hurting and pain! I just wanted to give him one final thrust to stop his suffering, and when he looked at me … and said 'please'… I … I felt like my heart broke, and something dark and heavy flowed inside, and I can't … seem to get it out. I want to get it out!" Rose cried and cried while Gleinguin just held her and let it all come out. Finally, she felt exhausted, wrung out, and he helped her back under the covers and tucked her in.

With a touch to her forehead, and a silent invocation to the god of slumber, Gleinguin said softly to the girl, "Sleep now, Rose. Sleep. And in the morning I think you will find that much of that darkness will have left, and the heaviness will be gone. Shh … rest now. Great Father and Great Mother watch over you, and you will find peace. You are blessed with many gifts from this encounter, Rose … many gifts, though you may not see them all right now. And, if my sight hasn't completely left me, greater things are still to come to you after this. Sleep now."

Gleinguin got up and gently closed the door behind him, leaving Rose in a heavy and deep sleep.

Chapter 10

When Rose awoke the next morning, it was as Gleinguin had said. Rose didn't feel like she carried a lead weight inside, though she still felt a bit sad and vulnerable.

Preemptively, Rose got up and washed her face and made her way to the practice hall before Meg sent someone to fetch her. Rose was in no mood to be ill-treated in order to motivate her into her practices.

Winter had turned harsh, lashing the borderlands with storm after storm as though the season refused to yield to the coming spring. Therefore, Rose's practice had been moved indoors to an open hall, nearly as large as the yard itself. Here Rose was expected to continue her training. Here she ran, hurdled, tumbled, and practiced her swordplay and mace work. She cast spears and javelins. The only thing she couldn't practice was the one thing she had yet to master – the lance. The hall was not suited to riding, and so her exercises with Grey Star were postponed, which Rose considered a mixed blessing. She deeply missed riding the wonderful warhorse, but she was also terribly frustrated with her practice with the lance.

The hall was unusually quiet when Rose arrived. The great hearths were still unbanked, and no fresh firewood had been heaped upon them to warm the space. Her footsteps echoed in the strange openness of the hall, and Rose felt a sudden apprehension as though another storm were ready to break with terrible crashes of thunder and lightning.

"Whenever I feel frightened," Meg had told her one day, "I find it comforting to do something ordinary, something routine, to help take my mind off of whatever may be bothering me." So Rose took it upon herself to stoke up the fires and load the hearths with wood. The familiar act did bring about a sense of comfort, and by the time she had the entire hall lit and warming, Rose felt much more centered and ready for whatever may come.

"I will see the girl now," said the woman dressed in grey robes.

Meg reacted to the order by trying to control herself. *Nimue,* that was the name the priestess had given.

"Lady Nimue," Meg said with restraint, "out of deference to the Lady of the Lake and the order of the Holy Isle, I will do as you ask. However, in this keep, I am mistress here and you are my guest. An honored guest, to be sure, but …"

Nimue tossed her mane of dark hair indignantly, "I do not have time, my lady, to play at pleasantries. If this girl is an – is the progeny of our renegade sister, she must come to the Sacred Isle for proper training. It … It would be very dangerous for her to remain ignorant of her heritage, and of her role in the skein of Destiny."

Meg rang for Liam, her steward, and gave instructions for him to fetch the girl. "And ask the druid, Gleinguin, to come as well, if you please," she told him quietly. *I, for one, though I respect the ancient orders, will not give up without a fight!*

Meg appraised the priestess who had come in answer to her letter asking if the Holy Isle was missing any initiates or novices. She saw a woman perhaps twenty years of age, tall and slender, but who emanated such power and force of will that it was like a mighty elm had come to life and walked her halls. Nimue possessed light grey eyes that shone with purpose, sharp and discerning, and hair the color of dark mahogany that hung down to her waist, unbound. She stood in place waiting, but with the energy of a brooding storm cloud.

Meg was looking for some similarity between her Rose and this priestess of Avalon, but couldn't find any clue that might tie them together in any way. Unless it were something about the eyes – a certain clarity – something that spoke of intensity beyond that of the norm, perhaps.

"Rose," Liam called to her when he found her. "You are wanted for an audience."

"An audience? With whom?" Rose asked as she stopped her tumbling practice.

Liam hesitated as though unsure of how much to say, but finally told Rose, "A priestess from the Sacred Isle has come. She wishes to see you. She has been quite … insistent … about it."

A priestess of Avalon? To see me? Rose wondered. *This must have something to do with my mother's pendant. But why now? How did they know where to look for me?*

Rose accompanied Liam through the corridors, and saw Gleinguin waiting outside Meg's private hall. He raised an eyebrow questioningly, but smiled and gave Rose a firm hug when they approached.

"I'm glad to see you up and about," the old healer said to Rose. "I trust a good night's rest did wonders for your spirit?"

Rose hugged him back, though she felt apprehensive about this meeting.

Liam opened the doors and escorted them into the hall.

Rose was struck immediately by the young woman who stared at her with such a piercing gaze, and she felt as if the woman were looking beyond her flesh and into her very soul.

"Rose," said Meg who remained seated in one of her carved wooden chairs, "This is Lady Nimue from the Sacred Isle, a priestess of Avalon. Lady Nimue, this is Rose."

Rose stepped forward after a small nod from Meg and curtsied as she had been taught when meeting nobility. "Your grace," she said.

Nimue stayed where she was, her eyes scrutinizing Rose. "Show me the medallion," she ordered.

Rose flinched slightly at the abruptness of the command, but Meg nodded again for Rose to comply. Rose reached inside her tunic and drew out her mother's pendant.

Nimue's face lost its composure when the pendant was visible, her intense gaze lifted from the girl to the chain she held. "So, it is true!" Nimue gasped. "Our sister had fallen so far from her teachings that she ..." Her eyes returned to Rose. "Are you the only child of our sister, Branwen?" she demanded.

Rose let the medallion drop onto her chest as she answered, "N-no. I have a ... a brother. Michael. Though ... I fear he may be dead." She looked at the ground, unable to face this fierce priestess and her penetrating stare while she felt so exposed and vulnerable.

"Two children?" Nimue asked incredulously. "We did not see ..." She stopped herself and glanced around at the others, noticing Gleinguin for the first time. "Forgive me, wise father, I ... the blessings of the Goddess upon you," she said to him and bowed slightly.

Gleinguin returned with a gesture of his own tradition, and returned the acknowledgement. "Blessing of the Great Father and Great Mother be upon you, too," he said. He looked at Rose and winked. "I take it we have a special flower in our garden, then?"

"Flower? Oh, yes ... Rose! Of course," Nimue replied.

Meg spoke up, "Lady Nimue, Gleinguin of Holywell, healer and druid."

"I acknowledge our brother, and his ancient ways," Nimue said formally.

"I am glad," Gleinguin responded with his usual charm. "Now that we have been introduced, perhaps we might have a seat, and perhaps something to drink? I'm an old man and ought to be indulged in such luxuries."

Nimue frowned briefly at the druid's lack of decorum, but refused to let herself be distracted.

"As you wish, father," said Meg as she motioned for the others to sit. She made a gesture for Rose to come and stand next to her, on her left side, which put her between Rose and the priestess. "Liam, please bring us some of the dried fruits and some cheese."

"And some ale!" Gleinguin put in, bringing a further frown from Nimue.

"And some ale, and mead for our guest," Meg instructed him. "And now, Rose, I guess it is time for some answers ..."

Rose was grateful for Meg's nearness. She tried to avoid the gaze of the priestess from Avalon, but found herself time and again drawn back to those intense grey eyes. *So, this woman knew my mother?*

"Tell me what you know about us, and about your mother, our sister," Nimue asked.

Rose wasn't sure where to start. "I ... don't really know much about my mother's religion," she admitted. The statement brought a look of displeasure from the visitor, surprised disappointment. "She taught me a few things – simple things, like prayers to the Ancient Ones and such, but nothing more than most people in my village who honor the old ways know. Those who haven't converted to the Christian God, that is. My younger brother, he was baptized in accordance with my father's faith, and given a Christian name, Michael, after one of the spirits of Poppa's religion. I believe he was a warrior of some sort."

Gleinguin offered, "An angel. One of the servants of the Most High, and yes, a champion of the Light."

Rose nodded in gratitude for the information, but the stern regard from Nimue made her grow self-conscious, and she stood silently.

"Go on, girl," ordered the priestess. "What else do you know? Did your mother ever intend to bring you to our isle? Who was your father? How did they meet? Speak!"

Meg interrupted the barrage of questions with a simple patting of Rose's hand. "Take your time, my dear. There's no rush ..."

Nimue glared at the older woman, but sat quietly waiting, as if she could silently will the information out of Rose.

With a deep breath to calm herself, a practice she had learned from Meg in order to center herself before exercise, Rose continued, "My mother was called 'Mary,' though I heard my father call her something else once. As I understood it, she had changed her name when they married – I thought out of respect for my father's religion. But now ..." She looked down at the medallion that had caused a new mystery to come into her life, "I'm not so sure if that was the only reason. My father was ... a bit of a mystery, to be honest." *Poppa!* Rose thought with fond remembrance, and sadness. "It wasn't until after ... after his death that I found some of his things hidden with my mother's pendant under the floorboards of their bedroom. The tunic of a Roman soldier, and a staff of office. I believe my father may have been a Legionary of Rome."

The statement brought a look of wonder to the eyes of Meg and a narrowing look from Nimue, who nodded as though Rose had imparted some vital piece of information.

"It is as I suspected," said Nimue half to herself. "You are the offspring of our renegade sister." Her gaze withdrew inwardly as she pondered, seeking guidance from within.

"Go on, Rose," asked Gleinguin gently, "I for one am curious to know more about the parents of so exceptional a child."

Meg smiled with the druid and motioned for Rose to continue.

"My father – Poppa – he was a very kind and loving man. He loved to tell stories. Wonderful stories! All kinds ... stories about ancient heroes, and about knights and kings. It is because of Poppa's stories that I began to dream about becoming a knight!"

"Don't be silly!" said Nimue suddenly. "The daughter of a High Priestess of Avalon a *knight*? No, my dear child, it cannot be. It will not be! I have asked for guidance, and the answer I receive is for you to accompany me back to the Sacred Isle where you will be trained in the proper duties and services of one of your blood."

There were several reactions to what the priestess of Avalon said. All of them heard the words "High Priestess," which was astonishing to both Meg and the old druid. But Rose also heard the "cannot be a knight" and "must accompany me back to Avalon" and felt as though she had been struck by lightning.

"But ... what about ... all my training!" Rose stammered. She looked down at Meg, who sat as though she had been struck as well, dumbly staring into space as the orders of the priestess registered.

I am to lose the girl to the Sacred Isle? Meg thought with a sadness that wrenched at her heart.

"Meg?" Rose implored. "Do I have to go? Have I no say in this?"

Gleinguin stood and tried to comfort her. "Whist! Whist, I say!" He banged his staff on the ground until everyone grew silent. "Well, I'm glad I still have that much magic left in me!" he joked trying to break the tension in the air.

Meg spoke, using her position of authority, "The girl cannot go."

Nimue went to interject, but Meg cut her off, "In accordance with our ancient traditions, as I have no heir of my own, I name this girl heir of all I own – lands and tithes, as well as the responsibilities that go with them! I declare it so, and so mote it be!"

Nimue stood stunned as though Meg's words had slapped her. "You cannot! This must not be!"

Meg stood and came down from her dais. She hobbled over and looked up at the young priestess and said, "Oh, but I am

The old druid moved next to the old woman and answered, "It is so." He bowed formally to Nimue, and took a step back, his face unusually serious for once.

This was all happening too fast for Rose, who stood in a whirlwind. *I ... I'm what? Meg has named me her heir?*

"Unless the heir agrees," said Nimue with anger flashing from her eyes. "She has the right to choose, and can dispose of the property as she wishes. If the girl – Rose – wishes it so, she may accompany me and take up the duties to which she was born." Nimue cast a glance at Rose. She knew it unlikely that she would choose to go with her. "I must warn you, however ... It is not wise to cross the servants of Destiny."

Gleinguin shook his head sadly. "Sister," he said gently but firmly, "Is this what we have become? Our duties are a sacred act, not the political wrangling of petty tyrants."

Nimue flushed at the rebuke.

"You should understand, wise father," she said as she stabbed a finger at Rose. "This child is an *abomination*! She should never have been born. The fact that she exists threatens the Skein!"

Gleinguin smiled softly, but held Nimue's gaze with his own. "I am not so versed in the ways of Destiny as those who serve on the Sacred Isle," he said, "but I am a servant of the Balance. I do not know what role this child has to play in the skein of Time, but I sense healing here, not danger. A chance for renewal. Hope."

Meg and Rose felt lost as the druid and the priestess spoke on a level beyond them, Rose most of all.

Nimue felt tempted to compel Rose, but knew that to do so would be to damage the girl beyond use if she was that set against going. She would have to make another appeal if she were to succeed in her endeavor.

"Forgive me," Nimue said putting on her most congenial face. "I have acted overly hasty in this. I would ask that you allow me to explain myself and my need to take this girl back to Avalon."

Gleinguin wanted to say "aggressive" rather than "hasty" but deemed it wiser to say nothing. Meg looked to him for guidance, and he shrugged to say in answer, "It can do no harm to listen."

"Very well," Meg said as she returned to her chair. "Perhaps you have more information for the child than she had for you?"

Rose felt the need to sit as well, but remained standing until Meg motioned for her to sit on her footstool.

Nimue walked slowly as she spoke. She weighed her words carefully, and resisted the impulse to expedite things by drawing on her powers as an emissary of the Goddess. "The girl's mother, our sister, Branwen, was not merely one of our sisterhood," she paused as she considered what she was about to relate. Nimue wondered if the listeners would understand the enormity of the betrayal, and ashamed that such a thing had occurred in the first place. "Branwen was one of Avalon's High Priestesses, second only to the Lady of the Lake, and stood to become the next Lady when the time came. But, somehow, Branwen was lured away from her place by, I assume, Rose's father, a centurion of the Roman Auxiliaries here in Britain. He had been injured defending the region against Saxon invaders and brought to Avalon for healing. What happened between them, I do not know. Only that our sister broke her vows and left the Sacred Isle with this man." Nimue looked again at Rose, seeing much of her mother in Rose's features – the eyes and hair, the pale skin, even her slender build.

"Isn't it possible she fell in love with him?" asked Meg.

Nimue refused to accept it. "We who serve the Goddess devote ourselves to Her alone! And those who are deemed most worthy, only those are accepted into the higher orders. They are expected to remain … pure. She was a vessel for the Goddess to fill. For this man to touch her, it was sacrilege!"

Rose couldn't believe what this priestess was saying. *Of course she loved him! How could it be wrong for Poppa to touch her? Poppa was always kissing Momma and holding her hand whenever they walked anywhere.*

"So, you don't know why she left, is that right?" asked Gleinguin.

Nimue nodded curtly. "I had hoped the child might be able to tell us what we did not already know."

Rose felt the stare from the priestess again and said, "Momma loved Poppa, and he her! That's all I can tell you."

"Nothing more?" Nimue pressed carefully.

"Rose?" Meg inquired, "Did your parents never tell you how they met? How they came to be together?"

"No. Never," Rose answered. "It didn't seem important. They just always seemed to be together, like they belonged that way."

Gleinguin spoke, "I still have not heard why it is so important for Rose to accompany you back to the Sacred Isle. The child is innocent, and at worst an unwitting danger, if danger she be at all."

"I had hoped my asking would be enough," Nimue replied with masked annoyance, "but, as you will … You have heard of this new king, this Arthur, yes? And of the wizard who helps counsel him?" They all responded they had. "And do you know that this wizard, this being who goes about in the form of a man, is the get of a demon upon … upon an innocent woman?"

"I have heard rumors, of course," said Meg.

"I can tell you, it is truth," replied Nimue tersely.

"It is also said that he is a member of our order," said Gleinguin, "though I have no such knowledge myself. None of my brothers know him to be a druid despite the common perception of him as one."

Nimue nodded, "He is no druid. Be assured of that. Merlin, or Myrddhin, is an emissary of Darkness, an agent of Chaos.

His coming was ... unforeseen ... but the damage he wreaks upon the Loom ... He must be stopped!"

"So, King Arthur is part of this ... damage?" asked Rose. "And how does this bear on my parents? Were they manipulated by this Merlin also?"

"That we do not know," Nimue admitted reluctantly. "Which is why I had hoped you might provide more insight. But, so it is ... And you, and your brother, are part of this unraveling. It is hard to explain to one who has not seen – who has never touched the Skein, nor had their eyes opened by the Goddess – but that is why you must come with me back to Avalon. You must return the thread your mother's leaving pulled free from the pattern. This Myrddhin ... he is like a great stone that has been cast through the warp and weave of Destiny, leaving a huge tear in the fabric of What Is To Be ..."

"And leaving you blind," said Gleinguin under his breath. But Nimue heard his remark and scowled at him. "No wonder you are so desperate to get the girl back with you! To help patch things up, as it were."

Nimue's eyes shone dangerously as she looked at the old man. "Brother," she said and allowed a hint of the Power to come through her voice, "what Merlin does threatens us all. He is a danger to the Ancient Ones, and the old ways. Already he has brought a bastard child onto the throne of England, and a Christian king at that! This new God, it is a Power unlike any this land has ever known before. People leave the old ways, abandon the old customs ..."

Gleinguin used some of his own craft to deflect some of Nimue's magic as he answered. "The sense I have is that this new God brings Light and healing, forces with which I am perhaps a bit more familiar than you. Is it not possible that what you fear – the loss of vision you have - is due to too much Light rather than too little?" ·

Nimue frowned in frustration. *What do I fear?* she asked herself not for the first time. *Is it that I feel the Powers may be fading away that drives me so? No! It is the Goddess, and I am her instrument. It is She who guides me and fills me with the importance of Her mission!* "The girl is part of this rift. Her birth is … a mistake. Branwen would never abandon the Goddess and betray her teachings for … for a man. A mere mortal …" It was unthinkable!

"How does Rose's returning with you change all this?" Meg asked.

Maybe it doesn't, Nimue thought to herself, *but at least she would be where we can watch her, keep her safe, and keep her from doing further damage.* "As I said," she replied, "By returning this thread back to where it can be rewoven into the fabric of What Is To Be. I don't expect one not versed in the mysteries to understand."

"And what of Michael?" Rose asked, looking up at the priestess with soulful eyes. "Is he another 'loose thread' that needs to be rewoven if he is still alive? Or if he's not, is that a good thing for you?"

Nimue wasn't sure how to respond. If the boy lived, he would be another fragment set free to work its own will upon the Skein of Destiny. He may be another element used to create further chaos and destruction to the pattern. *And if he's already dead? Does that serve the Goddess or the forces of Chaos?* "It would be important to bring him to the Isle as well," she replied, "if only for his own protection."

Meg looked at Rose. "It is up to you, my dear. You have to make the choice: Do you stay and complete your training? Or do you go with this priestess to Avalon and become an Initiate like your mother?"

Rose looked down at the pendant hanging on her breast. *Momma, how I wish you were here to give me guidance!* "When must I let you know?" she asked Nimue.

"I return there at once," Nimue answered. "You may accompany me, or come later if that is your choosing." She didn't want to push too hard, sensing the way the current was flowing. "But, come spring, for that is when the next group of Initiates will take their first vows and begin service. You are already several years past the age when you should have begun training. But so it is. You have until then."

Nimue stood, giving Rose one last look. "I hope you will forgive my demeanor at our first meeting," she said. "But what I do, I do out of necessity. When you – if you decide to come and see for yourself, the Goddess might be so gracious as to give you a taste of what it is we do. Then you might understand."

Rose looked to Meg and Gleinguin for guidance, but they looked back making it clear the choice was hers, though Meg's eyes held a certain sadness to them.

"Then I choose to stay. At least until spring," Rose told them, bringing a smile from the old woman.

Nimue nodded in acceptance. "Very well, daughter of Branwen. Rose. But do not turn away from what is in thy blood so lightly!" She gestured toward the pendant, "That does not come as a gift but as a responsibility. Wear it as a reminder, not only of your mother, but of She Who Is Mother of Us All."

They escorted Nimue to the courtyard and saw her mounted. Dark clouds had gathered, and another storm readied itself to unleash its fury on the land as she departed.

"I can't say which causes me greater consternation," said Gleinguin half-jokingly. "Those storm clouds, or that priestess from the Sacred Isle."

Meg took the old druid's arm, and he walked with her back inside. "She did have rather a strong personality, didn't she?" Meg replied. "It makes me wonder why the Lady chose to send her. Why not one with a little more ..."

"Subtlety?" Gleinguin finished for her.

"That's a nice way to put it," Meg answered back. "What do you think of what she said?"

Gleinguin glanced at his companion, seeing the look of seriousness on her face, as he said, "About Rose and her brother? I don't know ... This news that Rose's mother was likely to be the next Lady of the Lake – that was quite a shock, I must confess!"

"And about the new High King, and his wizard?"

175

"Mmm ... I doubt that this Myrddhin is the High King's wizard. I rather suspect it may be that Arthur is this wizard's new High King."

"But do you believe this priestess that Myrddhin is a threat? A danger to the land?"

Gleinguin shook his head. "No. I fear that this priestess is blinded by her own fears and suspicions. What the truth may be, I do not know. But I suspect that Rose is no instrument of Chaos, whatever the answer is."

Meg squeezed his arm. "Good! Because I would hate to think I had just made an agent of evil heir to all I own!"

"I get the feeling," Gleinguin said, "that you had planned on doing this anyway, giving your land and keep to Rose."

Meg nodded. "I am getting too old for this," she confessed. "And I have felt ... it is like I am getting frayed and thin. My hips ache worse and worse every year, and with the cold here ..."

"I know how you feel," Gleinguin said to her. "If only I might squeeze out one more year as well as the last. But that isn't Nature's way. The old must give way to the new, when it is time."

Meg felt a sudden heaviness come over her, but she kept walking, determined not to be stopped by an enemy against whom she had no chance of winning.

"So, she has left?" Rose asked as the pair returned. "Am I free to stay?"

Meg took her chair, easing herself into it slowly, and nodded.

Gleinguin took his stool and picked up his mug of ale while he nibbled some bread and cheese.

Rose looked back and forth, confused by the somber atmosphere. Then, to Meg she asked, "Did you mean it ... what you said? About ... about my being your ... heir?"

Meg nodded and smiled distantly, preoccupied with her thoughts about other things. "Yes, my dear. I did indeed mean it. I will name you my heir – once you have finished your training, that is! If you are to be mistress of this hold, there is a great deal more for you to master than the sword, let me tell you!"

Rose was speechless, and threw her arms around the old woman, and cried in gratitude for Meg's extreme generosity.

"There, there," Meg said as she stroked Rose's hair, "this should be a happy occasion! Nothing to cry about … Besides, it isn't seemly to cry over such things, not when you must prepare yourself for what is to come and all that. If we have only until spring, then you must work even harder at your skills! And I must begin to teach you weapons other than those we have focused on so far." Meg shook off Rose's embraces and stood up as she felt re-energized by necessity. "Well, don't just stand there gaping, child! We have work to do!"

Chapter 11

The next several weeks went by all too fast for Rose. Meg seemed to double her already busy training and tried to expose Rose to as much of her vast store of knowledge as possible. Rose was also shown the manorial duties that would become hers one day. There were tasks to which she did not take very quickly, though Meg constantly reassured her she'd be fine.

"Just leave it to Liam to work out the details," she would tell Rose. "Your duty is to decide on the 'What' more than the 'How' of things."

Rose did her best to absorb it all.

As spring came nearer, the weather turned wetter, and so Meg turned Rose out of doors to practice in the rain. It wasn't until Rose caught a terrible cold, and Gleinguin had to be sent for that Meg eased up her driven pace of instruction.

"Meg," Gleinguin told her with his usual gentleness, "Rose is only human, after all, despite her knack for learning things so quickly. And you, your time is not yet come. You have years left in you if I am not mistaken!"

Meg was somewhat comforted by the healer's comment, but still felt time was her enemy in this. "I may be here longer than you, old man," she responded with her sarcastic humor, "but Rose won't be. And I fear ... I fear she won't be ready by the time she must leave."

"If she chooses to leave," Gleinguin said.

"Oh, I think she may," said Meg sadly.

"Rose!" Daffyd called to her through the pouring rain.

Rose turned Gray Star and looked in the direction of the voice, and saw the man waving to her to come back to the gates.

"What now?" she wondered, dreading some further task being heaped on her. "Come on, Star, let's hope it is a call for food and shelter, eh?"

She trotted the warhorse back to the gate and as she leaned down, water ran off her helm. In this weather Rose wore only the suit of heavy quilted armor she had first begun her training in. The water would only rust the metal practice armor, and she would have to spend hours cleaning and polishing it with lard to help protect it from further damage.

Just like the old woman, Rose thought wryly as she remembered the first time Meg had forced her to wear plate armor. *It wasn't until much later I found out the suit she'd given me was deliberately heavier than normal, from thicker steel. Armor suitable for a giant, perhaps, but not for me!* A scowl crossed her features as the thought of a man big enough to comfortably wear such a suit made her think of Carados. *I've not had time to think of him for a while now!* Rose realized with a shock. *Was it only a year ago that Michael and I, and Poppa, had watched as the soldiers rode past on their way south to fight with the High King? Has it been so little time since I buried you, Poppa? It seems much longer ...*

"The Mistress wants to see you! She said to rub down your mount, dry yourself, and wear something nice before you come and see her."

Wear something nice? Rose had to double check if she had heard the man correctly. He nodded, then ran back toward the warehouse where he had other duties as well as a chance to stay out of the downpour.

Rose patted the horse and kicked him into a canter back to the stables. "Well, old friend, looks like you get your wish after all!" *And I might just take a warm bath, if it is that important that I dress nicely!* Rose thought with mild amusement. *Let Meg wait for me this once!*

Carados sat like a great stone statue on the back of his horse waiting on the strand of beach. The fading storm continued to blow in from the west, sending waves high up on the shoreline, and the men with him ignored the water that occasionally ran over their boots. They carried torches that sputtered and flickered in the wind, threatening to go out, while their faces looked out into the grey coast expectantly.

A man shouted and pointed toward the water where a dark spot appeared on the horizon, followed by another and then another.

One of the soldiers ran up to the giant and said, "My lord, they have arrived!"

About damn time! Carados thought irritably and kicked his horse into motion toward the water's edge where the Saxon longboats were just now beginning to beach.

A large bear of a man leapt over the gunwale and strode through the knee-high waves as Carados swung down from his mount. The two men grasped each other's forearm in greeting.

"A dangerous crossing!" said the other man with a smile like an animal, his accent thick and heavy. "But well worth the danger, ja?"

Carados forced himself to smile back. "So your lord agrees to my terms?"

The Saxon commander nodded his head while his men dragged the heavy boats further onto shore and began to unload supplies – bronze axes and shields, swords, spears, animal skins, and food. "Ja, it is agreeable to King Wihtgar. You grant us safe landing, and lands once we help you overthrow this king of yours."

Carados smiled grimly, "Yes. Good." He climbed back onto his horse, turned it landward, then kicked it into a gallop as he headed back toward the lands of Royns, King of Norgales. *Come spring, we may begin to gather an army with which we may rid ourselves of this bastard once and for all!*

Not being known as a strategic thinker, Carados served lords who already had powerful followings of their own. But he plotted, nonetheless. *Once we have beaten Arthur, whom do you think these Saxons will remember as the one to whom they owe thanks? Ha!*

Carados smiled deliciously as he thought about how the other lords would react once he pressed his own claim for land and the title of "king". King Mark of Cornwall was too shrewd and clever for Carados' liking, and he felt he might have little chance of wresting his lands away from him once Mark was made High King. Of course, Lot of Orkney would also make his own bid for the High Throne, and Carados had enough savvy to recognize that the country would be ripe for warfare for many years to come. He and his men would be valuable assets to whichever side offered him the best deal. *And Lot's wife is a comely woman, with a few years of breeding children still left in her,* he mused. *Let Mark have the South – I'll take the North!*

"I have a surprise for you," Meg said to Rose once she had finished washing and getting dressed.

Rose wore a long gown of dusky red velvet that accented the highlights in her hair and brought out some color in her otherwise pale skin. She was surprised that Meg wasn't angry with her for taking so long, but the older woman seemed unusually cheerful, and Rose wondered if she had been drinking.

"One that I had expected to take a little longer than it has, so the timing is something of note ..." Meg motioned for Rose to come join her at her chair, and took Rose's hands when the girl was near her.

"Rose, I have been training knights, and men and boys who would become knights, for more years than I care to recall. I take them under my wing for one year, and in that time I perfect their skills so far as I am able. I then release them back into the wild. Hopefully as a force for Good in the world, and so many of them have proven to be. Most, but not all." A look of regret crossed over Meg's face briefly.

Rose felt herself grow suddenly very still. There was a growing sense of impending significance, some great change was about to take place, and she didn't know what it would be. She nearly held her breath, waiting for some storm to break, or lightning to strike, or something … something … to break this bubble of expectation that suddenly grew up around her.

A few of the guardsmen came in carrying a huge bundle tied up in heavy canvas, which clanked and clattered mutely as they carried it. Behind came Sion ap Gwdion with a slight smile he was trying to conceal on his face, though his eyes betrayed him. With them came the old healer, Gleinguin, whose eyes also shone with a mischievous glint, walking with his yew staff as usual.

Meg's grip tightened slightly on Rose's hand, then she stood. "Rose, please come and kneel before me here," she indicated a step down from her dais. Meg's steward came up bearing a small wood box and stood waiting to Meg's left, while Gleinguin came and stood to Meg's right.

Sion ap Gwdion stopped behind Rose, and motioned for the guardsmen to set down their bundle and stand aside at attention.

For Rose, the world slowed down as in a dream, much like it had the night Carados' reavers took Poppa and Michael from her. Everything seemed to take on an odd clarity, and it was as if everyone and everything shone with some internal luminescence.

"Am I … are you going to … *knight* me?" Rose asked in breathless wonder.

Gleinguin laughed, and so did the rest of the retainers present. Meg smiled and looked down at Rose. "No, goodness! I am no king, nor am I even a knight myself. I can't grant the title of 'knight' on anyone!" She chuckled.

Rose looked crestfallen, confused.

"I said I cannot bestow the title of 'knight,' " Meg clarified, "I can, however, do as I have done for many long years …"

"Many," chimed in Gleinguin with a wink at Meg, and a small nod of his head.

"… And that is to train knights and, if the mood comes over me, present them with gifts to help them in their quests." With that, she gestured toward the bundle.

Sion nodded to the guards, and they carefully opened up the canvas ties and lay open the bundle they had brought with them. Meg smiled with pleasure at Rose's wide-eyed look of wonder, as well as the gasps from the others, as they looked upon what she had gifted upon Rose.

Rose saw before her, bright and shiny and polished like fine silver, a suit of armor – breastplate and greaves, gauntlets, helm – an entire ensemble suitable for a prince! At least, to her eyes it was a princely gift.

"Behold, Rose! This is no ordinary armor!" Meg stepped down proudly and offered Rose her hand. Rose stood and accompanied Meg as the older woman pointed out the craftsmanship and special points about the suit.

"Note: there is no adornment, no fancy decorations, nothing to catch a blade or point of a weapon. Men seem to enjoy strutting about like peacocks in their armor, which is often more suitable for a parade than for battle! But this … pick it up, Rose!"

Rose lifted the breastplate and was amazed at how light it was!

"Yes," said Meg knowingly. "That's right. It is very light. And the padding has been tailor made to accommodate your build, my dear. This armor will allow you much greater mobility and flexibility than a heavier suit would. Remember, you're not to try to take a blow full on. Your strategy is …"

"Deflect and avoid," Rose said by rote, though she could hardly take her eyes off the gift in front of her.

Meg looked at Rose, and with some seriousness said, "Always remember that. It will save your life, and I won't have wasted my time on you."

Rose looked at the other woman, looking down into her face as she stood a head taller than Meg. "I don't know what to say. This is … most generous. Too generous! I …"

"Can't say 'No,' " Meg finished for her.

"Well," said Sion as he came up next to them, "Ye surely cannot have anyone else using it, that's for sure. Less ye find another girl to train!"

Rose was overwhelmed by Meg's generosity and choked back the tears of gratitude that were threatening to overwhelm her. "Thank you," she managed to choke out at last. Sion squeezed her shoulder, and Rose squeezed Meg's hand.

Gleinguin coughed and made a gesture toward the steward for Meg to see.

"Ah, yes! Oh, dear, I … I hope you're not too overwhelmed just yet, my dear Rose! But, I will need to sit for this. I'm getting too old for all this excitement."

"You're not either," Rose said as she helped Meg back to her chair. "I'm sure you could best me two tries out of three any day of the week."

Meg wasn't so sure, but took the compliment graciously. Her steward bowed and handed over the small wood box. When Meg opened it, Rose saw that it was a writing box, containing a few sheets of parchment or vellum, a small inkwell, and some quills. Inside was a very ornate sheet, written mostly in Latin, though Rose could make out a few of the words here and there.

Meg took out the sheet and looked it over before turning to look at Rose quite seriously. She paused as if considering, but shook her head as if to dispel any doubts about what she was about to do.

"Rose, I ... just realized, I don't even know your father's name!" Meg shook her head again as if disappointed at herself.

"My father's name was 'Lucas,' my lady," Rose answered.

Meg nodded. "Very well, then. Rose, daughter of Lucas and Mary, also called Branwen," Gleinguin nodded as Meg made sure to include all the information that had been made known. "Be it hereby known that I, Megan, daughter of Bryn, having no children of my own, do herewith bestow all rights and title to my lands and estate upon Rose, daughter of Lucas and Branwen, this date, by my own hand and attested to by my seal." Here Meg signed her name with one of the quills and affixed her signet upon the wax seal her steward prepared for her. "And witnessed by Gleinguin, druid and healer, and Sion ap Gwdion, my sergeant-at-arms, as well as my steward, Liam." Meg paused and took a deep breath as if relieved to have this over. "Well, Rose? What do you think?"

Rose stood as if transfixed.

" 'Thank you!' is the customary response," nudged Gleinguin with a smile. He came down and gave Rose a big hug and congratulated her. "You should be very happy! It's not every day something like this takes place."

Rose looked up at the old grey-haired healer, and said, "I ... I ... don't ... understand ..."

Gleinguin nodded his head very slowly as if demonstrating the move for Rose who was still in shock. "Yes," he said, "I think you do! And it is all very real, my dear child. Congratulations!"

Sion patted Rose on the back, then snapped to attention and called for the guardsmen to fall in line. Together, they all saluted first Rose, then Meg, and bowed and stepped back to their rest position.

Rose looked again at Meg and said, "But ... why?"

Meg frowned unsuccessfully, her eyes betraying too much fun at Rose's expense. "Why? I told you. I have no children of my own. And shouldn't you be saying 'Thank you, my lady,' and not 'why?' "

"Thank you, my lady!" Rose said. "But, I still don't understand why ... why me?"

"Because, my dear, I wish it so," Meg answered Rose using her customary "I-am-in-charge-here" tone. She couldn't help but try to bait the girl. But then, in a more serious manner, she beckoned Rose closer and took her hands. "Rose, my dear ... I am getting too old for this line of work." Rose started to protest but Meg stopped her, as she had a few months ago when the two had only begun to know each other. *Only a few months! How much things have changed in so short a time!* Meg realized. "My people love you. My servants love you. And I ..." Meg couldn't quite say it, "I respect their intuition. You are the only person I have ever met who understood things the way I do. And, much as you may protest it, I honestly feel you can go further than I ever could. Now, now, now! Don't argue with me! In this, you will not win. Not that you have won any of our other debates, but no matter. I have no children of my own, and I am free to do with this keep as I like. And you ... you are the closest thing I will ever have to a daughter, and you are certainly capable of continuing the training that I have always done here."

Rose knelt down and placed her head on Meg's lap when she heard her say how she was "the closest thing to a daughter," touched beyond words at Meg's generosity and affection, difficult as it may be for her to demonstrate them. And her tears of gratitude rolled down her face, leaving small stains in Meg's velvet robes.

"I don't know what to say," Rose said. "This is all ... so much! More than I feel I deserve. I am practically a stranger to you, and yet you took me in, nursed me back to health, took me under your guidance and protection, and now ... now you gift me with all of this!" Rose gestured around the room. "I know you wanted to give me a choice, once spring came ..."

"Rose, look at me," Meg told the girl. "I may be old, but I'm not senile. I know what I am doing. Something in me says that this is the right thing to do, and I have learned over the years to trust that voice. It's not something I can teach you, but I can tell you: trust what you find in your heart. It will never mislead you. Though, at times, the path may seem darker and more dangerous than the one you expected to find yourself on, it always serves a higher purpose than our own. The gods will do what they will do," Meg made a gesture toward Gleinguin with that last part. "He can tell you the same. Believe me, my dear, I don't do this lightly. I have thought this over, and discussed it with all those who served as witnesses here."

Meg fought back her own tears and motioned for Rose to stand up. The two of them stood looking at each other for a moment without speaking, in loving regard.

"Now," said Meg at last before her composure dissolved, "A celebration! A feast, with music and dancing, and displays of skill! Only, this time, Rose, you are not to compete but simply to enjoy."

"As you wish, my lady," Rose replied and curtsied respectfully. "I will do all you ask, and more."

Michael kept his immovable face on as he recognized the giant who rode up out of the darkness into Meraugis' camp. He knew this man to be the leader of the war party that had come to his farm the night he had been captured. Michael watched closely, trying to memorize every detail so that, perhaps, he might one day find out what had happened to his sister and father.

The giant practically leapt from his saddle and demanded to see Meraugis. Michael, as Meraugis' personal squire, was the one to escort Carados to see his master. He stood aside and kept his eyes, like those of the mute, fixed in a distant stare while Meraugis and this man spoke.

"You ... you have news, yes?" Meraugis asked dreamily. He had taken to consuming the potions from Queen Morgawse regularly now, often leaving Michael to handle the day-to-day business despite Michael's young age.

Carados looked at the bastard son of King Mark with narrowed eyes. "Yes. Wihtgar has agreed to send warriors in the spring. By early summer, we should be ready to mount our forces." Carados hated dealing with Meraugis, even more so now what with his mute butler and this strange youth who attended him.

"Ah, spring!" Meraugis said gaily, "Such a lovely time, don't you think? Yes, my lord? Yes, the spring ... perfect time to ... to ..."

"Tell your father that I will have my men ready," Carados said brusquely. He wanted to finish his business and get away from this pewling, this degenerate, as soon as possible. "We can launch our campaign by summer. Tell him!"

Carados strode from the tent and called for his mount.

"Excuse me, my lord," came a soft voice behind him.

Carados turned and saw Meraugis' youth standing in front of his master's pavilion, his sharp eyes looking as though they gazed beyond him. The child made Carados uneasy, and that made him angry.

"What do you want?" he barked.

"Forgive me, my lord Carados," the youth pronounced his name carefully, as though to make sure he had it right, "But my master has asked me what he is to tell his father regarding whom you intend to back once this campaign is over?"

Ah, just like King Mark not to waste any time, thought Carados. "Tell him, he may count on my sword, as always," he answered. *Let him ponder that!*

Michael nodded and bowed as if to go. But then he stopped and looked Carados in the eye and asked, "Does that mean, my lord, that King Lot may *also* count on your support?"

Carados' face grew tense, and he wanted to grab his axe from off his horse and cut the boy in half, but he controlled himself. *Is Meraugis as clever as his father? Does he already suspect what my plans may be?* Carados recognized the danger immediately and tried his best to cover. "Of course, as always. My services have gone to both kings against our mutual enemy."

Michael smiled with shrewd understanding and bowed again. "Thank you, my lord Carados. My master will be greatly relieved by that, as he has a special understanding with the house of King Lot." This time he did retire to his master's pavilion, though he had no intention of sharing what he had discerned from the giant's visit.

Carados stood for a moment, tempted to stride into the pavilion and kill Meraugis himself in case the bastard betrayed him. But his fear of how that might break his alliance with Meraugis' father stayed his hand. Once his horse arrived, Carados climbed into the saddle and rode for his own lands, itching for the relaxation of the arena.

So, thought Michael, *this Carados has ambitions of his own. Of course he'll be of service to both Lothian and Cornwall – until Arthur is overthrown, that is. Then what? If it were me ... Yes! I'd make myself indispensable, then ask for whatever I wanted as I pit the main rivals one against the other. Who knows? They may so weaken each other that I could become the strongest player and take everything myself!* Michael nodded to himself in conclusion, confident in his reasoning. Wasn't it what he, himself, had done already in Meraugis' household?

"Siddon!" he called out. The page appeared at once, his eyes carefully averted to avoid looking at Michael directly lest he seem challenging. "Spread the word, we strike camp in the morning and make for Cornwall."

"Y-yes, Squire!" chirped the lad and dashed away, all too happy to be off without trouble.

Michael went and checked on his master, glad to see Meraugis in one of his frequent lethargies. The opened decanter of drugged liquor sat on his bedside stand. He wasn't sleeping, but gazed up at the roof of the pavilion, gently waving an arm back and forth as though following the track of some invisible butterfly.

And what of him? Michael wondered. *How will King Mark react to the presence of his son, seeing how far he has fallen? Will he still find him useful?* For Michael early on decided that Meraugis was merely a pawn or knight in his father's game. Why else would he send his bastard as an emissary, unless King Mark was too blind to see the obvious weaknesses and vices in his own son? And Michael very much doubted that King Mark of Cornwall was that big a fool.

Rose sat to Meg's left at the head table, enjoying the music and feasting that had been given in her honor. It was like a dream come true! But one thing took some of the magic out of the night for her – the realization that her time here was over. In a little less than two weeks she must decide whether or not she will leave the Welsh borderlands and journey to the Sacred Isle, or stay and help manage Meg's estate and learn all she can.

Meg, on the other hand, seemed oblivious to the fact that Rose may be leaving and kept her focus instead on the pleasures of the evening. She laughed, and drank, and banged the table with abandon as she watched the tumblers and jugglers. She listened to the harpers, crying when they played something sad, and laughing when they played something gay. Meg had discovered a troupe of performers were nearby, making a circuit of the borderlands on their way south, and had invited them to come and perform.

"Ladies and gentlemen!" cried the Master of the Players. "I bring to you a modern wonder! A bit of magic discovered by me and mine as we traveled the lands of the mystic East. A marvel witnessed by the kings of Gaul, Germany, and Brittany! I present ... a shadow play!" With that, he asked that most of the torches in the great hall be extinguished, and a huge sheet of light canvas was set up masking the Players from their audience. With lanterns and torches set behind them, the Players cast shadows upon the fabric and made shapes and monsters on its surface. Some of them were delightful, and others grotesque and frightening. The audience made noises of delight, or gasped in fear. Their reactions became part of the performance. Cut-out figures on sticks in the shapes of men on horses could be seen moving over rolling landscapes, with their bony arms raising and falling in mock battle against shadow infantry who fell before them like wheat before a scythe.

Rose sat entranced as the scene changed, and the story became that of Arthur as he drew the sword from the anvil and stone. The puppets waved and cheered, or moved in a manner to suggest their clear opposition to his claim. Rose witnessed various battles against the rebel lords and felt a shock go through her body as she recognized one that was larger than the others, a giant on horseback compared to the shadow figures around it. She watched as the shadows moved into a forest where they were ambushed, and Rose felt herself wishing that the giant would get trapped, cornered, and killed as was happening to so many of the other figures. She leaned forward as though straining to see beyond the fabric, nearly coming out of her chair. And the shadows moved and flowed in front of her. The shadows of Arthur's forces were joined by others and drove the rebel puppets until they broke. But the giant and several other shadows turned back, harrying the pursuit while the other rebels fled, scattering. The little stick arms raised and fell, raised and fell, until everyone watching was sure that a torrent of blood must be ready to flow out from under the curtain.

The scene changed again, and Rose began to tremble as the puppets followed the giant, and showed him burning and pillaging village after village. It was as if Rose truly were enspelled, unable to look away, while the shadows played out what had happened to her family. The audience hissed and shouted at him as he moved about the surface of the fabric, and several men got up angrily as they witnessed the shadow reavings and shook their fists as they yelled at the curtain.

Rose could feel her heart hammering in her chest and the blood rushing to her ears, as she watched one shadow that came forward to fight the giant, its little stick spear in its hand. *Poppa!* Rose wanted it to stop, wanted to cry out, wanted to run, but she could only watch as the shadows fought. The giant on horseback wheeled and attacked, and Rose heard a scream when the little stick axe came down on the puppet head. She felt hands on her, and she began to fight them off, only then realizing it was her own voice screaming, "Stop! Stop it! Poppa! Oh, please!!!"

The shadow curtain seemed to loom larger until it became all Rose could see. She heard voices around her, men's and women's, but couldn't make out what they were saying. It made her recall the cries and lamentations she heard when she had made her way back to the farm, only to find Poppa' body and the ruins of their barn and home. The shadows changed again. They flowed and grew larger in Rose's eyes until they were man-sized. This time they showed boats landing on a shore. The giant was there, and he greeted a stick figure that jumped out of the boats. The figures coming from the longboats bore spears and the circular shields of the Saxons, and Rose knew what she was being shown, but she kept muttering, "Please … Stop it … Please …" while she watched. But the shadow play went on and on. Shadow Saxons readied stick weapons, and the giant led them as they fell upon a group of villagers, killed them all, and then moved on. Through magic or the mastery of the players, the shadows became distorted until it appeared a huge pack of ravening wolves roamed the land, destroying homes, families, and armies. The shadow of the giant grew larger and larger until it made the entire room go dark. Rose felt the room tip, and something struck her head, and she fell into deeper blackness.

"Rose? Rose? Are you all right?" Meg's concerned voice finally came through into Rose's consciousness, followed by light that filtered through her closed eyelids.

Rose felt rough but gentle hands cradling her neck, and caught the scent of earth and herbs that permeated the rough fabric under her head. She knew it had to be Gleinguin in whose lap she lay. His strong hands helped her to sit up, and Rose could feel a dull throb on her right temple. She winced as she lifted up a hand and felt a lump there.

"What happened?" she asked weakly, feeling a little nauseous as she spoke.

"You fainted," said Gleinguin with warm concern.

Rose noticed that the hall was clear; all signs of the revelry already cleared away, the players gone.

"I … I did? What about the … Where did the players go?"

Meg answered, "They left about an hour ago. They gave their apologies, and the Master of the Players offered to return the money I had given them if they had caused any harm."

"I … the shadow play … It seemed … so real …" Rose tried to tell them what she had experienced. "I remember some men getting up and shouting at the curtain, and the giant … Carados! I remember, he was there! They were showing what had happened to … to my family!"

Meg and Gleinguin glanced nervously at each other, and Meg spoke, "Rose – what are you talking about?"

Rose looked at the two of them, and saw their concerned stare back at her, "The … the shadow play! About King Arthur, and the rebel lords, and the battles …"

"Rose," said Gleinguin, "the Players performed the Epic of Lugh – a Welsh folktale. They never did anything about Arthur, or the rebel lords."

Rose looked at him quizzically, feeling a little panic, "But … no! I saw it! I saw him, Carados! I saw his shadow on the … on the … the …"

Meg glanced at Gleinguin, who merely shook his head, and put a gentle hand on Rose's shoulder as if ready to catch her should she faint again. "Rose," Meg said, "Tell me what it was you saw. Something obviously happened. I know that. You're not the kind to faint over nothing. At first I was afraid it was something you'd eaten. or that you had had too much to drink. But now … I don't know. So, what did you see?"

193

Gleinguin asked Rose to lie back down and close her eyes while he cradled her head. A warm cloth was brought, and he carefully dabbed at the lump and soothed her forehead. He entered a light, healing trance, just enough to add some of his energy to hers so that Rose might more easily recall what she had seen yet remain calm. "Rose? I want you to breathe deeply and slowly, all right? Just take it in, and let it out, slowly but naturally. Breathe while you close your eyes, and see what you saw before."

Rose did as they asked and slowly recounted for them what she had witnessed. By the time she had finished, she felt very light and sleepy, and asked if it would be okay for her to go to bed.

Gleinguin helped her up, and one of the servants walked with her to her room, though the healer was fairly certain Rose wouldn't faint again.

"What do you make of that?" Meg asked him as he walked her back to her rooms.

Gleinguin shook his head. "I don't know what to make of it. I don't know if it is something within her that called up the images, or if some magic is at work here."

"Magic?" Meg asked.

"Well, of a kind … Except that if there were, I expect that I'd have felt it somehow while it was happening. Usually magic upsets the natural order of things, and you can't do that without my knowing about it!"

"So you think this might be a power inside of Rose?"

Gleinguin thought for a moment before answering. "I don't get that sense either, really. It's not as if some power came up inside her and overwhelmed her. It's more as if … How do I put it? More as if something touched Rose's mind just enough, just enough to let it see these things on its own. It's hard to describe."

Meg thought for a moment as something else struck her. "There is something else. Now that I think about it, have you ever known a player to turn down money, let alone offer to give any back?"

Gleinguin admitted that he didn't.

"Don't you think that a little odd?" she asked him.

"So, you think possibly this player had something to do with this? But how? As I said, if magic were at work here, I think I'd feel it."

"I don't know," Meg confessed. "And I'm no mage or priestess myself, so I have to trust your word on that. But, the timing is interesting to note."

"How so?" asked the old healer.

"Well, Rose is, I am sure, beginning to question what she will do next. Will she stay here? Leave and wander the forest? Or will she go to Avalon?"

"Hmm," considered Gleinguin. "So you think possibly the Sacred Isle had something to do with this?"

"It is a possibility. Though I doubt that reminding Rose of what it is she has to want revenge for could serve their interests. But, who else would have any interest in our Rose?"

Gleinguin couldn't think of an answer, nor could Meg, though both of them pondered the question as they went their separate ways to bed.

Chapter 12

The morning came, bright and clear. Everything seemed brighter as though the series of rains had washed all the dirt and grime from the countryside. Colors were brighter, scents fresher, and the air felt crisp and clean.

For Rose, however, it made little difference. Some deep knowing inside herself knew that her time with Meg was at an end, even if only temporarily. The first day of spring was still a little less than two weeks away, but Rose knew it was time for her to go.

But go where? she wondered to herself, desperately seeking an answer.

A gentle knock came on the door, and Rose identified immediately whom it would be.

"Come in, wise father!" she called as she finished pulling on her wool robe, which covered the quilted tunic she had out of habit gotten into as soon as she awoke.

Gleinguin pushed his head through the door and smiled at her, though it faded once he saw the look in Rose's eye.

"My dear, what's the matter?" he asked with concern as he entered the room.

Rose fought the urge to be hugged by the old man, much as she wanted to feel his strong arms protectively about her, warding off the unknown. But Gleinguin couldn't be there for her all the time, and Rose recognized it was time she stopped behaving like a child and accept the responsibilities and duties of the young adult she had become.

"Nothing's wrong," Rose lied.

Gleinguin, however, wasn't fooled. There was a guardedness about her that had only been there when Rose felt insecure, or was beating herself up for not mastering something as fast as she wanted. He had learned that sometimes the best thing one could offer was silence and a willingness to listen when and if the other party felt safe enough to talk.

Rose glanced at the old healer as he watched her with his deep, grey eyes. It was like being watched by a forest, and it caused Rose to remember the first time she had encountered the druid. She could vividly recall the shade of this dear man as his spirit went forth and found her in that grove somewhere in the borderlands of the Dead. The sense of loving care that he radiated now was just as undeniable, and Rose felt ashamed for shutting him out. But she felt she had to be strong if she was going to be able to make a break with everything she had come to adopt as her second home.

"I need to go," she told him softly, not really sure if he would say anything to stop her but half-hoping he might. "I don't know where yet, exactly. I've thought about going to Avalon, but ..." Rose shrugged in uncertainty.

"You don't feel pulled there, is that it?" Gleinguin finally asked. His voice conveyed his understanding of her dilemma.

"Yes," Rose nodded and pulled out a sack into which she began stuffing clothes. "I simply don't know where I am going. I only know that I have to go!"

A browned and weathered hand helped hold open the bag Rose was trying to fill as Gleinguin spoke. "I felt the same once I had finished my training," he told her. "It was as if I were trying to hold back a river that had become overly full, and I was overrunning my banks."

He gave Rose a glance as he asked, "Have you told Meg, yet?"

Rose sighed, and sat down on the bed. "No. I know I need to, it's just … It is so hard to do! I … I know she loves me, and I love her, too, but …"

"Rose, it is because Meg loves you that she will understand your decision. It ought to make it easier to tell her, not harder."

"I know! But, it just feels – well, it hurts, you know? I'm going to miss her more than she can imagine. And you. And Sion, and Liam, and, well, *everybody*!" Rose got up and grabbed another handful of clothing, some leggings and another cloak.

"And we will miss you more than you will know," Gleinguin responded. "But, Rose, it isn't forever, right? You are the heir to this estate, and have responsibilities to the people here, don't you? So, we'll see you again. In the gods' own time."

'But where will I go, if not to Avalon?" Rose asked with frustration.

"I can't answer that for you," Gleinguin replied. "Only you can know. Trust in yourself, Rose. Trust in your heart."

My heart? He sounds just like Meg.

"Talk to Meg, Rose. Believe me, she'll understand. And she won't stand in your way, no matter what you decide."

But what if I want her to? she wondered privately. "I couldn't leave without saying 'Goodbye' anyhow. Meg would have me tracked down if I did."

"You're probably right," Gleinguin agreed with a smile.

Rose found Meg out in the small, walled garden, speaking with the man who tended the trees and bushes for her.

"Ah, Rose! How opportune! I was just asking Sulwyn here if he would plant some of your name's sakes right through here," Meg said as Rose drew close.

Rose smiled faintly at the compliment, though it also made it feel harder to say what she had come here to tell Meg.

"Ay, m'lady," the gardener said with a bow and a quick touch of his fingers to his brow to the two women. "I'll have 'em springin' up in no time!" he said as he gathered up his tools and departed.

As Meg turned and looked at Rose, her face flushed with enthusiasm. She was practically glowing, drinking in the wonderful sunlight and fresh air. "This has always been my favorite time of year!" Meg exclaimed and did a little twirl as though she were many years younger than she was.

"My lady," Rose started to say, but Meg stopped her.

" 'My lady?' Rose, it isn't like you to address me so formally. Whatever is the matter?" Meg's smile faded just a bit, and she put her hand on Rose's arm as she regarded her for a moment. "Usually it is 'old woman' or just plain old 'Meg' with a slight roll of your eyes, like this," and Meg rolled her eyes imitation of Rose. But her playful mood didn't catch on with Rose, and she said, "Uh-oh ... I get the feeling I'm not going to like this."

Rose looked Meg in the eye, and keeping her voice very calm, she said, "Meg ... the time has come for me to go."

The simpleness and sincerity of the statement caught Meg by surprise, and she felt herself practically stumble under the impact of it. "Go? But, you still have two weeks to decide! You haven't made up your mind already have you? About going to the Sacred Isle?"

Rose shook her head, "No, Meg, I haven't. It's not that. It's just – I feel I have to go. I don't know where, but I feel like something inside me is struggling to get out, and I have to leave to let it go. I don't know where it wants to go, only that I can't stay here!"

Meg looked at Rose with sympathetic eyes. "It feels like you're a young chick and its time to break out of the shell, eh?"

Rose nodded.

"I know the feeling," Meg said sadly. Then, with a bit of a forced cheeriness, she said, "Thank the gods I don't have to push you out of the nest, as I understand so many parents have to do with their children when they reach a certain age!"

Rose smiled a little at that.

"Well," said Meg more seriously. "How soon?"

"Today," answered Rose. "Or tomorrow, but no later than that, I think."

Meg nodded as she thought it over. "And then what? Where do you think you might go?"

"I'm not sure," Rose answered truthfully. "I guess east? North? I really am not sure."

"Let me make a suggestion, then, if I may. Spend the night as a knight would before embarking on a quest. Fast. See a priest, or Gleinguin, and ask for a blessing. Then spend the night in solitary vigil. I'll have Liam send you some tea that will help you remain alert, and pack provisions to last you for a couple of days, at least. And Sion will ready Seren Llwyd for you, as well as a pony to carry your gear. You don't expect your warhorse to carry you and everything else as well, do you?"

Rose felt both grateful and relieved at the same time. "Thank you," she said, "for understanding."

Meg looked at Rose and said, "Of course I understand! You don't think you're the first person to ever feel the need to leave home, do you? Plus, it is about time for me to go off for a bit by myself. You know … To see if a young lad wanting to become a knight chances my way, and to carry on my tradition."

"I'm sorry I won't be there to join you," Rose said sincerely. "I guess it would be a good idea for me to accompany you on one of these trips sometime."

"Sometime, but not now," Meg told her. "Rose, there is a small shrine, a chapel people call it, called the Green Chapel. It is a bit south and east of here, maybe a week's ride, maybe less. It is a common starting place for young knights going on adventure. Why don't you start there before deciding on whether or not you will continue on to the Sacred Isle and their priestesses?"

"The Green Chapel?" Rose asked. "Very well, old woman. If you recommend it, then I shall go there."

Meg slapped Rose playfully on the back of the head for calling her "old woman," but then took Rose's arm, and the two of them strolled about the gardens, enjoying the beauty of the day and the final experience of each other's company.

"Good!" said the strange old man sitting in the woods. He dragged on his clay pipe before rising to his feet, brushing the dirt and leaves from off his robes. "She's on her way! But this old rag will never do!" he exclaimed as he looked down at his clothes and examined his arms as he stretched them out in front of him. "This might be better," he said and looked himself over anew. Where before had stood a lean old man with a long, grey beard shot through with white, now stood a youth of perhaps twenty years of age, with short dark hair, and short beard with overly long mustachios that hung down from the corners of his lips in the Celtic fashion. His robes had become a worn and faded cloth shirt and woolen leggings with knee-high boots of soft leather laced with leather cord. Where he had once held his pipe he now held a large wood axe. He hefted it over his shoulder as he picked his way through the foliage and neared the ancient stone structure the locals regarded as sacred.

"There is something peaceful about this place," he remarked as he leaned his axe on a log and sat before a small fire over which cooked a rabbit on a spit. He glanced at the stone building, partially collapsed but obviously the work of man despite the huge stone blocks and lack of Roman-style adornment. This was a place that had been here long before the Romans, even before the tribes that had become the peoples of Britain gathered together and named a High King for the land.

The man became aware of being watched and sensed the presence of the *Sidhe* – one of the fairy people who dwelt both in this world and slightly outside of it. A brownie, he knew, who watched him with wary but curious eyes, seemingly invisible as he blended so deeply into the woods behind the stranger.

The man reached to his belt and opened a small pouch that hung there. He drew forth a small wood, stoppered flask. He uncorked the top, raised the opening to his nose, and inhaled deeply. He let out a loud satisfied sigh before taking a sip from the mouth of the flask. He carefully poured out a libation to the Old Gods, as well as for the spirits he knew still inhabited this place despite the encroachment of Man.

The brownie caught the scent of the alcohol, and it slipped swiftly yet cautiously closer, its nose all aquiver as it breathed in the odor of the liquor the stranger had poured. It looked out of the side of its eye, but the stranger either wasn't aware of its presence, or was deliberately ignoring the brownie. It wasn't sure which. Then it noticed the man's hand with the flask slowly drifting closer to where it squatted, unsure whether to bolt or accept the stranger's offering. It decided to accept, snatching the flask out of the man's hand and skittering back several paces before up-ending the flask and swallowing a huge swig of the potent brew.

The man only smiled, glad that the brownie had taken his gift, for he knew that the "little people" often repaid small kindnesses with kindnesses of their own. Sometimes that simply meant leaving a stranger unmolested. But that was enough.

The brownie crept closer, flask in one hand, the other held slightly before it as it neared this stranger, ready to bolt should he move suddenly. His smell was odd – not a Man smell, but something richer, earthier. Pleasant. Safe. It slowly settled itself next to the man who was not a Man on the log he used as a bench, and stared into the fire where the man kept his gaze. He took another swig of the delicious liquor the stranger had given him. It relaxed, its tiny potbelly hanging out in front, serving as a convenient place to rest its free hand while the two sat watching the flames.

"Hurry up, laddie! It will be the Second Coming by the time we reach Camelot at the pace we're going!" Gawaine shouted at the rider several yards behind him.

Gaheris sighed, wondering what his brother's hurry was since the delay was due in large part to their mother and her excessive baggage train. That, and the decision to travel before the spring had come. The Orkney party with all its attendant horses, wagons, tents, pavilions, crates and boxes and chests had been bogged down several times in sleet, snow, mud, and rain ever since leaving Lothian. To Gaheris it felt as if God Himself were trying to tell them to turn back. They even lost a wagon and some horses in a flash flood fording one of the river crossings on their way south.

"Don't blame me!" he shouted back to Gawaine. "If you want to make it there any faster, then maybe you should have a word with our mother, the Queen."

He wasn't sure, but it looked to Gaheris as if Gawaine flinched slightly as he heard what Gaheris said. As expected, he merely raised one hand and gestured rudely but refused to turn around or wait for his brother to catch up.

I'm not surprised, Gaheris thought to himself. *Just like Gawaine to talk big, but when it comes to Mother, he's as scared as anyone. So much for the big, brave knight!*

"Hold up!" came a call from far behind the two of them, and Gaheris passed the order along to Gawaine who stopped his horse and sat as though the entire world were attached to his back and dragging him down. The Queen had ordered the caravan to stop and pitch camp for the day.

"Probably her ass is sore from so much sitting," Gaheris muttered to himself as he turned back, though he waited for Gawaine to draw up along side of him so they could ride back to the others together. "Women," he heard Gawaine say as he rode past.

Men were already busy setting up tents and the royal family's pavilions by the time the pair reached the main body of the camp. Morgawse was seated at the long table, a feast spread as though she were still back at home and not out in the middle of nowhere under open sky. Agravaine and Gareth were there, too, already helping themselves to the food and drink. Morgawse didn't even bother to look up as Gaheris and Gawaine dismounted and sat down at the family table.

"Have a nice ride?" Agravaine asked with his usual smirk.

Gareth, though, was glad to see the pair returned. Agravaine was a terrible bore who never wanted to do anything with him, and he longed for the opportunity to ride with his other two brothers. He also envied them the fact that they could so easily get free of Mother's watchful eyes. In greeting, he threw a quince at Gaheris, who looked unhappy as he sat down. And Gawaine was unusually quiet and looked disgruntled. "Can I ride with you next time?" he asked hopefully as the pair reached for the food and drink without enthusiasm.

"Of course not! You stay here near Mommy, where you're safe," Morgawse said before the boys could respond.

"Mother," said Gaheris with annoyance. "He's old enough to be a page at least. Why not let him ride with Gawaine and me so I can teach him what he needs to know?"

Morgawse shot Gaheris an angry glare, but covered it up to avoid any squabbling. "I appreciate your offer, Gaheris. That's very considerate of you. But I have very expensive tutors for your brother. They are teaching him everything he needs to know. Skill at arms isn't the only thing that distinguishes a fine leader, you know. History, politics, finances – these are the concerns of a good ruler as well!"

"I don't mind, Ma," Gawaine said through a mouthful of food, half-hoping she wouldn't hear him. "The runt can ride along. He's more fun than the Ice Pope here," he indicated Gaheris.

Ice Pope? Gaheris didn't understand the insult, but was hurt by the comment anyway.

"If you're not happy with your service, you are free to find somebody else," Gaheris said defensively. "Except that I don't think anyone else would want to do it!"

Gawaine was in no mood and knocked Gaheris off the bench with a sweep of his powerful arm. "Take that back!" he shouted and jumped up from his seat, fists raised and ready to pummel his brother.

"Never!" Gaheris yelled as he got up and ducked under his brother's arms in a tackle. "You're the biggest, loudest, most ..." The two boys wrestled and threw punches at each other, Gaheris taking quite a few bad hits from Gawaine who not only outweighed him, but was probably one of the strongest men Gaheris knew next to his father.

"Stop it!" shouted Morgawse. "Boys! I order you to stop!"

Agravaine sat and watched the whole spectacle with mild amusement, but made no move to interfere. Gareth was horrified and joined his mother in yelling at the two to stop.

"I am sick and tired of listening to your stories! And your complaining," Gaheris said through gritted teeth as he tried to land a few punches of his own.

Gawaine gripped Gaheris around the waist and lifted him up in a bear hug, squeezing the air out of his younger brother. "Tired of me, eh? You think I complain, is that it? You think I'm a big bag of wind, eh? Let's see how much wind you've got inside you, ye little shit!"

Gareth screamed, which brought everyone to a standstill. "Stop it! Please, don't! You're killing him!"

Gawaine caught himself, feeling the blood drain from his head, and stood as though someone had thrown cold water over him bringing him back to his senses. Gaheris was straining to get out of his grip, but his face had gone pale, and he had a look in his eyes Gawaine had seen before in enemies he had killed – a look of confusion coupled with fear. He set Gaheris down, then with atypical gentleness helped him to the bench on which they had both been sitting when their tempers erupted, asking, "Are you all right? Here, sit down. I'll get ye a drink of ale."

Gaheris gasped and sucked in air once he was free of his brother's deadly hug. He was stunned by how quickly things got out of hand and grateful for Gareth's cry to put an end to it.

Gawaine returned with a mug and placed it in Gaheris' hand, holding it while he helped lift it and made him take a sip or two.

"I'm sorry," he said. "I ... ye know me ... I've got a terrible temper. I get carried away, ye know? I ... I'm sorry."

Gaheris nodded that he understood and forgave him, though he couldn't speak yet, but sat taking deep breathes.

Morgawse came over and slapped Gawaine on the face. He merely took it with stone-faced passivity. When he didn't react, she hit him again, then once more before he finally looked at her, his right eye twitching a little as he fought the anger that wanted to strike her back.

"Now that I have your attention," she said coldly, "not only am I your mother, but your Queen as well. And when I order you to do something, I expect to be obeyed! Is that clear?"

Gawaine's face turned red, but he only nodded slowly.

"Is that clear?" Morgawse repeated to Gaheris, who did the same. "Good. And do you think the two of you are the proper teachers for your youngest brother? To teach him good manners and courtly behavior?" It was clear she did not.

To Gareth she said, "Let this be a lesson to you. You'd be better off behaving more like Agravaine than either one of these two scoundrels. I know you admire Gawaine, but look at him! No self-control. No discipline. And Gaheris? Disobedient and disrespectful. Especially to me! Me! Who brought him into this world and only wants what is best for him, for all of you. And this is how I have been repaid, time and time again. You are a disappointment to your father and me, both of you. I won't have you embarrass me in front of the High King. Why I'd be ashamed to acknowledge you as my own if you behave like this in Camelot!" She turned and walked off, dismissing them without another word.

Agravaine stood up ready to say something smart, but one look from Gawaine and he decided it would be better not to press his luck, so he bowed and followed their mother.

Gareth came over sadly and sat down next to Gaheris and Gawaine. "I'm sorry," he said as he became choked with emotion. "I didn't mean to start anything! I just wanted to get away from Mommy and Aggy. I just wanted to ride with you two, that's all!"

The two older brothers looked at Gareth and felt guilty for their behavior.

"It's not your fault, runt," said Gawaine.

"No, you're all right," said Gaheris trying to comfort his brother. "I understand. Dull as ..." he tried to joke.

Gareth answered lamely, "Gawaine's sword."

The two boys smiled weakly at each other, while Gawaine missed the joke but sat appreciating the lighter mood.

"I'm sorry, too, Gawaine ... for what I said," Gaheris apologized.

Gawaine shook his head and said, "No – ye're right. Who would want to be my squire with such a temper as mine? I guess I should be glad ye've stuck it out as long as ye did."

Gaheris could see how hurt Gawaine was by the idea that nobody liked him, and he had a sudden empathy for his brother.

"No, G, I wasn't right. You're one of the bravest, most generous men I know next to Da, and your reputation as a warrior is unsurpassed. Anyone would be glad to have the honor to serve as your squire!"

Gawaine gave his younger brother an appreciative glance, trying to hide his watery eyes lest he seem unmanly. "Thanks, Gaheris. I know I've been a bit of a brute lately. To tell ye the truth, I feel a wee homesick. Y'see, there's this little serving wench I've been dallying, and it's been a while ..."

Gareth rolled his eyes, "Yuck! Why would you miss spending time with a girl? Don't you want to be on adventure? Don't you want to visit Camelot and see the High King? I can hardly wait! I'll bet it's got walls as thick as a road, and towers as tall as a tree!"

Gaheris had to laugh, but sensed that Gawaine's pain was deeper than he let on. Deeper than anyone even suspected.

"It's okay, G. Gareth's right – won't it be grand, the Orkney boys loose in Camelot? The city won't know what hit it!" Gaheris tried to coax his brother out of his mood, and it seemed to work. If there was one thing he knew about his brother Gawaine, it was that his moods changed as swiftly as the weather, and was more often open and free than the irritable, dour person he'd been.

Gawaine broke into his familiar grin as he thought about it, and it broadened as he saw the excitement in Gareth's eyes. He reached out and tousled the boy's hair and said, "Aye! What a time it will be! And I bet there are lasses as comely as the ones at home. Nay, better, though I'd have a hard time admitting that any women in the world were fairer than our northern breed – but 'tis the heart of the kingdoms after all! Why wouldn't it have the best of everything?"

Gaheris could see Gawaine getting caught up in his grandiose fantasies already, but was glad to have his familiar brother back again and so listened with enjoyment as Gawaine predicted impossible and incredible sights and sounds of the Golden City of Camelot.

"G, there is one thing I'd like to know," Gaheris said as he and Gawaine and their youngest brother strolled through the camp.

"Eh? What's that?" Gawaine asked.

"Ice Pope?" Gaheris asked and made a gesture of incomprehension.

Gawaine grinned bashfully, and dropped his head a little, as he answered, "Ach, that! Well, 'ice' because ye seem a bit cold and distant sometimes, and 'pope' because, well … ye can be a bit self-righteous at times. I know it isn't particularly clever, but it was the best I could do in the moment."

Gaheris let the comment sink in despite the initial hurt at being described as cold and self-righteous. *Is that how people see me?* he wondered. He felt a firm hand on his shoulder and looked up at his oldest brother who regarded him with serious eyes.

"Don't let it get to ye, laddie. I did nay mean it, really."

Gaheris touched his brother's hand in thanks, but still felt himself pull away inside. "I don't mean to be distant," he explained himself, "but – I just don't seem to feel I belong in this family, somehow. I'm not as strong as you, nor as bright as Agravaine – and everybody seems to love Gareth here. But me? I just seem so different from you all. Even father ..."

"Da? You think you're not like him at all?" Gawaine exchanged a look with Gareth, who only shrugged his shoulders as he shook his head in disbelief.

"What? What is it?" Gaheris asked the other two.

Gawaine looked Gaheris over and said, "Laddie, if there's anyone in the family who's like Da, it's you." Before Gaheris could disagree, Gawaine held up his hands to stop him and continued. "I know, I have Da's temper, and the old man could probably still give me one hell of a good thrashing in hand-to-hand fighting, but you ... you've got Da's sensibilities. You care about people the same way he does. And I'm not the only one who knows it."

Gaheris looked at Gareth, but Gawaine said, "Not him, ye dolt! Da has said so, though I guess never in your hearing. It used to make me angry, and I used to think Da loved you more than the rest of us, but now I don't. He just felt you had a better understanding of what it meant to be royalty than the rest of us. Even Agravaine, whom ye'd think would be the most likely to rule of us all. But no, Da has said that ye were the one who'd make the best choice as King of Lothian and Orkney should it come down to it. Why? Because you love the people, and you care about their welfare. Me? Hell, I've no mind for such things. Give me a sword and a horse, and I'm as happy as a pig in a mud hole. Agravaine would squander the kingdom in fancy clothes and food, all the things to feed his fancy, and we'd be paupers in a week!"

Gareth and Gaheris both laughed at that.

"Thank you," Gaheris said with sincerity. "I ... never knew he felt that way about me. He always seemed troubled whenever he was around me, and we always ended up talking about you and your exploits and adventures. I always thought he loved *you* best, not me."

Gawaine nodded, "Aye, we're not the best at making our-selves clear, our family. No matter that Da and I can weep in a blink, or when we hear a sad melody, we don't tend to tell the people we care about the most what we really feel."

Gareth piped in, "And here I thought Mom and Pop loved *me* the most of all!"

This made all three of them laugh out loud, and they hugged each other brotherly, with claps on the back in emphasis.

"Come on!" said Gawaine and lifted Gareth up and put him on his shoulder. "Before Ma has a chance to say otherwise, let's go for a brief jaunt, just the three of us! What do ye say?"

Gaheris and Gareth made exclamations of enthusiasm, and the trio went off to the horses, carefully avoiding their mother's pavilion.

Morgawse stopped in shock as she entered her pavilion, for seated on the cushions was a slender woman dressed in the grey robes of Avalon. She recognized her, but had to take a moment to gather herself due to the audacity she displayed at making herself at home in her tent!

"Greetings, sister," the woman said without getting up from where she sat. "You seem to be doing well."

Morgawse refused to look at her sister until she had poured herself some brandywine and taken her chair. "What is it, Mor-gana?" she asked impatiently. "Has the Sacred Isle turned you out at last?"

Smiling slightly, Morgana let the barb go by without notice. "The Sacred Mother has no authority over me, as you well know, since I never took my final vows to become a priestess in actuality."

"And yet you wear the robes of a votive to the Goddess. Why is that?" Morgawse asked critically.

"Suffice it to say that I serve the Goddess in my own fash-ion," Morgana answered cryptically. "Which is why I've come, though I suppose you're disappointed I haven't come merely out of love for you, my oldest sister."

Morgawse wanted to scratch Morgana's eyes out for the subtle way she said "oldest," knowing it would irritate her. Morgana knew quite well her sister's vanity and had a knack for playing on her vulnerabilities.

"Oh, I'm sorry, sister," Morgana said lightly. "I didn't mean that you were *old* by that! Only, well, the fact is you were born long before I was."

"You don't need to make a point of it!" Morgawse hissed in response.

Morgana smiled wickedly and at last rose up from her place among the cushions. Morgawse hated her even more for the fact that Morgana still possessed the slender waist and glowing skin of youth, unmolested by pregnancies and childbirth. Her sister had always been "slender as a reed" as their mother would say, and still had lustrous black hair, long limbs, and ample bosom to be found attractive by most men. *More desirable than me, though?* she wondered, and the thought ate at her heart.

"Good to see you, too," Morgana said with mock sincerity.

"Tell me why you've come, then go!" Morgawse said in annoyance. "I'll allow you this one audience only because of the common blood we share. But never again! In future you must sue for my attention like any other petitioner."

"Tsk, tsk, tsk," Morgana clucked her tongue. "And here I came to warn you about the path you plan to choose. Is that gratitude? Where's the devotion to the Mother of Us All?"

What Morgana said sent chills through Morgawse, who knew her sister to have been blessed with second sight even as a child.

"What do you mean? What path was I going to choose?"

"With your own brother – well, half-brother, but still, isn't that incest?" Morgana asked with a knowing shake of her head.

How could she know about that? How could she know what I had planned ... unless ... Did the Goddess reveal this to her? But how? Morgana's not a priestess of Avalon. "I don't know what you are talking about," Morgawse lied.

"Still," Morgana went on as though she hadn't heard her sister, "in some ancient cultures such things were common between members of the royal family. In Egypt, they say, brother and sister were married in order to ensure the bloodline remained pure. Is that what you were thinking, Morgawse? To start a new, royal bloodline? A pure one? Or is it just lust and the gratification of your own perverse desires that would lead you down such a path?"

Morgana's directness startled Morgawse who felt exposed, as though all the blackness of her soul were laid open to Morgana's scrutiny. She covered her mouth with one hand as she gasped, "How could you …?"

"But I do know," Morgana lost all sense of play and became quite serious, and seemed filled with a presence that loomed like a huge shadow, which filled the tent as she spoke. "I know, and I see, and I plan. Your petty ambitions mean nothing to the Mother of Us All, Morgawse. You are nothing to her. You are just another thread in the hands of She Who Spins. But I, I am a tool of She Who Measures. I know, and I come to bring warning. Do this thing, and you will destroy Arthur and all he builds, all he will achieve. This much I can see, though Arthur is unaware that he is outside the Skein of Time. Merlin Emrys has changed the future of What Is to Be and now works to create What *May* Be. The Old Ways are dying, and I for one wish to make sure I survive the changes."

"Whatever do you mean?" Morgawse asked with all sincerity. The presence that spoke through her sister made her forget everything else, all their past annoyances with each other. Only the sense of import behind what Morgana was relaying had any meaning right now. *I can undo Arthur? How? By creating a new royal bloodline?*

Morgana stood facing her sister, her eyes rolled back until only the whites showed, deep in trance, while something else spoke through her. "Beware! Beware! The path is dangerous, and all roads lead to bloodshed in the end … a son shall kill his mother … a serpent shall slay the dragon … fire shall come from across the seas, wolves rave the land! A rose shall fell a giant with its thorn ... darkness will fall upon the land because of the pride of two brothers, and one brother shall slay the other ...The Grail! Ah, the Grail! Its Light hurts us! It is too bright! Too bright! I cannot see! I cannot see ... I cannot ... see ..." Morgana collapsed as the presence left her, exhausted by being used so.

Morgawse went to her sister, all sibling rivalry and pettiness forgotten. She cradled Morgana's head and asked, "How? How do I do this? How do I ruin Arthur? *How?*" But Morgana was too far out of it, the god or goddess gone that had been speaking through her. Morgana began to tremble and spasm, and Morgawse knew a fear unlike any she had ever felt before, exposed and vulnerable before this power, and unable to do anything for her sister other than hold her until the seizures stopped. Foam dribbled from the corners of Morgana's mouth, and Morgawse felt an impulse to grab a cup and collect it for future use in spells or potions, but resisted the temptation.

"Wh-where? Morgawse? Ah, yes ... that's right," Morgana spoke weakly as she came back from her trance. A brief look crossed over her features, the look of an innocent child glad to be held in the arms of a loving mother, safe and cared for, before her face grew taught and the customary mocking smile played about her lips. Her eyes regained their usual knowing gleam, and she brushed away her sister's hands and sat up. "Water. From a spring or stream. Fresh," she demanded, though without strength.

"Y-yes, of course!" Morgawse got up and called for a page to bring a pitcher of fresh rainwater collected in a barrel. She was tempted to help her sister stand, but Morgana waved her away disdainfully and waited, resting on the cushions, until the water came.

"You watch me with new eyes," she finally spoke to Morgawse. "I don't know what the Goddess said through me, or God. I only know that I go where I am bidden, and I give myself wholly to the Power to use as It will. That is why I never joined the cult at Avalon. My Path is a solitary one, and only I may walk it."

"You don't remember any of it?" Morgawse asked, half hoping it were true but not finding herself able to trust Morgana completely.

"No, not really … I remember seeing you come in, and I know we exchanged our usual pleasantries with each other," Morgana made it clear she had no great love for Morgawse either, "but the rest … no. I gather from the look in your eyes, however, it was something of use to you. Something from which you will benefit, I am sure."

Morgawse's mind was already working, trying to look ahead in the limited way she could with just her own brilliant thinking and planning. *Oh, what I wouldn't give to have just a little of Morgana's second sight!* "Oh, well, yes … you know. The usual kinds of things tinkers and fortunetellers might say. 'Great love and wealth' and all that."

"I know you lie," Morgana said and stared at her sister angrily. "The Powers do not use me lightly, and would not have guided me to you just to tell you something you could guess by breathing on a mirror or gazing into a bowl of water by starlight. But, I can also see you have no intention of being honest with me, despite our tie as sisters. So, I will depart as soon as I have rested. Being mortal, the God or Goddess' use of me takes quite a bit out of me, and I must recover. This was – one of the more powerful tellings, that much I do know."

Morgawse tried to think quickly of a lie to tell, only to decide it would be of no use against Morgana's sight, so she deferred instead. "I will have one of my stewards show you to a pavilion, where you may rest yourself, and provide for your comfort. Perhaps, once you are rested and I have had time to think about what you have told me, I may relay the god's message to you so that you may stay informed."

Morgana inclined her head in assent, and the two sat in silence as she waited to be shown her resting place.

It was a clear, cold morning as Rose dressed herself in quilted padding, then donned the light armor with which Meg had gifted her.

So, this is it! she thought, and took a deep breath. *Is this what it means to become an adult? To face the unknown?*

Her baggage had been collected by stewards and delivered to Sion ap Gwdion who oversaw the outfitting of Seren Llwyd and Rose's pony. Everything was ready. Rose had done as Meg asked. She had asked Gleinguin for a blessing and spent the night in solitary vigil, cold and frightened by the reality of the next day's departure. Gleinguin had given her three beeswax candles to light and recommended she focus on their flames, and let her worries be lifted away as the flames consumed the wax. It had taken a while, but Rose finally settled into a meditative state, and it had helped. Morning had come all too soon, however, and all that was left for Rose to do was to make her way downstairs, mount her horse, and say her goodbyes.

Rose took out her mother's pendant, said a final prayer asking for the guidance and protection of her parent's spirits, then tucked it back inside and made her way down. As she walked, it almost felt to Rose as if she walked a stranger's halls. Seeing these corridors possibly for the last time made them seem like new, and she noticed things she had never seen before. The details of the tapestries stood out in stark detail even though Rose had walked past them hundreds of times during her months here. The cracks in the mortar, the spacing of the windows and the angle of the dim light coming through them ... everything held an unspoken significance to Rose on this day.

She opened the wide front doors, and paused. Waiting in the cold pre-dawn grayness were a handful of figures: Meg, dressed in a fur robe against the cold; Gleinguin in his familiar wool and yew staff; Liam, Meg's steward – *and mine as well*, Rose reminded herself – and Sion ap Gwdion who held the reins to Gray Star. Rose half-expected a grander send off, but also felt that this handful of people were the most important in her life, and was glad to have a more intimate farewell.

Liam bowed, and Gleinguin inclined his head while Sion touched hand to brow in salute as Rose approached. Meg merely stood gazing at Rose steadily, but without betraying any emotion at all.

Liam stepped forward and said, "Don't worry about a thing, young miss. We'll have everything in order by the time you come back."

If I come back, Rose thought, but appreciated Liam's steadfast certainty that things would go as planned. *That's Liam – never ruffled, always prepared.* Rose took his hand, which made the older gentleman blush in surprise for once, and he smiled just a bit, but no more than might be seemly between mistress and servant. "Thank you, Liam," Rose said. "I am sure you will do as you have always done – your best."

Gleinguin was next, and he gave Rose a deep, warm hug, for which she so ever so thankful. The old healer had become almost an uncle to Rose, and she loved him dearly. She breathed in the incense and earthy smells of his robes, and enjoyed the warmth of his body as she let herself be enveloped by the old man.

"Blessings of the Great Father and Great Mother be upon you, child," he said. "May the Light shine upon you and guide your way."

"Thank you, wise father," was all Rose could say. But it seemed enough, and she stepped back and regarded the old man lovingly before moving on to Meg.

This was the hardest goodbye of all, and Rose could tell Meg was doing her best to remain stoic.

"Rose," Meg started to say, then stopped. Her eyes said everything, searching Rose's. So Rose embraced the older woman, and kissed her on the cheek, and whispered into her ear, "Thank you, old woman, for everything."

She stepped back, and Meg smiled at the "old woman" comment.

"I ought to give you a good thrashing for that," she said to Rose with a smile. "But, I trust that you'll encounter plenty of that out there in the wide world, knowing you and your smart attitude."

"I love you, too," Rose answered back, and she saw tears form in Meg's eyes, and the old woman blinked them away lest she lose her composure.

Sion came up and placed the reins into Rose's hand and gave her a quick glance, before saying, "I've made sure the saddle is girthed tight, but not too tight. And ye've got three good, stout lances on the little buck here, as well as a mace, extra bed roll, cooking pot, flint and steel, tinder box, a few torches ..."

Rose touched the sergeant-at-arms lightly on the arm, and said, "Sion, I'll be all right. Thank you. I've had good instructors – the best!"

Sion became unusually embarrassed all of a sudden, and uncharacteristically gave Rose a quick, tight hug and squeeze, before stepping back and assuming his parade rest stance.

This is it! Rose thought, and climbed up onto Grey Star's back. She took one last look around and then down at the four people who had become her second family. She raised an arm in salute, kicked her heels, and clucked at Grey Star and then turned herself and the pony out away from the compound. She sat straight and tall and drew the hood of her cloak further over her head, not only to ward off the morning's chill but in hopes that no one would see her tears.

Chapter 13

The ride to where Meg had said the Green Chapel could be found took less time than Rose anticipated. The weather had remained relatively mild, with only an occasional shower, and the going was easy. The hardest times were at night when Rose had to make camp by herself. The first night she had barely slept at all, startled by the frequent cries and crashes through the brush by unseen animals. She kept close to her small fire, spear close at hand, and hobbled the horses nearby both to protect them and to feel the comfort of something known.

The closer Rose got to the chapel, the more densely-wooded the region became. Mists clung to the trees and ground, and the woods became darker and more mysterious.

"I'm spooking myself," Rose commented and surprised herself at the muffled sound of her own voice. It had been five days since she had left Meg's keep, and all those she loved, behind.

The exact location of the chapel Meg did not know, but explained that this was part of the quest. "What sort of quest would it be if there were huge signs saying 'Adventure this way?' " So Rose hoped she might find some local inhabitants in order to inquire, but had seen no one for the past three days. Once she had left the Welsh borderlands, Rose had seen no sign of man – no farms, no woodcutters, no coal burners, nothing. And it had given her time to consider what she wanted to do once this visit to the Green Chapel was over.

Do I want to go to Avalon? she asked herself frequently. But the image of the stern priestess made her reconsider. *Why would I want to turn out like* that?

"Halloo!" a voice cried.

The sudden intrusion of another human voice startled Rose, and she turned Grey Star about in a flash, drawing her sword as she did so. Looking about, Rose spotted a man approaching dressed in ragged clothing, his arms held aside to show he carried no weapons.

"Sir Knight!" the man waved at Rose indicating he wanted her to follow him. Rose felt a mixture of delight and annoyance at being mistaken for a male, but ignored it as she cantered toward the man.

The man, however, ran deeper into the woods as Rose approached, glancing over his shoulder to make sure she followed.

"Here, now!" Rose called after him. "Hold up! What is it you want?"

"This way," was all the man would yell, and kept just at the edge of Rose's vision.

This is an odd way to ask for help, Rose thought. *Why doesn't he stand still and let me catch up to him?*

She had her answer as she rode into a small clearing where the man waited. He smiled wickedly as five other men threatened Rose from both sides. They wore remnants of armor, in very poor condition at that, but the weapons they carried looked serviceable enough – swords, maces, and one bore a long pole-arm weapon, his hold showing that he knew how to wield it.

Ah, gods! This is a great way to start, isn't it?

"My thanks, good Sir Knight!" the man shouted as he picked up a spear of his own and stood on top of a tree stump in front of Rose. "Very kind of you to oblige!"

Rose scowled and put on her most dangerous voice, which sounded very odd to her but she hoped she might pass for a more experienced knight. "Brigands, eh? And just what is it you would have of me?"

The leader of the small band showed his teeth as he grinned and motioned at the men about him. "As you can see, we outnumber you six to one. All we ask is that you give us your weapons, armor, mounts, and anything else of value you might carry, and in return we shall let you leave with your life."

Six to one? Rose considered her odds. *And if they've had military training, as it appears they have, then I guess I'd have little choice even though I am mounted.*

"Well, what are you waiting for, my fine fellow? Off with that fancy armor of yours and give over your mount and pony, and this can still prove to be a good day for us all!"

"I was only considering whether or not I'd let you live!" Rose bluffed. "I know so many ways to kill a man, I was debating which would give me the greatest pleasure in ending your miserable lives!"

The men around her laughed and "ooh-ed" in mockery.

Rose stroked Grey Star thinking, *Between you and me, my friend, I'd never hand you over to the likes of them if I had any other choice. You'd as likely end up in their stew pots as their beast of burden.*

The leader stepped down off his stump, using his spear as a staff as he leaned on it gazing up at Rose.

"You look too young to have seen any action, lad, though I credit your attempt at lying," he said. "I've no desire to kill you, boy, but I will if you don't do as I say right now."

The men closed in from both sides, and Rose readied her sword as Grey Star reared up and slashed at the nearest men with his hooves. The men to Rose's left backed away to avoid being hit by the horse, but the men on her right, which included the man with the pole weapon, came on very fast. The leader kicked at the man nearest him who brandished a mace and got him moving to threaten Rose should she turn her horse.

Without thinking, Rose grabbed a javelin from out of the quiver that hung on her mount's left and cast it at the man ahead of her while she slashed her blade at the pole weapon which threatened to unhorse her. *If I were wearing any other armor, once they got me down I'd be cut to pieces. At least with this I have a chance! But let's pray I don't have to find out.*

The javelin caught the man with the mace full in the chest, and he fell with a stunned expression on his face. The leader cursed and yelled at his men to kill Rose.

Rose managed to parry the pole weapon, but it kept her distracted as the leader and the other men closed in on her. Grey Star reared again and struck one of the other brigands as he took a swing at Rose, crushing his shoulder and taking him out of the fight. It took everything Rose had to keep her seat and continue to parry the most pressing threat, but she knew it would only be a matter of time before the men had her. Out of the corner of her eye, she saw the spear coming at her. Instinctively, Rose leaned back and the tip glanced off her armor, and Meg's voice came back to her: "Deflect and avoid. Never take a direct blow if you can avoid it!"

Close! Rose said to herself, and it was then she noticed that the fight was now down to four to one. *At least I'm giving them one hell of a good fight!*

The man with the pole weapon managed to get its hook onto Rose's shoulder, and he pulled to unhorse her. But Grey Star responded to the shift in Rose's weight by moving toward the man, who couldn't get out of the way fast enough and tripped as he backed up hurriedly. The horse trampled the man, and the fight was now three to one. Rose was trying to shake the hook of the weapon off her in case one of the other brigands seized it and succeeded in unhorsing her. But the leader saw his chance and threatened Rose's mount while he shouted for the other two to get Rose down from the beast's back. As Rose struggled, she saw a young man with a large wood axe step out from the trees and bring it down on the leader. The blow bit through the man's neck, nearly severing the head from the trunk, and he fell in a spout of blood. The last two men on seeing their leader felled, and so many of their companions downed, turned, grabbed the injured man, and fled.

"My thanks," Rose said as she regained her breath. The fighting had taken only moments, but she felt like she had been exercising for nearly an hour the way her heart hammered so.

The young man merely nodded as he wiped the blood from off his ax and tipped the body of the lead brigand over so it lay face up.

"Anyone you know?" he asked casually, as though he were asking Rose about the weather or the price of cabbage.

The stranger's voice was rich and deep, and Rose glanced at him. She liked him immediately.

"No ... no one I know," was all she could think to say.

The man was quite tall, and well-proportioned. He had the long mustache of the Celtic tribes and a tanned, pleasant face. His eyes sparkled, and yet Rose wasn't sure of their color – green? Blue? They seemed as though they could be either or both.

"Well, not surprised," the man said. He slung the ax over his shoulder and stood regarding Rose patiently.

Rose felt flustered and embarrassed as she finally pried the pole-arm off her shoulder. "Not surprised? Why? Are there lots of brigands in these woods?"

"Oh, it's full of them!" the woodsman laughed. "Thick as the trees, which is why it was a good thing I was here to help cut them down," he joked.

Who is this man? Rose wondered. "You seem comfortable with this sort of thing."

The young man seemed puzzled by her remark. "What? With the killing? Isn't that what *you* do?" he asked.

Again, Rose felt a flush of embarrassment. "No, it isn't what I do!" she replied sharply, shocked at her own reaction. "I ... I mean, well, unless I have to, of course. To ... to enforce the King's Justice and all that ..." *If I'm going to play the part, I might as well do it all the way!*

The young man nodded as though satisfied with her response. "Nice way to begin your adventuring," he said as he turned to leave. Then with a glance over his shoulder, and a look that made Rose's heart beat louder, he said, "If I were one for omens and portents, I'd say this was rather an auspicious day for you."

Rose climbed down from Grey Star in order to check him over for injuries, and to make sure all her gear was still in place on Willum, her pony. "How do you mean?" she asked lightly, trying to behave as if this were all very ordinary to her.

"Well, here you are, a youth looking to prove himself, off on a quest of some sort. You come to the Green Chapel, and – poof! Just like that, you take on six men at once! And succeed? One for the legends, I tell you!"

Rose smiled despite the gravity of what had just transpired. The stench of death hung in the air. She longed to get away from the sight of the fallen men, and the lifeless corpses that lay staring at the sky with vacant eyes. "Green Chapel? So, I'm close to it?"

The young woodsman jerked a thumb over his shoulder and said, "Maybe a bow shot in that direction. I'm camping there, if you'd like to join me? I've a nice brace of quail ready to roast, and some fresh greens and turnips, as well as wonderful morels with which to make gravy. And some powerful *poteen* to sip, if you're the type who likes a wee nip every now and then."

Rose stopped as she considered. The food sounded wonderful, and the young man was certainly personable enough. But, would she be able to maintain the pretense of being both a male and a knight? Or, at least the former, which gave her some small protection out here on her own? "I … I appreciate the offer, and I might just take you up on it. For a bite, anyway. Once I visit the chapel, I'm not sure where I'll be off to. But, I must visit there first, then I'll see."

"Good enough," the young man said and touched his finger to his brow in salute. The gesture brought a pang of homesickness to Rose, who blinked as her eyes became watery. The woodsman left, and Rose made a note of the direction he headed.

"What do you think, Seren? Should we go join this mysterious and handsome stranger and take him up on his offer of food and drink?"

Grey Star merely neighed and snorted, stomping his hooves as Rose checked him over. One of the brigands had managed to cut the beast, probably the leader with his spear, though Rose couldn't think of when it might have happened. But she made sure to rub some of the salve Gleinguin had given her into it just to help it heal that much more quickly.

"You were very brave," she told the horse, "and I probably owe you my life. I hope I am worthy of your actions."

The horse lowered his head, and pushed his nose into her as if to say, "Of course!"

Once Rose had double checked her gear, she took a moment to look over the carnage. Three dead men lay abandoned on the ground, and Rose couldn't help but feel the waste of it all. "Why couldn't they have just let me alone?" she asked regretfully. But, she didn't feel right just leaving them there to be scavenged by ravens and the like. So, she got out a small trowel and began to dig shallow graves for the three men and hoped their companions didn't decide to come back and seek revenge.

"This is one thing you never hear about in fairy tales," she mused.

The day was past the midpoint, and her work made her stomach growl, which caused Rose to consider once again the offer of the woodsman.

I guess it wouldn't hurt to have a bite or two before I visit this chapel. And Meg didn't tell me what I was supposed to do once I got there, only that it was a frequent starting place for questing knights.

Leading Grey Star and Willum, Rose walked in the direction the man had pointed.

"Ah, I see you've decided to join me! Excellent timing, too, I must say! The quail are just now done, and the gravy is ready.

Like a sip of poteen?" the young man asked as he proffered a small wooden flask.

"Thank you," Rose said, then caught herself as she realized she had used her own voice and not the affected one she had used earlier. "I ... I mean, thank you, that is very kind," deeper and more masculine.

The youth simply grinned and handed over the flask, then turned his attention back to his cooking.

He seems perfectly at home out here, Rose admired. *Unafraid of all the bandits and beasts that might be about. He's more concerned that his meal doesn't burn than he is in getting robbed or killed.*

Rose saw the odd structure at the edge of the clearing and asked, "Is that the chapel?" It looked more like a ruin than anything else.

"Huh? Oh, yeah ... that's it. The Green Chapel, or the Chapel of the Woods some people call it. Don't know why except for maybe the feel of the place. Seems kind of reverent here, doesn't it? Peaceful."

Rose had to agree. There was no sense of danger despite her recent encounter and what the woodsman had said about brigands here about. The structure itself was made of mammoth stone blocks, mostly fallen, but there was a dark entryway visible – mysterious and inviting.

"Yes," Rose replied, "It does seem very peaceful here."

The young man blew on his fingers as he worked the quail onto some wooden plates, and garnished it with some turnips and the fresh greens he had mentioned.

"Gravy?" he asked.

"Please," Rose said. The food smelled wonderful, and she accepted the plate gratefully.

"May I, if you're not going to have any?" the youth said as he indicated the flask Rose still carried.

"Oh, sorry ... of course."

He accepted it with a dazzling smile and took a deep swig. He let out a contented sigh as he lowered it, then gazed at Rose with his sparkling blue-green eyes.

"Sure you wouldn't care for a nip?"

Rose smiled back and accepted the flask, trying to imitate the manner in which the young woodsman had drunk, and nearly choked as fiery liquid burned down her throat.

The woodsman took the flask back and stoppered it while he laughed at Rose's discomfort.

"Takes a wee getting used to," he said, but without mocking. He sat and started eating his meal, slowly, savoring every bite.

Rose sat and recovered from the sip of liquor, then tasted the food. It was as delightful as it smelled!

"You're a very good cook," she commented, and felt a small pang of pleasure when he seemed to brighten at her compliment.

"Thank you," he said. Then, "You seem very young to be a knight. If you don't mind my saying, and I mean nothing untoward by it, but you are the fairest youth I have ever seen in my whole life!"

Rose blushed at the statement, made all the more awkward by her trying to maintain the appearance of a young male. *He thinks I'm fair? How should I respond to that?*

Coughing once or twice as she tried to find her "male" voice again, Rose said, "No offense taken, I am sure. I ... uh ... have been told that before, by other men. Many, in fact!" *Ah, gods! Why did I say that? Now he'll think I like men. Which I do! Just, well, not like that ...*

"I didn't mean to embarrass you," the man said ingenuously.

"No ... you didn't! I mean, not at all," Rose flustered.

"No, no, no ... I can see that I did, and I apologize. I'm not being a very good host, it seems."

Rose tried to wave off the woodsman, assuring him that everything was fine. "No, really. I haven't been told that by very many people, and so it is nice to hear. But I don't take anything from it, all right?"

The woodsman sat down again, a playful grin returning to his face. "I am a poor host! I haven't even asked you your name yet!"

"Ros-," Rose started to respond, "Rochedon. Yes, Roche-don, of ... Holywell." She hoped she had covered her mistake in time.

"Well, welcome Ros – Rochedon of Holywell," the woods-man said looking Rose in the eye, and winking. "My name is Emrys. A pleasure to make your acquaintance."

So, he knows I'm lying about my name ... Does he know anything else about me? "The pleasure is all mine, Master Emrys," she said.

"Rochedon ...," the man paused, mulling over the name. "I've heard of a duke by the name of Rochedon. Any rela-tion?"

"No! No, none at all. Just a coincidence is all," Rose felt shaken, discomfited by the man even though he seemed very honest and straightforward.

"Obviously you couldn't be the same *Rochedon*," the woods-man continued, "You're much too young to be father of a girl who'd be about your age." He laughed.

Rose froze, her appetite all but disappeared. *Girl about my age? Is he – does he know I'm a girl? But, why would he play with me so?*

After a moment had passed where neither spoke, the woods-man turned his attention back to his campfire and opened up his flask to sip, much to the relief of Rose.

She ate the rest of her meal, though it had lost its savor, and thanked the woodsman with a brief nod of her head.

"I ... uh, guess I'll be on my way," she said, trying to act as casual as possible.

"Aren't you going to visit the shrine?" Emrys asked, glanc-ing up at her as if he didn't care whether she did or didn't.

"Oh, yes, of course!" she replied. "That's what I came here for, after all!" Rose headed directly for the darkened lintel.

"Don't you need a lantern, or a torch?" he called after her, a quizzical look on his face. "Or can you see in the dark like a demon or a cat?"

See in the dark? Oh, there's so much I don't know about this place! What am I supposed to do here? And this youth is making me crazy with his questions and his charm. I hardly know what I'm doing, anymore!

"Torch? Yes, I have torches. Of course I have torches, who doesn't?" Rose fumbled around the baggage on Willum until she found some torches carefully wrapped by Sion. *Thank you!* Rose said silently as she took them out, as well as the flint and steel from the tinderbox. Lighting one, Rose ducked under the heavy stone doorway and saw steps leading down into the earth.

"It goes quite a ways," she heard Emrys call after her. "And watch out for broken steps! If you fall, it might be some time before anybody found you down there in the dark."

Placing her hand on the wall to her right, Rose descended slowly and carefully. After about thirty paces, the sloping ceiling blocked the light from above, and Rose thought she heard the sound of dripping water from further ahead, though the sound was distant. *In this place, who can tell where the sounds are coming from?*

Another twenty paces or so and the ceiling began to disappear from view. Obviously the steps continued down into some huge natural cavern or high-ceilinged hall of some sort. The darkness seemed to envelope the light of the torch, and Rose felt like her entire universe had shrunk down to just the little globe of light she bore in her hand. It cast its radiance maybe three or four steps ahead of her, but the rest was black void.

An odd shimmer appeared in the darkness ahead of her. It rippled and fluctuated, and Rose realized she was seeing the reflection of her torchlight off water.

Pool, or lake? she wondered. The steps ended at the edge of the water, and Rose stood there as her torch burned dimmer and dimmer. *What now? Am I supposed to wait here, or go back? Or am I supposed to swim out into that blackness? And gods know what may be under the surface of that ...*

Rose's questioning was cut short as a white boat carved into the likeness of a swan slowly drifted to the water's edge right in front of her. Her mouth hung open in wonder, and her heart hammered in fear at the sight of it.

This is just like the stories Poppa would tell Michael and I – about the Fairy Realm and all that! But, do I get in? What was it that Poppa said happened to people who entered the Fairy Kingdom? Didn't they always come to some mischief in the end?

But the pull of the unknown outweighed Rose's fear, and with dreamlike steps, she climbed into the boat and sat down. Immediately the little boat began to drift away from the shore, and once again Rose was lost in a small ball of light. She could be drifting here, or somewhere between the stars, there was no way to know, no sense of direction. Time lost all meaning save for the flicker of the torch as it burned lower and lower. Before it could go out, however, Rose used it to light a fresh one, glad that she had brought along more than one.

Merlin Emrys took out his clay pipe. His form shifted, fluctuating from that of the young woodcutter to that of the old man, and sometimes even to that of a young boy with bright golden hair and cherubic face, while he had himself a smoke and gazed into the flames.

So, she's got courage, too! he remarked to himself. *And now she goes where even I cannot see … I hope she fares well! For in that Place, I would not be able to intervene.*

The boat drifted but with a purpose. Rose could tell that she was moving in some direction, though she had no way of knowing how or where. She kept her eyes open for any change, any sign that she was nearing safety or danger.

At last, Rose thought she detected a change in the horizon in front of her – a light bluish glow, like sunlight through ice. The boat moved toward a small, dark bay, encircled by walls of jagged rock. She prayed the boat would land her safely and not be cast up on the teeth of unseen rocks below. In her armor, she'd sink like a lead weight and never be heard from again.

But the boat sailed into the tiny bay without incident and gently ground onto the shore. Taking a deep breath and tucking her last torch under her arm to light should her recent one burn out, as it was likely to do shortly, Rose stepped out of the boat and onto the strange shore.

The shingle was firm but yielding sand, black like the rocks about her. The blue-white glow seemed to come from somewhere on top of the cliffs, and Rose could just barely detect a slightly lighter, grey trail leading from the shore up a winding path toward the cliff top.

I guess I follow the trail.

With a cautious tread, Rose began her slow ascent up the path.

Upon reaching the top, Rose stopped and gasped. The bluish glow emanated from a vaguely defined region in front of her, about the size of a small village. It lacked clear edges, as if Rose were seeing a village at night through a falling sheet of heavy rain. But she could also make out small, dim forms moving about beyond the veil. Human, or humanoid, certainly, but of various shapes and sizes from as small as a cat to as large as a house.

The Fairy World! Rose's torch flickered out, and the sudden loss of its familiar warm light startled her out of her reverie. However, the glow from beyond the veil cast enough cool radiance that she was in no danger of stumbling over anything in the dark.

A form that started out small and extremely blurred gradually grew in both size and sharpness in front of Rose, and she realized it was the shape of a woman roughly her size, perhaps a head shorter, and it was approaching the veil which separated Rose from the other side.

A voice like liquid music spoke to her, "What do you seek here, child of fire and steel? Why is it you have come to the

Moonlit Lands? Do you wish to dance with us, and praise the Moon Goddess, and learn her secret ways? Or have you come to exchange gifts, from our world to yours?"

Without thinking, Rose answered, "Gifts? I ... I would exchange gifts ... yes."

"Of service or of craft?" came the liquid voice.

The woman's voice pulled at Rose like the current of a stream, soothing and refreshing, and Rose took an unconscious step forward.

"Stop!" the woman's voice hissed. "You must not pierce the veil!"

The sharpness of her tone shocked Rose out of her trance like a slap of cold water. She backed up a step or two and reached instinctively for her sword but did not draw it.

"A gift of service? Or of craft?" the voice asked again.

Rose thought hard, trying to remember the stories Poppa had told her. Bargaining with the fairy was always done at great risk to the mortal bargainer, seldom with a good outcome. *Why am I here?* she asked herself.

"You seek answers," came the woman's voice, slightly mocking. "Most children of fire and steel come seeking power, or the satisfaction of desires. What is it you desire, child of clay? Isn't it – revenge?"

Rose felt a shock go through her as the fairy woman spoke this, and the small, almost forgotten spark of vengeance rekindled inside her, and Rose felt the blood rush into her head. Her hand clenched and unclenched on the sword hilt, longing to draw it forth and cleave and hack as a blood lust washed over her.

The fairy woman's mocking laughter echoed in Rose's ears. "So much anger in one so young!"

Rose flushed with both anger and embarrassment. "I did not come to be mocked!" she shouted. "I came for ..."

"Adventure," mocked the voice, again. *"Answers. Power. Vengeance. Love ..."* Voices seemed to come from all around Rose, and she spun about trying to see if any fairy threatened her

from unseen quarters. "Service or craft?" the woman's voice asked again with a hint of impatience.

"I seek ..." Rose shouted to shut out the chanting voices, which immediately fell silent, and the air was filled with expectant tension, "answers. Does my brother live? And how may I find him? And, lastly, how may I defeat Carados, the giant?"

"Three questions, two of service, certainly – and the last? Service or craft?" The voice seemed to be pondering this last, and Rose thought she could hear whispered conferencing in a tongue she did not understand. "We shall deem it a question of craft, for what you seek – be it knowledge or otherwise – is a weapon against this giant. Sooth?"

"Yes," Rose admitted uncomfortably. Her thirst for vengeance had cooled somewhat as she had come to learn the realities of bloodshed over the past months. *But Poppa deserves no less*, she told herself, *and Michael, too, if he did not survive.*

Again Rose heard the whispered conference between beings she could not see. And then the woman's voice answered, "A weapon for a weapon shall be the trade for the third. But for the first two, what service will you exchange for service?"

Rose considered carefully if half of what was in Poppa's stories was true. "I will answer you two questions in exchange for the two you answer me," she offered, feeling the possibility it was a mistake to be so vague when dealing with these folk.

"Done!" cried the voice with a tone like that of a merchant wanting to close a deal before the customer backs out, realizing they've been taken. "In answer to the first: Yes. In answer to the second: by seeking him. And in payment of the third – well, ye must trade your sword for the weapon we shall give you, then ye must answer our questions!"

Rose unbuckled her sword belt, and with a tentative gesture she passed it gingerly through the veil. Inhuman hands snatched the sword from her grasp, and in its place Rose felt something soft, like silk or fine linen, and withdrew her hand to look at her prize.

What's this? A piece of cloth? "You promised me a weapon!" she exclaimed, feeling tricked already.

"But we have," came the mocking voice. "Oh, that we have ... And now 'tis time for your service!"

"But, you did not answer fairly to my questions!" Rose felt frustrated and cheated.

"But we did, child of clay! Both our responses were fair answers to thy questions! Is it the fault of the Moonlight People that ye did not ask them specifically enough to suit ye?" This was followed by titters of laughter, which made Rose angrier.

"Very well!" she shouted. "Then ask thy questions, and let me be done with you!"

"Oh, we did not say when we would ask," came the liquid voice teasingly, "only that ye would owe us the answer to two questions." More laughter.

"Ask!" Rose demanded, and as she felt her anger rise, she felt a cold burning on her chest, underneath her armor. *What the-? What is that?* she wondered irritably.

"Child of clay, speak not so to we of the Moonlight Lands! We have shown ye great favor by what we have gifted ye with! Do not be ungrateful."

The burning on Rose's chest became even more uncomfortable. Rose pulled on the chain holding her mother's pendant, and it came forth burning like silver fire, casting a brilliant glow all about Rose. By its light, Rose saw her own face reflected in the surface of the veil, which shifted and flickered like a waterfall. She gasped as she saw the anger in her own face, tense and twisted with rage, one hand poised to draw the sword that used to hang at her waist. In her left hand, she saw the piece of white cloth the fairy had given her in trade, and it shimmered softly like white samite.

"Tricked!" shrieked the voices Rose had heard before. "'Tis we have been tricked! Come stealing our gifts when ye have your own clan beneath the Lake! Aaah!" The voices screamed in piercing tones, and Rose had to cover her ears. She scrambled back away from the flickering veil. The ground shook once, twice, slow and steady like the footfalls of an invisible giant, and Rose saw dark shadows looming larger, coming closer to the curtain of falling light and shadow.

Time to flee! Rose shouted at herself, thankful for the light cast from her mother's pendant as she made her way hurriedly down the grey trail back to the shore and the strange boat. *I pray it will carry me back!*

Rose jumped into the boat, and it immediately pulled itself away from shore, and turned heading Rose knew not where, but hoped it would carry her back to her own world. The further she got from the shore, the dimmer her mother's amulet became, until it stopped shining all together, and Rose drifted in pitch blackness. She kept her last remaining torch until such time as she should feel the boat land, fearful of being lost forever in this underworld and darkness.

The boat scraped as it drew up on shore once again. Sure enough, when she lit her torch, there were the stone steps she had come down. *How long ago?* Rose wondered. *Have I already spent many years in that other place, and all I know are old or dead?* But when she reached the top, Rose could see the strange woodsman still at his fire, smoking a pipe. And her horses looked like they hadn't moved from where she had hobbled them, still grazing.

The woodsman glanced over, then leapt to his feet with a broad grin as he saw Rose emerge from the ruins.

"Saints be praised!" he exclaimed and approached Rose with arms held wide for an embrace. "You came back!"

Rose blushed at the unexpected welcome, but accepted the young man's hug. She felt her heart knocking in her chest as he did so. The experience below had taken its toll on her, and she felt shaken, ready to collapse.

"You look like you've seen a ghost!" the youth said, and held Rose's arm with concern. "Here, sit by my fire and have a sip of poteen. If nothing else, it can shock you right out of any enchantment you may be under!" He offered the wood flask to Rose, who took it thankfully and carefully sipped the potent brew.

"My thanks," she said as she returned the flask to its owner.

"Well?" the youth asked, his eyes bright and shiny, waiting.

"Well, what?" Rose asked suddenly feeling very tired.

"What happened? I've never been down myself. Don't have the courage, to be honest. But then, I'm no knight! So, what happened? What did you see?" He sat as expectantly as Rose had when she begged Poppa for a tale or two, and she had to smile at his openness and enthusiasm.

"I ... don't know if I should talk about it," Rose answered him. She felt sorry when his face fell, clearly disappointed. "But maybe I will ... *later*," she clarified when he got excited again.

The woodsman nodded and shrugged, "No matter! If you will, you will! If not, well, maybe I'll have to venture down myself one day ..."

This must be how Poppa felt when Michael and I would pester him for stories, Rose mused, and memories as well as the poteen made her feel warm inside. *What a tale my experiences would make! If only you were here, Poppa ... You'd be so proud of me! And wouldn't Michael be jealous? He'd want to know all about it. What did they wear? How did they speak? All that.*

Merlin watched the girl as she slowly drifted asleep in front of the fire. He knew she carried something of powerful magic tucked under her armor, and with great care, he eased the cloth out and wondered at it.

Am Bratach Sidhe! A Fairy flag! Merlin was surprised by the power of such a gift. *The girl has no sense of what it is she carries.*

A sudden flood of paternal concern filled him, and he got up and pulled the saddle blanket from off of Willum and gingerly laid it over Rose. He carefully replaced the fairy gift back under Rose's breastplate. Then he unpacked the horse and pony, while he clucked to them and let them know he was no danger as he worked. They nickered and pushed their noses under his hand, each wanting to be stroked once he was done with the other.

"There, there," he said. "You've a good mistress! I'm sure she pays plenty of attention to you. What's that? Not enough, you say? Well, I'll see what I can do about that. But, let her rest now, all right? She's earned it."

He gazed at Rose while she slept and enjoyed the look of peace and tranquility that came over her features as she slid deeper into the world of dreams. "I felt the same way about Arthur, not so long ago," he said to himself. "Children! What a blessing and a curse to parents. To both love and hate the same creature at the same time? Love because, well, we do love them; and hate because we love them so much they have too much power over us. What I wouldn't give to be able to over-look them and not give a damn what happens to them, one way or the other!" But he considered, and then amended himself. "No. Given the choice, I'd still do as I do! God help me, but Mankind does need so much help and guidance! How did they ever survive the other dark times, eh?" He chuckled to himself, feeling both compassion and sympathy for mortals. "Sleep well, my thorny Rose! For dark times are a'coming, and you'll need your strength for the battles ahead!"

Chapter 14

Michael was extremely nervous as he stood waiting, while attending his master in the great hall of Meraugis' father, King Mark of Cornwall. They had moved with as much speed as Michael could muster out of Meraugis' caravan once they had word from Carados that the Saxon army would begin landing on the Welsh coast under the protection of King Royns.

Michael saw a large map of Britain laid out on the huge table, with small figurines bearing the flags of great houses set here and there denoting where enemy and ally were last known to be encamped. He made mental notes of corrections that ought to be made. Perhaps his keen wits and memory for detail might make him a valuable asset to Mark, and he could be released from service under his ever more unstable, lethargic master.

Meraugis winced at the brightness of the hall. The sunlight streamed in from open galleries above where archers stood on guard. His face was haggard, and his coloring more pale than usual, and he felt his skin begin to itch. "I need another drink," he said to himself, ready to order Michael to fetch him more of the precious liquor given him by Queen Morgawse, but his father entered before he could do so.

King Mark made no special welcome for his bastard son and treated him more like a special servitor than a potential heir. Michael noted the man's keen eyes and sharp face.

Like a fox! he said to himself. *Isn't that what some people call him? "King Fox?"*

With barely a glance at his bastard son, Mark said, "What's the matter? Are you ill from your journey?" But his attention stayed focused on the map in front of him, his face drawn in concentration as he motioned for Dinas, his seneschal, to move this piece or that about it.

"N – no, father," Meraugis replied weakly, stammering and swaying just a bit.

Mark looked angrily at Meraugis. "*Father?* Have I given you permission to call me that – *ever?*"

Meraugis dropped his head, as he waited for the usual whipping that followed his father's displeasure.

Mark stood, his hands opening and closing in wrath.

"N-no, m-m-my lord!" Meraugis quickly answered, hoping to avert his father's dark mood.

Mark stared at his son a moment before sitting down again. "No, *what*? No, you aren't sick from your journey? Or no, I have not ever given you permission to address me in the familiar?"

"N-no, your majesty. I mean, yes – I am ill from my journey! And no, I have no permission to ever address you familiarly," Meraugis looked green and tucked one hand under his armpit to keep from shaking.

"And who is that?" Mark demanded with a gesture at Michael. "I don't recall seeing him before? Another new plaything you've picked up from some brothel?" It was clear Mark did not approve of his bastard son's vices.

"My name is Michael, your majesty," Michael spoke up before Meraugis could answer. "I am thy son's servant, and his special squire. I …"

Mark's eyes flashed dangerously, poisonously at Michael and he stopped, wondering what he had said or done to offend the king.

"My *what*?" King Mark asked through gritted teeth.

Oh, shit! Michael realized his error, *not his son! His emissary? His servant?* He floundered for an answer. *Quick, you fool!*

Michael was saved by Meraugis suddenly bursting out in a shriek, slapping at his arms and face, waving his hands as though he were trying to ward off an attack. "Ahhhh!" he screamed.

Mark's face went pale, and he looked at Meraugis with a horrified expression and raised an arm in signal to his archers should they need to intervene.

Michael had seen his master like this once before, an after-effect of the potent drugs Meraugis had become addicted to. He seized him and helped him to lie down, while he pulled a napkin out of his sleeve and stuffed it into Meraugis' mouth.

"It's all right, your majesty! It is part of his illness. He'll be fine in a few moments, though he will be extremely weak and need to rest," Michael explained. Meraugis began to convulse and became bathed in sweat, as Michael held him until the trembling stopped.

Michael saw the king regard him with apparent wonder, perhaps even appreciation though he couldn't be sure.

"You have seen him like ... like this before?" Mark asked him, taking his seat once again.

"Yes, your majesty, several times," Michael lied. "It began shortly after we left the castle of King Lot in Orkney. I fear he may have contracted some serious ailment which has only become worse while we traveled through inclement weather to bring you the news of our findings."

King Mark was shrewd enough to note the "*our* findings," and his gaze narrowed as he looked at his son's "squire." *A spy of Lot's and that damnable queen of his, Morgawse? Just like her to use poison! And on my own flesh-and-blood!*

"Guards!" Mark called for his footmen, and the archers overhead knocked arrows to their bows, ready to draw should he give the command. "Take Lord Meraugis to his rooms and send for my surgeon to attend him. And take this boy, this 'squire' of his, and put him in the dungeon! I will have to see what part he may be playing in this affair once I have time."

Dungeon? "But, my lord! Your majesty!" Michael pleaded, but he could tell that King Mark had made up his mind and that he was doomed. "I have done nothing, your highness! Ask him! Ask your son! *Ask* him!"

With a dismissive wave of his hand, King Mark gestured for them to take Meraugis and Michael away.

Michael couldn't believe the change in his fortune. He practically had charge of Meraugis' entire retinue, and now … now he was being put in chains and locked away to rot. Perhaps even to be tortured. *Ah, God! How cruel Fate can be!*

It seemed an eternity before Michael heard footsteps approaching his darkened cell, and the torchlight blinded him when the door was opened, though he was certain King Mark was among those who had entered the room. He was hungry and thirsty; his arms were sore from the chains that held him upright against the wall and he longed to put them down.

"Please," he said weakly, "your majesty! I know nothing. I swear, I have done nothing but help your s-!"

A fist impacted his stomach, and Michael gagged from the unexpected blow.

"Haven't you learned he is not to be called that?" came Mark's voice from the shadows. Michael saw blurred figures moving, one of which must have been King Mark as he stepped away from him.

As his vision cleared, Michael saw that Mark was attended by three other men. One of them held the torch while another set about stoking up a small brazier of coals, then placing irons into them. The last man stood nearby, sword at hand, as insurance against Michael knew not what. He was no warrior, and his arms would be useless to fight with if he got free of the chains by some miracle.

"Have you asked him?" Michael pleaded. "Just ask him! He'll tell you I can be trusted!"

A fist lashed out and struck him across the face.

"You will speak only when questioned!" came a man's voice.

"I have asked," came Mark's voice from the darkness. "I have asked his other servants, and they have told me some very interesting things regarding you and my bastard."

Oh, no ... And so my sins come to roost, Michael thought. *All those I manipulated and used, everyone with even the pettiest complaint against me, can have their revenge. And there's not a damn thing I can do about it! Except, maybe, tell the truth?*

"If ... if you believe me to be a spy ..." Michael waited for the blow to come, but saw Mark gesture for the man to hold his fist for a moment, "then I tell you, it is true. It's true! But, I spied for you ... for Lord Meraugis, not for any of thine enemies! I can tell you everything that has taken place since I first came into his service. I can repeat, word-for-word, every conversation that has taken place in my hearing. I can tell you - !" He saw the king motion, and the man stepped closer to strike him again. "I can tell you that you've got forces for the King of Scotland in the wrong places! And that you underestimate his strength!" He closed his eyes, but the blow never came. When he opened them, he saw that the man had stepped back, and Mark stood where he could look into Michael's eyes, though still a safe distance back should he try anything.

"And what else can you tell me?" the king demanded, and glanced at the hot irons. "Why should I believe anything you say that comes without pain? Pain, as I'm sure you know, is a good guarantor of honesty in times as these."

"You have forces for Lot in Orkney and Lothian, but you do not know that Lot has sent his wife and sons to King Arthur to sue for peace."

Mark's eyes grew wide for a moment, then narrowed as he studied the boy with shrewdness. "Again, that could be a clever lie ..."

"And lord Carados? He intends to betray you once the Saxons have landed on Welsh soil."

"Lies! All lies!" Mark hissed, though he began to pace and stroked his beard as he considered what Michael had said. *Damn him! It sounds like truth, though. Carados? I've had my suspicions. But Lot and that queen of his? This must be her doing. I know Lot … he hates Arthur as much as I do. He'd never do such a thing! But Morgawse now … Yes, she might do something as clever as that. Set me up as the guilty one, claiming how the rebellion was all my doing … yes, she might at that.*

"And say that I believe you … then what?" King Mark asked Michael, watching him closely.

"For starters, you discredit the lies those others told about me in Meraugis' household," Michael felt he had nothing to lose, so why not shoot for the Moon?

Mark smiled, and the image of a fox came back to Michael once again.

"And what else? Provided that I believe you, that is?"

"You take me into your service, as special agent to the king – an emissary, or squire, I care not so long as you get me away from that … from my lord Meraugis."

Mark considered, looking at Michael the whole time.

"We'll see," he finally said. With a gesture at the three men with him, he left Michael alone, once again in the dark save for the glow of the burning coals and the hot irons that remained in them.

I guess that's supposed to be a reminder of what's in store for me should he find out I've lied to him.

Another eternity passed before the sound of his cell door being opened awakened Michael. His weakened condition and sheer exhaustion had taken their toll and he had fallen asleep despite the discomfort of his chains.

Only two men entered this time – King Mark and one other, whom Michael recognized as Meraugis' butler, the mute. Mark motioned for the mute to take Michael down from his chains, and the man immediately did so.

"You are quite a boy," Mark commented mysteriously. "Your fellows hate you to the point of wishing you dead, and yet as I understand it you have conducted Meraugis' affairs with great skill and efficiency. This despite, as I sense it, your loathing to be in his service ... hating him nearly as much as I detest the fact that he is my issue." King Mark had an unreadable expression on his face as he regarded Michael.

Michael shook his head, struggling to speak, but Mark cut him off.

"Don't try to deny it! I know enough to recognize a lie when I hear it. Beings such as we are too practiced at it to be easily deceived by another."

He considers me to be like him? Michael wondered. *Have I become like the very people I hate?*

The mute helped Michael stand, holding his arm to support him as they made their way up the winding staircase to light and air.

"You have him to thank," King Mark indicated the mute. "He serves as my eyes and ears in Meraugis' household, as shall you."

Michael looked at the large mute with new respect and gratitude.

"Thank you," he mouthed silently to the man, whose impassive face never changed, though Michael thought he saw a slight relaxation about the eyes in reply.

"You would be of less service to me should you suddenly be removed from thy master's service and entered into mine," Mark continued as they made their way to the front steps of his main hall.

And you don't trust me enough not to be spying for someone else, or potentially to betray you, Michael thought but listened attentively.

King Mark brought Michael and the manservant to a tiny cell, like that used by monks, where Michael could rest while he recovered his strength. He made signs for the man to fetch food for the boy, and some wine.

"My thanks, your majesty," Michael said and bowed in a courtly manner. He caught himself as he began to stumble, losing his balance a little.

Mark regarded him shrewdly, the fox-like smile playing about his face. "Don't thank me, boy," he said in response. "You played a dangerous game, but it is one that I am a master at. And I have respect for those who can play it nearly as well as I do. I recognize potential when I see it."

Michael remained silent, sensing that this was what Mark wanted. Obedience and servitude.

Mark went on, "You shall continue to serve as Lord Meraugis' personal squire." Michael's face fell, but he tried to mask it, unsuccessfully. "And you will continue to see to it that his household runs as smoothly as it has. He is of blood royale, bastard though he be, and I will not have him served as anything less. In exchange for your life and livelihood, you will become another set of eyes and ears within his retinue, reporting back to me anything that may be of note.

"Once you have eaten and refreshed yourself, you will attend me for the moment in my great hall where, as I am sure you noticed, I have battle plans laid out. You will impart any and all information you possess in order that I may correct my battle lines and make plans accordingly. Is that understood?"

Michael bowed again in acquiescence.

"Good! We understand one another, then," King Mark finished. "In one hour! Be sure that you are not late!"

"As you wish, sire," was Michael's response.

"Oh, and one last thing," King Mark said as if it he suddenly remembered a minor detail. "Who has been poisoning Meraugis' food or drink?" He looked at Michael as though trying to read his mind.

"Queen Morgawse," Michael replied nearly at once. "Though it is not a poison, particularly. A drug of some kind, yes, but I doubt that the Queen of Lothian intended to kill your ... my master. At least, not yet."

Mark appreciated the boy's perceptiveness and mentally made a note to add a poison taster into Meraugis' retinue. With a satisfied nod, he said, "You will fill me in on everything you witnessed in that traitor Lot's household. You said you could produce a ground plan of his fortress? Good! Then come in one hour. No more! Tardiness is something I detest, and I am not a man who disciplines lightly."

Michael bowed once again as Mark turned and strode briskly away.

Suddenly overcome by weakness, he sat on the edge of the hard pallet and thought, *What have I gotten myself into? What a fool I was to try to play a game with people like these! Poppa? Rose? Forgive me if I have become someone you would be ashamed of! Lord knows, I hardly know myself anymore ...* And, for the first time in many a long while, Michael let himself weep. He held himself and rocked back and forth while he waited for the mute to return.

Rose had a troubled rest. Once again she sensed the prowling presence of the great beast in the wilderness of her mind, casting about for prey. This time, however, she felt comforted by a maternal presence that seemed to enfold her, keeping the darkness at bay.

Momma? Rose wondered in her dream state. *Is that you?*

Yes, my darling Rose, came the reply, though without words but in the felt-sense of dreams. *Go, my dear, and fulfill thy destiny!*

But what is my destiny? Rose called out as her mother's presence dissipated like morning mist. *What is it I am to do?!*

Even as thy heart directs ... bring Hope back to a world falling into Darkness ... the voice whispered as it faded, and Rose awoke.

Loud snoring came from the sleeping form of the young woodsman, who lay with his back to her and the fire. Rose was surprised to find her blanket cast over her and wondered at the young man who extended such care and generosity to a stranger. A momentary panic came over her, and Rose cast about trying to find the fairy cloth she had won. She found it still safely tucked under her armor and let out a sigh of relief.

It was still dark, but the fire burned bright and warm, and Rose stood up and stretched her stiff arms and legs.

I would have thought it impossible to sleep in unyielding armor before, she thought to herself, *but now I know otherwise.*

Rose silently crept to her pony, who nickered at her as she came near. Rose saw that her packs had been unloaded, and the horses hobbled and left to graze on the sparse grass available.

As carefully as she could not to disturb the youth, though she doubted she could have awakened him over the din of his own snoring, Rose took out some of her cooking supplies, and set about making some biscuits and herbal tea. While she sat waiting for the water to heat, Rose removed her armor and carefully rubbed it to remove any spots that showed signs of rust, and then applied the light grease Meg had given her to help protect against further water damage.

"The grease also helps to slide a blade away," Meg had told her. *"So be sure to take the time to polish and oil your armor every morning and night!"*

Rose missed the old woman, and her terse way of speaking.

"Something smells good!" came a cheerful voice, and Rose looked up as the woodsman rolled over, bits of twigs and grass stuck to his beard and face. She had to smile, and he smiled warmly back.

"Ah, now, what a wonderful thing to awaken to!" he said with a playful lilt. "Good food and a pretty smile!"

Rose blushed at the compliment, and this time the awkwardness about her masking as a boy didn't even occur to her.

"Not even sunrise yet! You're an early riser! Don't know if that's a good thing or bad," he joked as he stood and stretched. He paced beyond the light of the fire, out where Rose could not see him, and she heard him sigh as he made water.

He has absolutely no sense of shame, doesn't he? Rose wondered with delight. *Everything just* is, *as though that's how it should be.*

A sudden crashing of branches followed by mild cursing could be heard as the young man floundered about in the darkness.

"Are you all right?" Rose asked and tried to keep from laughing.

"Eh? Oh, fine, fine!" came the call back. "Just thought I'd see if I couldn't add to our meal with a few berries or something!"

Rose smiled and shouted into the darkness, "Wouldn't that be easier to do in the daylight?"

"Of course!" came the reply. "If you wanted to do things the *easy* way!"

Rose saw the reflection of the firelight in his eyes before he emerged from the darkness, briars and leaves clinging to his clothes, and a fresh tear in his pant leg, as the woodsman came back holding a briar branch thick with berries in his hand.

"What's so funny?" he asked without pretense. "Is getting wounded fetching breakfast a thing to cause laughter?"

"Oh, you're bleeding!" Rose set down her armor, grease, and rag, and stood up to examine his cuts and scrapes. "Here, sit down! Let me take that from you," as she carefully took the berry branch from him. "Now, sit down and let me put some ointment on you."

The young man sat, held his hand out, and tried to not make faces as Rose washed his cuts and put some of Gleinguin's salve into them.

Once she was done, Rose noticed the youth looking at her strangely, and she smiled as she stood up from him to put back her medical supplies.

"You're not a lad, are you?" he said with an unfathomable expression.

Rose stopped in her tracks. *Of course! Without my armor, he can see I'm no boy. Rose, what were you thinking?* She turned and looked at him, feeling uncomfortable with the way in which he stared at her.

"Obviously, I am not," she said and stared back at him. *What now?*

He gazed at her for several heartbeats, then with a light smirk he said, "Thank God! I was beginning to think I was becoming attracted to boys!"

His response broke the tension, and Rose felt she could relax a bit. But now that part of her protection was gone she wasn't sure she liked him knowing the truth.

Rose put back her supplies and sat back down to resume polishing her armor, ignoring the look she was getting.

"Well?" he asked, and pulled the log over so he could sit and watch her as he finished making the biscuits and tea.

"Well, what?" Rose asked and tried to concentrate even harder on her task.

"What do you mean, 'Well, what?' I mean, let's hear the tale!" He looked at her with the same eagerness he had displayed when Rose first emerged from the chapel.

"I don't have any tale," Rose replied, but then stopped and looked at him. The sheer wonder in his expression softened her defenses, and she reconsidered. "Do you really want to hear how I came to be dressed as a knight, wandering the forest and coming to the Chapel in the Woods?"

"Yes!" he responded enthusiastically.

"Very well," Rose said. And she carefully and slowly told him her story. She told him how she had always dreamed of being a knight because of her Poppa's wonderful stories, and of how he came to be murdered and her brother stolen away. She told him how she had pursued Carados with the intention of killing him, and of her capture. Rose told him how Carados beat her half to death, then had her taken out into the woods to be killed, and how Meg and her hunters happened to come by and save her. And as she related her tale, the young woodsman shook his head sadly when Rose was telling something sad, or nodded appreciatively when Rose was speaking of something positive. And his sheer regard for her made it easier and easier for Rose to tell her whole story, and she told him everything, even the shameful parts of her story, such as the killing of Taulurd and the death of the hunters in her party. When she had done, the skies had lightened, and the biscuits had burned, but neither one had noticed.

"And so, I came here. I had no idea what to expect, save what Meg had told me. And now, now I have some answers, and more questions that I suppose can only be answered in time," Rose finished her story. She felt relieved to have finally explained it to someone, wholly and completely, and it was as if some weight which had been pressing her down had been removed.

The woodsman gazed at Rose with warm regard and shook his head in disbelief at her story and the courage and strength Rose had demonstrated at every turn.

"And so, here you are," he said in wonder. After a moment's silence, he asked, "And what will you do now?"

Rose looked off into the distance and said, "I have to find my brother, somehow. If the fairies can be believed, then Michael is alive, and the only way to find him is by seeking him. I only wish I knew where!" She slapped the ground with frustration. "The Fairy Folk tricked me, and now I have no sword, only this ..." and she withdrew the piece of cloth, which the woodsman took and admired while she went on. "Maybe I should go to the priestesses of Avalon, though not for the reason Nimue had given me. But to see if they can trace where my brother is."

The woodsman shook his head as he handed back the piece of cloth. "I wouldn't go there, if I were you," he said. "If they had knowledge of him, they wouldn't have been so surprised when you mentioned he had been born."

Rose frowned at what the woodsman said because he was right. "Then, I don't know where to begin!" she exclaimed.

"Don't you?" he asked her.

"What do you mean?"

The woodsman shrugged and said, "I don't know ... It just seems to me that, well, one place to start looking would be with this Carados fellow. I don't mean ask this giant of yours directly," he explained as Rose got a confused expression on her face, "but if your brother was captured and not killed by his reavers, then maybe he's still captive to one of them? Or been sold off, as these reavers are like to do?"

What Emrys said made sense. It would be extremely dangerous, though, to enter Carados' lands and begin to make inquiries. Rose had to think it over.

"I tell you what – and I must be mad to even make the suggestion, but ..." the woodsman said, "if it's someone to watch your back, I'll join you. If you want, that is."

Rose looked at him with appreciation, but wasn't sure if she should risk anyone else's life in this.

"No! Hear me out!" he said and indicated the clearing about them. "I'm rather bored doing what I'm doing for the time being. And, who ever heard of a knight without a squire? Eh? So, that's what I'll be! The squire of Roche – well, what is your name, after all?"

Rose smiled appreciatively as she answered.

"Ah, excellent! The symbol of Love and Renewal!" Emrys said brightly.

"I am no knight," Rose started to say.

"Tut! And I shall be no real squire, but only the two of us need know that! You look a knight in that armor of yours. You certainly can fight like a knight. If you look the part and can act the part, who is to say you are not what you claim to be? Even I was fooled!"

Rose thought it over. *It would be nice to have a companion, even though it will be risky. But, he has a point. If I dress as a knight and have a squire, wouldn't that make it all that much more convincing?*

"Very well, squire Emrys. But," Rose paused for emphasis, "you will do exactly as I tell you, without question? For the safety of all concerned?"

Emrys smiled wryly, and said, "Without question? Well, I have to question that … mostly because I doubt my own ability not to question anything. But, for the sake of the role? Very well!" He stood up, then sat down again. "Master Rochedon? Is it all right if we break our fast before we risk life and limb on this quest of yours?"

Rose laughed. "I guess some questions are worth asking," she joked, and felt a tremendous sense of hope spring up within her at the prospect of this odd woodsman joining her. "So, yes, it is a good idea not to face danger on an empty stomach."

"This will be such an adventure!" Emrys jumped up and did a quick jig of joy. "You know, I've always wanted to be an actor! I wonder if this may begin a whole new life for me?"

"That's the last of them," said the guardsman as he reported in. "King Wihtgar has sent five longboats' worth of warriors, about 300 men in all."

"Is that all?" snuffed King Royns and glared at Carados who towered over him.

Carados laughed grimly and asked, "How many more do you need, my lord? You know these Saxon warriors fight like three men apiece. Plus, you will have my own forces as well as mercenaries paid for by King Mark."

Royns scoffed, "And why does he not join me directly, eh? Why all this skulking about, staying in the shadows, instead of coming into the open and declaring his support for me and my men?"

Carados shrugged. "It's not for me to say, my lord. King Mark has his own concerns, as you know, of which your campaign is but the first."

"Aye, he treats me as his opening gambit, that much I know!" Royns scowled.

"But, my lord, your majesty, you stand to gain by your part in this. You will eliminate an old enemy of yours, King Leodegrance of Cameliard, as well as a potential ally to the bastard king, Arthur."

King Royns stumped about, looking for all intents and purposes to be truly the dwarf Carados considered him to be. Royns was as short and squat in stature as Carados was tall. "True. And yet ..." He did not entirely trust King Mark, nor his emissary, Carados, nor further still these Saxon warriors sent by King Wihtgar.

Carados' drew his face down into a scowl as well. He had little patience for cowards, and Royns liked to play things safe but still demand a lion's share of the spoils. Carados spoke without trying to hide his own mood. "Your majesty acts as though he was about to engage the High King himself, and all his allies, in this war and not just a petty kingdom, independent and isolated. It should be no great challenge for you and your men, plus these mercenaries, let alone my own seasoned fighters, to take Cameliard and claim all King Leodegrance's lands for your own."

King Royns stopped and stared at the giant of a man, hating the bargain he had made, and hating further that he had asked for aid. There was something in what Carados just said that struck a nerve, and Royns would rather take the time to puzzle it out than leap into the fray. *Battle against Arthur and all his allies? Not again. Not so soon, in any event. Not after the defeat he made on us when all eleven of us rebelled! Still*, he thought about it, *Leodegrance would not be expecting a fight and shouldn't have many men ready to defend his keep. A quick action might just succeed, and then ... ah, the gloating I could do after I have added his beard to the trim of my cloak! As well as the prize of the Table Round that Uther gifted to Leodegrance. A symbol of the old High King's favor!*

"Very well," Royns relented. "Sergeant! Assemble the men! Two weeks from now, we move against Cameliard."

Carados smiled like a wolf and nodded, "A wise choice, your majesty. Success!" He saluted the smaller man and left the hall in order to meet up with his own troops. The plan was to come at Cameliard from three sides. His forces and those of King Mark would screen the surrounding countryside. They would cut off Leodegrance from outside help should word manage to get out about the attack and some ally attempt to lift the siege. Meanwhile, King Royns and his men, supplemented by 300 Saxon warriors who would fight to the death, would besiege Cameliard itself. Carados felt sure that, should all go as planned, Cameliard would fall within a week, maybe even as little as three days. At worst, a month should the crafty king manage to hole up and Royns and Carados' men have to lay siege. That would be a little riskier, because the longer the war lasted, the more likely someone would attempt to break the besieger's lines and aid Cameliard.

Unless that is what Mark is planning on ...the idea just occurred to Carados as he spurred his mount. *Is that why Mark is staying out of this directly? Is he saving his thousands of men to come at an enemy, catching them between our forces like a hammer and anvil? But whom?* Carados shook off that line of thinking. It was too much for him, and too indirect. *Give me an open battle and let me loose my axe ... that's all I need! All I have ever needed! Strength of arm and blade!*

Chapter 15

"Oh I knew a fair maiden
she had golden hair
and a smile as bright as
a midsummer morn!"

Emrys sang as he and Rose made a leisurely way through the woods. He had a pleasant voice, with a wonderfully rich timber, and a range that went from deep bass to very high tenor. Rose marveled that such a talented young man should spend his life as a woodcutter.

"Master Emrys," Rose started, but he cut her off.

"Squire Emrys, remember?" as he made a sweeping gesture, careful not to stumble as he did so while leading Rose's pony.

"*Squire* Emrys," Rose corrected herself, "how is it that you came to be a woodsman and not a minstrel or bard?"

Emrys shuddered. "Bard? Barding takes far too much time. Well, that is if one is talking about a proper bard in the traditional Celtic sense. As for a minstrel, well … I have sung for a meal every now and then. Or for the favor of a pretty damsel!"

Rose blushed at the compliment she felt certain he had directed at her. The nature of their relationship was quite odd, and Rose found herself feeling the same frustrations she had while undergoing her training with Meg's men. *Here I am, an apparently attractive young woman, and yet I feel strange and uncomfortable relating to men as anything but ... well,* one *of them. Sion seemed attracted to me, but kept a respectful distance. And Emrys? He's like no man I've ever met before ... like* no one *I've ever met before. And yet, despite the occasional flirtatious comment, he doesn't press me for any particular response. Why is that? Am I fated to be forever a maiden, never a maid?*

Emrys stopped humming his little ditty as he saw Rose's face become saddened by some private reverie.

"You've a habit of doing that," he commented.

Rose looked aside at him. "Doing what?"

"Growing silent and withdrawn over God knows what, and I am left wondering, 'Have I done something to offend her?' "

"Offend me? Never ... no, nothing like that! I apologize. I am ... a bit preoccupied is all."

He seemed to accept her word, and went back to humming his song.

"Emrys," Rose said at last, "do you think I'm fair?"

Emrys smiled wryly and said, "By fair do you mean just and even-handed? Or are you asking if I think you're pretty?"

It was an awkward moment for Rose, and she suddenly felt very self-conscious. But she also felt a strong need for reassurance, so she replied, "I ... uhm ... mean, yes ... do you think I am ... pretty?"

Emrys stopped, and it took Rose a moment to realize he wasn't leading Willum any longer, and she turned Grey Star around.

"What is it?" she asked.

"Do you doubt that you are beautiful?" he asked her almost as if he couldn't believe it.

"Well, yes, sometimes ... I don't know ... I mean, I've spent a lot of time around young men and boys, and yet no one ... no one ever treated me as anything but an equal."

"And you would want them to treat you how, exactly?" he asked in reply.

255

Rose flustered, "I don't know! But more, well, like a woman, sometimes, I guess. You know what I mean!"

Emrys replied, "I'm not sure I do. Do you mean that you want to be, what? Put on a pedestal? Worshipped and admired from afar? Treated like an object of desire, but not as a person with feelings, wants, needs, fears, and who eats, sleeps, and has to use a chamber pot?"

Rose felt he was mocking her a little, and it made her a bit angry. This was something that she was sensitive about, and Rose didn't appreciate Emrys making fun of her.

"Never mind!" she said in a huff. "I am sorry I asked!"

"No!" Emrys cried after her as Rose kicked Grey Star into a trot. She reigned in but refused to look back at him. "My lady," he said gently, "you are as lovely as thy name. Does that suffice?"

Rose glanced back expecting to see him with that smirk upon his face. Instead, she saw that he was quite serious and was watching her as if to make sure she accepted his apology.

"Do you mean it?" she asked tentatively.

He flashed her his brightest smile and gestured toward the sky, "May Heaven strike me down if what I speak is untrue!" Then he tipped his head back, arms flung wide while waiting for the thunderbolt that never came.

Rose laughed, and Emrys lowered his head and arms to look at her.

"Rose," Emrys said, "You are as fair a maiden as any in the land. Do not think that because you do what others might consider 'man's work' that you are any less a lady."

Rose felt a tickle of pleasure at what Emrys said, as well as how he said it. *He thinks I'm beautiful!* she thrilled inside.

"Thank you," Rose said at last, "Squire."

"My pleasure," Emrys responded, "*Master* Rochedon."

That night as they sat near the fire, having eaten another of Emrys' wonderful meals, so good Rose felt he must be using magic somehow in order to create them, Rose talked about the days ahead.

"I guess I've made up my mind about Avalon," she said.

"Ah, you mean because we travel in the opposite direction in order to find your brother?" Emrys asked, and took out his pipe and loaded it up.

"I … I had a dream the other night … and I remember my mother saying to me I had to follow my heart …"

"A wise woman, your mother," Emrys commented and blew a smoke ring.

Rose nodded as she went on, "And I do feel that this is something I must do, you know? I have to find Michael, if he truly is alive."

Emrys spoke, "Oh, I'd believe it if the fairy folk told you so. They did answer your question fairly, even though it lacked the specificity you desired in response."

"And there's something more," Rose continued, gazing into the flames as if she might conjure up a vision there like she had as a child listening to Poppa's stories. "It's hard to describe, really. But I feel like all of this, everything that has happened to me, has been for a reason. Like I am *supposed* to become a knight and all! But why, I don't know …"

"Isn't it enough that you desire it in order to be so?" Emrys asked as he scrunched down lower to rest his head on his bed-roll and closed his eyes as he listened.

Rose wasn't sure what he meant, and so she asked him.

Emrys leaned up on one elbow and looked at her with one eye that seemed to glow with the reflection of the firelight. "I mean, isn't it enough for you to be happy that you are becoming a knight simply because you dreamed you would like to be one someday? Must it have any other purpose than that? Look at me! I desired to be a woodcutter, and so I was. Now, I desire to be the squire to a beautiful lady who poses as a knight, and so I am! Does it change the world for anyone but me? I doubt it. But, it makes me happy, and that's all that really matters to me in the end. My world is what I want it to be, and who could possibly want more than that?"

"Then I envy you," Rose replied. "Everything just seems to be perfect with you around. No matter the weather, rain or shine, it's perfect to you! You accept everything just as it is, and ... and ... it frustrates me to no end that I cannot find the same peace in simply *being* that you do!"

Emrys laughed. "It isn't that you can't, Rose ... only that you haven't. There's a huge difference in that, if you take the time to see it."

Rose didn't know what to say. Emrys' words rang true, but Rose couldn't seem to grasp them and take them into herself, into the deeper resources of her being and make them her own. Something blocked her acceptance of the truth, and she couldn't figure out what it was, exactly. A sense of something dark, something that hungered, that lurked within her, and she knew she didn't want to face whatever it was right now. It seemed too painful.

"Goodnight, Master Rochedon," Emrys said as he put out his pipe and rolled over on his side. In short order, loud snoring came from his side of the camp, and Rose was left to ponder the shadows on her own.

Rose had another dream that night. This time, it was her father whom she saw. He was sitting on a horse, tall and erect like he had the night he fought the giant and died. He sat at the edge of Rose's camp as though he had been waiting for her to notice him.

Poppa? Rose wanted to cry out to him but couldn't seem to move or speak.

Poppa sat, and as Rose watched, a pack of wolves entered the little hollow where she had her camp, and Rose felt terribly afraid, frozen like the night she had watched Carados strike Poppa down.

Poppa sat unconcerned until a rider on a dark horse came into the clearing, surrounded by the wolves like a hunter with his hounds. Rose knew who it was – *Carados!*

But Poppa still sat unmoving, and Carados and the wolves went past him as though he wasn't there, as much a ghost as they were shadows. Carados and his wolves traveled east, and after they had gone by, Poppa turned his horse and headed northwest.

Poppa! Poppa, am I to follow you? What do you want me to do? Rose cried out. Poppa's ghost vanished into the darkness of the wood, and Rose struggled to move or make a sound. *Am I to follow you?*

She awoke with a stifled cry, and looked around her in the dark. The glow of the campfire coals were the only source of light, and Emrys looked to be nothing but a shadow on the far side of the fire ... shadow and smoke.

"Emrys!" Rose made a whispering cry. "Wake up! Emrys?"

Emrys stirred, and his shadow seemed to take on substance. "Eh? What is it Rose? Are you all right?" he sat up and rubbed his eyes.

Rose felt relieved by his presence. She took a moment to calm herself down, suddenly embarrassed by her fright.

"Nothing," she said at last. "I ... just had a bad dream is all."

"Bad dream?" Emrys asked, concerned. "Do you want to talk about it? Sometimes we get useful information from our dreams. I only wish I could have a dream about buried gold sometime that turned out to be true!"

Rose thought it over, but then said, "No. Thank you. I'm all right. It was just a dream is all. I'll ... maybe I'll tell you about it in the morning."

Emrys made a small grumbling noise as he answered, "Very well. All part of the job I suppose ..."

"Follow your heart," isn't that what Momma told me? And like Michael, Poppa certainly is in my heart ... Maybe I am supposed to

follow him. So, does that mean we go northwest rather than further east into Carados' lands? If we headed the way Poppa went, where would that take us?

"Cameliard!" King Leodegrance shouted out the rallying cry. "Cameliard!" He rushed along the battlements and killed the enemy who had managed to gain the wall. He pushed the siege ladders over sending more warriors back to the ground or to their deaths.

The attack had come suddenly, but as Fortune would have it, he happened to have recalled his armies from the field and so was more heavily garrisoned than he might otherwise have been. King Leodegrance recognized the banner of Royns and knew that this would be a fight to the death. Royns and he had been bitter rivals for many years, ever since the passing of Uther Pendragon, and Royns had gone so far as to try to have him poisoned.

"Father!" came the cry of a female voice from somewhere behind him, and Leodegrance turned to see a fresh breach of warriors clamber over the battlement. Gwynnefer, Leodegrance's only child, dressed in light mail and armed with sword and shield herself, fought bravely against the attackers who were trying to hold their position as more warriors climbed up behind to reinforce them. His heart swelled with pride as he watched her dispatch one of the wild Saxon warriors, kicking his body off the walls and blocking the attack of the burly warrior who took his place.

"Cameliard!" he shouted again and fought his way back to his daughter's side. Back to back they warred against Royns' men as they waited for reinforcements to relieve them. Leodegrance had not rested in he knew not how many hours, nor did he know when the last time Gwynnefer had taken any food or sleep.

"Get back to the keep!" he ordered her with a shove.

Gwynnefer gave him one weary look, nodded, and made her way down the broken and battered stairs to the courtyard and proceeded to make her way to the main hall. She knew better than to argue with her father. No matter how much she loved him, she trusted his judgment in such matters. A tired fighter could be a liability in a prolonged battle, and she could help tend to the wounded and dying as well as she could fight at her father's side. And while Gwynnefer could fight with sword and shield as well as any man in her father's retinue, she was not in shape and was tiring quickly. What she lacked in physical strength, she made up for in agility and speed. But, she lacked the endurance to sustain her against seasoned fighters.

"I hope aid comes soon!" said one of the sergeants as Gwynnefer entered the main hall. After the siege had begun, it had been converted to a hospital, and wounded soldiers lined the walls, pallets having replaced the dining benches. Healers and priests made their rounds, bandaging this one's wounds or administering that one's final rite. Gwynnefer checked the bandages on the sergeant who had spoken, and in a hushed voice said, "I pray for that, too ... but it would be best to keep such wishes to ourselves. Everyone knows what we face, the rest is in the God's hands."

The sergeant winced as she bit the gut with which she had sown up his wounds, half suspecting that the daughter of his king had deliberately been less than gentle in order to impress her point. But, he understood the importance of what Gwynnefer had said.

"Riders travel even now to our allies, and father has sent to the High King for aid. You know my father's men. They are as crafty and guileful as my father, and I am confident that aid will come – never fear!"

The sergeant grasped Gwynnefer's hands and kissed them in homage, "You have your father's strength, Princess. God bless you and keep you!"

Gwynnefer had a momentary flash prompted by the soldier's sudden emotion, and it seemed to her as though it presaged something yet to come. She had a sense of other knights, king and princes and noble men all, kneeling and paying her homage. And the feeling was bittersweet, tinged with a sense of doom.

"My lady, what is it?" the sergeant asked with concern.

Gwynnefer shook her head and smiled weakly. "Nothing. Thank you! I just … it was nothing. Thank you for your compliment, but if you would truly show your appreciation for all my father has done, then I ask that you return to your station as soon as you are able."

The sergeant stood and saluted. "I will go even now!" he declared, inspired by the strength of purpose Gwynnefer radiated. He took three steps before collapsing, however, and Gwynnefer had to help him back to his pallet. The soldier covered his face in shame at his weakness, but Gwynnefer patted his hands and said, "I said as soon as you are able, not right away. You've lost too much blood to be able to fight for now. It is nothing to be ashamed of! You've fought bravely, and I will tell my father of your courage and love for him, and how much you were willing to ignore your condition in order to be of service. But for now, rest. Recover your strength. You will be needed in the future, if not right now."

Gwynnefer made rounds of the wounded and dying, and spoke words of encouragement and hope as she went. Men whispered to each other, not only of her beauty, but also of the greatness of her heart and spirit. "She is truly her father's daughter," was the highest praise Gwynnefer overheard, and she felt flushed with pride, not for herself, but for her father, King Leodegrance, and the tremendous love of his people.

"Lord God," she prayed after she had finished making her rounds. "Send us Thy aid! Let help come … from above or from earthly means, I care not! But do not let the dreams of my father die due to the treachery of those who are envious of him!" And to herself she added, *And let it come soon!*

"Whoa!" Rose reined Grey Star in and jumped from the saddle to join Emrys who waited, crouched down behind a screen of brush and peering over the top of a hillock. "What do you see?" she whispered to him.

Emrys merely pointed.

Rose looked and saw numerous watch fires spread about the plain ahead. Tents and pavilions were set up, and an army of hundreds, possibly thousands, camped outside the walls of a besieged fortress.

"Whose keep is that, do you know?" she asked.

"Leodegrance of Cameliard," Emrys whispered back. "A good man. Fair and just. One who dreams of a united kingdom once again, though he has not given his support to Arthur as of yet."

"And what of those?" Rose indicated the banners flying over the pavilions. "Do you know who the besiegers are?"

"Mmmm, Royns of Norgales, an old enemy of King Leodegrance, and … I can't quite make out the others. It looks like there are a few hundred Saxons among them, however. I've not seen the like since the days of Vortigern."

"Vortigern? Wasn't he the king Uther Pendragon warred against? How could you remember that? He was king before you were born," Rose puzzled.

Emrys flashed a wry smile and said, "I may be older than I look," and winked. "Or maybe I just have such a vivid imagination that I think I've seen armies like these before from tales my father used to tell me."

"My Po-," Rose started to say when Emrys clamped his hand over her mouth and shook his head. Rose started to struggle at first, but then froze when she saw why Emrys had stopped her from speaking. A scout came through the brush, and he walked with his eyes scanning the ground, pausing to crouch down every now and then and put his hand to the ground. Rose had seen Meg's hunters do the same and knew the man was checking the freshness of the tracks he had found.

Why doesn't he see us? Rose wondered. The scout was no more than ten paces away and yet he seemed oblivious to both Rose and Emrys, as well as Grey Star and Willum. *Does he just not care that strangers are a bowshot away from his camp?*

The scout seemed troubled by whatever he had found and stood up looking around. He retraced his steps, then doubled back over the same area again, this time paying even closer attention. He stopped at the same place he had before, and his confusion was even more evident when he stood. The scout put fingers to his mouth and whistled three times. Presently, two more scouts entered the clearing and held a whispered conference.

Rose's heart began to race within her chest, and she wanted to ready herself for a fight. Once again, Rose regretted the loss of her sword and berated herself for leaving the rest of her weaponry packed on the animals. Emrys, on the other hand, just held her still, and Rose could feel the heat of his body radiating through his hand and arm. He felt very warm, and Rose wondered if he might be feverish his hand was so hot. However, this was a secondary concern next to the presence of now three possible enemies all standing only feet away, and not one of them seemed to notice or care about Rose and her party.

How is this possible? she wondered.

After a few moments, the three scouts split up, one heading further along to the right, another to Rose's left, and the third walked right past where Emrys and Rose lay "hidden." He passed so close, Rose could have reached out and touched the man if she hadn't feared it breaking whatever spell these men must have been under not to notice them.

"That was close," Emrys said.

"Close doesn't capture half of it," Rose replied and got up to gather the reins of both animals. "I don't understand why they didn't see us! I thought for sure we were as good as dead."

Emrys shrugged. "Maybe the gods are watching over us. Or The God? What does it matter? The important thing is *we* are all right! Nothing happened to us, and that's enough for me."

Once again Rose marveled at the manner in which Emrys seemed to take everything in stride. *This was a veritable miracle, and all he cares about is that it didn't ruin his day?*

"What do we do about it now, that's what I want to know?" Rose said as she pulled a spear off of Grey Star just to have something ready in case their incredible luck didn't last through a second encounter.

"Well," said Emrys, "unless you think you can lift a siege single-handedly, which maybe you can, I don't know, then I would suggest we go and get help."

Rose knew he was right even though it meant abandoning the quest for her brother, at least for the moment. *But who could I go to for help?* Rose knew right away the one person to whom she could go, and she climbed onto Grey Star hurriedly.

"Get on!" she ordered Emrys and made room for him to ride behind her. "I know who will help." Then, praying they ran into no further scouts or sentries, Rose kicked Grey Star into a gallop with Willum following and headed for Meg's keep.

"What is it? What's all the commotion?" Morgawse demanded as she opened the curtain of her palanquin. She squinted as one of her outriders rode up, his horse in a lather. The man leapt off the back of his mount, ran up to his queen, and getting down on one knee, he relayed his message.

"Your Highness," the man said catching his breath, "Arthur, the High King, apologizes for not being able to receive you at this time. He rides even now to the aid of King Leodegrance, and word is out to all corners of his kingdom for allies to come to his banner and lift a siege on Cameliard!"

Morgawse felt like she had just been slapped in the face. *Not receive me? After all this time I have spent traveling to see him, and he "can't receive me?"*

With a cold glare, Morgawse said, "And just what does the High King expect me to do? Travel with him into battle? We just recently have been enemies, but my husband now sends me, his Queen, and all his sons to the house of his one-time enemy to ask forgiveness, and the High King says he cannot receive me?"

265

The messenger did not know what to say even though Morgawse stared at the man as if he might have a satisfactory answer. "Your majesty, my Queen, what is it you would have me relay to the High King? Shall I tell him you are displeased with his response?"

Morgawse wanted to flay the man slowly for his insolence, but another thought came to her. "No. Tell his Highness, the High King, that the sons of King Lot will demonstrate their love and fealty by joining him in this battle. Let it become clear to all that we know and accept our duty to he who is rightfully King!" *Yes, though who is rightfully king is not my bastard half-brother! Let him hold the seat for a little while. It is one of my blood who shall be the rightful heir!*

Gratefully the messenger bowed his head and then got up and ran for a fresh horse and rode off.

Morgawse signaled for one of her captains, and the man rode up to her palanquin and saluted.

"Your Highness?" he asked. "What is thy desire?"

"When that courier returns," Morgawse said lazily, "have him skinned alive. He has insulted me, and I think needs to be taught a lesson. Oh, and bring me his hide once it has been washed. I would like to keep it." With that, she closed the curtains and began to plot on how to be revenged on Arthur.

"Yahoo!" Gawaine let out a loud whoop. "Have ye heard, laddie? Mother has agreed for us to join Arthur in battle! At last, a little action!"

Gaheris was surprised, not only by Gawaine's reaction but also by his mother's decision. "Are you sure?" he asked. "I thought you agreed that Father would never willingly make peace with Arthur?"

Gawaine looked puzzled by the question. "Well, uh ... yeah! What are ye saying?"

Agravaine sighed and put his feet up on the dining table, pushing aside the remnants of his meal to do so. "He means,

dung head, that only a few months ago we were Arthur's enemies, and now we are being sent as his allies? Doesn't that strike
you as a little hypocritical? Unless, that is, Mother is going to
ask one of us to put poison in Arthur's food, or a blade in his
kidneys when he isn't looking."

"Aye, that'd be your way wouldn't it?" Gawaine retorted.
"Just like you to do it a woman's way! Ye don't dare to face a
man in open battle, blade against blade. No, that might put a
scratch in that fancy armor of yours, or worse still maybe on
that pasty face!"

Agravaine merely smirked, refusing to take Gawaine's bait.
"So long as my enemy is dead, why should I care how he got
that way?"

Gaheris was appalled, and wanted no part in further bick-
ering. "Please, G, Aggie, just this once, can't we all just get
along?"

"Do you think I'll get to go?" Gareth asked excitedly. "I
could serve as squire to one of you! Gaheris? Gawaine?"

"What about me?" Agravaine asked, insulted. "How is it that
you don't ask if you can be my squire?"

Gareth swallowed, suddenly ashamed. He hadn't meant to
hurt Agravaine's feelings; it simply never occurred to him that
his second oldest brother would even say, "Yes."

"Not that you'd make a very good one," Agravaine finished.
Seeing the hurt on Gareth's face seemed to satisfy him, and he
let the issue go.

"Oh, now don't go insulting the wee one!" Gawaine warned.
"Or you'll have me to answer to! Pa isn't here to keep you in
line, but I am! And as the oldest, it is my job to be the man of
the house."

Agravaine snorted in disdain, and Gaheris put a restraining
hand on Gawaine's arm.

"G, let it go. Please," he said.

Through clenched teeth, Gawaine responded, "Agravaine,
I tell ye this: stay out of my way. Even though we share the
same blood, I swear, in the field, if you ever get in my way,

I will take you down without regard for the fact that we are brothers."

For once, Agravaine had nothing to say. He recognized that, for whatever reason, he and Gawaine had crossed a line, and there would be no going back. And while he had no real love for his brother, he had no hatred for him either. So, Agravaine decided to remain silent.

"You can serve me," Gaheris said. Gareth's face lit up at that, but Gaheris added, "As long as Mother says it is okay."

Gareth's face fell. "Oh, she'll never let me go ..." he said sadly.

"Maybe not, and this once I might agree," Gaheris tried to explain. "This is a real battle we'll be going into, not a pleasant jaunt. You'd have to stay behind with the baggage anyway."

Gareth sniffed, "I don't care! I'm tired of never getting to go and have any adventures!"

"Well, I'm not going to wait around while the three of you ask her permission," Gawaine exclaimed. "For myself, I will show this High King of ours what a son of Lot can do!" With that Gawaine strode from the tent and called for an attendant to fetch him his horse.

"I'd better go after him," Gaheris sighed. "At least one of us better watch his back. G may have a reputation as a great warrior already, but he's not the most strategically-minded of us all."

Agravaine flashed a smile and said, "No, I believe that honor is mine. But he does have a point – if Mother wants us to join Arthur, then it must be for some deeper reason. And what better way to gain his trust? If nothing else, a successful military action might just show this High King why the lands of Lothian and Orkney shall remain independent of his rule. And if he wants our assistance in the future, he can petition for it like anyone else!"

Gaheris wanted to point out that Arthur deserved their respect and fealty, but he knew that it would fall on deaf ears. Instead, he went to Gawaine's tent to help him pack.

Is that what Mother wants? For us to gain Arthur's trust in order to betray him later on? Sounds like the way her mind works. And Agravaine's. Gaheris felt a chill go up his spine at the thought. *So I best watch both Gawaine's back, and Arthur's!*

"You understand your mission?" King Mark asked, directing the question more at his bastard son's servant than at Meraugis. "Do not engage Leodegrance's forces unless you have no other choice. You are to remain in the back and prevent anyone from lifting the siege. Should anyone attempt to do so, you are to catch them between your forces and those of Carados and his Saxon mercenaries. You are the hammer and they shall be the anvil."

"Y-yes, fa- your Highness," Meraugis answered weakly. He was still pale and drawn having gone through several weeks of terrible withdrawals. The drugs Morgawse had given him had taken some time to be purged from his system, and Meraugis still felt the occasional desire to partake of the elixirs his Queen had given him. He doubted that Morgawse had meant to poison him, believing instead that this was some jealousy of his father's, and that was why he had been forced to give them up. It had been a living hell, and the image of Morgawse was the only thing Meraugis felt sustained him through the ordeal. *Father must want her for himself, that's what it is! Yes. No wonder! He wants her for himself, and he probably had me poisoned once I got here. And then tried to convince me that it was my beloved, my goddess, my Queen who had poisoned me! Oh, but I am too smart for you, my father, dear. Cleverer than you!*

King Mark glanced at Michael, who indicated he understood with a slight nod of his head.

"Good. Then go at once! Remember, Fortune favors the strong. Be swift and decisive, and you shall earn my love."

Is that directed at Meraugis, or at me? Michael wondered as they left King Mark's hall. *I wonder if he knows Meraugis could care less for his love than for his power?*

Michael felt the heavy purse tucked under his shirt. It had been given to him by one of Mark's agents, and Michael was to use that gold to help sustain King Mark's network of spies and contacts throughout the realms. He was also given the task of recruiting more agents and nobles to Mark's cause. The King of Cornwall wanted to be sure of his backing before he pushed for the High Kingship and pressed his claim after Arthur was overthrown.

And that's who you suppose will come to Leodegrance's aid, don't you? Michael thought. *If Arthur arrives, you plan to be rid of Arthur, Leodegrance, and anyone else who may be a threat to you all in one fell swoop. Does that mean Carados as well? Possibly. For who would be left besides Lot to challenge you, then?*

Meraugis' retinue departed without delay and marched at a forced pace in the direction of Cameliard.

"Michael!" Meraugis called petulantly.

"My lord?" Michael inquired as he rode alongside his master.

Meraugis cast a sidelong glance at Michael, then stared straight ahead as though he could will himself to be in the presence of his beloved Queen once again.

"Bring me a draught of her majesty's liquor," Meraugis ordered.

"But, my lord," Michael began to say. Then, "As you wish, my lord." He turned and rode back to the baggage train in order to fetch his master's drink. *If you wish to destroy yourself, then so be it. I certainly won't stand in your way!*

Meraugis watched Michael's back as he rode to fulfill his master's desire. "Don't think I don't know who helped my father," he said quietly. "But I'll have my revenge, on the both of you!" Meraugis spat.

Once again Meraugis let his mind wander in fantasy as he dreamed of being with Morgawse, feeling her hands upon his brow – *the brow that burned so recently with longing for you!* – and of her hungry kisses upon his lips. And he listened to her in his mind as together he and his imaginary Queen planned and plotted. It was with a surprising restraint that Meraugis took the cup of wine from Michael without slashing the boy's throat, much as the thought appealed to him. Instead, he smiled his old familiar smile at the lad.

"Is ... is everything all right, my lord?" Michael asked. He sensed something behind Meraugis' façade, and it disturbed him.

"No, my sweet," Meraugis replied as he imagined all kinds of slow and horrible ways to hurt the boy. "Everything is just fine."

Chapter 16

"Let me think this over," Meg said. She had been somewhat surprised when Rose had returned, and with a stranger who called himself Rose's squire no less! But more than this was Rose's request that Meg assemble as many of her retainers and hunters as possible and send them to the aid of King Leodegrance.

"But, Meg!" Rose pleaded, "Without assistance, Cameliard will fall. And Emrys tells me that King Royns is not a man to be trusted."

Emrys, Meg pondered. *Where have I heard that name before?* She cast a glance at the handsome young man who accompanied her Rose. "Rose, you don't understand. It isn't that simple! Sending men off to hunt down the occasional beast marauding my lands is one thing. But to send men into battle is quite another! King Royns is a powerful lord and has allies with Ireland and others. Have you ever stopped to consider what the repercussions might be should I take sides in this?"

Rose scowled, confused by Meg's reluctance to get involved. "Meg, wasn't it you who taught me that it is a knight's duty to uphold the King's peace? That I have a responsibility to take action if I am capable of stopping someone from doing harm?"

Meg sighed. Rose simply didn't understand politics. "It goes beyond that," she tried to explain. "My people pay me with their loyalty and respect, and I grant them protection so far as I am able. In turn, I owe my fealty to the King of Gwynedd, and what actions I take reflect on him. If I go to war against Royns, it could draw my king into a war he had no desire to embark upon."

"Then send to him!" Rose implored. "Only I doubt that Cameliard has that much time to wait for a messenger to go and come back, then wait to assemble the men, *then* march against Royns in the field."

"And what would you suggest?" Meg asked. "Send what few men I have to their deaths because I was reluctant to wait until I had enough men to make a sizable force?"

Rose paced as she tried to think. Time was of the essence, she knew, but was there a way to successfully aid Cameliard with a very small force? And what did Rose know of field battle? She had led men once before in the hunt after Taulurd the troll. But, a war? Rose wasn't as certain of her abilities to command troops of men. Her experience was with smaller groups of hunters … "I have an idea!" she said aloud and approached Meg. "I think I know how I can help lift the siege, and I only need about 60 of your best archers to do it!"

Meg looked at Rose and remarked on the confidence the girl radiated. *At least I can hear her out*, she thought. "All right, Rose, what do you propose?"

It took Rose only a few minutes to outline her plan to Meg, who was struck by the simplicity of it. It was not the kind of thing Meg herself was likely to have come up with, though when she looked back, she wondered why she had never thought of it before. Then again, that was one of Rose's strengths to begin with – the ability to think in non-conventional ways.

"Do you think it will work?" Rose asked when she had finished, unsure of Meg's response.

Meg nodded and said, "Yes, I believe it could. It will be very dangerous, of course, but yes, I think it could work."

Rose felt a flush of pride, and thanked Meg for her help. "I owe it mostly to you. To be honest, it was you who planted the seed in my mind months ago. You told me that you had used the men as skirmishers before. This is just an extension of that idea."

"You'll need every arrow I can dig up, however, in order for this to work. You'll be going through quite a lot of them before this is all over."

"But as long as we don't engage, I think we'll be successful. Strike and run, strike and run. If we pull enough of Royns' men away from the siege to pursue us, it has to help. Even if it only gains King Leodegrance an extra day or two, at least we can do that much for him! And you can claim you had no knowledge of my intentions when I took your hunters with me. That way your king has no need to become involved since we are not declaring war. A hunting party – a very large hunting party, granted, but a hunting party, nothing more."

"Rose," Meg wanted to warn the girl, but thought better of it. "Be careful," is all she could say.

"Of course," Rose smiled and hugged the old woman. "I have every intention of coming back. You did make me heir to all you own, didn't you? I intend to inherit just to annoy you."

Meg smiled back, and bat the girl on the head. "Don't be too sure that I won't have given it all away and left you nothing but my chamber pot!" she replied. "Now, tell me more about your encounter in the Green Chapel. You say you gave up your sword for a piece of cloth?"

Rose repeated her adventure in the Underworld and her encounter with the People of the Moonlit Lands. Meg marveled at the workmanship of the cloth, and asked Rose if she noticed the design embedded in the weaving.

"What design? Where?" Rose asked as she examined the flag. "To be honest, I never really took that close a look at this. I was sure the fairy folk had cheated me, giving me this in place of my sword."

Meg lifted the cloth up so that the sunlight could shine through it. And there, subtly worked into the fabric so that it would barely be visible unless seen in such a fashion, was the outline of a huge rose in bloom. Rose gasped when she saw it.

"But, what do you think it means?" she asked as Meg lowered the flag and handed it back.

Meg shook her head. "I don't know what to make of it. If Gleinguin were here, he might be able to tell. But he is away at services in Holywell. I will send for him if you wish?"

Rose would have loved to see the old healer and feel the comfort of his embrace once again, especially before embarking on such a risky venture. But she knew there was no time. "No, but give him my love when you see him," she said.

Sion entered and saluted both Rose and Meg and informed them that preparations were underway. Rose should be able to depart in two days with enough men and weapons to serve her plan.

Rose felt an odd emotion as she looked upon his rugged features once again. Sion was as respectful and distant as ever, but Rose found herself wondering what it would be like to run her hand over his face, to feel the stubble of his beard. Even more, she felt a desire to feel his tough, callused hands on her face and skin.

"My lady?" Sion asked as Rose continued to stare at him. "Is everything all right?"

Rose blushed in embarrassment, and flustered, "Of course! Yes! Everything is fine!"

"Will you be needing me for anything else?" he asked.

"No, thank you, Sion," Meg answered for the girl. "You may return to your post." Then to Rose she said with a mischievous grin, "Unless you need help turning down your bed, perhaps, my dear?"

Rose blushed again and put her hands to her face to cover her embarrassment. "Am I that obvious?"

Meg patted her hand and took Rose by the arm as they walked out of the hall and along the corridors. "Only to me, my child. I doubt Sion has any idea what was going on in that mind of yours. But, don't worry! It's only natural for you to feel that way. Why, Rose, you're a young woman now! And part of being a young woman is to want to fall in love, and feel the breathless passion of a young lover as you tussle together. You do know about that, don't you?"

Rose fell silent. She suddenly felt very awkward and uncomfortable.

Meg hugged the girl as they walked and said, "Rose, Rose, Rose … There is so much to know and experience in this world of ours. I remember … well, let's just say I know what it is you are going through."

"Thank you," Rose replied. "Meg … is this … Do you think I am in love?"

Meg laughed, then stopped when she saw how serious Rose was being. "My child, there's no way I can answer that for you. Love? Lust? Who can say? It may be one, or both. But it is nothing to fear, either way. You're a beautiful young woman, Rose, and sooner or later, you will experience love, and perhaps even heartbreak …" Meg paused as she thought back to her own first experiences. "But so what? The important thing is to be true to yourself."

" *'Follow your heart,'* " Rose murmured.

"Yes, exactly!" Meg said not realizing Rose hadn't meant to say that aloud. "Follow your heart. Isn't that what brought you here in the first place?"

Rose came back to herself with a small start. "I'm sorry? What? Oh, yes … well, it was Fate that brought me here, wasn't it? I didn't find you or seek you out. You found me."

"Fate. Chance. God's will … or the gods' … who knows? The point is you took the opportunity to pursue your dream, and look at you now! Leading men into battle, helping to maintain the King's peace. If I had the power, I'd grant you the title of knight. And Rose, what a knight you are! A knight with heart. The best kind of knight I could ever hope to train."

Rose's mood lifted as she took in Meg's compliment, and the two walked arm in arm in silence, enjoying each other's company in the few hours before Rose must rest and then depart.

Let me be worthy of that honor! Rose prayed silently.

"Mother has decided to follow," Gaheris told Gawaine as the two made camp, greased their armor, and made sure of their weapons.

"Ye sound surprised," Gawaine grunted and spat on his polish rag.

Gaheris looked outside their tent to check if any guards might be within earshot before replying. "I am surprised, I admit. Do you want to know her reason? 'In case his majesty, the High King, should have need of a healer!' "

Gawaine shook his head, "I don't understand. Why is that so suspicious to you?'

"We both know Mother has no great love for the King. Do you … do you think it is what Agravaine said? That she means to poison him?" Gaheris asked.

Gawaine exhaled through pursed lips before answering. "I wouldn't put it past her. Between you and me, I sometimes wonder if Ma has a serpent's egg for a heart."

"Shouldn't we do something?"

"And what would ye have us do, eh? Accuse the Queen of Lothian and Orkney of treason? With what proof? Our suspicions? No. Just keep an eye out, like ye said. Arthur is like any other man, and as likely to die from a sword to the head in battle as from poison by our mother."

Gawaine's answer made Gaheris uneasy, but he knew Gawaine was right. With no proof, what could he do? And what damage it might do to them all, Gaheris, Gawaine, and the rest of the family, to accuse their own mother of treachery.

Footsteps approached the tent, and Gawaine and Gaheris stopped talking.

A gentle voice asked, "May I enter?"

Gawaine suddenly became unusually nervous and nearly dropped his armor, while Gaheris' eyes grew wide in recognition of the owner of that voice.

"Y-yes, certainly," Gawaine managed to stutter as he waved to Gaheris to open the flap wider and admit their visitor. "Please, your Majesty! Be our guest!"

Ducking his head under the eave, Arthur smiled wanly as he entered the small tent.

"Not a lot of room in here, is there?" he said. Gaheris indicated for the High King to take his cot, which Arthur did and acknowledged his gratitude with a slight nod of his head.

There was an awkward moment of silence as the three regarded each other. Gaheris suddenly realized that he had forgotten to bow to the King and went down on one knee, followed by Gawaine who also realized his lack of courtly obeisance.

"Please, please," said Arthur almost ashamedly. "There's no need for that here. Not now, anyhow." The High King seemed embarrassed by their manners.

Gaheris and Gawaine stood, and Arthur motioned for them to sit. Gaheris looked at the man he had only seen once before, and that as a child, but he still felt the incredible presence Arthur had. He saw the same gentle face, not much older than his brother, Gawaine, by more than a year or two; the same well trimmed beard and shoulder-length hair that in the sunlight would shine reddish-gold. And he saw the same welcoming smile he remembered from his childhood. A smile that had made a young and nervous boy feel at home and accepted.

"I know it's late," Arthur apologized, "but I wanted to see my nephews and thank them for riding with me to battle." He looked at them with a mixture of sadness and appreciation. "I would rather have welcomed you in Camelot, as your mother intended, but ... well, duty calls ..."

Gawaine sat trying to think of what to say. The presence of the High King, his uncle, Arthur, made his usual charm desert him. Gaheris answered for the two of them, "My King, we have come as our duty bids. And our love."

Arthur looked at Gaheris and was glad for his response. "Love ..." he mused. "Yes, though I fear there has been too little love between thy father and me since my ... since I became King."

There was another awkward silence.

Finally, Arthur cleared his throat and said, "Your mother looks well! I am grateful for her offer to tend the wounded this battle is likely to cause. I must confess, though, I am a bit surprised that she has left Lot's side. I understand he is still recovering from the blow Kay gave him. Ah, what a fight that was!" He remembered whom his audience was and stopped in embarrassment. "Please, forgive me ... I didn't mean ... I don't wish to cause you or yours any further harm."

Gawaine clenched his jaw, but stopped Gaheris from speaking with an upheld hand. "M'lord, your Majesty, it does us nay harm for ye to speak of our Father's prowess in battle. Win or lose, we know our father a brave and noble man!"

Arthur measured Gawaine with an appraising look before he smiled and said, "Spoken like a true son of Lot. I pray the Lord grant me such fine sons, one day, that will defend the honor of their family with such surety!" With that, Arthur extended his hand, an offer of truce or friendship.

Gawaine stared at the outstretched hand, then up at Arthur's eyes, and to Gaheris' astonishment, seized it with a firm grip of his own. Tears welled up in Gaheris' eyes, and relief washed over him at the actions of his brother ... a burst of pride.

"And I pray that the Lord grant me the power to show you the true strength and courage of we Orkney breed! In battle, there's nay better to have at your side than a son of Lot!"

Arthur laughed, his face relaxing, and he patted Gawaine on the shoulders. "I've no doubt of that," he said. "And I welcome you to ride at my side in the defense of Cameliard. As High King, it is my right to have a Champion. Perhaps that will be you?"

Gawaine was speechless and knelt in gratitude for the offer. He kissed Arthur's hand, and tears of pride rolled down his cheeks. Arthur gripped Gawaine's hands for a moment, then let them go. He looked over at Gaheris. "You've grown since last I saw you. Of course, I have as well … only around here," he indicated his stomach, "more than this way," as Arthur indicated height.

Gaheris returned the smile and said, "My King, you look as fit as ever. But, yes, I have grown, and I am ready to serve you. With all my heart, I am ready to serve you."

"With two such fine warriors at my side, what need have I for any other forces? The three of us together should be able to face most anything." Arthur laughed, but his mood became more somber as he thought about the conflict ahead. However, he had no desire for his mood to infect the others, for Arthur knew that men who were inspired fought better than men who despaired. The weariness he felt from the constant battling was his own demon to fight. So Arthur stood and took each of their hands again in thanks, and departed. He slipped out into the camp to make his rounds of the men. He knew each of them by name, and called to them and joked to keep their spirits up. The Orkney brothers watched him from the opening of their tent until Arthur was too distant, obscured by smoke and the dark for them to see.

Gawaine whistled. "So, that's our Uncle Arthur – the High King! Whew!"

Gaheris nodded in agreement. "Just as I remember him. Noble and just. And humble."

Gawaine sat down and practically attacked his armor with renewed vigor. "What are ye waiting for, ye git? If we are to ride at the side of the King, I'll be damned if I'll do it in shoddy armor! Where's the buffing compound? I want my armor to sparkle like sunlight off the surface of a lake when we ride into battle."

Gaheris tossed the small jar to his brother and joked, "You sound just like Agravaine."

Gawaine scowled, but playfully replied, "Ach! Don't be comparing me to that fancy popinjay! No matter how brightly I shine my armor, that git will claim I but reflected *his* brilliance!"

The two worked on their armor and double-checked their weapons, unwilling to sleep, ready for the morning to come and an opportunity to ride at their uncle's side.

The time spent with Meg passed all too quickly for Rose. Archers and hunters were assembled and outfitted as if they were going on a prolonged hunt. Each man carried four quivers of arrows, plus Meg had made sure there was a handful of men who could handle fletching and repairing the arrows they used up.

Sion had overseen the provisioning as well and gave periodic reports to both Meg and to Rose. Rose found herself looking forward to and dreading each of those visits. But Sion was perfunctory in his duties and came and went with no apparent indication that he was aware of Rose's dilemma. It was actually somewhat of a relief to Rose when the time had come to leave. She wanted to jump on Grey Star's back and ride away as soon as possible before she made a fool of herself mooning over a man who was many years her elder, and, in all likelihood, already had a lover. *Maybe more?* But Rose didn't even like to imagine it, and so she kept herself busy with vigorous exercises.

Emrys had dug up a new sword for her from somewhere and Rose took every opportunity she could to practice with it. She also spent time improving her casting skills with both spear and javelin, since she knew that these could be her edge against warriors much larger and stronger than she.

The sword was long and narrow with an incredible balance slightly toward the tip. Rose was delighted when he brought it to her. When she asked him where he found it, Emrys only gave a mischievous grin and said, "Oh, well, you know ... I have a knack for finding such things."

"You didn't steal it from Meg, did you?" Rose asked as she tested the weapon's swing.

"From Meg? No," was his reply. Rose felt that there was something he wasn't telling her. But as long as it wasn't stolen from Meg or one of her retainers, Rose didn't mind. She had too many other things to think about, not the least of which was whether or not her plan would work. And if she could handle the responsibility for the lives entrusted to her.

"I also took the liberty to have this done up for you," Emrys said and handed Rose a surcoat. Rose marveled at the design sewn onto it: a sword, point down, split the field; on the right side was a gold cup or goblet and on the left a large red rose in full bloom. "I thought I'd take the liberty to make up your crest, *Master* Rochedon. I know I am no sanctioned herald, and so it isn't a patent of course, but …"

"I love it!" Rose exclaimed, and hugged him. "It is the most beautiful … most wonderful … I don't know what to say!"

Emrys accepted all her hugs and even stuck his cheek out waiting for her to kiss it, though Rose didn't catch on. "You've said all you need to say," he responded with a flourishing bow.

Rose donned the surcoat over her armor, the gift Meg had given her, and had Emrys fasten the fairy flag onto a lance to serve as a standard as they rode out of Meg's keep. It was just like the time she and Michael and Poppa had gone to watch the soldiers march past, only this time it was Rose at whom people waved and cheered. She even saw little boys and girls point and look up at her with wide-eyed wonder, and Rose felt a sense of pride and sat taller in her saddle. She made a point to acknowledge each and every person close enough to reach a hand down and thank as she rode past. One little girl ran up to her, and Rose stopped as the little girl's mother ran and picked her up and apologized for the child's behavior.

"No," Rose said and stopped Grey Star. She reached out and asked if she might hold the child. Nervous but not wishing to offend, the mother agreed and handed her child up to Rose.

The little girl was thrilled and could hardly sit still as she squirmed to get comfortable on Rose's lap.

"So, what is it you would like to be when you grow up?" Rose asked as the child turned her head this way and that, and waved at her friends who were no doubt envious of where she sat. "Do you want to be a knight one day, too?"

The little girl turned her head and made a face. "No!" she answered as if the idea were the last thing she would want. "I want to be a princess and have knights rescue me!"

Rose was stunned by the little girl's answer for a moment. But then she began to laugh, and it was the lightest and most free Rose had felt in many months as she handed the child back to her mother. Rose laughed so hard, tears began to trickle down her cheeks, but she waved and smiled as she rode by.

Emrys ran up alongside and asked, "Rose, are you alright?"

Rose giggled and said, "I am more than alright. Everything is ... perfect!"

Emrys nodded in understanding, and fell back into place behind her leading Willum.

"Everything is just perfect!" Rose sighed to herself as the keep fell from sight behind her.

"Perfect. Just perfect!" Michael complained as he made his way back from the lines to Meraugis' tent. "I don't know how Mark plans to rule an entire country when he can't even hire decent soldie-..."

Michael stopped short as he neared the front of Meraugis' tent. Something was wrong, but he couldn't put his finger on exactly what it was. A sense of pressure, a tightness in his stomach, but nothing tangible.

Michael entered the tent, surprised to see a woman in grey robes seated to the right of his master, who was nodding his head at whatever the woman had been saying to him. They spoke in low tones so Michael hadn't overheard the last part of their conversation, but they both stopped and looked at him as soon as he entered.

"Well, what is it?" Meraugis demanded impatiently. "As you can see, I have a guest!"

Michael took in the woman Meraugis indicated and felt he should recognize her somehow. There was a deep sensuousness to the woman's face, and she radiated power unlike any Michael had experienced before. The woman sat regarding Michael silently but unwaveringly, and he felt she was looking at his soul. The idea made him uneasy so he turned his attention back to Meraugis.

"Forgive me, my lord, for the intrusion," Michael said. "I came to inform you that the men are in position, the pickets have been formed, the sentries posted, and scouts sent out on patrol."

Meraugis sat gazing at Michael with an odd glint in his eye and his customary smirk. "Thank you, my pet. Yes. Excellently well done. You have everything in order, don't you? So competent, my dear little Michael, aren't we?"

"My lord, if there is anything more I can do …? Do you wish for me to attend you and … your guest?" Michael asked.

Meraugis thought, *So you can spy on me for my dear, dear Father? No, my sweet. Not this time!* Then aloud, "No, thank you, Michael my dear. But I will call you if I have need."

Something had changed between Michael and his master since the caravan had departed King Mark's lands. While Meraugis continued to allow Michael to run the day-to-day affairs of his camp and retinue, he kept Michael at a distance relying more and more on his old mute butler to attend him personally. Michael wasn't too concerned about it at first as he simply gathered information about Meraugis from the mute at the end of the day. But, still something felt uncertain, and he wanted to figure out exactly what it was before it was "too late".

Michael bowed and prepared to leave when the woman spoke.

"He isn't telling you everything," she said in a deep, rich voice.

Michael froze, stunned not only by the words but also by the sureness with which they had been spoken. He felt rooted like a rabbit caught in a snare as the woman stood with a fluid gracefulness and approached him. Her eyes locked with his, and Michael found he couldn't look away, much as he wanted to do so.

"Sharp eyes ... quick, clear, intelligent this one ..." she said as she loomed over him. Her eyes grew wide for a moment as though she had seen or sensed something that surprised her. The woman flinched, stepping away from Michael as though she had nearly stepped on a snake. Her face lost its passivity, turning into a snarl, and she hissed like an angry cat. "Whose child is this?" She turned to Meraugis who regarded her with the frightened expression of a little boy in the presence of his worst nightmare. "Whose child is this?" she demanded again.

Meraugis slipped from his chair, crouching under her gaze, and stammered, "I don't know! Believe me, I don't know! He is a devil-child for all I know! Please, Mistress ... Morgana ... Goddess! I don't know!" Meraugis whimpered and cringed, covering his head and crying while Morgana towered over him.

She turned back to Michael and drew upon her powers as she cautiously came nearer to him. Michael could feel it, and it made his skin crawl even as he felt his soul shrink from it like the nearness of a hot brand held too close to the skin – dangerous and harmful.

Morgana gazed once more into Michael's eyes, and it seemed as though her eyes became his whole world, falling into them through their cold, steel grayness and into the black depths of her pupils. "Yes, you know me now, don't you?" Morgana whispered as she slipped herself around the boy like a serpent entwining its prey. She flicked his ear with her tongue as she continued to whisper into Michael's ear, into his Mind. "I am Goddess, Mother, Fate. I am the Womb from which you came and the Tomb to which you shall go. I know you – or shall know you – to the very core will I know you ..."

Michael trembled, his heart hammered in his chest, faster and faster until it seemed it could go no more. Blood trickled from his nose – he could feel it dripping off his lower lip – but still he was unable to move or even make a sound. There was no escaping, even into his mind as he had learned to do under

Meraugis' abuse. Only this horrifying sense of invasion, this sense of rape, exposed layer by layer, a living death. *Am I dying?* Michael wondered. *Is this what it feels like to die? This blackness and exposure?* Every memory passed through him, from his very earliest experiences as an infant, even to those of being in his mother's womb, his birth, the shock of cold air as he was brought forth into the world ... being held by his mother and passed from hand to hand as the midwives all took turns cleaning him and cradling him ... the sense of profound fulfillment suckling at his mother's breast ... the pain of cutting his first tooth ... more, more memories and all the feelings that came with them passed through Michael, witnessed by this invading presence in his Mind that held him captive. It went on, from infancy to childhood – the playing and fighting with his sister, the stories and laughter from Poppa, even memories of Momma before she died, laughing like a little girl at the charm of their Poppa as he danced or sang for them all ... the time he and Rose caught their first trout ... wondering at the difference between his body and Rose's as they went swimming at the swimming hole ... the time they watched the soldiers, and the sadness and confusion and hurt over Poppa's departure on his birthday ... and the night the reavers came and took him away from the life he had known, away from happiness and laughter and joy ... Michael wanted to weep, could feel tears slipping from his eyes and running down his cheeks even as the blood had from his nose, but he was denied the ability to enjoy the release of the sadness and loss he felt. All he could do was re-experience it, and it went on and on and on until Michael thought, *I must be in Hell.*

At last, it just ended, and Michael was adrift in the void. *I am dead,* he thought. There was no more pain, no more sensation, no more memory or feeling. He simply *was*, without form or weight – mere Consciousness. And in that void, Michael became aware of a slight glow or shimmer that slowly became clearer and more distinct within his awareness. Michael knew without thought, without language, just pure knowing that what he was seeing was the Fabric of Reality, the Skein of Time, and that he existed outside of it. He was beyond it, without knowing how or why. But Michael was also filled with a sense of purpose, that he drifted outside the Skein for a reason – a reason too profound even to be comprehensible to him in this state of pure knowing. And another knowing came to him then, too, and it was: *Rose is still alive! And she is looking for me!* Michael knew that Rose, like himself, existed outside the Skein, and yet she was also part of it at the same time. Rose somehow linked both worlds, both realities, and Michael knew that he could find her, find her in person, if he could get back into the Skein himself. But something blocked him – something dark, something blind and wounded that groped in the void, running its hands which were not hands over the Fabric of Reality as though seeking something, and he knew that this was the Power that had emanated from Morgana. This was the Power that worked through her and that stood between him and his return to the world. And Michael felt a profound sympathy for this Power, the Being that groped in the dark. His heart filled with Compassion, and he understood that this Power, whatever it was, was afraid – simply afraid, as he had been, and was trying to get back to a place it knew and felt safe inside. Willing it to be so, Michael moved nearer the Being, and he sensed an opening that would allow him to return to his body if he but chose to do so. It meant slipping past the Being, and Michael feared that the Power might follow him through, or worse capture him as he tried to go by. But his desire to see Rose, to find his sister, was too strong, and he followed his desire back. The Being clutched at him, but Michael slipped by unharmed, and fell into a different, deeper blackness.

Emrys suddenly stopped, and he nearly stumbled, bringing the line of men and animals to a halt.

Rose turned around and became quite concerned as she saw the expression on Emrys' face. "Emrys?" she asked. "What is it? What's the matter?"

Emrys looked up at Rose, and his face was uncharacteristically sad, with tears forming in his eyes as he answered her cryptically. "Rose, I am so sorry."

Rose felt a shudder go through her, and she got down off of Gray Star and approached her squire. "Emrys, what is it? You say that as though ... as if somebody just died. What do ..." Rose stopped because Emrys' eyes looked away as soon as she said "just died," and Rose felt a panic come up inside her. "Is it ... is it Michael? Is it my brother? Emrys, what is it?"

But Emrys kept his eyes averted as he said, "Your brother still lives. But ... Rose ... I ... I cannot tell you more. Things must be what they will be. I have no power over that. Not this time."

Rose grabbed Emrys by the shoulder and made him look at her. "What do you mean? How do you know this? How do you know my brother is all right or not? Emrys? And what do you mean you have no power over this? What are you talking about?"

Emrys looked Rose in the eye, his demeanor serious. Lacking his usual playfulness or optimism, he said, "My dear Rose, if you would find your brother, then we must go on as you intended."

"What aren't you telling me?" Rose demanded, shaking Emrys a little, but he made no further reply.

Frustrated and frightened, Rose climbed back onto Grey Star's back and kicked her horse into a gallop.

The men shouted after her to stop, but Emrys held up his hand and quieted them down, saying, "She goes to meet her Destiny. If you would be there to assist her, then we must keep on as Rose has asked. Do not fear ... we will be there in the hour of need. Trust me! Rose has not abandoned us, nor shall we be abandoning her by marching on to the agreed upon point. By tonight, we shall see our lady once more. And Rose shall be rewarded for her bravery, by the hand of the High King no less, or my name is not Emrys!"

Chapter 17

Rose rode hard and fast, wishing she could sense her brother and know exactly where to find him. Emrys' reaction frightened her, and Rose felt as though Time were slipping away from her. *I must find him!* she thought, *Before – before it is too late.*

Grey Star began to fight Rose's control, however. He slowed her pace and made Rose work very hard to keep the beast moving forward.

"What is it?" she demanded and kicked her heels into the horse, but Grey Star finally stopped and reared up, neighing. The horse snorted and stomped its hooves, and Rose had to turn the beast in a circle as it refused to go forward any longer. "Seren? What is it? What's wrong?" Rose felt a tickle of danger and seized a javelin from its quiver just as she heard the whistle of an arrow whip by her. *Damn it!* Rose realized that the horse had been trying to warn her of danger and that she had been too preoccupied and headstrong to listen.

The arrow had come from Rose's right and from behind, so she leapt off her mount and ran to the shelter of a large tree pressing her back against it. Another arrow struck the bole of the tree with a loud *thunk!* just as Rose gained its shelter. *Too close!* Rose could feel the adrenalin coursing through her veins, and her senses became heightened, aware of every rustle of leaves, every breath of wind. *What a fool I was to rush off like that.*

Now what chance do I have to find Michael with some enemy scout out there ready to pick me off like some poor hind the moment I expose myself? Armor or no, I'm stuck.

Grey Star snorted again, and Rose prayed that the scout would at least leave the beast unmolested. *No reason Seren Ll-wyd should suffer because of my recklessness.* Rose heard the crack of a twig, and she froze, ready to dodge or cast her weapon as the opportunity arose. But there was no further sound, and Rose realized the scout was trying to move into position to cut her down where she crouched. She also realized the irony of the situation. *Here I am, pinned down by an archer, exactly as I planned to do to Royns and his men. At least I know it is an effective strategy!*

"All right! Come out!" yelled a voice. "I know you're there, and there's no chance for you to escape. Step out where I can see you and surrender yourself."

He can't see me! Rose began to think quickly. *That means he must be either this way, or that way ... but how close?*

"Your beast has gotten away, so don't think about trying to make a break for it. I'd be able to shoot you down before you got three paces anyway!" the voice shouted. Rose was able to discern which side it was coming from, but she still had no idea of the distance. She had a plan, a very dangerous and reckless plan, but one she hoped would catch the scout by surprise.

There was another rustle of leaves further off to Rose's right, and Rose knew it was now or never. With a quick prayer to the gods, Rose launched herself in the direction of the rustle. She heard a surprised grunt and saw the scout as he pulled back his bowstring and fired in her direction. Rose saw the arrow leave the string and could see its trajectory coming straight at her. It was as if everything had gone into slow motion, very surreal, and Rose's body simply shifted so that the arrow glanced away from her before it contacted her shoulder. Had she wanted to, Rose felt she could have snatched the arrow with her bare hands, things seemed so clear to her. The archer was already fumbling for a second arrow, his face strained with concentration and surprise, as time seemed to catch up to Rose, and she bowled him over in a tackle. Rose thrust her plated shoulder into the man's face as she connected, and his head snapped back, his nose broken by the impact, and he went down unconscious.

Rose stood over him panting, catching her breath, and counting her blessings at her incredible good luck. A moment later, Grey Star trotted into view, and Rose looked at the fairy flag waving on the lance tied to the horse's back. What was it the People of the Moonlit Lands had told her? Something about it bringing good luck to its owner? "Well, maybe I did get the good end of the deal after all," Rose said to herself as she checked the scout over for weapons.

Rose put the javelin back in place, then rechecked her armor and supplies making sure everything was secure before dragging the unconscious man out and tying him up with a length of leather cord. Rose intended to question him, though she felt sure he'd never reveal anything to her without torture, and Rose knew she could never torture anybody. Except maybe Carados, but she might find herself unable to harm even him in such a fashion. Such helpless victimization sickened her.

Splashing some water on the scout's face, Rose got him to come to after a few minutes.

"Spuh! Wha' ... what the?" the man sputtered as he regained consciousness. When he saw Rose squatting down in front of him, his own weapons in her hands, he spat at her. "Ptuh! What do you want? What ... why, you're a ... a ..."

"Woman?" Rose finished for him. "That's right, I am. You just got beaten by a girl! How does that feel, eh?" Rose watched him as the information sank in. "But obviously I'm like no girl you've ever met before. I'm a little more – dangerous." As she said that, she thrust the man's dirk into the ground between his legs, far too close for the scout's comfort. He flinched and crept his crotch back a hand's width, eyes wary and watchful for Rose's next move. "Now, I'd like to know – whom do you serve? To whom do you owe allegiance?"

The man considered carefully while Rose plucked the dirk from the ground and played with its edge looking at him. He opted to remain silent, refusing to answer.

"You know," Rose said casually. "I used to live on a farm. I've helped my Poppa geld animals before. I always thought, 'That must be really painful,' you know? It doesn't take much. Just pulled down, and a quick- ..." Rose made a swift cutting motion, and saw the man wince. "Even if it doesn't hurt all that much, or for very long, I do know one thing. I know that that beast will never sire any children." Rose squatted and slashed the blade in front of the man's waist.

The scout tried to slide back further away from her, but he backed into the stump of a tree and could go no further. He swallowed, looking up at Rose and attempting to gauge her seriousness.

"Look, I ... uh," he said. "I'm just a volunteer is all, all right? You know, just out here because I'm good at tracking and hunting. When the army came by looking for conscripts, I figured it was either volunteer or get volunteered against my will, if you take my meaning."

"Oh, so trying to kill me was ... what? Nothing personal? Just doing my bit?" Rose asked with a scowl.

"Well, uh ... yeah, exactly! Nothing personal."

"So I suppose if I were to make a gelding out of you," Rose stood and pulled out a sharpening stone from her kit, "I could say the same thing. You know, nothing personal, just doing my bit for King and country."

The scout swallowed again and began to sweat. "Hey, listen! Really! I don't ... don't know anything, anything useful. So, uhm ... just, uh, let me go, okay? Or take me in, I don't care. Just please, please don't!"

Rose began to run the dirk over the stone slowly. "Poppa always said, 'If you want to spare the animal any hurt, make sure your knife is good and sharp, and heat it over a flame to help seal the wound as quick as you can.' Poppa was like that,"

Rose said, "before reavers came and killed him. Men like you who were 'just doing their bit,' nothing personal."

Rose saw that the scout was beginning to shake, and she felt proud of herself for bluffing so well. She could sense that this man was not like Carados, nor like the reavers who had destroyed her farm and family. This was, as far as she could tell, just an average man who perhaps hoped to win a little fame and honor by fighting for whomever he happened to live near.

"All I want to know," Rose said as she put the stone away and tucked the dirk into her belt, "is whom you were scouting for. To whom do you swear allegiance?"

The scout looked at Rose's face for a moment, and then finally answered, "Royns. King Royns of Norgales. But I swear to you, had I known you were a woman, I would never have shot at you."

"And why is that?" Rose asked. "Am I not a threat just because I am a woman? As you can see, a woman can do plenty of damage to a man."

The scout thought about it, then said, "I ... just never thought about it before. It just seems wrong, somehow. Women shouldn't be out fighting, that's man's work! Women are what we fight for ... to protect. At least, that's what I fight for. To keep my family safe and maybe add some more land to keep ourselves fed through the winter."

Rose knew he was telling the truth, and sympathized. *Is that what most men fight and die for? Land? The concept that they are protecting and providing for their families?* There didn't seem anything particularly ugly or evil in that. "One more question," Rose crouched down and looked the scout in the eye. "How many scouts are you aware of between here and Cameliard? How often do they patrol, and how far apart?"

The scout licked his lips, wondering if he should say anything more or not. To tell this woman warrior more might endanger other scouts, and he'd be a traitor then, not just a captive. "I ... can't say. Kill me if you must, but I will not betray anyone because of my clumsiness and lack of skill."

Rose stood and looked down at him with the darkest scowl she could muster. But she knew he was sincere, and that the only way she would get any more information would be to hurt him in earnest, and that she wouldn't do. "A fair answer," she said. "I suppose I should kill you to keep you from calling for help after I am gone, or of wriggling free, but I'll have to risk it. Like you, I do what I must because people I love are in danger, and so I don't have time to dally here with you."

Rose gathered up the scout's bow and arrows and tied them onto her horse. Using extra gut that she found on the scout to replace a broken bowstring, Rose tied the scout more firmly. She rolled him face down and tied his hands to his feet, and then looped a length of cord around the man's neck in a slipknot. "The more you struggle, the tighter this will get," Rose warned him. "If your friends don't happen by in the next few hours or so, some of mine will. They will see to it that you are taken care of, never fear. You'll not be harmed nor sold into slavery, nothing like that. You'll be treated fairly, more fairly I think than the man you serve would treat us. In any case, fare well!"

"Lady?" the scout called after Rose, "Whom should I say captured me? By what name are you known?"

Rose paused, then said, "Tell anyone who comes after me that it was the Rose of Camelot who captured you. Yes, I rather like that! Ha!" Rose laughed, clucked at Grey Star to get the animal into a trot and moved off.

"Hold your position!" Carados roared at his men. "Or by the gods, I'll tear your hearts out myself!" He spurred his horse along the line of pikemen and looked across the field to where Arthur and his forces had broken through the outer pickets. Carados longed to charge across and engage the High King directly, but he understood Mark's plan and knew his best chances of success lay in holding his position. Let Mark's mercenaries drive Arthur onto his spears, trapped between two hostile armies.

Arthur had come swiftly, as he always seemed to do, and had cut through the outer lines of their defenses quickly. But the High King had also, in Carados' opinion, behaved too rashly and too recklessly and now was cut off by the extra men King Mark had sent for just such an opportunity.

"Come on! Come on!" Carados muttered, as restless as his mount. The men were eager to engage in the fighting as well and shifted impatiently. The dozen or so Saxons he had hand-picked to become his own personal bodyguard looked at him with dark faces, curious as to why they were not engaging the enemy. "You'll get your chance, never fear!" he shouted at them. "Revenge for Octa and Horsa!" At this, the Saxons grinned and gripped their great spears, even more eager for a fight.

The line of Arthur's men broke and came flooding toward Carados' position at last, a tide of men, steel, and horses. Carados swung his mount and raised his axe as a signal to the other horsemen of his company. "Remember Bedgrayn!" he yelled. In moments the world was a chaos of screams, shouts, and the smell of sweat, blood, and spilled entrails. To Carados it was a warrior's paradise.

Gaheris rode at Arthur's back while Gawaine protected Arthur's flank. The three fought bravely and well, as did Kay and several other of Arthur's knights. But Gaheris was tiring. It had been a long while since he had seen this much exercise, and he regretted his early departure from Meg's training. Her instruction had been of tremendous help, though, and he knew he had only managed to keep up with his uncle and his brother because of it.

"Camelot!" shouted Arthur as he charged headlong into another fray. He was like a god of war in Gaheris' eyes. It was almost as though Arthur glowed in battle. And Gawaine? Gawaine seemed to grow in strength with each engagement as if his strength, like the sun, increased with each passing moment. He swung his sword so savagely that he was almost a danger to anyone around him, friend or foe, but with such deadly force that he hewed through armor and mail as though they were wood.

"Arthur! My King!" Gaheris shouted trying to get Arthur's attention and alert him to the danger he perceived they were in. "We have come too far! We must wait for reinforcements!" But Arthur either couldn't hear or chose not to respond, only lifted up his visor briefly and flashed a smile, then lowered it again and set to with the enemy who had rushed him. Gaheris had no choice but to ride to his aid while Gawaine helped beat back the men trying to pull Arthur from his mount.

"Quite a battle, little brother, eh?" Gawaine asked as the three fought side by side. His sword dripped with blood and gore and was badly chipped as well. Gawaine himself had a gash upon his thigh, but paid it no mind, and laughed when Gaheris pointed it out to him. "'Tis nothing! Just a scratch." He did, however, allow his brother to wrap a cloth around it when there was a small break in the fighting.

"You fight bravely," Arthur said and lifted his visor to survey how the battle was going. His face seemed alive, radiant even, and Gaheris marveled at these two men who seemed more like children at play than soldiers or men of war.

"My King, shouldn't we wait for reinforcements?" Gaheris asked.

"Reinforcements?" Arthur nearly laughed but did not want to embarrass his nephew. "We *are* the reinforcements!"

Gawaine grinned and adjusted his shield strap.

"Or, if you prefer, we ride to gather our reinforcements from the castle itself," Arthur pointed at the walls in the distance. "If we can get close enough, King Leodegrance I'm sure will sally forth and assist us."

Gaheris was confused, so Arthur explained quickly before closing his visor, readying his shield and signaling for his men to charge the next line. "We have the element of speed, and so I utilize it to the fullest. How else do you think we could have come so far so fast? Camelot!" he shouted and kicked his horse into a charge.

Gawaine followed suit, and Gaheris did likewise, once again trying to keep up with the two madmen with whom he rode.

Michael awoke to shouting and the clash of metal. The smell of smoke stung his nostrils, and he coughed once or twice before opening his eyes. The daylight hurt for a moment, and his body felt extraordinarily heavy until Michael realized it was due to the weight of a female body draped over him.

Who-? Where am I? Then the memory came back to him. *Morgana! But what has happened to her? And where is Meraugis?*

Michael crawled out from under the comatose Morgana, noting the spot of drool that had stained his surcoat from her unconscious mouth. He checked her quickly and saw that she breathed. But she remained strangely unresponsive. He laid her head on a pillow, then stood and tried to take in what was happening.

A battle? But with whom? And so soon? Could it be-?

Michael rushed to the opening and ducked down as he heard riders charge past lest they mistake him for a soldier. He saw the camp in total disarray. Some of the baggage was burning, and men were forming lines to try and put it out before it spread. Other tents had been knocked down or burned, and Mark's men hurried from place to place. Meraugis was nowhere to be seen, and for that Michael felt strangely relieved.

"Master Michael?" shouted one of the pages as he recognized Michael. "Thank the heavens! What shall we do? The King has charged through like a storm, leaving wreckage and death behind."

"Which king?" Michael asked as he approached the lad. The boy was perhaps seven or eight, and clearly frightened.

"Arthur ... the High King, who else?" the boy answered. "Master, are you all right?"

Michael wavered a bit, still unsteady after his experience with the witch, Morgana. "I'll be fine. I just need a moment ..." He felt small hands under his arms to support him, and Michael was grateful for the assistance.

"What's your name?" he asked the page. Michael knew he aught to know, but for the first time his exceptional memory seemed to fail him.

"Thomas," the boy replied. "Don't you remember me, sir?"

It suddenly struck Michael how odd it was to be called "sir" when he was still but a youth himself, only a few years older than the boys who served under him.

"Do you know where our master is? Did you see where Lord Meraugis went?"

Thomas shook his head. "No, Master Michael. I ... I think I saw him ride that way, in the direction of where the High King went, but with all the knights in their armor, I can't be sure. They all look the same to me!"

I need to teach the pages some heraldry, then, Michael thought to himself. *They should be able to recognize who's who from the insignia.*

"You're a good lad, Thomas," Michael said feeling much older than his years. "I want to ask you one more thing – do you know how close the fighting is?"

Thomas' eyes grew wide for a moment as he replied, "Very!"

Michael pondered, the memory of his experience when he was ... dead? ... and the sense of how close he was to his sister beckoned to him. Rose was close, very close to this place. *But where? How do I find her?*

"Master Michael?" Thomas asked with concern.

Michael knew what he had to do, or at least attempt to do, and had a sense that it meant not coming back ... at least, not into Meraugis' service again, for which he was thankful.

"Page Thomas, I'm going to do something for you. I am promoting you to squire. And I will tell you this: in my tent, beneath the spare tunics I keep in my chest, there is a small leather bag. It will feel heavy. Please fetch that for me and come right back."

Thomas was stunned with the unexpected promotion, but ran off to do as Michael had asked.

If I'm going to leave, a little gold would certainly prove helpful in starting a new life!

Thomas came back right away and handed the pouch of King Mark's gold over to Michael. Michael opened it and counted out ten shiny gold coins and placed them into Thomas' hands.

"Consider this as an advance on your future pay," he told the boy, though that much gold would have taken the lad a lifetime to earn. Michael stood and waited for the world to stop swaying before he said, "Have a good life, Master Thomas! God knows we deserve it." With that, Michael walked off, pausing occasionally to wait for his dizziness to pass. He saw the dead, as he made his way through the camp, and felt his heart grow sad and heavy when he recognized the body of the mute butler lying near the outskirts of the camp. His throat had been cut, most probably by their mad master, Meraugis, himself. Michael said a silent prayer for the man's spirit, for he had been one of the few people Michael considered a friend in the past year.

And for me, Lord, Michael prayed, *Help me find my sister! Let me go home!*

Carefully slipping from tree to tree, Michael followed the path the riders had made. He knew where they were headed, and he wondered how far they would make it.

"Arthur! Arthur!" Carados bellowed as he fought. Arthur and his forces had turned aside and ridden along the line of pikemen at the last second, drawing Carados and his knights out into the open and away from the foot soldiers. Unlike the last time they had faced each other, Carados was determined to engage Arthur one-on-one. But, like the last time they had fought, Arthur kept slipping away while Carados was forced to engage one or another of Arthur's fellow knights.

This time it was Carados' turn to ride too far from his reinforcements. His bodyguard had fallen far behind as he charged into the midst of Arthur's men. Trumpets blared, and Carados looked to see his line being attacked by archers on the flank. *This can't be happening!* he thought as he watched the far edge of his line disintegrate into chaos. *Fools! Let them die if they're too cowardly to stand and fight!*

"Arthur!" he growled and whirled his mount around to engage the next of Arthur's men.

"I'm not he," said a knight with a northern accent, "but if ye'd like t'have a go at him, then ye'll have to have a go at me!" and charged, brandishing his sword.

"More meat for my hounds," Carados said as he charged as well.

The two men met with a shock, horses rearing and slashing at each other with hooves while their riders met sword to axe. They exchanged a furious round of blows, Carados landing a hard knock on the knight's right shoulder. So hard he thought he might have gotten through the armor, or at least numb the knight's sword arm. But the knight stubbornly held onto his weapon and bashed his shield into Carados with such force that it pushed both Carados and his mount away for a moment.

"Ach! Now ye've made me mad!" said the knight. He lifted his visor and shook his arm as though shaking off the effects of the blow. Carados thought he recognized the face for it bore a resemblance to King Lot.

"You must be a son of that traitor, Lot," Carados taunted. "Which one are you? Not that ape son of his ... what is his name?"

"Gawaine!" Gawaine answered, his face turning red with rage. "Aye, I be he! And who might you be, ye great shite? King of Turds?"

Carados' voice growled with danger as he answered, "I am Carados! And I am your death!"

Gawaine lowered his visor, and the two men charged each other once again. Gawaine's blows were wild but powerful, and Carados had to use all his skill to avoid being struck by any of them. He used every trick he knew, but Gawaine was fighting so blindly, so instinctively, that he failed to be drawn in by any attempt to leave an opening that Carados could strike through. Not only that, but for the first time in his life, Carados found himself on the defensive. One of Gawaine's wild blows struck Carados' horse, flashing through the barding covering the horse's neck, and it collapsed. Carados was caught by surprise as the great beast fell over, and he was pinned beneath its weight.

"Ye're whose death?" Gawaine taunted back. However, Gawaine himself was forced to turn and fight as more of Carados' men gained the field, and he was drawn away from the giant. "I'll be back, don't ye worry!" he shouted while Carados struggled to free himself from under his horse.

Gwynnefer heard the trumpets blare and hurried out to see what was going on. Her father, King Leodegrance, came down from off the walls and called for his horse and knights.

"Father, what is it?" Gwynnefer shouted to him. "What's going on?"

Leodegrance gave her a weary smile and shouted back, "The King! The High King approaches our walls! Help has come at last!" With a cheer, he and a small band of horsemen rode out through the gates where a slightly larger group of knights were battling with a much larger group of footmen. Together, the High King's forces and those of Cameliard cut down or drove off enough men that they were able to make it back to the keep.

"The King! The High King has been injured!" cried one of the knights in Arthur's retinue. The knight threw off his helm, exposing a handsome youth with a concerned expression written all over his face, and helped the King down from off his horse.

"Help me get him inside!" Gaheris yelled, "And bring your best surgeons!"

Gwynnefer hurried over and helped take the other side of Arthur from Gaheris, and the two of them carried him inside.

Arthur's face was quite ashen, and Gwynnefer saw that he had a terrible gash across his left ribs. Remnants of Arthur's shield, mere splinters and ruined wood, testified to the violence of the fighting in which he had been engaged.

"Help me take off his armor," she said softly but firmly to the knight helping her. "I am one of my father's best surgeons, and I will make sure your king survives."

Gaheris looked at the fair daughter of Leodegrance, and with tears in his eyes he pleaded, "Please be sure that you do! The future – all the hope for the future – lies with this man."

Gwynnefer was surprised by the youth's earnestness, and she realized that here was a knight who loved this king as much as she loved her father. Gwynnefer touched Gaheris on the hand and said, "If it is within God's will that he live, I will do everything I can to be an instrument of that healing. Now, please go ... I have work to do."

Gaheris reluctantly stepped away. He wiped the tears from his eyes, strode back into the courtyard, and called for his horse.

"Hold on!" King Leodegrance said. "And where do you think you're going?"

"Forgive me, my lord," Gaheris answered, then realized to whom he was speaking. "I mean, your majesty! But my brother, Gawaine, is still out there, and I must go look for him."

Leodegrance frowned and pulled on his mustache a bit. "Such loyalty and love is commendable, but foolish. It has grown dark outside, and the enemy controls the countryside. Rushing out, alone, is almost certain death ... or, at the very least, capture." He held up his hands as Gaheris began to protest. "I understand! Believe me, I understand how hard it is to remain behind when someone you love is in danger.

But a dead soldier is no one's rescue, do you understand? I have my own scouts out there who may be able to assist him, if God grants it so. And if thy brother is as crafty as he is skilled at battle, then he might just survive long enough to see the morn."

Gaheris fought with himself. What King Leodegrance said made sense, but he couldn't just abandon Gawaine to whatever Fate had in store without doing something. He grew silent and remained seated on his horse.

"If I have to," Leodegrance said, "I will have you arrested for disobeying the orders of the King and thrown into the stockade. But I don't think that will be necessary, do you? Not for the son of King Lot." He stood regarding Gaheris with very serious eyes, and Gaheris knew he would do exactly that.

With a sigh, Gaheris dismounted, and held his hands out for the guards to take him. "If that is the only way, then that is what you must do. I do not consider it a dishonor to be imprisoned for loving my brother so much I would defy a king in order to save him."

Leodegrance clasped Gaheris on the shoulder and said, "By God! I heard that you Orkneys were a stubborn lot, but now I see it is true! Ha! No, my lad, no prison for you. I believe we may still have fighting to do ere the sun rises again, and your sword will be needed. Who knows? We may need to sally forth and rescue your brother after all. Trust in God's plan, my boy, for the Lord knows all and has prepared our place at His table when it is time."

Gaheris reluctantly agreed.

"All right, now, lads!" Emrys said as the company neared the agreed-upon meeting place. "We've managed to elude or kill enough sentries and scouts, thanks to great, good Fortune, and now we have a chance to do what we came here to do."

"But what about our lady?" cried someone. "Shouldn't we wait for Rose to come back?"

Emrys looked around at the group, and it was plain to see they were all worried about Rose. He knew that such a distraction might dishearten the men, and he had to do something about that.

"I promise you, as my name is Emrys, we will see her again! But not until after we have struck a blow against her enemy. Think how proud she will be when we show her how well her plan has worked! Think of the reward when we, small band that we are – a mere handful compared to the armies gathered out there around the castle – when we help raise the siege! What legends they will tell of us then, eh? What glory will be heaped upon our names! Emlyn and Rodric, Rhys and Daffyd! When people shall say, 'Do you remember the time when King Leodegrance and the High King were trapped by enemies at Cameliard? And how that group of brave and courageous men, for the love of a woman warrior, lifted the siege?' Think of how thy children, and thy children's children shall revel in the fact that their father, their uncle, cousin or brother, was here on this day!"

"And what about you, Emrys? Don't leave yourself out if it!" called a voice.

"Oh, I think my name will survive long after I am gone," Emrys said, "for this and for other things I have done. And that I plan to do. Let's not forget that, either – that we all have other things we plan to do in the future. This is but one of many. Today we strike a blow to help ensure the future – a future we long to see!"

"What shall we do, then, Emrys?" asked one.

"Yes, what exactly are we to do?" asked another.

Emrys smiled, and in a quiet voice, he said, "Why, we go to create chaos! What else? We are to cast stones at the bee's hive, and run like a bear through the woods to avoid being stung. Then we can come back and collect the sweet, sweet honey!"

"Sounds kind of cowardly to me," said someone.

"Cowardly? Is it cowardly to survive? Is it cowardly to use your brains and achieve a victory simply because you thought of a better, more effective way to kill your fellow man than to stand and bang away at him with pots and pans? No, I say! No!

What we do has been done before, and shall be done again. Strike and run! Harry and harass! I'm not saying it won't be dangerous – of course not. Some of you may not ever see home again. But that's been true every time you get out of bed! Hell, that's been true every time you get *into* bed for that matter, for who knows when their time has come?"

"They say the wizard, Merlin, knows," said someone.

Emrys smiled faintly at that. "I say if Merlin knows, good for Merlin! But as for me, I don't know, and in not knowing I take advantage of every moment I have because I don't know if it will be my last. I create the life I want, and I do my best to accept my life as it is. Who could ask for more? And right now, I want to make Rose proud!"

There was a murmur of agreement and the men readied their equipment, checking bows and quivers, tightening straps, double checking knives, and so on.

"On we go!" Emrys said. The men split into four groups of about fifteen men each. They slipped off into the woods, moving as soundlessly as possible and blending in to their surroundings.

Unbeknownst to the men, Emrys used a little magic to help shroud their passage from searching eyes. It was because of him that they had come this far without any warning being passed along, and why their scouts had managed to neutralize or kill the enemy sentries and outriders so easily. He was tempted to drop his façade and use his powers more openly, especially as they neared the larger encampments, but he restrained himself. *I still have a surprise or two that I could spring!* Merlin thought to himself and smirked.

Rose knew she was nearing the enemy encampments, and so she dismounted and walked Grey Star, trying to be as silent as possible. She had already dispatched two scouts, catching them off guard, though Rose wasn't sure how long her incredible good luck was going to last. It was better to plan on it not lasting than to come to rely on it too much. So she proceeded cautiously.

Not long after, Rose heard sounds of battle. As she neared the edge of the woods, she could see the enemy lines set up to screen Cameliard from outside aid. Rose watched as knights in armor fought their way through the outer defenses, and then pause before riding in to engage more troops further along.

"All right, Seren, this is it I guess. Time to really put some of Meg's training to use!" Rose said as she climbed back onto Grey Star's back and slid on her helm. Rose tightened her shield, and tucked a lance under her arm. She removed the fairy flag and tucked it under her breastplate, and took a moment to kiss her mother's pendant.

Momma, wherever you are, watch over me now! And Poppa, too!

With that, Rose gave Grey Star a kick, and they sped along the ground in the direction of those whom Rose took to be the knights come to help lift the siege. They were quite a distance away, and as she got nearer, Rose had to engage foot soldiers who broke their lines and charged her.

She killed three men with her lance before she had to drop it, the last man still impaled on it, and drew her sword.

"Camelot!" she cried and lashed out with her weapon. The sword had always been one of Rose's best weapons, and this sword responded in her hand like an extension of herself. It flashed under an exposed helm or into an opening in the armor, taking one man in the throat and another under the armpit. She cut through pikes and pole arms as well as through flesh and bone. Through it all, Rose felt detached, once more experiencing that sense of flow she had felt before. Men came and went in tides, and it all seemed so natural and easy. She did not pause to think about the ruined flesh she left behind, or the lives that were ended in her wake. Dream-like, Rose rode on.

The next time Rose became aware of her surroundings, she had reached a small knot of warriors besieging a knight on horseback who fought savagely, cursing and shouting insults at his attackers.

"C'mon, ye mangy dogs! What, do ye not dare to attack an unarmed man? My sword's little more than a bit of steel by now. Are ye afraid of a dull sword?" With that, he staved in the skull of one of the burly mercenaries with the blunt and pitted sword, and bashed his shield into the ones trying to take him from his left side. Rose charged in, killing men from behind before they realized there were now two opponents.

"You look like you could use some help!" Rose yelled at the knight as she maneuvered Grey Star into a protective posture between the knight and fresh warriors who were closing in.

"Aye, I guess I could at that," said the knight with a tired laugh. "But don't go thinking I couldn't handle this lot for a little longer with nothing but my bare hands if I needed to!"

Rose didn't doubt it, but she could also see that the knight's blows were having less and less effect. He was covered with a dozen cuts, and some of them still bled freely. And his sword was so badly damaged it was of practically no use.

"Here!" Rose shouted and handed her sword to him as she pulled a javelin from out of its quiver. With a strong cast, she caught the foremost warrior in the chest and he staggered and fell with a stunned expression on his face.

"My thanks!" said the knight. "Though this little twig hardly seems capable of doing a lot of damage! I'm afraid it'll break in half on the first skull I hit."

"It won't, never fear!" Rose answered back. The knight's humor was refreshing, and Rose admired his courage for joking in the face of battle.

"Gawaine hight," he shouted at her as he turned his weary mount around and attacked the newest batch of soldiers.

Gawaine? Rose recognized the name at once. "I knew your brother!" she shouted back. "My name's Roch-..." she didn't have time to finish before they were battling for their lives. Grey Star reared and smashed the face of one warrior, while Rose thrust her spear into the neck of another. Whirling it about, she batted the spear thrust at her with the butt end of her own, twirled the spear around and slashed the arm of the soldier carrying it cutting him deeply. While the blow wasn't likely to be fatal, it certainly took him out of the fight.

"Nicely done, Ross!" Gawaine said appreciatively. Apparently he had only heard part of Rose's name.

"Thank you!" she shouted back. Rose dispatched two more warriors before realizing that things had grown quiet. Looking around, she saw that they had managed to kill the entire party that had come out to fight, and also that Gawaine seemed to be sitting his horse oddly.

"Sir Gawaine, are you all right?" she asked as she rode closer to him.

"Eh?" came Gawaine's voice. He sounded absolutely exhausted, and wavered in the saddle.

"Sir Gawaine? We're safe now. We've beaten them all … for now, at least."

Gawaine nodded his head. "Good, because there's something I'm afraid I'm going to do now …"

"What's that?" Rose asked just as Gawaine's body tipped sideways and toppled to the ground.

"Oh, gods," Rose muttered.

Rose slipped off of Grey Star and knelt down by the fallen knight. She removed his helm, and was relieved to see that he was still breathing. But his color wasn't good, and he was breathing shallowly.

"Brave, brave man," Rose said quietly. "Let's see what I can do for you."

Already the day had worn, and the daylight was falling. Rose was glad for that because now would be the time when soldiers would come looking for their fallen and injured comrades. In the shadows, she might be able to hide with Gawaine until her own scouts caught up to them.

"Awright!" said a voice dangerously from behind Rose. "Stand up and surrender, knight! For we've got the drop on ye!"

Chapter 18

Rose stood up slowly so as not to take an arrow in the back.

"Tha's right," said the voice, "Nice 'n easy ... no need to get yerself kil't. Ye've fought bravely and well, I'm sure, but now ye're my prisoner."

I know that voice! Rose thought. It was with all the control she could muster that Rose prevented herself from rushing the man who stood behind her when she turned around. "Emlyn?" she said, "I have never been so glad to see or hear anyone before in my Life!"

The grizzled old hunter who stood with arrow knocked and ready lowered his bow slightly and squinted at his captive in the fading light. "Lass?"

Rose wanted to both laugh and cry at the same time, and she stepped forward and kissed the old man right on the lips and then on both cheeks before seizing him in a tight hug. "Oh, thank the gods, it is you!" she cried. Rose hurried back to the fallen Gawaine and began to loosen his armor. "Where are the others? How far behind?"

Emlyn took a moment to gather his wits before answering with a jerk of his thumb toward the woods to their west. "Maybe three good bowshots that way," he said with his slow drawl, "though things didn't go quite as well as we would've liked."

Rose looked at him as it registered with her what he was saying. "How many?" she asked softly. Heaviness filled her at the realization that more good men had fought and died on her behalf.

"A dozen or so dead," Emlyn answered, "and maybe twice that injured. Half of those are still able to fight, though." He wanted to try and give Rose some good news in all of this. "Don't fret yerself, lass," he said. "They fought like badgers, they did. Oh, ye'd have been proud of 'em!"

Gawaine moaned a little as Rose removed some of his armor so that she could bind up what wounds were still bleeding.

"And what of Emrys?" she asked, fearful of the answer.

"Oh, he's fine," Emlyn replied and shook his head. "Thanks to him, we kept things from going too sour. Why, if it weren't for him, we wouldn't have nearly so many left! But I'll let him tell you himself, for if I'm not mistaken that's some of our boys right now."

Rose looked up as a handful of dark silhouettes emerged from the dusk, bows ready and heads scanning this way and that for danger. Emrys' eyes glowed like a cat's, from what source Rose did not know nor did she think to question, but she felt relieved at the sight of him hale and whole.

"Rose? Thank heaven we found you! Are you all right?" he asked, his customary smirk slightly strained with the concern he felt.

"I'm fine, but I need help with this knight," Rose answered him.

Emrys crouched down next to her and put a hand on Gawaine's forehead. The gesture reminded Rose of Gleinguin, and she suddenly felt a surge of homesickness sweep over her.

"He'll live," Emrys said flatly. "Though he will be in no shape to fight for a few days. It would be a good thing to get him back to our camp as soon as possible, however."

Rose stood as some of the men came and helped lift the unconscious knight to carry him back to their camp.

"Rose," Emrys began to say, but Rose interrupted him.

"Emlyn told me. I know," she said.

"But it worked, Rose!" Emrys said, "That's what I want you to know. Your plan worked! Until they charged us, that is."

"Didn't you fall back? That was what I planned. Just hit them enough to get them to break their lines and follow us, then run like hell and cut them down as we fall back." She asked her questions angrily, but Emrys knew she was angry with herself and not with him.

"We did, Rose. We did exactly as you had planned. I set the men up in staggered columns so that one group could cover the retreat of the others falling back. It worked beautifully for the first few waves, but then ... then their cavalry charged us and ... and we simply couldn't get away fast enough."

Rose stopped, and Emrys stopped with her watching her expectantly.

"I ... I should have planned better. I knew ... I thought that the archers could stop the cavalry, too. In fact, it was against their mounted knights I based the idea of using archers. They are so accustomed to being able to ride through lines of unarmored men and feeling themselves to be nearly invulnerable except against each other, I just thought ... I thought we could stop them by taking down their mounts, if nothing else." Rose felt so frustrated with herself that she wanted to punch the nearest tree with her fist just to vent it.

"We did, Rose. And it worked at first, like I said. But, these bows just aren't powerful enough to punch through heavy plate at such distances. Maybe, if we had heavier bows, yes ... but we didn't. What arrows hit the horses did take those knights out of the battle, and some of those were easy to kill because they couldn't get up and maneuver in that armor of theirs. But enough got by unharmed ... it turned into a rout."

Rose wanted to beat herself up. "My fault. It's my fault ..."

Emrys grabbed Rose by the shoulder and said firmly, "Rose, your plan worked! Even though it became a rout, the knights, and the footmen who support them, chased us into the woods. They broke their lines and followed us! We cut down many more times their number than they did of ours. Far more than many generals would consider 'acceptable losses,' don't you see? And our actions helped the High King to reach the castle. Without us, he would have been beaten back into a retreat."

"Acceptable losses? No loss is acceptable!" Rose answered back.

Emrys sighed and sympathized with the girl. "Rose, in a perfect world, no man would ever have to lose his life in warfare. But this isn't a perfect world, and battle is nothing more than organized chaos. It is those who adapt to that chaos the best who survive or prevail. A lot of it is luck more than planning, though planning isn't unimportant."

"I don't want a lecture in philosophy or military strategy right now," Rose said and began to walk on again.

Emrys walked with her in silence while the men followed behind leading Grey Star and Gawaine's mount.

It wasn't long before Rose smelled smoke and the scent of meat cooking. With a heavy heart, she braced herself for the reunion ahead.

"Hey! They're back!" someone shouted, and word spread quickly. Men began to gather, many of them bandaged or wounded. *Too many*, thought Rose. They gathered and watched her as she went from man to man, thanking them for their bravery this day. One of her men brought her a list of the dead, and Rose thanked him for his duty while she looked over the list of names.

"I want to thank you all for your actions!" Rose started. "Thanks to you, the High King was able to reach Cameliard with a small group of knights. More are on their way, or so I understand. We helped buy King Leodegrance another day, at least. You should be very proud of what you achieved today!"

"And what about you?" somebody shouted. "I hear you rescued the great Gawaine from certain death!"

A murmur went through the camp in response.

"She did!" Emrys stood up and shouted over them. "Your lady fought bravely and well. Thanks to her, one of the greatest knights who ever lived shall live to see his fame and honor grow! Rose has helped ensure that the flower of knighthood will endure, and the legends of this time shall pass on from generation to generation until the ending of Time!"

Rose looked up at Emrys. He seemed so sure of what he was saying, Rose could feel it ... it was as if Emrys spoke prophecy, not just a speech to rally the men.

"How can you be so sure?" she asked him quietly.

Emrys looked down at her and flashed his usual, mischievous grin. "Oh, I have ways of knowing," he said mysteriously.

"Who are you?" Rose finally asked him. "Who are you, Emrys?"

"I wish I could give you an answer," he finally replied after a pause. "Do any of us really know who we are, let alone anyone else? I don't know ... Sometimes I think this is all God's way of having fun, and that I am just another of His imaginary friends."

One of the men began to shout, "Rose! Rose! Rose!" It was soon picked up by the others, including many of those too injured to have gotten up and joined the circle around the fire where Rose was sitting. Her name echoed into the night, a roar that followed the fire and wood smoke up into the sky. Rose felt her heaviness leave her and stood up taking Emrys place on a tree stump so that the men might see her better.

The moment was magical. A dream come true. But as sometimes happens, dreams turn into a nightmare with but the smallest of shifts. And so it was for Rose.

Michael stumbled through the dark, fearful of running into some of Meraugis' scouts, or those of Royns or their allies. He was also afraid of breaking his leg tripping over a root or stump, but his certainty that he would be reunited with his sister grew stronger and stronger.

Rose! How do I find you? he wondered.

At that moment, Michael heard a noise like the call of dozens of men, and they were chanting one name over and over again – "Rose! Rose! Rose!" At first, Michael thought he was delirious, but he realized that he wasn't imagining it. The sound was coming from not too far away, and he made his way cautiously towards it. Finally, Michael perceived fire-light coming through the trees. He could see the faces of the men who were calling his sister's name, shouting it out to the night. And he could see that several of them were injured from recent battling, and his curiosity overcame his sense of caution.

Who are these men? And why are they shouting out Rose's name? Are they shouting out for my sister?

Suddenly, Michael felt a hand grasp him by the back of his hair and felt the edge of a very sharp knife pressed to his throat.

"Well, my lovely little Michael! About time you showed up. Come to join your friends, yes? The people you were spying for? Eh?" Meraugis hissed into Michael's ear, and the knife pressed harder into Michael's skin. Hard enough that it began to bleed.

Clamping his hand over the boy's mouth, Meraugis dragged Michael back away from the trees circling the camp. His hand felt slick with sweat and blood. For one instant Michael caught a glimpse of his sister – she was standing in the firelight, el-evated on a tree stump, turning this way and that as the men chanted her name.

Rose! Dressed in armor? What does it all mean? But his ques-tions were the least of his concerns right now.

Meraugis held Michael with an iron grip, hurting the boy as he held him still while one of Rose's scouts walked his patrol right past them.

"If you even whimper, I'll slit your throat," Meraugis warned Michael in a whisper.

They waited for several moments after the scout had passed before Meraugis lifted the boy and crept closer to Rose's camp to spy.

Michael's eyes grew wide, and he longed to call out, but Meraugis kept his hand clamped over his mouth while he held Michael in front of him as a human shield.

"You know that bitch?" he asked Michael in a tight whisper. "Is she the one you have been spying for? Naughty boy! You'll have to be punished for that."

Rose had just begun to quiet the men when a huge figure emerged from the woods. It was an armored knight, a giant of a man who whirled a great axe overhead as he hurtled toward her with a cry. Six Saxon warriors rushed behind him with their heavy spears thrusting and killing men as they came. For an instant, Rose was reminded of her vision, and she saw Carados as the huge ravening wolf of her nightmares and the Saxon warriors as his pack ravaging the land.

Carados was upon her before she knew it. Her men were scrambling to draw swords and daggers to defend themselves from the unexpected onslaught, since their bows had been unstrung in order to maintain and repair their weapons during the night.

Rose dived off the stump as Carados' weapon crashed down where she had been standing. Rose could feel the impact shudder through the ground from the force of it.

Carados? Rose was completely caught off guard. *Of course! My dreams! They warned me that he was behind this.*

"Die, little knight!" Carados roared as he swung his axe like a scythe. He cut down two men who were rushing to Rose's aid as she scrambled to stand up.

Rose cast about for a weapon and saw a flash of steel as Emrys tossed a sword to her before slipping away to engage some of the enemy who were pouring into the camp.

Why didn't we have warning? Rose wanted to know as she readied her sword against the giant. But all her attention was needed as Carados bore down on her.

315

The giant fought savagely, and Rose was sore pressed to avoid his blows. Carados reminded her a bit of the fight against Taulurd the troll, but where Taulurd had fought with blind rage, Carados had years of practice and skill. He feinted and parried with his heavy weapon, and the shock of those blows nearly numbed Rose's arm when sword met axe.

"Die!" Carados grunted as he swung again and again. "Die! Die! Die!"

Rose quickly noted that Carados was signaling his blows with every word, and his blows were falling hard and regular, relentless in their attack. But Rose knew that it was probably a trick, and she refused to be drawn in by it.

"Beware of a warrior who is too obvious in his attacks," Meg had said, *"It is most likely a trap. Any warrior who has survived for any length of time knows that success comes through unpredictability. Repetitious movements are a distraction for something else."*

Rose decided to try a little surprise of her own. She had been falling back, parrying and deflecting each of Carados' blows as they rained down on her. This time, Rose stepped in as Carados stepped forward at the same time. She made a quick thrust with the tip of her sword at the giant's face and was gratified when Carados made a surprised grunt as he pulled back to avoid being blinded. However, he swept Rose's blade aside with his axe and gave Rose a heavy blow across the face with the back of his mailed fist. Rose staggered from the impact. It was through sheer instinct that she managed to take the next blow from Carados' axe with her sword by directing the force of the blow with a glancing movement into the ground. For a split second, Carados was over extended and slightly off balance. Rose seized the opportunity and spun, striking Carados in the back with her sword blade. While it failed to pierce the giant's armor it did manage to make him stagger forward a step or two before regaining his balance. And now Rose was on the attack.

Rose struck – thrust, thrust, slash – utilizing her greater speed and agility, the two qualities Meg had told her would be to her advantage, especially over heavier and stronger knights like Carados. Carados had to parry and counter, narrowly avoiding a dangerous thrust toward his crotch where the armor was weaker, defended mostly by heavy chain and not the thicker plate armor covering the rest of his body. Rose went for those weak points – crotch, throat, armpits, and face – and kept Carados on the defensive for the moment. She could tell he was used to a more physically aggressive style of fighting, strength against strength, though he was no sluggard in adjusting to Rose's quicker attacks.

"So, we know how to fight, eh?" he said and laughed. "But you fight like a dancer, not like a warrior. What's the matter, afraid to fight like a man?"

Rose tossed her head to clear the sweat from her eyes. "Maybe you haven't noticed, but I'm not a man," she replied. "Though I suppose a beast like you can hardly tell the difference." With that, she launched another flurry of attacks.

Carados, however, was ready for her this time. While it took all his skill to counter Rose's attacks, Carados refused to give ground and took great risks in avoiding Rose's thrusts. And it was Rose's turn to be surprised as Carados pinned her sword to the ground with the head of his axe and seized her shield arm with his, and lifted. The move wrenched Rose's arm painfully, and Carados dropped his axe in order to grab Rose in a deadly embrace as he twisted, nearly pulling Rose's arm from the socket.

"Ahhh!" Rose cried. Spots swam in her vision for a second, and pain flared along her left shoulder and back.

With a wicked grin, Carados released her and shoved her away from him as he stooped to pick up both his axe and her sword, hefting one in each hand.

"Maybe I shouldn't kill you," Carados growled. "Maybe I should skin you from that metal armor of yours and show you what a man can do. I like that! Yes, I'll make you my own personal slave, and bed you whenever I wish."

"I'd rather die!" Rose shouted back. Her eyes were blurred with tears from the pain in her shoulder, and she fought it back.

"As you wish," Carados answered with a grim smile.

The fire was to Rose's back, and the dancing light made Carados' features twist and shift, and he looked more like a wolf than ever.

"You don't remember me, do you?" Rose asked before the giant came to finish her off. "No … why would you?"

"What difference does it make?" Carados asked as he strode forward weapons ready.

Rose laughed sardonically, "Because I want you to know why it is that I am going to kill you." She stared at the giant as he loomed larger and larger.

It was Carados' turn to laugh as he said, "Kill *me*? You're going to kill me? Ha! That's good. Girl, I have been killing men longer than you've been alive. What makes you think that you can kill me?"

"Because to kill me like this would be a coward's way, not the way of a great warrior. Great warrior? Ha! Carados, slayer of women and children, that's all you are. Slayer of farmers and peasants and little boys." Rose spat as Carados stopped a mere three steps away.

Carados' eyes narrowed dangerously, and he stared down at Rose while she kept her eyes locked on his.

"That defiance! That face. Yes, I know you now! You're that little boy who came to kill me, what – about a year ago, yes? Ah! I remember now. I thought you were a boy at the time, the way you were dressed and the anger that you showed. You should be dead by now, shouldn't you? I thought I had ordered you to be killed."

"You did, but I managed to escape, thanks to Fate, or the gods, or God. I don't know which," Rose replied with restraint.

"And look at you now!" Carados grinned wickedly. "So, is this what Arthur has stooped to? Recruiting girls and old men? What are you supposed to be? A knight? A warrior?" He laughed again.

"I'm not a knight – not yet. But I will be, one day. Once I kill you," Rose said with a calmness that surprised her.

"Well, then, little knight, what are you waiting for? Come, come and kill me. Isn't that all you have lived for? Didn't you swear an oath on your father's grave or some such nonsense?" Carados tossed Rose her sword and backed away a step or two. "That's right – I remember. You spat in my face and said that you had sworn to kill me because I killed your daddy. That was it, wasn't it?"

Clenching her teeth against the pain, Rose picked up her sword and steadied herself as she looked at her enemy, Carados. He grinned at her with his wolfish grin and held his arms out in mockery, daring her to attack.

Rose felt a sense of calm pervade her entire being. Time slowed down, and suddenly Carados was no longer her enemy but her partner – a partner in an intricate and deadly dance. She no longer felt the rage, the anger and hurt and frustration that had fueled her when she had first begun down this path. Instead, she felt an incredible sense of peace, a belonging and rightness that went beyond words.

I am an instrument, Rose said to herself. *What was it Gleinguin had told me after I had killed Taulurd the troll? Something about how I had merely been an instrument to help restore order and balance? That's what I am, now – an instrument of Justice!*

"I am Rose," she said clearly and evenly. "Daughter of Lucas and Branwen, sister of Michael, and I will kill you." She pulled the fairy flag out from under her armor and tied it around her shield arm with her teeth. She wasn't sure if it made any difference or not, but it seemed as though the pain diminished slightly. Just enough so as not to be excruciating, though by no means making the pain disappear. Under her breastplate, Rose could feel the comforting coolness of her mother's amulet.

Momma? Poppa? Be with me now!

The noise of battle in the camp faded away. The world for Rose became the small patch of ground illuminated by the smoking fire beside her, and her opponent, Carados, who stood ready and waiting.

And so it begins, Rose heard a voice in her mind say.

Rose closed with Carados swiftly and fluidly, striking with her sword in similar fashion to her attacks before – thrusting at joints and exposed gaps in the giant's armor. This time though, Rose could almost feel Carados' moves before he made them, and she flowed with each as if they were merely steps in a larger dance. Thrust and counter, parry and evade, it all became one great flow. Carados landed a blow on Rose's armor, and the force penetrated, cutting Rose. But it seemed as if that was exactly where it was supposed to come in this deadly dance of theirs. Wounds and pain were all a part of it. Rose watched as her sword found a gap, pierced the giant's defenses, and drew blood from Carados' leg, wounding him behind his right knee. Carados' cursed, favoring his other leg as they turned and moved. Rose was aware of Carados' breathing, how he was beginning to breath harder and more labored while her own movements seemed nearly effortless. His expression grew darker and more serious as he had to focus more and more energy into meeting Rose's attacks and defending his vulnerable points, while looking for openings of his own. He tried once again to use his greater size and strength to his advantage and attempted to seize Rose in a bear hug. But Rose simply slid through it, turned, and cut Carados on his left wrist as the blade slid through the overlapping plate. He cursed, pulled his hand away and brought his axe down at Rose's head.

Carados knew that his earlier engagement with Gawaine, and being trapped beneath his horse, had taken a toll on him - more than he expected. And he also realized that this girl, this female warrior, was far more skilled than he had anticipated.

Is she a valkyrie? he wondered. *Is this how they come to gather up their chosen warriors?* The idea pleased him if it were so. *How glorious to die in battle, proving my worth to those who would claim me!*

Carados began to fight with renewed vigor, finding a second wind and enjoying the contest between himself and Rose regardless of the outcome.

Rose could feel something shift in the rhythm and flow of their mortal pas-de-deux. Carados began to fight with more ease than before, much like her own. And the sense of distance Rose had, began to slip away. She became aware of the aches and bruises, the cuts and wounds that covered her body, more and more with each passing moment. Rose became more a participant in her own battle than the observer she had been before.

Blood dripped from her shoulder and side even as it ran from wounds on Carados' arms and legs. Something dripped into her right eye, blood or sweat Rose couldn't tell which, but it blinded her momentarily on that side. Carados seemed to sense it, and he slammed Rose's face with his elbow, knocking her to the ground. Rose tasted blood in her mouth, reminded of the other beating Carados had given her at their first meeting. She scrambled back as his axe crashed down upon her, rolling first to her left, then to her right as he followed trying to finish her off. Carados raised his axe for the third time, readying a blow that would cleave Rose down the center when Rose thrust her sword as she had done in her battle with Sion ap Gwdion, right into the giant's thigh, and felt it connect. Looking up, Rose saw that she had managed to slip the blade into a gap in the metal covering Carados' right thigh, and the blade had been driven deep into his leg. Blood spurt from the wound as Carados continued the momentum of his swing. But it lacked the driving force behind it and he toppled over Rose as it carried him forward.

Rose crawled out from under the giant and tried to roll him over but her left arm was simply too painful, so she tugged her sword free of the giant and stood panting over him. "This is for Poppa," Rose said as she prepared to slay Carados by splitting his skull with her sword. But at that moment she heard a familiar voice call her name.

"Rose?"

Rose turned in the direction of the sound unbelieving as she saw Michael and a stranger emerge from the trees. Michael's eyes were wide with fear, almost pleading for Rose to help, and she saw the man behind him had a dagger to Michael's throat.

"We know each other, then do we?" the man said with a silky voice. Rose recognized him as the crazed youth who had captured her when she had tried to sneak into Carados' castle.

"You?" she said and stepped in their direction.

"Ah, ah, ah!" Meraugis warned Rose by pulling Michael's head back and raising the blade so it would be more visible. "Be nice or I slit your little pet's throat."

Rose stopped and held her arms out to show she was no threat.

"Drop your sword!" Meraugis ordered.

Rose hesitated, but Michael's eyes implored, and Rose complied. The sword fell, the hilt landing over her right foot.

"Now, order your men to surrender," Meraugis commanded and he licked his lips. He walked Michael closer to Rose, using the boy as a shield in case Rose tried anything. "Your men are losing anyway. Surrender now, and you can save the handful that remains to await my lord's pleasure. Oh, won't father be pleased?" He kissed Michael on the side of his face, but the boy tried to pull away.

Carados lifted himself up from the ground. He felt weak; could feel his strength ebbing away as it poured out of him from the wound in his thigh.

Stupid bitch forgot to finish me off! he said to himself. *Big mistake. The mistake of the weak and the foolish.*

His vision was dimmed and growing worse as he looked in the direction of the voices he had heard. He thought he recognized one, and the other was that of the girl. Carados pulled a throwing axe from his belt and moved a step forward. He saw Meraugis, the girl knight, and what he thought was Meraugis' squire all standing in a small knot.

So, Mark was in on this betrayal as well! Carados thought. He readied his axe and threw, not caring which of the three he hit so long as he killed one of them. The throw cost him the last of his strength, but Carados sped it with his curse before he collapsed.

"Rose!" Michael cried suddenly in warning.

Everything happened so fast – Michael pushed himself away from Meraugis who lost his grip on the boy in surprise. Rose kicked the sword from the ground into her hand and swung it at Michael's captor as Michael slipped away from him. She brought it down with a cleaving motion that bit through Meraugis' shoulder and into his chest. Michael made a soft grunt behind her and fell to the ground.

"Michael?" Rose screamed and turned to see what had happened.

Michael gagged, bringing up blood. He looked to his sister with sad, pained eyes. "I'm sorry," he croaked before the life went out of him.

"Michael? No!" Rose cried and went to him.

The ground thundered as horsemen rode into the camp. Rose drew her dagger, the only weapon she had left to her as her sword was stuck inside Meraugis' body, and readied herself in front of Michael's body protectively. She heard screams as men were slain by lance and sword or trampled under hooves.

A knight in dark armor rode up and halted his horse next to Rose and Michael. The man wore a chain coif over his head and looked down at the pair with curiosity. "In the name of Arthur, the High King, I arrest you for treason. Surrender to me now or feel the wrath of the King's justice!"

The knight scowled at Rose. Another knight, a balding man with grizzled beard, rode up, and the two had a whispered conference. The knight in dark armor seemed surprised by whatever the other man conveyed, and he glanced at Rose with a puzzled look before reigning back his horse to make room for a new figure who approached from the direction of Rose's encampment. An old man with a long white beard came into the light bearing a carved staff that looked to be made of pure ivory. His eyes glowed with reflected firelight, and Rose felt she ought to recognize him but didn't know how or why.

"Excellently well done, Kay!" he said with a mischievous grin, "And right on time, as always. Any longer and these friends to the High King would have gone to meet their maker, and we would have suffered greater losses in the time to come."

Kay frowned as he answered. "I got here as soon as humanly possible, old wizard. If you wanted me here any faster you should have spirited me and my men here like you do yourself. How is it that you are always where the bloodshed is heaviest?"

Merlin shrugged and smiled mysteriously. "Just lucky, I guess. Call it your God's sense of humor. In any case, weary as you may be both of travel and battle, there's one more fight ahead before this night's work is done."

"Who said I am weary of battle?" Kay asked clearly irked.

"Forgive me," Merlin said and bowed. "I forget to whom I speak. You have this young knight to thank for having purchased you the time to bring reinforcements to free Arthur and King Leodegrance from the net surrounding them. It was her plan to cut a hole in that net and wreak what havoc she could on the lines of your enemies."

Kay looked down at Rose and said grumpily, "My thanks to you, boy. I shall be sure my brother hears of this. The crown owes you a debt of gratitude, and we will pay you, never fear."

Rose dropped to the ground and cradled Michael's body in her arms. Her grief overcame her, and she wept, washing Michael's face with her tears.

"Oh, Michael!" she cried. "Why? Why did this have to happen? Why?"

Merlin crouched and placed his hand on the boy's forehead, the same gesture Rose had seen Emrys make on the fallen Gawaine.

Of course! Merlin is a druid, isn't he? Isn't that what Gleinguin said? Or that people believed him to be so?

"Sleep now," Merlin said softly to the boy. "Sleep without dreams, for your dreams have been too unhappy and painful of late. Sleep in peace and oblivion now." Merlin looked at Rose sadly. "I am sorry for your loss, my child. Truly, if it were within my power, dear Rose, I would have seen to it that things did not unfold in such a manner."

"How ... how do you know of me? What do you know of me?" Rose asked.

"Much," was all Merlin would answer as he gazed at her softly. "I am needed elsewhere at the moment, however," he said suddenly and straightened. "But, we will see each other again. And soon!" And he vanished.

Kay snorted and said, "Just like Merlin, always one for dramatics. He should have been a performer, he loves spectacle so!" he kicked his horse and called for his men to follow him.

"Wait!" Rose called after him. When he stopped and turned, she said, "What of me and my men?"

Kay answered sourly, "You and your men have the King's thanks, what more do you need? If you can fight, then follow. If not, then stay and tend your wounded and dying. I have no time to waste on explaining what should be evident to anyone with even a basic understanding of warfare." So saying, Kay rode off in the direction of Leodegrance's keep with his men.

Rose bent down to her brother, and her grief for his loss was greater than anything else right now. She startled when a hand touched her shoulder, and she readied a punch at the man crouching over her.

"Emrys!" she clutched the man in a tight embrace and cried on his shoulder. "Where have you been?"

"Good to see you, too," he replied. "I can't be in two places at once, now can I?" Emrys looked down at the boy cradled in Rose's lap and he became serious. "Your brother? Rose, I am so sorry."

Rose nodded and wiped Michael's hair away from his face. "He died trying to protect me. There was nothing I could do. It ... it all happened so fast ..."

Emrys placed a gentle hand on Rose's shoulder in sympathy. "I'm not surprised. Courage seems to run in your family. Why, I remember your mother- ..."

Rose wiped her eyes and said, "You knew my mother? How is that possible?"

Emrys glanced away quickly to recover. "Did I say I knew her? I mean, from what you've told me of her ... she seems to have been a very courageous lady. And your Poppa. It's no wonder they had such exceptional children." He paused and looked at Michael's face in repose. "Rose, would you like for Michael to be buried here at Cameliard? He'd be welcome with all the other heroes who have fallen here this day."

Rose considered but she knew it wasn't what she wanted, nor what Michael would have wanted, either. "No," she replied. "I know a little place ... a farm, or there used to be a year or so ago – a farm with an apple orchard where Michael and I ..." she couldn't continue as tears choked her. Emrys waited in respectful silence for her to continue. "That's where I buried Poppa. And that's where Momma's buried, too. It's all we wanted ... to just ... go home."

Emrys nodded in understanding. "As you wish, so be it. Home we shall take him once this is all over."

He stood and looked around the camp. The dawn light was beginning to break and a pre-morning mist began to rise hiding the dead and dying strewn about the grounds. Emrys went to fetch the men who had survived the night's attack to help gather up the dead and to help assist the wounded.

Carados' body was numb and cold when the woman appeared to him. He had been left for dead when the soldiers of his enemies had gone about looking for their fallen comrades.

"*Valkyrie?*" he said hoarsely and reached his hand toward the figure.

The woman was dressed in a long grey robe. She did not look like the warrior women Carados had heard described to him. Her face was too sensuous, her figure too slender and alluring. But her eyes, her eyes had the look of death, penetrating and inescapable.

The woman bent down to him, her hands stretched out until they were pressed upon the wound in his thigh. Pain flared through him, and Carados fought the groan that wanted to escape.

I mustn't show any weakness! Not if I am to be deemed worthy of Valhalla!

"Not yet," the woman muttered under her breath. "No, not yet. No Valhalla for you, not yet. You still have work to do. Yes. For the Goddess, for She Who Cuts, do you still have a purpose to fulfill." A pleasing warmth poured into Carados' leg, and he felt all his aches and pains slowly fade away. When the woman stood, he was still weak but had the pleasant afterglow he normally felt after an exceptionally good workout or combat.

"Rise!" the woman commanded him, and he found himself responding as though he dreamed. "Go to the coast. There shall you take one of the longboats King Wihtgar sent with his warriors and return with it to the Saxon homeland. In time you will return, but not now. Now you must leave all you own, all you have won with your own might, for all that you might hope to achieve. Go! Now!"

Carados walked like a shadow, feeling as though he floated across the battlefield. Bodies lay strewn all about, dismembered and disemboweled, Saxons and Britons, Welsh and Northern men locked in mortal struggle to the very end. He could feel their ghosts there, too, as he passed amongst them heading for the coast.

It would be many days' journey, but Carados' body followed the grey woman's will, though his will was not set against it. *In order to gain all I hope to achieve isn't that what she told me? I have much that I hope to achieve, much that I desire in this life still! Not the least of which is to set the bastard king's head on a pike and take the land for my own. And let's not forget Mark and his betrayal! No,*

I have many things left to do. What do I care which god or goddess desires it, so long as I am the tool of that destruction?

Chapter 19

"They're coming!" came the shout of a lookout from one of the watchtowers of Cameliard's battlements.

King Leodegrance walked along the wall, readying his men. "Archers ready!" he yelled. "At range – fire!"

Dozens of flaming arrows arced toward the oncoming horde in a deadly hail. They killed and injured many of the attackers but did not slow their advance as they merely ran over their dead or dying comrades in order to gain the walls.

"Again! Ready – fire!" Leodegrance ordered once more.

More of the enemy fell to the rain of flaming arrows, but now most of the men were at the walls, and threw up siege ladders or tossed up grappling hooks with heavy rope.

"Prepare the walls! Defenders to the walls!"

Men rushed into position as they had for several nights, now. They were tired and exhausted, but every one of them knew that to do any less meant letting the enemy win. More than that, they feared disappointing their beloved king.

Poles were used to push over ladders before climbers could gain the wall, and axes cut at ropes to dislodge the grappling lines. But Royns' men attacked relentlessly in several places, and Leodegrance had to spread his men thin in order to try and hold the battlements. "Hold position!" he ordered, though he knew that sooner or later he'd have to fall back to the main keep. *Let it be later rather than sooner,* he prayed.

In the main keep, Gwynnefer tended to the wounded Arthur. He had lost a lot of blood, and she was still picking splinters of wood from the open wound before sewing up the wound and holding a poultice to it to draw out any fever or infection. Arthur groaned and tossed in delirium, gripping the bed sheets in his thrashing. Gwynnefer prayed as she worked and poured her total concentration into this man that so many followed already.

The hope of the future – that was what that young knight said, wasn't it? This man was the hope of the future? She had promised to do all that was within her power; the rest was up to God.

She wiped Arthur's brow with a cool, moist rag in an attempt to sooth him. He already was burning with fever! If he made it through the night, Arthur stood a good chance of surviving. But it would require a constant vigil, and Gwynnefer hoped she had the strength to see him through it.

Lord? Help see that my father and his men fight bravely and well!

Gaheris heard the trumpets blare and looked up as Leodegrance gave the order for him and his men to ride out. He had listened as the fighting continued outside and was tempted to dismount in order to assist the defenders on the walls. But King Leodegrance had given him charge of the sally force and told him to be ready to ride out at a moment's notice.

"We may not have time for more than one attack, so we have to make it count. Royns and his allies outnumber us, so every man we lose is like the loss of ten – more with every day that passes and more are taken away from duties elsewhere," Leodegrance had said. "Our only advantage right now is that we hold the walls. Once we lose that, his superior numbers will make quick work of taking the keep, and we are lost. All of us."

"I will do my best," Gaheris had said. He knew that there was a lot riding on this.

"Sally port, ready!" shouted the king. "Open!"

Gaheris pulled his sword free and kicked his horse into a gallop, leading the small band of mounted knights out to join with those of the High King's brother, Kay. "Lothian!" he shouted as his battle cry.

Gaheris and his men turned to the right, and together with Kay and his knights they charged the men at the foot of the wall. Despite their speed on horseback, the men at the foot of the wall were stubbornly displaced making the knights fight brutally for every yard they cleared. Knights were pulled from horseback by small groups of footmen and killed, too many for the knights to fend off at once. Seeing this, other men broke from their concealment and rushed to the aid of their fellows hoping for a share in both the spoils and the glory, adding to the danger.

"Fall back! Fall back!" Kay gave the order. They were forced to leave a handful of their number behind, killed or captured while they regrouped.

"If they want a fight, they'll get one," Kay swore. "Wedge formation! Snap to! We'll teach these dogs a thing or two," Kay barked his orders. "I will take the point, as it is the place of highest honor and greatest danger. Follow me. Stay tight, once we have broken through the line, I want two columns to sweep right and left and back to center. Understood? We break their formation, kill them on each side, then regroup. I don't want anyone going solo on me trying to claim all the glory for himself."

"That's his job," quipped someone in the group.

"Who said that?" Kay demanded. "Hervis, was that you? I know your voice, old man, don't think I don't. While Arthur may love you for what he takes to be your wisdom, I know you to simply have a smart mouth. Now, prove yourself worthy of my brother's love, and we'll put this all behind us, okay? Charge!"

The group surged forward like one great weapon directed at the wall of men who stood waiting for them. They rode through the gap created by Kay and the more experienced knights at the front. Gaheris turned with nearly half the forces and attacked the footmen trying to get themselves organized on that side. The knights used their greater speed and force to decimate the unorganized opposition before turning and heading back to the point they had initially broken through and riding away a short distance.

"Once more!" Kay shouted, and they turned back toward the reforming wall of men.

Once again, the wedge broke through and they killed men on each side before whirling and dashing away.

"Dare we risk it one more time?" Kay asked as he caught his breath.

"No, I don't think so," answered a man with a heavy North Country dialect. "Look! They're already bringing up the pole-arms. Dung heads! If they had thought to do that earlier, they could've saved themselves a lot of dead and injured."

Murmurs of agreement went round the group of knights, and men began to argue over what would be the best tactic to have employed to beat them. Gaheris marveled at this group of men in whose company he found himself. Here he was riding with Kay, Arthur's brother and seneschal – a figure out of legend! And there was King Pellinore. Dozens of the world's greatest knights and heroes, and they argued over battle like men watching a hurling competition!

"Very well! Back to the castle! We've bought King Leodegrance a brief reprieve in which to catch his wind. Let's hope it was enough of one for us to do the same!" Kay gave the order to fall back, and they rode in a loose formation back to the gatehouse and into the courtyard.

Royns cursed, tearing his hair in frustration. "Damn that Mark! Mercenaries he promised me, not these cowards who run at the first sign of resistance! And where are all my Saxon warriors? That damned Carados kept most of them to himself. Uses my gold to buy his armies, then abandons me when the time comes to use them. Oh, I was a fool to ever agree to this!"

"My king?" Royns' captain asked, "What are your orders? The men keep being repelled from the walls, but Leodegrance cannot maintain them forever. Surely he must be over extended by now."

Royns pouted and squinted at the dark walls of Cameliard as if trying to divine the state of the defenders within.

If only Leodegrance had been caught with his pants down like I intended, he thought, *then even now I'd be adding his beard to the hem of my cloak! If – if, if, if! If only Mark had hired more competent men, or had not held his men back from joining in the siege to begin with. If he had added his men to those I had brought expecting the easy victory that damned Carados promised. If! If only I could bend the world to my will – as easy to play God as to dream it! Fie!*

"What do you suggest?" Royns asked the captain petulantly.

The captain ignored his master's tone and answered honestly, "My king, we came without the proper equipment to take the castle by force. Ladders we can construct in short order, yes, but not catapults or ballista. Nor do we have the crew to man them. What we can do we are doing, and in my estimation we could gain the walls by the morning or as late as tomorrow afternoon. But-,"

"But," Royns interrupted, "but the cost will be so heavy that it might be better to withdraw now rather than face retribution by the High King later, yes? Fah! Mark did this to me, damn his eyes. This is all his fault!" Royns stomped his foot in emphasis. "To have come this far – agk!" Royns stomped again in frustration. "And the High King is in there, too! If I win – *if* I win, then I could add both their beards to my cloak. And claim the Table Round that Uther gave that fool Leodegrance. Wouldn't that make up for the loss of men, eh? I could be High King, and that would be-...."

"So, what are your orders, my liege?"

Royns narrowed his eyes in concentration, looking like a rat as he sucked his teeth and thought. "Give the order," he finally said. "Tell the men to fall back. We return to Norgales, and we'd best prepare our defenses for the retaliation that is sure to follow."

He sulked and stomped his foot one last time, pulling on his beard. "Damn that Mark! And thrice damned be that lackey of his, Carados!"

Rose heard the trumpets sounding the retreat. She paused from sharpening her sword and stood. "Is that – is that what I think it is?" she asked.

Emrys smiled brightly and jumped in the air in a jig. "It is! It is! They're falling back! The enemy is retreating. The siege is broken!"

A "hurrah!" sounded through the camp by the men who still had strength to cheer.

Gawaine muttered to himself, "And I had to miss it all! Damn!" He beat the ground with his fist before wincing at the pain it caused him. "Of course, getting my ass out of the fire was probably a good thing. Thank you, Ross!"

Rose smiled weakly at the big northerner. He still hadn't realized that Rose was a girl, and she had not had the heart to tell him. "You're welcome," she replied. Her loss made her sad and heavy, and not even Gawaine's gregariousness could overcome it.

"The High King's baggage train is coming through, lass," Emlyn reported to Rose. The old hunter had his left arm in a sling but insisted on continuing his duties despite his injuries. None of the men blamed Rose for what had happened; they all took responsibility for themselves. "Mayhap they have a healer or surgeon among them, or supplies at least."

Rose stood and walked to where the caravan would pass through. Gawaine got up and followed her, resting every few yards or so.

"Aye, one of the best healers is with that baggage. Me mum! She's kept my family fit and whole ever since I was weaned."

"Queen Morgawse? She works as a healer?" Rose inquired.

Gawaine grinned proudly and said, "Aye, why not? She's a mother and wife as well as Queen of Lothian and Orkney. And with such kin as my brothers and me, let alone my Da, she'd have to know how to sew up an injury or two. Life is never boring on the North Sea Coast!"

The outrider from the caravan paused and spoke with Rose and Gawaine and told them that the Queen was in a hurry to get to Cameliard where her skills were needed to tend the High King himself.

"Arthur's been injured?" Gawaine said. "Ach! Then what are ye doin' waggin' yer tongue at us who can stand and breathe? Get a move on, ye git! Where's my horse?"

Rose held Gawaine's arm to steady him before he fell over. "Perhaps, Sir Gawaine, you might consider walking a bit? I don't think you're ready to sit a saddle just yet."

"Why I ... oh, ye're right, Ross. It may be undignified but right now I care more for the comfort of my bum than my honor. Don't ever tell anyone I said that, though, or I'll have to box your ears!"

Rose smiled despite herself and said, "Your secret's safe with me, my lord."

"My lord? No, Ross, that'd be my Da. I'm not lord yet, nor do I wish to be for some time yet! There's too much I want to see and do before I get chained down with running a kingdom and all that."

Rose helped Gawaine walk back to the camp before securing a ride on a wagon for Gawaine and her own injured or dying that needed further care.

Arthur woke from a fevered sleep. He saw a young woman wringing a damp cloth into a bowl at his bedside. "Are you an angel?" he asked weakly. He felt a deep attraction when she smiled shyly at him.

"Shhh, my lord," she said and replaced the cool rag on his brow. "You're injured and need to rest."

"What is thy name, fair maiden?" he asked and reached for her hand with his own. He had no strength, but guided it to his lips to kiss before releasing it. The touch of her skin made Arthur feel a peace he had never known. A peace that had eluded him despite all the years he had fought to find it.

"Gwynnefer," the maiden answered softly. "I am daughter to King Leodegrance, the man you came here to save. I ... well, we all owe you a debt of gratitude for saving the man we love."

"Love ..." Arthur said in a whisper as he fell back to sleep. "Yes, love ..."

"About time we showed up," Morgawse said haughtily to the driver of her wagon. "The High King is in danger, and you ride as though we are returning home from market!"

"Mother, please!" Gaheris tried to calm her. "King Leodegrance desires to welcome you before you go to tend to Arthur, the High King. His daughter -..."

"His daughter? I am a Queen, not some silly princess to some minor lordling! The High King would be better tended by someone of my breeding and station than some little ..."

"Ah, Lady Morgawse, your majesty!" said King Leodegrance as he walked from the barracks. He bowed in courtly manner, no more nor less than befitted their comparative stations. "Welcome to Cameliard! I thank you for your generous offer to assist in tending to the High King. My daughter has no small skill herself ... indeed, is one of the best surgeons I have if a father may be so bold as to speak well of one of his children."

Morgawse curtsied slightly and replied, "Your majesty. Of course, why shouldn't a parent speak well of their child? I am proud of all my sons, brave knights all – or will be. Allow me to introduce my son, Agravaine."

Agravaine strode forward and gave a curt bow before returning to his mother's side.

"My son Gaheris you already know," she said casually giving Gaheris a cursory glance. "And this … this is my treasure, my little joy, Gareth."

Gareth was pushed from where he hid behind his mother and bowed shyly. "Y-your majesty," he said and backed away wishing he could hide. King Leodegrance frightened the boy. He reminded Gareth of one of Daddy's drill sergeants in both bearing and perfunctory manners.

"And what of thy son, Gawaine? Where is he? I owe him a debt of gratitude as well, or so I understand. He fought bravely with the High King until they became separated during the fighting."

Morgawse blushed with embarrassment and said, "My lord, my eldest son, Gawaine, has chosen to … to arrive by means other than I deem fitting for a son of King Lot, and a knight and warrior. He was injured during the fighting, you see, and was too hurt to sit a horse as is proper."

Leodegrance smiled in understanding and responded with courteous grace. "No matter, my lady. His reputation goes before him, and I am sure he will more than exceed it when I meet him in person. For now, be welcome. Rest. Refresh yourselves. We will be a while in rebuilding what damage was done during this siege, but I trust that my steward shall be able to accommodate thy desires."

Morgawse put on one of her appreciative smiles and said, "Thank you, your majesty. For myself, however, I cannot rest until I see how fares the High King, my brother. I am too distraught with concern for his health and well-being to rest, or even eat, until I see him with my own eyes."

Leodegrance bowed slightly in assent. "Then I shall have you taken to him as soon as possible. Torrance? Please show her majesty to her rooms where she can at least freshen up a bit from her grueling journey, then conduct her to the High King so that she might relieve my daughter who sits watch over him."

"Very well, my lord," answered King Leodegrance's steward.

Morgawse spoke to Gaheris, "Watch your brother for me while I am busy, will you? Keep him out of harm's way and out from under foot while his majesty has his men doing whatever needs to be done to restore their keep to order."

Gaheris wanted to protest, but knew that it would do no good so he acquiesced quietly. Gareth shouted with glee and ran to Gaheris' side. He took his brother by the hand and dragged him in the direction of the stables.

"Yippee! I want to see the mounts while the knights exercise them. Can we, Gaheris? Can we?"

Gaheris stumbled along after his little brother and said without enthusiasm, "Whatever you want, Gareth. Whatever you want." He cast a searching glance at his mother in an attempt to divine her motivations, but without success.

Morgawse followed the steward and had him wait outside her apartments while she splashed a little water on her face and washed her hands in rose water. She took a moment to look over her grimoires one last time to make sure of the incantations she intended to use on her half-brother, Arthur, in fulfillment of the prophecy her sister had made.

A new royal bloodline – and a pure line, at that!

Composing herself after anointing herself with the musky perfume she concocted in order to sway men's minds and bodies, Morgawse went with Torrance to where the High King lay sleeping under the watchful care of Leodegrance's daughter.

Gwynnefer stirred as she heard steps approaching, and wiped her bleary eyes. It had been a long, troublesome night. Arthur still burned with fever though he no longer thrashed and moaned. Gwynnefer smiled at the memory of his first words to her, *"Are you an angel?"* She was flattered despite her experience with men and their tendency to develop an attraction to whoever nurses them to health. *They're such boys, some-*

times, she thought with humor. *Still looking for mommy to kiss their hurts and make it all better.*

Gwynnefer's musings were stopped short when she saw the woman who accompanied her father's steward. Gwynnefer knew that she herself was pretty, but this strange woman made her look skinny and pale by comparison. The woman exuded power and sensuality and made Gwynnefer feel like a little girl and not the young woman that she was.

"My lady? This is her majesty, Queen Morgawse of Lothian, a healer as well as a royal mother. She has come to take over for you in order that you might rest," Torrance introduced the woman who looked at Gwynnefer with a measuring regard.

Gwynnefer curtsied and said, "I thank you, your highness. This is indeed most generous of you."

Morgawse looked the girl up and down before responding. "It is my pleasure, princess. I can do no less for the man who is both High King and my brother."

Brother? Oh, yes, of course, Gwynnefer thought, *on her mother's side. The High King is her half-brother, the supposed son of Uther Pendragon and Queen Morgawse's mother, Ygraine.*

"He's still weak," she explained to the Queen of Lothian, "but resting comfortably. I have some herbs and teas to help-…"

Morgawse waved impatiently. "Yes, yes, I know all that. I've raised four boys, some are already in their manhood, and I know a thing or two about how to care for an injured body. I am a healer myself, you know. As was my mother before me."

Gwynnefer feared she had somehow given offense and said apologetically, "Then I will take your leave." Curtsying again, she departed, though something bothered her about the way Queen Morgawse looked at her before turning her attention to Arthur. Gwynnefer watched for a moment as Morgawse lifted the bandages to check the wound for signs of infection or gangrene, her face harsh and serious. Morgawse seemed to sense she was being watched and looked up from her inspection. To Gwynnefer it almost seemed as if a mask was suddenly slipped over the Queen's face, for her critical expression was swiftly replaced by a gracious, too cheerful smile.

Gwynnefer made one final curtsy then left, disturbed and uneasy but without any good reason why.

Morgawse dismissed Torrance, telling the steward she would be all right and would call if she needed anything brought to her.

Once she was alone, the façade dropped, and Morgawse became cold and calculating once again. Reaching into her bodice, she pulled forth a small iron dagger. Muttering her incantations, she placed the dagger point down into the wooden bowl at Arthur's bedside while she poured fresh water over it and let it run down over her hand, down the dagger, and into the bowl. Morgawse crushed some herbs she had brought with her, dropped the crumbs into the water, and stirred it a little with the dagger blade.

One last ingredient, she thought to herself and winced a little as she cut the space between her middle and ring finger to draw blood. She allowed six drops to fall into her mixture before pulling her hand away. The blood slowly ran down the back of her hand, and Morgawse felt her heat rise at the sight of it.

"Gwynnefer?" Arthur asked weakly as he began to wake.

Morgawse was tempted to simply be direct in her course of actions and slay her helpless half-brother with the dagger in her hand. But something more powerful stirred within her, ambition and desire, and she said gently, "Hush, my king, hush … Here, drink this. This will slake thy thirst." And she offered Arthur the bowl with her potion in it.

As Arthur took a few sips, he made a face at the bitterness of the herbs contained therein. But Morgawse made him finish it all as she held the bowl to his lips and tilted it up and up until it was all gone.

Arthur lay back, exhausted. His face was pale, and he broke into a cold sweat, his muscles becoming more rigid.

No! I've poisoned him! Morgawse feared when she saw the effect her potion was having on him. But his color began to deepen, and his eyes opened, alert but glassy, and he looked at Morgawse in a manner she knew all too well.

"Yes, my king?" Morgawse purred as she began to undress, letting Arthur take in her nakedness. "What is thy desire, my lord?" she said as she slid into bed with him.

"Gwynnefer?" Arthur said, confused. His voice was deep and nearly growled with sexuality. He kissed Morgawse savagely, ignorant of the pain from his wounds. All else was forgotten as he pulled this woman to him, his need to satisfy his lust more powerful than anything else.

"Yes," Morgawse crooned to him as she caressed him and fanned his desires to the fullest. "Yes, my king. Yes!"

Morgawse felt as though she herself had become entrapped by her own spell, the instrument of powers too strong for her to deny, either. Locked together, man and woman, half-brother and half-sister, the two coupled and made love. Morgawse drew Arthur deeper and deeper inside of her and caused his wounds to bleed afresh. She wiped his blood over herself and over him in her uncontrollable passion, licking it up and kissing him as he continued to thrust and thrust and thrust. "A true king shall be born of this union!" she cried. "A true bloodline shall rise and take the throne!"

Is this what Morgana feels? Morgawse wondered as she surrendered to her own desires. *This sense of power and release at the same time? Intoxicating! Is that me speaking, or is something speaking through me?* It didn't matter. Morgawse didn't care.

Once Arthur had finished, shooting his seed deep inside of her, Morgawse kept herself wrapped around him panting, slowing her breath and cooling herself down. She no longer cared whether he lived or died, but fear of discovery, lest her plans unravel too soon, made her wash herself down with the water and cloth at hand.

Arthur had fallen into a comatose sleep, shallow and strained. For appearances sake, Morgawse wiped him free of blood, too, and applied the poultice to the wounds that had broken open during their lovemaking.

"Sleep now, my brother," she said softly. "Wake or not, no matter. But know this – a child of thine and mine shall rule all of England. Hold it for a while, if you live, but I have seen it. I have been told it! And it shall come to pass." Morgawse placed a hand over her abdomen as though it already carried their child.

"Gawaine!" Gaheris shouted and ran to greet his brother as the former was helped down from the back of a wagon bearing the injured and dying.

"Brother!" Gawaine said and returned the hug, though he cringed a bit and said, "Easy, now, laddie. I've seen a hell of a spot of trouble and have the wounds to prove it."

"I'm sure you do," Gaheris said. He was glad to have his brother back in one piece.

Gawaine ruffled Gareth's hair as the youngest of the Orkney brood hugged him.

"Ross? Come here a sec, won't you?" Gawaine waved Rose over to meet his family.

Gaheris stopped as he recognized the features of the knight who came toward them. "You? I don't believe it!"

Rose blushed, suddenly embarrassed that Gaheris should see her again after all this time in such fashion. "Yes, my lord Gaheris. And I remember you, very well," Rose said noncommittally. She didn't want to embarrass the great Gawaine with the fact that she was really a woman.

"Ah, you two know each other, do ye?" Gawaine asked and was pleased. "Then I don't need to introduce you, except maybe for the wee tyke here. This is Gareth, who will one day, no doubt, be a knight as well. Maybe even as great as his big, older brother Gawaine, eh?"

Rose bowed her head and extended her hand to the young one. "I'm pleased to meet you," she said.

Gareth eyed Rose oddly, cocking his head and closely looking at her hand before taking it tentatively with his own. "Are you really a knight?" he asked, curiously.

Rose laughed nervously and said, "Well, not yet. I've not been formally knighted, no. But I do fight for the King's justice, and I hope one day to be knighted. Maybe even by the High King one day."

"Ah, wouldn't that be great?" Gawaine agreed and clasped a hand on Rose's shoulder. "Ross, aren't you uncomfortable in all that armor? Why don't ye take it off for the nonce? The danger is past, for now."

Rose blushed again as she made excuses. "I – uh, forgive me, Sir Gawaine. I will once I have seen to it that my men are cared for and billeted. Until then, I am reluctant to relieve myself of my armor and duties for the sake of my own comfort."

"Spoken like a true knight," Gaheris said with a knowing smile. "Allow me to help you, *Ross*." He gestured down a hall, and Rose followed where he directed.

After they were out of sight of the others, Gaheris began to laugh out loud. "Ha! I don't believe it. You? Gawaine will never live this down. The rumor is that you saved my brother when he was surrounded and outnumbered? And that thanks to you he was given medical attention when he needed it?"

Rose gave an embarrassed smile, saying, "It's true. At least, that much of it. I know how men tend to exaggerate their stories. No doubt I will have grown in size and strength, as will the number of the enemy we overcame, by the time I leave here."

"Rose?" Gaheris shook his head in disbelief. "The last time I saw you, you were still weak and very ill. The last thing I expected was to find you here, in full armor no less. How? You must tell me everything that happened after I left Lady Autumne's keep."

Rose recounted much of her adventures as they walked. She excluded some things, especially the things she herself had a hard time accepting like the dreams and visions. But other than that, she related most of what she had experienced since the time Gaheris had left Meg's training.

"She really made you her heir?" he asked incredulously. "You must be quite exceptional, then, which I must say I rather tend to believe given the circumstances and all. Incredible!"

Gaheris' smile brought back the dreamy, wistful feelings Rose had felt the first time she watched him from her window.

"You know, it's funny," she confessed to him, "but you were part of my inspiration to do this … become a knight and all."

Gaheris looked at her with questioning eyes.

"It's true! From the first moment I saw you, there was just something wonderful and magical about you. The way you moved, the way you sit a horse. I remember watching you from my window and I … I thought you beautiful."

It was Gaheris' turn to blush. "Really? Beautiful? I don't think anyone has ever called me that before."

"Not even your mother?" Rose asked.

Gaheris grew quiet at the mention of his mother. "No, not even my mother," he said.

Rose sensed that she had brought up a sore spot, and she wanted to switch the conversation.

"Gawaine fights like a troll! Did you know that? And I should know, I've fought one myself."

Gaheris turned to her unbelieving. "A troll? You're kidding!"

Rose became embarrassed and a little ashamed as she recalled how she had managed to kill Taulurd. "I … uhm … It wasn't as great as it may seem. Gleinguin, Meg's healer, he told me that I should respect even those I killed. I … I didn't fight honorably, but yes, I did fight and kill a troll."

Gaheris whistled in admiration. "Whew! And you say Gawaine fights like one, eh? I'll have to remember that. I can always tease him with it."

"He's like no one else, isn't he?" Rose said. "You must be very proud to be his brother."

"Oh, I am," Gaheris admitted. "When he's not being so proud of himself. He complains about my brother Agravaine, how cocky *he* is … G should really look at himself once in a while."

Rose listened and appreciated the talk. It was nice to find somebody who seemed to accept her for who she was, and who could appreciate all that she had gone through. As they stopped outside the rooms King Leodegrance had assigned to her and her men, Rose found herself wishing this moment could last forever. She suddenly felt very self-conscious, fumbling for things to say, but reluctant for the conversation to come to an end.

"Well, uh, this is it … Thank you for walking with me. And the talk!" Rose said and looked away. Her heart was beating loudly, and her palms felt hot and wet. She was sure Gaheris would notice, but he seemed preoccupied by something at the moment himself.

"Oh, you're welcome," he said and touched Rose on the arm.

Rose looked into Gaheris' beautiful blue eyes, and her mouth went dry. "You won't tell Gawaine, will you? About my being a girl and all?"

Gaheris smiled and said, "Not unless I really feel the need to embarrass him. Until that happens, your secret is safe with me. He'll have to find out, eventually. After the events of the past few days, you're bound to come to the attention of some king or other. I'm sure somebody is going to want to knight you."

Rose's eyes grew wide as she realized Gaheris was right. *I really will be a knight, then! Oh, Michael – Poppa – how I wish you could be here to see it!*

A tear rolled down her cheek, and Gaheris watched it fall.

"Rose, I'm sorry. I … you must really miss him. Your brother, right? I … it's all right." Gaheris stepped forward and Rose let herself be embraced by him. Everything she had been keeping at bay, all the hurt and grief and stress, it all came flooding out. Gaheris held her as she wept, and his heart went out to her.

"It's all right, Rose," he said and stroked her hair. "Everything's all right, now. You'll be fine."

"I tried," she wept. "I tried to do everything right. I tried to do my best! And still, people got killed. I didn't want them to. I didn't want for any of this to happen. I just wanted my brother back! I just wanted to be able to go home!"

"Shhh," Gaheris comforted her. "Rose, you did more than anyone could have asked. You did things people wouldn't believe! And you did them all for love. You're a champion, Rose, as surely as any figure out of history or legend."

As her tears faded, Rose looked up at Gaheris. "Stay with me," she said. "Please, just ... I just want to be held for a while. Until I fall asleep. Is that okay? Please – I don't want to be alone."

Gaheris wiped her eyes and said, "It's fine. Yes, it's all right. I'll hold you until you fall asleep. Don't worry, Rose, everything will be all right."

He helped her to stand and opened the door for her. Her men spoke her name in salute as she entered, but softly when they saw that she had been weeping. They watched as the handsome young man some of them recalled from Meg's keep helped Rose remove her armor, then to a cot, and no one said a word or thought it strange when he lay down next to her. Gaheris let Rose curl up against him while he stroked her hair until she fell asleep, exhausted emotionally and physically.

Emrys watched with bright and curious eyes, but kept his thoughts to himself. *So strong and yet so fragile ... She is aptly named.*

He felt that he should be doing something, but had an odd lethargy. It was the same feeling Emrys got before a storm came, a feeling of pressure building, indistinct yet undeniable. It was almost as if an invisible hand held him in place, trapped by an invisible jar from which he would want to escape if only he was aware of it being there. It was a feeling that overcame him from time to time, and Merlin knew it had something to do with his own Fate, and he was loath to think too deeply upon it. *Whatever I can do I do! Everything else is out of my hands, and I must merely accept it. Make the best of what I know, and what I have right here, right now. The Future must tend to itself. Well, with the occasional nudge every now and then, yes – but even in that, am I really independent? Or am I simply caught in the Loom that weaves the Loom I think I am free of?* He laughed, and the men near him simply thought him odd in a way Merlin was used to as he enjoyed his own private reverie.

Chapter 20

When Rose awoke, Gaheris was gone. It had taken no time at all for her to fall asleep, comforted and protected by the presence of the young son of King Lot. Rose had slept deeply, without dreams – at least, none she could recall.

"My lady?" said one of her men as he brought her a wash-basin and pitcher.

Rose nodded in thanks and allowed the man to pour the water for her as she washed her face and hands. Another man from her retinue, Theodorus – a descendant of a Roman soldier who had married and settled down in the wild borderlands of Wales – offered Rose a plate of hard cheese and dried fruits. Rose realized that all the men watched her with concerned eyes, careful of her welfare and well-being. It touched her more than they could possibly know.

"Thank you," she said softly, and Theodorus smiled and backed away.

Emrys came over and sat on the edge of Rose's cot, giving Rose a flask of wine that had been shared by the others while she rested.

"Have a good sleep?" he asked and regarded her with his usual cheer.

Rose still felt tired, more due to her grief than her physical body, but otherwise she felt fine. "Yes, very good," she answered.

"The men have been wondering when we will be heading home," Emrys said.

Home? Rose thought. *How nice it would be to be back home.* "I don't know," she confessed. "As soon as the men are ready to travel, I guess. We have ... we have many to take back with us so that they may have the proper rites performed, and I must see what Meg can do to provide for the families of the fallen. And then ..."

"And what about you, Rose?" Emrys asked more pointedly. "What about your own dead?"

Rose fell silent as the responsibility sunk in. "Yes," she said quietly to Emrys. "I must go home, too. To bury Michael with Momma and Poppa. It ... it seems only fitting. I'd kind of like to see the old stead one more time."

Emrys agreed and touched Rose's hand briefly. "We still have some time to spend here, though," he told her. "And there are those who will want to thank you before you leave."

Rose understood. And the nearer the realization of her dream came to being a reality, the more Rose wanted to shrink from it. Once she was knighted, what would become of her then?

Emrys stood and took his leave, explaining that he was going to arrange for transport back to Meg's keep for the dead and those still too injured to walk or ride on horseback.

Once he was outside of Rose's quarters, Emrys shifted to his guise as Merlin, wizard and seer. He passed quickly through the corridors of Cameliard, and anxiousness grew within him as he neared the High King's apartment.

Merlin paused outside the door, a sudden presentiment of evil washing over him. He hurried into the next room where he saw Queen Morgawse watching over the sleeping Arthur.

"Who dares-?" Morgawse stood and regarded Merlin impe-riously. "Oh, it's only you, old man. What do you want?"

Merlin's vision came to him in that moment – of fire and bloodshed, of friendships and betrayals, and of the dark child who would bring about the destruction of all he had hoped to build through Arthur.

"What have you done?" he demanded fearfully. "Morgawse, what have you done?"

Morgawse laughed evilly and placed her hands over her belly once again as if trying to sense the being growing there. "I fulfill my destiny, old man, just like you! I serve the Powers, the Ancient Ones, and they have filled my vessel with the seed of the High King. It is my child, that of me and my half-brother, who shall rule all the realms one day."

Merlin nearly staggered under the impact of the visions that assaulted him. He became almost like Morgana in trance, the power of them nearly too much for his half-mortal frame to bear. "A serpent shall hatch from this union … and the Dragon shall fall … Darkness shall claim the memory of this Golden Age and mankind will fall into barbarity and ignorance … the Ancient Ones shall fall into disregard, their ways forgotten … but Hope shall endure … Hope shall endure … Hope – shall – endure!"

Morgawse grew fearful as she witnessed Merlin's transfor-mation. His words filled her with fear even though they echoed much of what Morgana had prophesied earlier. But Merlin gave new meaning to what her sister had said.

"What do you mean, old fool, that the Ancient Ones will be forgotten? I bear the hope of the future! My child is that hope. I, like my sister Morgana, am a servant to the Old Ones, the Ancient Ways. You speak nonsense when you say that they shall be forgotten!" Morgawse laughed nervously in denial.

Merlin's visions faded, but he recalled them all. As well as the ways in which he might be able to salvage at least some of the good that would come from all of this.

Drawing on his own Power, Merlin seemed to grow in size, looming over Morgawse like a huge shadow, a being of smoke and flame. "Girl, you know nothing! All you seek to achieve is but Dust and Destruction. Death shall be thy end, by the hands of thine own child. A more fitting curse I could not pronounce on anyone. But it is not my sentence upon you but that of your own making." Merlin began to shrink and became more solid, returning to his form as the wizened old mage. "I almost pity you, Morgawse," he said as the Power left him. "You are nothing but an angry little girl demanding love and attention, and feeling she has to force the world to give her what she deserves, ignorant of what it is she truly desires."

Morgawse covered her uncertainty by reacting with defiance and false confidence. "We shall see, old wizard! We shall see. When my brother wakes, tell him what we have done. I only wish I could be there to see his face when he realizes he has sinned against his God, damned in the eyes of his beliefs. But not mine. He shall be damned, but I … I and my child, we shall be saved! We shall save the very gods he seeks to destroy!"

"Go now, Morgawse," Merlin spoke quietly yet firmly. "What evil you seek to inflict shall find you instead. Now go!"

Puffing herself up with all her royal indignation, Morgawse leaned over the bed and kissed Arthur on the lips one last time, and smiled wickedly at the old man as she did so, then left. Her musk smelled like decay, heavy and cloying to Merlin's nostrils, and he held his breath until the scent dissipated.

Merlin rushed to Arthur's side and reached out with his hands, placing one over Arthur's heart and the other on his brow as Merlin called upon those healing energies to which he was allowed. Power flowed through him and brought a sense of peace and calm to Merlin as it healed his own emotions even as it healed the spirit of the man into whom they flowed.

Arthur's breathing deepened, becoming easier, and his face relaxed as he passed into restful slumber. His fever left him, and his color became more normal.

Merlin took a deep breath, thankful he had arrived when he did. *But why was I denied knowledge of this event?* he wondered.

Why does this new God allow me so much, and yet deny me when there is great need?

Arthur stirred and groaned as he awoke. "Merlin? What are you doing here?" he asked weakly. "And what am I doing here? And where exactly is here, by the way?"

Merlin smiled and gave Arthur a sip of water as he answered his liege. "Cameliard, your majesty. Don't you remember? You went to lift the siege ..."

Arthur frowned as he tried to recall. "Oh, yes ... I remember now ... I remember a number of fights ... battles ... I got wounded!" Arthur turned and examined his side where his hurts were most grievous. "And there was a girl, a maiden ... I thought she was an angel. She watched over me in the night. And, and ... I thought ... I must have dreamed it ... I thought we made love. Can you believe it? Fanciful, I suppose, to dream of making love to an angel. But it seemed so real!"

Devil more like it, Merlin thought but kept it to himself. "Yes, your majesty. But you need to rest a little more before you resume thy duties. This angel of yours, did she have a name?"

Arthur thought for a moment, struggling to recall, but finally the name came to him, and he smiled as he spoke it, "Gwynnefer."

"Gwynnefer," Merlin repeated. "She is real, my king, and I suppose she is something of an angel. King Leodegrance will be glad to hear you think of his daughter in such manner, I dare say."

"King Leodegrance's daughter? Oh, but she is beautiful. Why, if I could, one day ... one day I'd make her my Queen! Once we have won enough peace for me to finally enjoy some of it, that is."

Merlin felt a stirring, something that tugged at his mind, but the recent taste of evil from Morgawse clouded his memory, and he supposed he was being suspicious of everyone and everything all of a sudden. "Yes, Arthur. That day will be soon. Peace, and a peaceable kingdom that shall endure in the memory of Men forever. This much I promise you."

Arthur lay back down and closed his eyes again. "Thank you, old friend," he said softly as he fell back asleep. "Thank you."

The days passed slowly for Rose. She and those of her men well enough to assist helped King Leodegrance in rebuilding some of the damage done to his castle during the siege. To Rose, it was not unlike when she had begun her training under Meg and fetched wood and supplies and carried them hither and thither. Rose was thankful for the distraction and went to bed exhausted every night. But the need to move on, to complete her journey and end her grieving, ate at her.

Gaheris came to visit, and Rose looked forward to the time she spent with the youth. They would talk for many hours; they shared hopes and dreams, fears and worries. Gaheris laughed when Rose told him she feared becoming a dried up old spinster since men did not look at her as a woman.

"Rose," he laughed. "How can you expect them to see you as a woman when you keep yourself disguised as a man?"

"What do you mean?" she asked.

"Well, you keep your form hidden by that armor or padded quilting most of the time, even when it isn't necessary, for one thing."

"I … I just feel more comfortable that way," Rose explained. "I feel that the more I grow accustomed to wearing it, the less awkward I feel and more capable of moving in it."

"And your hair. You keep it cut short, like a boy's, instead of letting it grow out like a maiden's."

Rose had her reasons for that, too. "It makes it easier to wear a helmet," she explained. "Plus it doesn't give an enemy much to grab hold of if they intend to fight dirty."

Gaheris shook his head good-naturedly. "Meg has taught you well, I can't deny! You have excellent reasons for almost everything, but I think it is because you don't trust in your own beauty. You prefer to stay hidden so that you don't have to risk someone rejecting you."

Rose was speechless. Something in what Gaheris said struck home. *Am I afraid? Is it just because I am afraid to be seen as a woman that I perceive the men don't see me that way?*

"And what about you?" Rose asked. "Can you see me that way?"

It was Gaheris' turn to feel put on the spot. "What do you mean?"

"Can you see me as beautiful, short hair and all? Or do I remind you too much of a boy to ... to want to kiss, if nothing else?"

Gaheris swallowed nervously. Never had he dealt with a woman so direct. "I must admit," he said, "the first time I saw you ... well, you were quite a mess ..."

Rose rolled her eyes and looked away, frustrated and embarrassed.

"No, now let me finish! That was at first. But, as you were recovering, I have to admit, young as you were, I would say ... yes, you were pretty. And I was in awe of your strength and courage."

"Really? But you left before I started my training. How could you see me as strong or courageous?"

"Because of the fight in you," Gaheris told her. "You have such spirit! I knew you'd recover. I had no doubts about that. And as for your beauty, I have no doubts on that account, either."

Rose looked into Gaheris eyes, and he looked back without looking away. "Do you mean it?"

Gaheris' look was steady as he said, "Yes."

Rose leaned forward, and her lips touched Gaheris' gently, tentatively at first. He returned the kiss, and their lips touched longer, more pleasantly.

As they separated slowly, Rose exhaled with a gentle, "Whoa ..." Her heart was beating loudly, and she felt exhilarated.

Gaheris smiled bashfully and asked, "Was that ... was that your first kiss?"

A little self-consciously, Rose admitted that it was.

"How was it?" he asked a bit unsure of himself.

"Wonderful!" Rose said and leaned her head against him.

Gaheris put his arm around her, and the two sat simply enjoying the candlelight and the time together.

"Rose?" Gaheris said gently. "Don't ever doubt it. That you're beautiful, I mean. One day, you'll meet someone and want to settle down, maybe have some children, I don't know, but it will happen. One day."

"Do you think I'll be like Meg?" she asked. "You know, with several lovers but not anyone more ... permanent?"

Gaheris smiled and kissed her hands. "I don't know, Rose. I suppose that depends on you and what choices you make. It depends on what you want, really."

"Follow my heart," Rose said softly.

"Yes, exactly. Follow your heart," Gaheris agreed.

The time for departing had come. Rose's men who were stronger were ready and eager to return home. They, like Rose, wanted to finish burying their dead and get on with their lives. Plans were made to put the dead and injured into wagons while Rose journeyed home with her brother's body, accompanied by Emrys, Gaheris, and one or two others of Rose's retinue that wanted to do so. They would catch up with the others most likely by the time they had reached Meg's keep, as they would be traveling lighter and faster.

On the night before her departure, King Leodegrance came and visited Rose and her men in their quarters. He invited them all to a feast to be held in honor of the High King and all the knights and soldiers who had answered Cameliard's call.

"I would like for you to be seated at the Table Round," King Leodegrance informed her. "A singular honor, one reserved for only the best and bravest of knights. It was a gift to me by the old High King, Uther Pendragon himself, for bravery in battle when we drove the Saxons from our lands all those years ago."

Rose was thankful and agreed to do as he wished. "But, my lord, your majesty, I must tell you ... I am no knight. Not yet. I have never been knighted by a king or lord or knight in the field."

Leodegrance pulled on his mustache as he considered. He was a man who lived very much by the forms and rules, and yet he felt he couldn't deny Rose a place at the Table. However, he could knight her, though he felt such privilege should either go to the High King or to one of the knights with whom Rose had fought alongside. "I'll see what I can do," he reassured her with a slight bow.

Emrys had the men clean and polish their gear and set to Rose's armor so that she might "be the brightest star shining in the heavenly panoply of knighthood ever gathered to date!"

Rose was so nervous, she almost felt ill. But she knew that to fail to appear would be a grave insult to her host. And so, she practiced the breathing meditations Meg had taught her to center herself before her exercises.

The feast was glorious! Rose felt as though she had walked right into one of Poppa's stories, with the shining armor and pennants hanging over the hall, and trenchers of food, whole boars and suckling pigs, fruits, and wine, wine, wine. It was too much, and Rose tried to take it all in, to remember every detail.

Emrys was strangely absent. Rose expected he, of all people, to be there when the wine and revelry began.

Trumpets announced the High King as he was helped into the hall. Gawaine walked to Arthur's right, supporting his uncle and king, while Merlin walked to Arthur's left. When they were seated, Merlin rapped his staff on the floor and shouted at all those gathered there, "We have a pretender in our midst!"

His words quieted down the throng, and he said aloud, "There is one among you who sits at this Table who has not been granted the title 'knight.' One who sits here who is not what he appears to be!"

Rose froze as she knew it was she the old wizard referred to.

"Master Rochedon, will you please stand and approach his majesty, King Arthur, Lord of Camelot, and ruler of the Britons?" Merlin gestured for Rose to come near them.

Rose stood, trembling inside but not wanting to show her fear to anyone. With hesitant steps, she drew near to Gawaine, Merlin, and the High King who sat regarding her strangely.

The hall was so quiet, Rose could almost hear the whisper of the pages as they asked one another what was going on.

"Master Rochedon, here in the presence of these witnesses, I ask you – what is thy true name and parentage?" Merlin's eyes looked at Rose like an eagle spotting prey.

"My name ..." Rose croaked and cleared her throat. "My name is ... Rose. I am the daughter of Branwen and Lucas. My brother ... my brother's name is Michael, and he died protecting me when enemies of the King attacked our camp."

Gawaine turned deep red and gripped his chair tightly. "A girl?" he muttered under his breath. "Ross is a girl?"

Rose looked in Gawaine's direction and bowed her head apologetically. He glanced away, but his debt to her was greater than his pride, and he looked back and acknowledged her.

"You came here why? You owe no fealty to King Leodegrance, so why did you come, risking life and limb, to the assistance of people unknown to you?"

"Because," Rose answered as she tried to find her voice. "Because it is my duty as a loyal subject to the High King – to do what I can to help uphold the peace, maintain the King's justice, and protect and serve those who are within my care."

Arthur nodded, as did Gawaine and many of those gathered there.

"A meet answer," Merlin said with a smile. "Fitting." He winked at Rose, and she was so surprised by it that she nearly forgot where she was. "As the High King did not witness for himself what feats you performed on his behalf, nor did King Leodegrance to whose aid you came, are there any gathered here who would like to give witness and testimony to the deeds of Rose, daughter of Branwen and Lucas?"

Gawaine stood and in a loud voice said, "Aye! That will I!" Then softly so that no one might hear, he muttered, "Though I didn't know it was a girl at the time ..."

Rose looked at Gawaine as he steadied himself before he told how Rose, whom he had called "Ross," rescued him from a dozen or more of the enemy, how bravely and skillfully she fought, and what aid and assistance she rendered to him after. "If it weren't for Ross here," he said ignoring his mistake, "I'd be more fodder for carrion to feed on. I owe her my life, and so my family owes her as well. To Ross!" he said and held up his cup to toast.

"Rose!" answered many voices in the hall. There was some laughter as knights joked about Gawaine's situation and his stubborn insistence on mispronouncing Rose's name.

"Based on that alone his majesty, King Arthur, could grant you the title of knight. But I sense there are more who would like to speak on Rose's behalf?" Merlin looked about the hall.

"I do," Gaheris said and stood from his seat. "This girl, this young woman, is perhaps one of the bravest, most coura-geous people I know ... next to my brother, Gawaine, that is. I met her first when she was beaten nearly to death by one of our enemy, Carados. But she survived. And like her name, she has flourished and come into bloom! Her skill with a sword is nearly without equal. Her training is of the best, by a woman out of legend that has trained some of those in this very hall, or whose reputations are known to all of us here. For all that Rose has suffered and overcome, for all that she embodies of what is best in the code of chivalry, I, too, say, cheers to Rose!"

Another round of "Rose!" went up as the men drank to her honor.

Rose was nearly in tears both of pride and gratitude for what these men said and felt about her.

"Is there anyone else who wishes to speak on Rose's behalf?" Merlin turned and looked about the hall. "Anyone? Last chance!"

A familiar voice called out from the shadows at the back of the hall. Merlin squinted and smiled mysteriously as he beckoned for the owner of the voice to step forward where they could all see him and speak.

This is where it gets tricky! he said to himself.

A young man strode into the hall, a woodsman's axe slung over his shoulder and a jaunty smile on his face.

"Emrys? Where have you been?" Rose called to him.

Emrys bowed and jumped up onto Rose's vacated chair so that everyone in the hall might see and hear him. "I can't be in two places at once," he answered Rose lightly, as if amused by the answer to a funny riddle.

Well, not at exactly *the same time*, Merlin said to himself enjoying his trick.

"I'd just like to say," Emrys went on, "that it has been my privilege and honor to serve as make-believe squire to this make-believe knight. This woman, this beautiful, loving, stubborn, strong-willed woman whose desire it was to become a knight ever since she heard the stories her Poppa told her about many of you gathered here in this very room – this woman has deserved the title of knight for many months, long before she ever lifted sword against those who came against Cameliard. Let me tell you ..." he went on. In the manner of the great bards, Emrys related Rose's life and adventures from the night Carados burned her farm and slew her father, to the hunt for Taulurd and the subsequent guilt she felt for slaying him, and even her adventures into the Underworld and the realm of the Sidhe. Emrys spoke as though he had seen and witnessed each and every one of these adventures. And he spoke so skillfully, with such poetry and artistry, that many were the knights who wiped away a tear from their eye at Rose's loss and pain, or who could not relate to her anguish and guilt. By the time he had finished, Rose was astonished herself at all she had seen and accomplished in but the span of a year. It seemed a lifetime of achievements, and yet it all made sense, somehow. It all wove together in a beautiful tapestry of magic, adventure, and experience that was greater than the sum of its parts.

"And so I say, three cheers for Rose! To Rose, the rose of Camelot!"

Cheers went up, and men banged on the table. Rose was overwhelmed by the noise and vibration that filled the hall.

Arthur smiled and eased himself from his chair carefully. He leaned forward so that Rose might hear him, and he said, "If I don't knight you, I think I'd have a riot on my hands!"

Rose smiled back and bowed.

"Kneel," Arthur prompted her before waving for silence. "My lords! Your majesty, and fellow knights," he said as loudly as he could. Arthur motioned, and Kay stepped forward with his sword. "By the power of Saint Michael and Saint George," he said as he laid his sword on each of Rose's shoulders, "by the might of this sword, the sword that proclaimed my true kingship when I pulled it forth from the anvil and stone, I do grant you, Rose, the right to bear arms; the right to enforce the King's will; to grant and meet justice; and to take arms against those who would do harm to his subjects! Arise, Sir ... uhm, er – *Lady* Rose!"

The cheering grew even louder than before as Rose kissed the blade of Arthur's sword, a sign of her fealty and oath of allegiance to him and the Throne of England.

Merlin helped Rose stand, and walked her back to her seat. Emrys had once again disappeared, but Merlin shouted so that Rose could hear, "Don't worry about him! He'll be back. Enjoy yourself! You've earned it!"

Rose ate and drank, and the world became a spinning blur of laughter, hands clapping her on the back, and brusque voices making rude jokes. She was so overwhelmed, Rose managed to put aside her grief and her desire for Poppa and Michael to be there to share it all with her, for the moment. In some way, Rose knew that they were there in spirit and rejoiced with her.

When Rose awoke, her head was killing her, and she felt nauseous and thirsty. One of the men offered her a wineskin, but the scent of the wine nearly made Rose throw up and she handed it back.

"Ohhh ..." she moaned. This felt worse than she had ever recalled feeling her entire life! *Well, maybe not as bad as when I was recovering from Carados' beating, but this is close.*

Emrys came and gave her a cup, pressing it upon her and making her drink it down. It was cool and crisp, with just the slightest flowery taste.

"Emrys?" Rose croaked. "Why aren't you feeling the same way I am?"

Emrys shrugged and smiled in his usual manner. "I've been there before, and I've learned my limits. It's funny," he said as he held Rose's head, and she vomited, "but most men never learn despite the number of times they wake up wishing some-one would come and put an end to their misery. All done? Good. Drink some more."

Rose was too weak to argue. The cool water actually felt good going down, and the second time it didn't make her sick. Her stomach began to settle, and Emrys handed her a bit of hard tack to nibble on.

"Eat this slowly," he told her while he cleaned up her mess. "The more you can get down, the better you will feel. Trust me on this!"

Rose did as he said, and when Emrys had gathered up all her gear, she followed him down the corridor and outside. The sunlight, however, made her head pound, and she felt a little sick again.

Blinking against the light, Rose saw Gaheris already mounted, and Theodorus and Emlyn as well. Two more horses awaited riders, and they had three ponies in tow, one of which had Michael's body draped over its back, wrapped in linen – a gift of King Leodegrance.

Arthur was there as well, along with King Leodegrance and Gawaine, Kay, and several of Arthur's knights.

Emrys helped her into the saddle, and the men smiled in sympathy for Rose's condition. A few there themselves were a bit green in the face.

"Fare you well, Lady Rose!" Arthur said and waved. "I trust that you will visit Camelot some day, or must I make that an order?"

Rose smiled wanly and replied, "I would like nothing better, your majesty. Perhaps, once I have gone home, I will do exactly that."

Arthur nodded. "Home … yes … It is a nice place to be when you get the time. Don't ever take it for granted."

Gawaine reached up and shook his brother's hand farewell. "Watch the lassie's back, will ye?" he said.

Gaheris took his brother's hand and squeezed it tight. "You know I will. And I'll see you soon. You need someone to watch your back as well."

Gawaine frowned a bit, but understood what Gaheris meant, and he smiled and slapped the horse to get it moving.

"I'll see you in Camelot, twit!" he shouted after them.

After they had ridden some distance away, Emrys rode along side of Rose and noticed that she seemed to be enjoying the fresh air and sunlight. Gaheris and Emlyn were discussing something to do with battle strategies, the older man feeling he had a whole new perspective that "the younger generation might benefit from."

"And what will you do now, my lady?" he asked.

"You mean after I have settled my affairs?" Rose asked him. She shook her head a bit, enjoying the breeze as it blew over her face. "I don't know, Emrys. I don't know. But as I've learned, anything is possible. You just have to follow your heart!" With that, she gave a laugh and kicked her horse into a faster trot. The others followed, and the group disappeared into the woods heading toward the remains of Rose's farm and the apple orchard that would be in full fruiting by the time they got there.

About the Author

James Philip Cox lives in Southern California. He holds a Master's degree in Spiritual Psychology from the University of Santa Monica, and a Bachelor's degree in Theatre Arts. James has been the artistic director of a classically based Shakespearean company, and studied with members of both the RSC and Britain's National Theater. He has long been a fan of Arthurian tales, and has been inspired by the writings of such people as Mary Stewart, J.R.R. Tolkein, and John Steinbeck.